GEARS

GORDON BONNET

Copyright © 2016 by Gordon Bonnet

All rights reserved.

No part of this book may be reproduced in any form or by any electronic or mechanical means, including information storage and retrieval systems, without written permission from the author, except for the use of brief quotations in a book review.

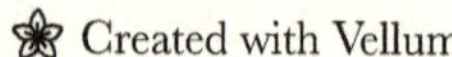 Created with Vellum

1

D ecember 20, 64 B.C.E.

MAYBE I'LL ACTUALLY GET off this godforsaken island alive.

Caelius Marcellinus barked a quick command at the slave leading the pair of mules. He was astonished, really, that he'd made it this far. The whole plan had gone as smoothly as the gears of the bronze mechanism that sat in the shadowed corner in the ramshackle shed, resting underneath a ragged sheet of canvas. Every part of the scheme to betray Priscus Gallo and his wife Livia worked just as he'd planned it in the past days and weeks. Arrange for a banquet in Gallo's honor, conveniently held on the other side of the island. Make certain that the host, an obsequious half-Greek named Silvanus, would press the two of them to stay overnight. Only Livia had looked suspicious, and gave Caelius a curious look from beneath those heavy-lidded eyes.

She didn't trust him. She'd never trusted him. But that meant he had to go through with it. If he didn't act, she'd still find some trifle of a justification for ending him.

After that, there'd be no stopping either of them.

Drug the slave guarding the shed where the mechanism sat. He thanked Caelius for the cup of wine, astonished that anyone thought to bring him some of the bounty Silvanus provided to his guests. He didn't dream that the crimson liquid held a full measure of the syrup of poppies Caelius had stolen from Gallo's home two weeks ago, the theft that had finally convinced him that he might actually get away with what he was planning. And now the slave sat with his back to the shed wall, mouth hanging open, snoring softly.

When they discovered the slave asleep and the mechanism gone, he'd probably be tied up and flogged, if Priscus Gallo didn't have him killed outright. Unfortunate to play on the man's trust in that way, but there was no other option. After all, it was one slave's life against...

...what? What exactly were Priscus and his wife planning? No way to be entirely sure, but the hints they'd let fall turned his blood to ice water. No—if the slave had to suffer for it, that was too bad. The thing had to be done, and tonight was his last chance. After tonight, he'd have to find a way to get off the island, but one thing at a time.

"Caelius." A half-spoken, half whisper in the dark sent his heart pounding against his ribs, even though it had been expected.

"What took you so long?" he hissed. "You should have been here as soon as the sun set."

"I arrived as soon as I could. You want to go through with this?"

"No choice now, Avilius." Caelius gestured toward the sleeping slave. "The wagon is waiting there, behind the copse down the hill. My slave will help you bring it up."

Avilius nodded and slipped away into the night.

There were too many people involved. Four slaves, and Avilius Blandus, a young friend who had recently finished out his service with the Roman garrison on the island but was still casting about for adventure. He was strong and well-muscled—Caelius had chosen him for that more than anything else—but could he be trusted?

Could anyone be trusted with this? He barely trusted himself.

There was a creak as the plodding mules led by Avilius and one slave pulled the wagon up alongside the shed. Caelius gave another glance at Gallo's slave. Still asleep, and would be for hours. He gave Avilius a small jerk of the head, and the two men entered the shed.

"What does it do?" Avilius asked, looking with awe at the low gleam of bronze where the canvas didn't quite cover the machine's gears and posts.

"Nothing good."

"But what?" The younger man's voice was heavy with excitement.

"What I am told," Caelius said, "is that it draws off a man's power and gives it to others. The recipients grow that much stronger."

"You wish to destroy this thing?" Avilius looked thunder-struck. "Why not use it? If it is true, what you say, a man who had it could be powerful beyond measure."

Suddenly Caelius felt weary, weary of the whole enterprise. Too late for that now, he had to follow through or it would all be for nothing, and Priscus and his wife would still have their revenge. If he was going to sell his life, at least he should get a good price for it. "The man who used it would profit, yes. But the others who stood in his way, what of them? The temptation to use such power would sow nothing but evil. Now help me to maneuver it onto the wagon."

Even with the three men straining their muscles to the utmost, Caelius, Avilius, and the slave were barely able to lift the machine into the bed of the cart. The axle sagged alarmingly under its weight.

"Now," Caelius said to the slave. "To the boats."

Avilius followed, but his expression was still dubious. It was clear he wasn't convinced. Even the presence of the device would be a sore temptation to a man like him, young and untested and full of blood and heat and his own body's strength.

So it was with no great surprise that he heard Avilius's voice behind him, before they had even gone halfway. "You said that Priscus is your enemy, and that is why you are doing this. Surely now that you have it in your possession, you could use his own weapon to destroy him, him and his wife both. Is there no way to reason with you?"

Caelius laughed without turning. "Reason? This is not about reason."

Another pause. "Then let me use it."

He gave a quick command to the slave, who halted the mules from their task, and turned to look at his young friend.

Avilius stood, legs apart, hands outstretched in a gesture of frustration. "Why? Why would you destroy something that could make you as a god?"

He should have known it would come to this.

He walked slowly toward Avilius, his voice low and melancholy. "Because men are not gods. They fool themselves ever to think they could be. As long as this thing exists, it will corrupt men into believing they could wield its power safely. They will betray each other, then trample the corpses of their friends to be the one to harness what it can do."

One step, then another. Avilius's handsome, open face was caught by the moonlight, and Caelius saw the anger building in his eyes. When the young man spoke, his voice was harsh, overloud in the quiet night. "Perhaps that is because you yourself are too weak and fearful to put your hand to the weapon that is within your grasp. If you are afraid to use it, I am not."

"You are a fool."

"You are a coward." Avilius's tone held scorn. "When you asked me to join you in this enterprise, you told me almost nothing but that you needed help on a secret and dangerous task. I foolishly agreed. I did not know that you were planning to throw away something that could bring you renown. Go back to your bookkeeping like the petty bureaucrat you are. Leave me this thing, or I will take it from you. Who will stop me? That fellow?" He laughed, and gestured toward the slave, who held the mules' tether, his face taut with apprehension.

"Avilius, listen to me. You do not even know how to harness the power this machine has. Nor do I. But I know enough to recognize my own ignorance, and what is best left alone."

"Listen to you?" He spat on the ground. "I should have known better than to listen to you when first you asked me to help you. Or better yet, I should have told Priscus Gallo himself that you were conspiring against him. He would have rewarded me, and he would have known what to do with the information."

"He would have taken what information you brought, and slain you where you stood. You do not know Gallo like I do."

"Again, the words of a coward. The difference between you and me is that I do not turn down what fate has brought into my grasp."

"No," Caelius said. They were face to face now, almost as close as lovers about to kiss, and he spoke in what was nearly a whisper. "The difference between you and me is that I know which weapons to use, and on whom." He stabbed forward with his right arm, and the thin-bladed dagger sunk deep between the younger man's ribs. Avilius's eyebrows drew together, and his mouth fell open in shock. He looked down at the knife protruding from his chest as if unable to believe it.

Caelius jerked the dagger out. Avilius fell to his knees in on the damp earth.

"Gods," he said, his voice slurred. A thread of blood, black in the pale moonlight, trickled from the corner of his mouth. "We could have been gods."

He pitched face down onto the ground.

"No doubt the gods themselves will explain to you the error of your thinking." He wiped the dagger blade on Avilius's toga, slipped it back into the sheath at his belt.

"Help me to get him on the cart," he said to the slave. Wide-eyed with fear and astonishment, the man complied, and Avilius's body joined the mechanism underneath its canvas shroud.

With a small gesture Caelius motioned for the slave to start the mules moving again.

Moments later he looked back, in part because he was still fearful of pursuit, and in part to see the dark blood stain on the road, the mark of the first man he had ever killed. But there was no one following them, and a curve in the path had already hidden the spot where he had murdered his friend from sight.

Too bad Avilius had to die. But it only made Caelius more certain that he was right. It had to be destroyed. In the hands of a man like Priscus, the evil that it could wreak would be beyond conception.

The wagon wheel slipped into a muddy rut with a thud, and the mechanism underneath its cover banged against the side of the wagon.

"Steady, fool," Caelius snarled at his own slave. "If the axle breaks, we will go no further, and our lives are both forfeit. What's in this wagon is worth your skin and mine put together."

Was Avilius right? Was he not a good man trying to do the right thing, but a coward? Perhaps he wasn't trying to stop two dangerous people from their evil plans, but a man who had simply lost his nerve. When Livia discovered how to build the thing—and the gods alone knew where she'd found that information, probably in one of those books or scrolls she hoarded so carefully—at first it had seemed like a game. Another one of her forays into magic that she'd become so fond of since her husband was exiled from Rome to this benighted outpost north of Crete.

It became apparent to him gradually that not only was she serious, she was going to succeed this time.

It was a foolish waste of time to try to parse his own motives. At this point, it was too late to turn back. The slave was drugged, the mechanism stolen, Avilius murdered. The die was cast. The game must be played to the end now, however it went.

The path sloped downward, and ahead he saw the sea, steel-gray and restless under a leaden sky. Figures moved on the quay, and Caelius had a panic-stricken moment before he recognized them as his three other slaves, sent ahead to prepare the ship once the wagon was loaded.

He called to them, and three faces turned. All registered apprehension, and one of them looked outright terrified. None understood what was happening, but they knew enough to realize that Caelius was up to something danger-ous, something to double-cross Priscus Gallo and his wife. And they also knew that if whatever it was went sour, they were going to bear the brunt of the punishment. The slaves always did.

The wagon creaked its way down the quay, up alongside the little ship.

"Put this man's body in. When you have done that, lift what is under the canvas in as well. Remember what I commanded you earlier. Take care with it, more care than if you were bearing your own child in your arms. And only handle it through the cloth. Touch it with your bare skin at your peril."

Caelius used a flint to light an oil lamp, hung it from a post on the side of the quay, and the slaves got to work. He alternated watching them, holding his breath in the moments that the heavy bronze clockwork hovered over the sea, and looking over his shoulder, expecting Priscus and Livia to show up at the head of a column of armed servants.

Avilius's body was easily hauled into the boat, but the mechanism was heavier and clumsier, and proved more of a challenge. There was a hollow thunk as the front corner of the mechanism struck the deck of the ship. The two slaves in front backed up, the two behind pushed it forward. Caelius closed his eyes and took a deep breath of relief.

Then the canvas on one corner slipped. The slave on that side—he was the one who had looked so scared earlier— gave a yelp as his hand jerked upwards. Reflexively, he grabbed onto the only hand-hold near, a bronze bar that jutted upwards from underneath the cloth.

A sizzling blue-white crackle, followed by a deafening thunderclap. The slave's body was thrown backwards, flailing like a bundle of rags, struck the bulwark, and flipped into the water with a splash. Caelius leaped forward onto the deck, heart thrumming in his chest. The other three slaves watched, wide-eyed and frozen in place.

He peered over the side. The slave's body floated face-downward, rocking gently in the restless surf.

No time to pull him out, see if he still lives. Fool. I warned him.

He pulled the canvas back over the exposed corner.

"Leave him. Row. Row it out where the water is deep. I will follow in the punt."

The remaining three slaves set the oars, one of them looking over his shoulder at his fallen comrade, and their muscles strained as they pulled at the handles to maneuver the laden boat out to sea.

By the time they were far enough out, the last of the light had faded from the overcast sky. Caelius followed the boat by the sound of its oars striking the water. His eyes were fooled by the shadows and the rocking of the punt, and invented pursuers tailing him, Priscus and Livia bent on rescuing their precious machine and taking their vengeance on him. But no ship appeared, no angry call came from behind.

Surely this had to be far enough. Had it been a summer day, he would have been able to see the deepening of the color of the sea, from turquoise to ultramarine to indigo, as they passed out over the edge of the shallows into the deeper water. Here, he had to guess at how far they'd come, and hope that his fear wasn't driving him to strike too soon, to leave the device in a place where it could be retrieved.

He had to do it now. His heart couldn't take more waiting, more fear, and more rowing in the dark.

He called out to the slaves, ahead of him in the darkness.

"That's enough. Stop. Let me catch up."

His aching shoulders made him certain that they had far outstripped him, but in only a few more strokes of the oars, he saw the shadowed outline of the ship, floating low with its heavy cargo, and the prow of the punt bumped gently into the hull.

"Climb in. Leave the oars. There is no room."

The three slaves scrambled into the punt. It was not meant for four men, and rocked alarmingly until they all were settled. But Caelius stood, and lifted by its handle a heavy axe that he had stowed in the punt earlier.

"You, hold onto the bulwark of the boat. Hold it firmly, mind you. If I lose balance and drop this axe into the sea, all of my planning will come to nothing."

Once the two boats were as steady as they could be, Caelius lifted the axe with weary arms.

Do I have enough strength to do this? I must. I have gotten this far, I can't turn back in failure now.

He swung the axe at the hull of the boat. The blade bit deeply into the wood, but not deeply enough. It took five hard swings to knock loose one of the boards. Two more, and a gaping hole in the side of the boat was letting in enough salt water that the deck was already flooded.

"Let it go. Unless you want to follow it to the bottom."

Now, to wait and watch until it sank. He had to be certain the thing was gone.

With the extra weight of the mechanism, it didn't take long. Soon the waves were cresting over the bulwarks. Suddenly the boat tipped backwards. The device, half underwater, sloshed the same way, sliding across the deck. The prow of the little ship angled up into the air, and the machine fell over on its side, pinning Avilius's body to the deck. Good—if the corpse went to the bottom with it, it was less likely the murder would be discovered.

Caelius watched until the pointed prow of the boat was sucked downward into the waiting ocean.

He let out a long, slow breath, waiting to see if the boat or Avilius's body would bob back up to the surface, but after a few minutes, nothing showed on the waves except the glint of moonlight.

The mechanism was gone.

"Take us back in," he commanded.

"I do not know the way." The slave's voice was thick with fear. "How can we know which way the island is in the dark?"

Suddenly Caelius's heart felt emptied, as if his concern for his own safety had followed the mechanism to the seabed. "I don't know. Guess. Anywhere you can find to make landfall." And maybe it would be better not to return to Antikythera at all. Was there somewhere close enough to row in a little punt, with no food and water? He didn't know. He was a petty bureaucrat, not a mariner. Whenever he had to make a voyage at sea, he was content to let others worry about such things.

But whether by luck or happenstance, it was less than an hour later that the slave in the prow of the boat called out.

Ahead was a little flickering light—the oil lamp Caelius had hung at the quay side. He closed his eyes and said a quick prayer of thanks to the gods for carrying his plan to fruition. He didn't take religion seriously, but at times like this, a quick nod in the gods' direction couldn't hurt.

The slaves climbed out before him, securing the punt to a ring on the side of the quay, one reaching out a hand to steady him as he joined them. He even favored the man with a smile.

"And now, to a well-earned bed."

The slave gave him a tentative, shy smile in return.

"Dog. What have you done with it?"

A harsh female voice, one that Caelius had heard compared to the croak of a raven, split the night air.

His stomach gave a painful clench.

"What?" His voice was weak, faltering.

"You heard me." Livia stepped into the light of the oil lamp, and behind her stood her glowering bear of a husband, Priscus Gallo. "Where have you and this slave filth of yours stowed it? Tell me quickly and perhaps we will give you the mercy of killing you with equal dispatch. As I have already done with my own fool of a slave who fell asleep and let you steal it. Priscus ran him through with a sword as he smiled in his dreams."

A hundred lies and evasions flickered through his head. None of them sounded plausible enough to convince a child, much less to dupe these two, whose guile, intelligence, and ruthlessness were known far and wide. It was with a measure of disbelief, as if he were listening to another's voice, that he heard his mouth say, "You are too late. The thing you seek is sunk to the seafloor. Unless you beg of Neptune to return it to you, it is out of your hands."

Priscus's voice, heavy and cold. "You would not dare."

A disembodied lightness filled him. That he was about to die, he had no doubt at all. The certainty, far from increasing his fear, made it evaporate entirely.

"But I did dare. It will trouble none but the fish, until finally it corrodes and its power is broken forever. What will happen to you then? Perhaps both of you will die with it, destroyed along with your precious mechanism..."

Livia gave an inarticulate scream, and flung out one hand toward him, fingers splayed.

Even though her device sat on its side, five miles out on the floor of the ocean, it was still intact now, its potency undiminished by distance. It would be years before the salt water ate into the bronze, pulled apart the gears and dials, dropping them into the muck where they would remain for two millennia.

Far too late to save him.

He saw the greenish ball of light approach him, shimmering like a rainbow, spreading out, reaching toward him with fingers made of lightning.

His last thought was, *I have done well. The lives taken were a fair price.* His face relaxed into a smile as he was thrown to a place where even Livia's rage could not follow.

2

FIXED INPUT CROWN GEAR: CALIBRATED

THURSDAY, July 23, 2015

BY THE TIME Dr. Lise Verhoeven made her second transfer on the London Underground, she was nearly certain that she was being followed.

Her pursuer was being careful not to appear threatening. That much was clear. But there were three individuals who were possibilities, unless whoever was tailing her was being even more stealthy than she suspected. In order of likelihood, they were: a conspicuously American twenty-something with tousled black hair and a backpack, who had followed her onto the train at Canons Park, and now had made two transfers with her, first at Wembley Park and then at Kings Cross St. Pancras; a tweedy university don type, almost comically stereotypical, who was reading a book of philosophy and watching her when he thought she wasn't looking; and a dowdy grandmother, with snowy-white hair and a flowered dress, who had bumped into her rather hard when she got on at Baker Street, apologized profusely, and now sat with her handbag in her lap, both hands primly clutching the strap, smiling in a benevolent way at her fellow travelers.

She was banking on the American. He seemed the type that they'd hire to follow her. The don looked like he wanted to ask her to lunch, and the grandma was light years away from threatening. Although she did have an odd accent herself.

"I'm so very sorry, dear, how clumsy I am," she'd said, in a fluttery, distressed fashion, when she collided with Lise. It hadn't sounded British, that was certain, but neither was it clearly American, or Australian, or any of the other accents of English with which Lise was familiar.

Of course, her pursuer might not be any of the three. It might be someone else entirely, someone completely unobtrusive.

Or no one at all. Perhaps she was simply being paranoid.

It was Armand Soileau who had put the wind up her at the meeting the previous day. She had been in attendance at a talk he was giving, part of an archaeological conference at his home university of Birkbeck. The topic of his presentation was the Antikythera Mechanism, a collection of fragmentary bronze gears and pins that had been recovered from a shipwreck in the Mediterranean Sea over a hundred years ago, and that most researchers believed to be a device for predicting the positions of planets and timing of eclipses. Lise's specialty was ancient timekeeping devices, especially in pre-Common-Era Greece and Eastern Europe, so both the relic and Soileau's talk were of special interest to her, if not to most of the other people in attendance. Although the audience was mostly composed of professors and students from the School of History, Classics, and Archaeology, the Antikythera Mechanism was an abstruse topic even in a room full of historians. Lise noticed that the applause welcoming Soileau to the podium was polite at best.

Honestly, it probably wasn't the topic. They were more likely put off by his self-congratulatory air. The arrogance rolled off the man in waves, as did his contempt for anyone he considered not at his level of erudition. Which was most everyone. He stood behind the podium, gripping it with both hands, well aware that at a little over two meters tall and 120 kilograms in weight, with a great swatch of wavy chestnut-brown hair and a flowing mustache, he couldn't help but be an imposing figure.

The first part of the talk went by without Lise taking more than cursory notice. She'd read Soileau's papers before, and there was little that he said that was new until nearly a half-hour had passed. By this time, only a few of the grad-uate students, most of whom depended on him for their stipends, were paying attention.

"Fragment D," Soileau said, showing a digital photograph of a corroded bronze gear encased in sediment, "is still of unknown purpose. M. T. Wright and others admit as much. The reconstruction by Freeth and Jones I find unconvincing. I posit that it, and the differential gears from Fragment A, are indications that the Antikythera Mecha-nism was once part of a much larger machine, of unknown purpose. What is certain is that it was not simply a hand-cranked astronomical calendar."

He said the last phrase in tones that were dripping with sarcasm, an effect accentuated by a French accent that twenty years of living in London had not been sufficient to modify.

This made Lise's attention suddenly snap back, full force. Her eyebrows rose at the confidence with which he made the pronouncement.

Whatever could he have meant by that?

But there was no further elaboration. He had already passed on to further details about the gear ratio in the device, and how the fragmentary bits might have fit together.

She listened patiently to the rest of the talk and decided not to confront him during the question-and-answer period, knowing from experience that Soileau tended to treat questions from his younger colleagues as the equivalent of being slapped across both cheeks with a gauntlet. The only attendee who asked him about his odd comment was an elderly gentleman with a thick German accent, who said, "Dr. Soileau, you say the Mechanism was not a calendar. How do you come to such a conclusion?"

Soileau gave the man a smile and a nod. "My dear Professor Vollenweider. I assure you I will have much to say about this at future conferences. I am currently at work on a paper that will elucidate much. You will forgive me for not being more forthcoming, but I hesitate to answer further when I have not, as they say, all of my own ducks in a row. I perhaps should not have mentioned that facet of my research at this point. I respectfully withdraw the comment, and would ask you to focus on the rest of the content of my presentation."

The old man seemed satisfied and inclined his head.

But Dr. Verhoeven was not to be so easily dissuaded. She went up to Soileau following the question-and-answer session, while wine was being served. After waiting nearly a half hour for him to deliver benedictions to his devotees and commence drinking his third glass of wine, she said to him, "Dr. Soileau, you said during your talk that you believe Antikythera to have been more than a calendar. What, might I ask, do you think its purpose was?"

"I believe, Miss Verhoeven, that I said its purpose was unknown."

Lise bristled slightly at his use of "Miss" rather than his reciprocating the honorific "Doctor," but she didn't let it show on her face. "Nevertheless," she said, "you must have some speculations. Someone with your expertise must have let your mind consider the possibilities. I understand your reluctance to put forth untested ideas in a formal talk, but informally, between colleagues…?" She trailed off, letting the implication speak for itself.

Was the flattery too obvious? Soileau gave her a benevolent smile.

"Oh, to be sure, I have ideas," he said and took a sip of his wine. His voice was already a little slurred from the alcohol he'd consumed. "About some of it, I will have more to say in due time. I said as much to Herr Vollenweider, you recall? However, there are parts of what I am researching that is perhaps not… not safe to discuss, not here in public."

Lise could not stop an amused chuckle. "Not safe?" she said. "Why would it not be safe?"

"Has it never occurred to you, Miss Verhoeven, that the Antikythera shipwreck may not have been an accident?"

Now her smile passed into incredulity. "No," she said. "I had never considered such a thing."

Soileau's face registered annoyance, but he maintained his urbane and condescending tone. "Well," he said, "I can see why such an idea would not have occurred to you." He placed considerable emphasis on the word "you," which was obnoxious even for him, and Lise wondered if the wine she'd seen him drink was all he'd had that evening.

"Nevertheless, Dr. Soileau," she began, but he waved her off.

"My research has revealed that the shipwreck at Antikythera was quite deliberate. It was, I believe, done so as to put the Mechanism itself out of commission, safely at the bottom of the sea."

"But why?" Lise said.

"Because of what it could do," Soileau said, his voice dropping to a whisper. "Because of what it could do again, if someone were to rebuild it."

"Which is?"

"Let me say simply that it was not a measurement device, it was a controlling device. A dangerous one, that people would go to great lengths to reconstruct. That they have not succeeded yet is perhaps due to the authority with which Freeth *et al.* have proclaimed that it was nothing more than an elaborate calendar."

"What is your evidence of this?" Lise said. The skepticism was clear in her own voice, but she decided that she didn't care. She was his equal, whether or not he acknowledged the fact.

Soileau looked at her for a time, wine glass poised in one hand, his eyes narrowing, his bushy right eyebrow lifting a little. "It would be unwise of me to tell you more," he said. "And unwise of you to inquire more. I have been fortunate myself that I have not been, what is the word…" He waved his hand about, and the wine in his glass sloshed around. A little of it splattered on the white tablecloth, staining it crimson. "… that I have not been hindered in my research. Perhaps they believe that leaving me to work is more fruitful toward their goals than stopping me would be. But you, on the other hand… they would consider you simply a liability."

"They?" Lise said. "Who are 'they'?"

"I believe, Miss Verhoeven, you have asked quite enough questions. I only say this because of concern over your safety, you understand. They have many ears, you know." He looked over Lise's shoulder and smiled, and said in a loud voice, "Metaxas, my dear friend! I am so delighted you came!" A tall, slender man, with curly black hair and small, steel-framed glasses, gave Soileau a frosty smile and a little bow. "I read your paper on the Riace bronzes. Masterful, my friend. Quite masterful."

The audience, Lise knew, was over. He turned away from her and refilled his wine glass.

The thought haunted her through the evening, however, and it disturbed her sleep as she tried to shut her mind off, lying in a comfortable bed in a friend's flat in Canons Park.

She had two more days in London before flying back home to Antwerp, and the only thing she could do to stop the questions forming in her mind was to promise herself that the next day, she'd try to fill in the ellipses in Soileau's tale.

After her friend had left for work the following morning and Lise was lingering over coffee, she sat with her laptop searching for anything that could give her clues about what Soileau had hinted at. She reread the Freeth and Jones paper that he had so roundly dismissed and dug up various other references on the topic. None of it answered her questions. If any archaeologists considered the Antikythera Mechanism to be more than an analog timekeeping device, they hadn't published their speculations.

That was when she thought of calling Georgios Metaxas, Soileau's colleague at Birkbeck, and another expert on Greek bronzes and early technology. She had met Metaxas at conferences before, and he seemed solid enough if a bit aloof and not especially friendly. He was there the previous evening, and must have heard the odd comment during Soileau's presentation. At least it was a better idea than trying to talk to Soileau himself, who by now was likely to be nursing a hangover.

She called the Department of History, Classics, and Archaeology, and after speaking to a secretary who was none too friendly herself, she was put through to Metaxas.

She hadn't expected to succeed this quickly. She'd thought that she would have to leave a message, and have time to formulate her questions more thoroughly while waiting for him to return her call. But here she was, cellphone in hand, an awkward silence developing after a cool voice said, "This is Metaxas," and waited for a response.

"This is Lise Verhoeven," she said, stumbling a little, and then clearing her throat. "I am a fellow archaeologist, and I saw you last evening at Professor Soileau's talk, although we did not get a chance to speak."

"I know who you are," Metaxas said.

Lise frowned. It sounded, to her ears, as if her name had only recently been the subject of discussion. But perhaps she was reading too much into Metaxas's words. He was notorious for disliking small talk, she knew.

"I wanted to discuss with you the allusion Dr. Soileau made, regarding an alternate model for the purpose of the Antikythera Mechanism."

"Soileau mentioned no alternate model. He said that he did not know what its purpose was."

"He suggested that he did know. After the talk was over, he spoke with me for a time. You may not have heard…"

"I heard what he said." There was a pause. "You should not put too much into what Dr. Soileau said last night. He was… shall we say… in his cups."

"Perhaps," Lise said. "But that doesn't mean he was lying."

"Why would you not ask Soileau himself?' Metaxas said, his voice taking on an annoyed edge. "If he knows more, then he would be the one to tell you, not me. Antikythera is hardly my area of study."

"I did ask," she said. "Soileau gave me hints that such knowledge might be dangerous."

There was no response for a moment. Then he said, a hint of amusement in his voice, "Dangerous? For what reason would a two-thousand-year-old relic be dangerous?"

"That's what I want to know."

"Then as I said, you should ask Soileau himself, if he gave you to understand that there was a reason to believe such… conjecture." The hint of a pause made Lise wonder if he had only at the last moment stopped himself from saying "nonsense" or "foolishness."

"You don't know, then? I thought that perhaps since you work together…"

"Perhaps Soileau was making you a victim of a joke," Metaxas said. "Unless you should find yourself being followed by sinister individuals on the Tube, I believe that you can conclude that Dr. Soileau was testing your credulity. Too much wine can make people act unwisely. I do not know what else to tell you, Miss Verhoeven."

Again the use of "Miss." Lise sneered at the phone, but said, in a controlled voice, "Thank you for your time, Dr. Metaxas," and ended the call.

THE COMBINATION OF THE MALEVOLENT "THEY" from Soileau, and Metaxas's jeering suggestion that she might be followed must have been what played upon her imagination, leading her to wonder which of her fellow passengers was following her with evil intent. Lise was an eminently practical woman, not usually prone to flights of fancy, but sitting on the train with the vague hints from her colleagues floating through her mind, she was spooked enough to be convinced of anything.

But she disembarked at Warren Street Station without incident. She gave a quick glance back at the three passengers she had suspected. The tweedy university don type was himself walking to the exit, as the train doors opened, and was giving her no further attention. The young American with the backpack was still in his seat, in enthusiastic conversation with a young redheaded woman who, as Lise looked, laughed and blushed at something he said.

The white-haired grandmother had fallen asleep.

Lise took a deep breath and chuckled to herself. So much for the evil machinations of Dr. Soileau's mysterious "They." She left the train with about fifteen other passengers, made her way to the escalators, and five minutes later, was walking toward Birkbeck and the day's slate of scholarly presentations.

She arrived early in the auditorium where the first talk was scheduled. It was to be a report of a recent discovery of a Bronze Age site near Tiryns, in southern Greece, something only tangentially connected with her own research. She seated herself near the front and looked around her. Even given that the presentation was not supposed to begin for twenty minutes, the hall was unusually empty. What few people were there were standing, clustered in knots of threes and fours, whispering to each other.

It became obvious that something was seriously wrong when only a half-dozen other people had arrived by the ten AM start time, and several of the ones who had been there earlier had already left. At ten minutes after ten, Dr. Niles Rayleigh, a venerable professor of archaeology who was one of the moderators of the conference, stepped to the podium. He had a stunned look in his pale blue eyes, and his skin was the color of whey.

"May I… may I have your attention, please," he said and passed a shaking hand through his thinning gray hair. "I… I'm afraid we are canceling the remainder of the presentations at the conference. I understand that… that many of you have come from a long way away, and we apologize for the inconvenience. We will reimburse you or your institution for the cost of the conference fee. I…" He stopped, cleared his throat, then opened his mouth, but no words would form.

"Dr. Rayleigh," Lise said. "Why? What has happened?"

"I am afraid… afraid that a terrible thing has happened." He swallowed. "Professor Armand Soileau, whom many of you know and have worked with closely, has… was found, this morning. In his office. He was found murdered."

"Murdered?" Lise said. The word came out in a squeak.

"He was struck with a heavy object in the center of his forehead, with considerable force," Dr. Rayleigh said. Lise wondered if he were going to faint, or vomit, but he swallowed, and continued. "He must have been killed instantly."

3

Main Drive Wheel: Position Calibrated, Drive Set In Motion

Eclipse Pointer: Engaged

Sunday, October 25, 2015

The Skipton Bible Church of Skipton, New York was about five hundred yards from Reverend Morris Bradley's front door, and he drove to and from church only in extreme weather. Today it was hardly extreme, but was certainly unpleasant, the chilly and gray breath of the dying year. The wind curled around the denuded maple trees, picking up drifts of brown leaves that only two weeks ago had been a fireworks display of red, yellow, and orange. He pulled his coat tighter around him, and squinted against a great gust that reached right through the wool and lining and chilled him to the skin. He passed through the old cemetery on the north side of the church, between simple grave markers whose writing was eroded with age and furred with moss. He offered up a quick prayer for the dead as he rounded the corner of the church, a habit he had formed as a young man whenever he was in sight of a cemetery.

He trotted up the stairs of the church and unlocked the massive mahogany front door. The church building was over a hundred years old, which meant that it was solidly constructed, but dimly lit and impossible to heat. He turned up the thermostat to 75 degrees and waited for the clunk and gurgle of the ancient boiler kicking on, then walked down the center aisle, the oak planks of the floor creaking under his shoes.

He went to his office, a small room at the back of the church, sat at his desk, and absently leafed through the notes for his sermon. The reading was from Revelation, chapter 13: "Then I stood on the sand of the sea. And I saw a beast rising up out of the sea, having seven heads and ten horns, and on his horns ten crowns, and on his heads a blasphemous name." In his sermon, he compared the beast to American society, with its love of material things and its general disdain of all matters spiritual. Keep your mind on God, and don't listen to the voice of the beast: "If anyone worships the beast or its image, or accepts its mark on his forehead or hand, he too will drink the wine of God's wrath."

That should satisfy the likes of Mrs. Anson. He looked up from his notes with a wry smile. Mrs. Anson loved the Book of Revelation, especially parts about the downfall of the wicked. She herself was a shrewish woman who rode herd on her husband and three children and anyone else who would listen to her, and one Sunday last summer Reverend Bradley had not been able to resist looking right at her while reading from St. Paul's letter to Titus: "Put them in mind to be ready to every good work, speak evil of no man, to be not brawlers, but gentle, showing all meekness unto all men." He doubted she'd taken his point, but there were more than one of the other members of the congregation who had. Joe Brumback, the Ansons' next door neighbor, shook Reverend Bradley's hand particularly warmly after that service ended.

Reverend Bradley heard a creak as the front door swung open, and he consulted his watch. Forty-five minutes till the service began. That was probably Karen Cromarty, the organist, coming in to warm up. He stood, wincing a little at the stiffness in his back, and walked into the nave of the church, to discuss the hymns for that morning's service.

It wasn't Karen. Sitting in one of the back pews was a young man, probably in his twenties. He was shivering uncontrollably. He had an untidy swatch of black hair which accentuated the sallowness of his complexion, and there were dark smudges beneath his eyes. With an effort Bradley ignored a sudden and inexplicable wash of fear rising in him, and went over and sat down next to the young man.

"What's the matter, son?" he said. "You look half frozen. Can I get you a jacket and something hot to drink?"

The man looked up, and their eyes locked for a moment. There was a flash of clear blue, a startling color on that pale face. His eyes were wide and terrified. Reverend Bradley suddenly thought that he had never seen anyone who looked as frightened.

"I'm not cold…" the young man struggled over the words. "I mean, I'm cold but that's not why I'm here. I need help…"

"What kind of help?"

"Can I stay here?"

The question caught Reverend Bradley entirely by surprise. "Here, in the church?" Reverend Bradley's perplexity, bordering on alarm, came through clearly. "We don't have the facilities to house… to have someone living here. There's a homeless shelter down in Colville, if…"

The young man gave him an irritated wave of the hand. "I have a place to live. It's not safe. I'm…" He swallowed, and the chattering of his teeth intensified, then subsided. "There are people who are going to kill me."

For a moment, the Reverend stared at the man in the pew. Love your neighbor as yourself, the Bible said. He needed to help this man. It was commanded by the Lord. As a minister of God, how could he refuse? But why did he feel a rising desire to show this man the door, watch him leave, never see him again?

"Maybe the police…?" he began, and immediately felt ashamed that he was trying to push the responsibility onto the secular authority.

The young man laughed bitterly. "Police. Don't you think I'd have gone to them if they could have done something? I'm not stupid. The police will ask too many questions."

"If you have nothing to hide…" Reverend Bradley said, but the man cut him off.

"Everyone has something to hide. Besides, if the police could help, do you think I would be talking to a frail old pastor in a drafty church in the sticks?"

This comment stung. "What can I do to help?" the Reverend asked, trying to keep the reluctance out of his voice.

Why *was* he reluctant? This young man looked pitiable, not dangerous.

"Let me stay here. Here in the church."

"Why?" The word came out in a bleat before Reverend Bradley could stop it.

"I told you."

"How do you know that the people you're running from won't find you here?"

Panic glittered behind the man's blue eyes. "It wouldn't occur to them. I hope."

A flutter of fear rippled across his skin. It was his duty to help those in need. But there was something about this situation that was wrong, wrong right through. Unbidden, he thought of a quote from the First Letter of John: "Beloved, believe not every spirit, but try the spirits whether they are of God: because many false prophets are gone out into the world."

"You need to tell me more," he said, and shame rose in him at how weak he sounded. "Without that, I can't... I'd have to talk to the church officers..."

In one startling movement, the man stood up. Reverend Bradley shied back like a startled horse. He looked up at the glittering blue eyes set in that ghostly face.

"I should have known. You religious are all alike."

"Son, I didn't mean..."

"I'm not your son," he spat. "All empty promises. I was a fool even to come here. You talk about fighting evil. You talk and talk. And if Satan was at the church door, you'd let him walk right in."

Reverend Bradley stood up, his mind whirling. "Now, young man, I didn't say I wouldn't help you... I just need... you need to tell me..."

"I've already told you too much. There are wheels within wheels. You should know that phrase. It comes from the Bible, right?" He gave a high, mirthless laugh. "Wheels within wheels."

"It's from the Book of Ezekiel, I believe..." Reverend Bradley said, but once again, the man cut him off.

"Doesn't matter where it comes from. You don't under-stand it. That's all your faith is. Talking about things without understanding them." He turned away. "I should have known you wouldn't be willing to do what it takes to stop the gears from turning." The shivering, which had subsided for a few minutes, struck him again, and he stood mute and trembling for a moment as if he were on the verge of a seizure. But he regained control of himself, walked down the aisle toward the door, and pulled it open. An icy gust of air and a few leaves swirled into the church.

Reverend Bradley raised his voice, and shouted, "If you need help, I'll help you..." but the wind rose and caught his words and tossed them away. The young man turned, and looked back at him for a moment, and then said some-thing, something that was so odd that at first Reverend

Bradley couldn't even comprehend what he'd said. He said it in a quiet, despairing voice, but it carried on the wind and the scraping of the leaves across the hardwood floor. Reverend Bradley tried to convince himself afterwards that he hadn't really heard what the man said, but that was a lie.

Then the door swung shut, and the reverend was alone.

THAT EVENING, Reverend Bradley couldn't remember any details about that morning's service. He expected it went well enough, but his mind wasn't there in the church. The only comparison he could make was to the way he'd felt when he'd had a concussion as a teenager. The whole world seemed vague, as if it weren't quite real, and nothing made any lasting impression on his mind. All that was fixed and solid from the entire day was the five-minute conversation with the young man in the back of the church. But he couldn't pin that down, either. The whole incident was dreamlike, surreal, its meaning always a little beyond his grasp.

But his mind kept returning to the last words the man had said before walking out of the door of the church, words that were to disturb his sleep that night, and for several nights hence—words that he repeatedly tried, and failed, to put rational meaning to.

"You just set the clockwork in motion. Remember that. And if you ever run into me again, don't believe a single thing I say."

4

Fixed Input Crown Gear: Engaged

Monday, October 26, 2015, through Tuesday, November 10, 2015

Transcript of telephone interview with Philip Dawson and Audrey Westerman:

PD: Ms. Westerman, you were Dr. Armand Soileau's secretary, is that correct?

AW: I am the secretary for the School of History, Classics, and Archaeology, yes. I was not Professor Soileau's personal secretary.

PD: How well did you know Dr. Soileau?

AW: I knew him in a professional capacity. We were not friends outside of the workplace if that is what you're asking.

PD: How much do you know about his personal life?

AW: I have met his wife, Corinne, and spoken with her at college events on more than one occasion. Other than that, Professor Soileau was not forthcoming about his life outside university. Nor, I might add, was it any of my business.

PD: What can you tell me about Dr. Georgios Metaxas?

AW: Can you clarify the question?

PD: Dr. Metaxas is currently on a sabbatical leave, is that correct?

AW: That is correct, yes.

PD: Do you know where he is?

AW: It is not the University's policy to monitor lecturers while they are on sabbatical.

PD: The answer is no, then.

AW: That is correct.

PD: Do you know of a woman from Belgium named Lise Verhoeven?

AW: I've never heard the name, so far as I recall.

PD: To what extent were you familiar with Armand Soileau's research?

AW: Part of my duties is to type and format scholarly papers by the professors in the department. I have become somewhat conversant with their research, although I am hardly an expert.

PD: Are you aware of anything about his research that might have put him in danger?

AW: (pause) I believe you are asking me whether I know of anything about him that could have been a motive for his murder?

PD: Yes.

AW: Let me assure you, Mr. Dawson, that I have already spoken with the police on this matter, and I was completely forthcoming with them. They were of the opinion that Professor Soileau's murder was a random event, perhaps a joy killing by a street thug. There is nothing I know of in his life or his work that would have been a reason to kill him. You are researching this for a television show, correct?

PD: That is correct, yes.

AW: Allow me to urge you not to sensationalize Professor Soileau's life. He was a brilliant academic, and like many brilliant academics, somewhat eccentric. The world is full of people who enjoy exaggerating claims and making capital on hints and whispers. Frankly, I find this kind of behavior to be repulsive, and if that is what you are planning, I want nothing to do with it.

PD: We are trying to be as accurate as possible…

AW: Then the police report should be sufficient for you. Good day, Mr. Dawson.

PD: Good day.

(call terminated)

Transcript of telephone interview with Philip Dawson and Shirley Robart:

PD: Mrs. Robart, you were romantically involved with Armand Soileau for some time, is that correct?

SR: I suppose that's right.

PD: You suppose?

SR: I mean, I guess it's common knowledge now. His wife knows. The police…

PD: Yes?

SR: The police pried into everything. They thought that I might have killed him.

PD: Why did they think that?

SR: I don't know. I loved Armand, for all of his faults, and he treated me well. I knew he wasn't going to leave his wife. He was clear on that. And he said that his wife knew that he was… that he had others on the side.

PD: Mistresses.

SR: Yes.

PD: Did he imply that his wife had no problem with this?

SR: He didn't say that, exactly. More that she knew and accepted it even though she didn't like it. He said that she understood his, you know, his needs. And that if it kept him happy, she could live with it.

PD: Did it surprise you when you found out that Corinne Soileau had no idea what was going on? And that he had other mistresses besides yourself?

SR: Yes. I could've been knocked over with a feather, I was that surprised. But even so, she didn't fuss, you know? A real lady, she is. And I didn't fuss, either. What would have been the point?

PD: You had an alibi for the time of the murder, is that correct?

SR: I did. My husband and I were in Lancaster, visiting his parents.

PD: Your husband?

SR: Now, don't take that tone with me. My husband and I have been through it all already. He's had affairs, I had an affair. We've patched it all up.

PD: I see.

SR: I really don't know who would have wanted to murder Armand. He was a wonderful man, quite generous, and a genius.

PD: What did you know about his research?

SR: Me? Nothing. He used to tell me about it, you know, after a few drinks and a tumble, when we were cuddling and talking, you know how you do? He'd tell me all sorts of things about the Greeks and the Romans and all. I didn't understand much of it, but I let him talk. Men like to have their women listen to them.

PD: Well, I think that's all the questions I have for you.

SR: If you want to interview me in person, I'd be happy to. This is going on a television show, right?

PD: Yes.

SR: That would be ever so exciting, being part of a television show. You'd have all of my friends watching it, I can promise you.

PD: We'll be in touch if that's an option, Mrs. Robart.

(call terminated)

TRANSCRIPT OF TELEPHONE conversation between Audrey Westerman and Corinne Soileau:

AW: Mrs. Soileau, I hope that my calling you is not out of line.

CS: Not at all, my dear, what is it?

AW: There is a man who is making himself a nuisance, and I thought I had ought to warn you. He works for one of those television series, about unsolved murders and mysteries and so forth. His name is Philip Dawson.

CS: He was inquiring about Armand's death?

AW: Yes. He asked me a great many questions, but I put him off. I didn't want you to be blindsided by a telephone call. I know how upsetting that could be, after all, you went through this summer.

CS: That was terribly, terribly thoughtful of you, Miss Westerman.

AW: So, he hasn't contacted you yet?

CS: No.

AW: He seemed to think that there was something in Professor Soileau's work that may have been the motive for his… for what happened.

CS: I cannot imagine what that could have been.

AW: Nor I. But I thought I might mention it.

CS: How very odd.

AW: He also asked about some of his colleagues. Professor Metaxas, of course. And another… do you know a Lise Verhoeven? She's not at the University, but he said she had some connection to Professor Soileau's research. I found her name mentioned in some of the literature, but I don't know that she ever collaborated with Professor Soileau.

CS: No, no, not that I am aware of. I do not recall his ever mentioning that name.

AW: I don't want to keep you. But I did want you to be forewarned if he calls.

CS: Thank you, my dear, and once more, let me thank you for your support after Armand's death. You are a true friend.

AW: If there is anything more I can do, please let me know.

CS: I will.

(call terminated)

Transcript of telephone interview with Philip Dawson and Jan Verhoeven:

PD: You are Lise Verhoeven's brother, is that correct?

JV: Yes, that is so.

PD: I have some questions about your sister's work if you don't mind.

JV: You may ask your questions.

PD: She did research on Greek archaeology?

JV: Yes. She was one of the most respected researchers in her field. She studied particularly the timekeeping devices and calendars that were made by Greeks and Romans, from antiquity.

PD: What was she working on at the time of her death?

JV: She was studying a device called the Antikythera Mechanism. It was, I believe, a bronze machine of some sort found in a shipwreck off the coast of Greece. You must understand, however, Mr. Dawson, I have little technical knowledge of my sister's work. You might be better off contacting one of her colleagues at the University.

PD: I'm more interested in the personal side of her research. Did you notice any changes in your sister's behavior before her death?

JV: I do not understand what you are asking.

PD: Did she act distracted? Afraid?

JV: Afraid? No. I do not believe that I ever saw Lise afraid of anything. But she did seem… how do you say it? I believe the word is obsessed. After she came back from a conference in London, I think it was perhaps three weeks before her death. She was intense in her research, completely absorbed. But she was passionate about her field of study. I did not think it was that unusual.

PD: After her death, did you wonder if there was some connection?

JV: A connection? How so? Lise's death was accidental, did you not know?

PD: There is some possibility that it may not have been an accident, that she might have been killed because of what she was studying.

JV: (swearing in Dutch)

PD: Mr. Verhoeven…

JV: What you are saying is ridiculous. Who would kill someone over an ancient relic, of no possible use to anyone?

PD: She had not spoken to you about the possibility of there being more to her research? Something of more than academic relevance?

JV: I don't… (pause)

PD: Yes?

JV: It is nothing, very likely, I think it is nothing. But the week before she died, she was speaking to my wife, and she said something peculiar. Lise visited us for supper, and she was talking with Marta, my wife, and she said… how did she put it? My wife asked her, making a joke, you know, if she had found the key to wind up the clock she was studying. And Lise said, "It wasn't wound with a key." Marta laughed, and said, "What did you use to wind it with, then?" And Lise tapped her forehead, and said, "Your brain."

PD: What did she mean by that?

JV: I do not know. At the time, I thought she was having her little joke with my wife. Lise had an odd sense of humor. But I do not understand why anyone would have killed because of what she was studying. What evidence do you have?

PD: There were two other researchers who were studying the Antikythera Mechanism. One was murdered this summer, and one is missing.

JV: (silence)

PD: Mr. Verhoeven?

JV: Why was I not told about this before?

PD: You said that the police considered your sister's death an accident. There would have been no reason to connect the deaths.

JV: I do not know what to tell you. That my sister might have been murdered, it is extraordinary.

PD: Is there anything else you can tell me about her work? Anything that might shed some light on a motive?

JV: No, nothing I know of. Perhaps if you called her colleagues at the University?

PD: I've spoken with the head of her department. She was as astonished as you were that her death might not have been an accident.

JV: Have you contacted the police about this?

PD: I still have very little to go on. I am reluctant to involve the police until I am more certain of my facts.

JV: I see.

PD: Do you have any idea of who else might know more?

JV: I will speak to my wife about this. She and Lise were very close. There might have been something Lise said to her that could be helpful.

PD: Thank you. I apologize if I've upset you, Mr. Verhoeven.

JV: Yes, yes. I understand. I will contact you if I find out anything further.

(call terminated)

TRANSCRIPT OF TELEPHONE conversation between Jan Verhoeven and Dr. Margarethe Bornstra (translated from Dutch):

JV: Dr. Bornstra, this is Jan Verhoeven, Lise's brother. I am sorry to call you at home, but I needed to speak with you.

MB: No apology needed, Mr. Verhoeven. What can I do for you?

JV: Today I received a call from an Englishman, a Mr. Dawson, regarding Lise's death. He said that he had spoken to you and that he told you that Lise may have been killed because of her research.

MB: I spoke with him, yes. What he said was nothing more than supposition. Speculation for a television show about unsolved murders.

JV: He did not tell me that he worked for a television show! He gave me to understand that he was some sort of private investigator.

MB: That is incorrect. He is a writer and researcher for a television series about sensational crimes that the police had been unable to solve. Those people, they are beneath contempt, the way they will lie to get people to talk.

JV: What did you tell him?

MB: Only that Lise was a brilliant researcher, and that she had been working on a study of Greek astronomical calendars before she died. Nothing more.

JV: He asked me a peculiar question. He asked if I had noticed a change in Lise's behavior before her death.

MB: What did you tell him?

JV: That Lise did appear more… more obsessed than usual. She was like a hound on a hare's trail. Do you know what line of research she was following?

MB: Only in general terms. She had copious notes on the Antikythera Mechanism, working toward a paper she intended to submit by the end of the year. All I know of it is that she said she had opened up a new area of research on it, something quite groundbreaking. She was working in collaboration with archaeologists in the UK and the United States. But since her death, all of our colleagues here in Antwerp have been involved in research of our own, and no one has picked up where she left off. Her notes, I believe, are still in storage at the University.

JV: He said that Lise's death was connected to the death of another researcher, in London, this summer.

MB: (pause) Do you mean Armand Soileau?

JV: He didn't mention a name.

MB: I cannot imagine that it is someone else. Soileau was murdered in July. But my understanding was that he was killed because of some kind of sexual indiscretion. An aggrieved mistress, or something of that sort.

JV: But if Dawson is correct, and Lise's death was also a murder…

MB: I do not know how that could be. What could possibly motivate two such murders?

JV: I have no idea.

MB: Perhaps it would be prudent to contact the police.

JV: I think it might. But what would we tell them? We have no evidence, only the questions this Dawson asked.

MB: (pause) It is most upsetting. I will give it some consideration, Mr. Verhoeven.

JV: Thank you. I appreciate your time, Dr. Bornstra.

(call terminated)

TRANSCRIPT OF TELEPHONE conversation between Dr. Margarethe Bornstra and Sabine Leeuwens (translated from Dutch):

. . .

MB: Miss Leeuwens, do you have a moment?

SL: Of course, Dr. Bornstra.

MB: I want to know what became of the research notes of Lise Verhoeven.

SL: I cleaned out her office after her brother took her personal belongings. I asked him if he wanted her academic files, and he said no, that they might be of use to the University. So I boxed them and put them in the closet next to Dr. Van Vleet's office, where we store old journals.

MB: Might you retrieve them for me?

SL: I would be happy to, Dr. Bornstra. Shall I put them in your office?

MB: Yes. But if you have time, would you go now and check on them?

SL: Of course. Shall I ring you back?

MB: No, Miss Leeuwens, I will hold.

(pause)

SL: Dr. Bornstra… I cannot imagine why, but the boxes are gone. There were three, I believe, containing all of the files from her cabinets. I know I labeled them carefully and placed them in the closet, perhaps two weeks after her death. I do not understand…

MB: Do not be distressed, Miss Leeuwens, I am sure you were as careful as always. Who else besides you has a key to that closet?

SL: Yourself, of course, and I believe that Mr. Kuyper does, as he manages the archives. And probably the custodians of the building. But Dr. Bornstra… (pause)

MB: Yes?

SL: Who would have taken Dr. Verhoeven's research notes?

MB: I do not know, Miss Leeuwens.

(call terminated)

5

MAIN DRIVE WHEEL: FIRST TURN

Wednesday, November 30, 2015

ON THE LAST day of November, Reverend Bradley climbed into the driver's seat of his aging Nissan station wagon. It wasn't that often that he made the thirty-mile trip down to Colville, the nearest good-sized town, but that morning he needed some washers to fix the chronic leak in his bathroom sink. He made a list of various other oddments—a box of nails, a bottle of wood glue, a bucket of ice-melt—that could be gotten at Colville Hardware. If the trip was necessary, may as well make it worth the drive.

He spent the drive mentally arranging his duties over the next few days, thinking about planning for the Christmas service, and praying. They were mostly prayers of thanksgiving for his health, his children, his ministry in the church, his congregation, and simple petitionaries—that he not hit a deer on the way to Colville; that the snow that had been threatening in the somber skies hold off till he got back home; that he would remember to get everything he'd come for and not have to make another trip to the hardware store anytime soon. He slipped a hand into his pants pocket and checked to make sure that he had his list. His memory was good for a man of sixty-eight, but lists didn't hurt.

The parking lot of the hardware store was only about a third full, typical for a weekday morning. Reverend Bradley pulled into an open spot, got out of his car, and walked past stacks of topsoil and bark mulch bags, covered with tarps for the winter and dusted with snow. He pulled open the glass-fronted door, and a welcoming blast of warm air brushed his face. Even on a middling-cold day like today, the heater of his car never warmed the interior very well.

He passed Christmas decorations, a large cage with three small kittens for sale, a table full of sale items ("They'd Make Perfect Gifts!" a handwritten sign proclaimed), and turned down the aisle toward the plumbing section. As he rounded the corner, he almost collided with a man who was bent over, examining an assortment of socket wrenches hanging from hooks on the wall.

"Oh, excuse me," Reverend Bradley said.

The man turned a smiling face up toward the Reverend. "No problem, sir."

Reverend Bradley's heart gave an uneven little gallop. It was the young man he'd talked to in the church. He looked different today. His face was fuller and had lost the deathly paleness, his hair was cut short and was neatly combed. But it was definitely the same man.

"Are you all right, sir?" the man asked.

"I..." Reverend Bradley began and stopped. "I'm sorry, it startled me. I didn't expect to see you again, I suppose."

The man's forehead wrinkled, but his smile didn't dim. "I'm sorry, you must be mistaking me for someone. I don't think we've met."

"A month ago. In the church. Skipton Bible Church."

The man shrugged, and shook his head. "Sorry. I've been through Skipton once or twice, but I've never been to church there."

A panicked voice in Reverend Bradley's head said, *Leave. Make your apologies and leave. Get out of here.* But he continued to stand there, looking at the man's face, as if hypnotized. "I... are you sure?"

"Quite sure," the man said, and looked a little puzzled. "Perhaps someone who looks like me?"

"No," said the reverend. "It was you."

"I assure you, it wasn't," the man said, and his smile faded a little.

Reverend Bradley could see the dawning irritation in the man's face—the look a basically nice person has when confronted on a bus or a street corner by someone who is off his rocker. *I said it wasn't me*, the man's face said. *Give it up and leave me alone.*

But somehow the Reverend couldn't stop himself. "You looked ill, you asked for help..."

The rest of the smile disappeared. "Look, I told you, I've never been to the church in Skipton..." He paused, and then all of a sudden, the irritated expression was gone, and was replaced by astonishment. "I wonder..." He trailed off, the question mark hanging in the air between them.

"What is it?"

"I have a... an identical twin brother. I haven't seen him or heard from him in ten years. He left home right when we graduated high school, supposedly heading for California. Did the guy in the church tell you his name?"

"No."

"Wouldn't that be something, if David was back in town," he said, looking away, his voice low and awestruck. "And in a church, no less. What did he say to you?"

"He told me somebody was trying to kill him, and he needed help. Then he got up and left before I could do anything to help him." *That isn't the whole truth*, thought Reverend Bradley guiltily, *but it's enough for now.*

"David was paranoid, that's for sure," the man said. "Our parents wanted him evaluated by a psychologist, but he left before they could get him there."

"Do you want me to... um, contact you? If he shows up again?"

The man hesitated. "I guess... I suppose I should know if he's in town. I don't know why he wouldn't have come to me first, but I suppose he has his reasons. But, yeah, I'd like to know. Do you have something to write with?"

Reverend Bradley reached into his pocket, found his shopping list, and handed it to the man. There was a pen on a chain on the counter behind them, next to several bins containing bulk nails. He picked it up and wrote, "Stephen Calhoun," and a phone number then handed the slip back.

"I'll call you if I see him again," Reverend Bradley said.

Stephen nodded, and said, "Thanks," and turned back to the socket wrenches.

A LITTLE DAZED, Reverend Bradley completed his shopping and climbed back in his car for the return drive to Skipton. He was pulling out of the parking lot when it came to him. Thunderstruck, he turned back toward the façade of the hardware store, looking for Stephen Calhoun, trying to convince himself that he hadn't dreamed the entire incident.

How could it not have occurred to me? he thought, his brain careening wildly. *Why didn't I think about it while I was talking to him?*

He drove along, mostly on auto-pilot, while his mind frantically searched his memory for what exactly Stephen had said to him in the hardware store. It had taken him by surprise. How could he have expected to run into the man in Colville Hardware?

The last words of the young man in the church were echoing in his skull. That low, despairing voice, somehow cutting through the sound of the wind rushing in the open door of the church, speaking of it being too late to help, of clockwork in motion, and of lies.

If you ever run into me again, don't believe a single thing I say.

Reverend Bradley pulled out the note with Stephen Calhoun's name and telephone number on it, held it before him in a trembling hand, and kept driving.

THE SOUTH END OF COLVILLE, New York is singularly unattractive. It is too far from Carlisle Lake to be scenic, and the flat topography, unusual for upstate New York, makes it both visually boring and prone to flooding. The result was that early in the town's development it had been relegated to run-down shops and low-rent housing. In the last two decades, following an impressive combined flood mitigation and urban renewal project, it had been taken over by strip malls and car dealerships. The stores were, by and large, more successful than the flood mitigation, and there were still parts of the area which became stagnant ponds whenever it rained more than three days in a row. This proved only a minor deterrent to the big box stores and fast food restaurants, which in the previous decade had sprung up like some sort of strange, rectangular fungi that thrived in the waterlogged soil. Their success did not make them attractive, however, and most of the people who drove down the main road through the south part of Colville did their business at the Home Depot, Walmart, or Eckerd's, and then kept on moving.

Ten years ago Louise Middlebury had attempted to bring a small pocket of charm to the seediest corner of the town, and had opened a florist's shop and nursery right off Route 7, in a narrow triangle of land hemmed in by a K-Mart SuperStore on one side and Petrillo Ford ("If Joe Petrillo didn't sell you your car, you paid too much!") on the other. She called it Robin's Nest Nursery and Florist.

The business struggled along, especially in winter, when all of her nursery stock were lying leafless and dormant in thick layers of mulch. Most of her business in December was in poinsettias, a flower which Louise frankly loathed, and in balsam fir wreaths, which at least smelled nice.

It was a little less than a month before Christmas, and business had been, if not brisk, at least enough to allow her to make her payments. Louise was unmarried and had no near relatives, significant others, or anyone else to pick up the pieces if the business were to go that way. She stood at the counter, twisting fragrant fir branches into circles, the sweet resinous smell all around her, wondering if she'd sell enough wreaths, cut flower arrangements, tropical house plants, and hideous poinsettias wrapped in red or green foil to make ends meet until May and the beginning of the growing season.

It was as she was musing on the fact that she'd not had a single customer that morning that the bell on the door jangled, and a man walked in. She looked up, and smiled in recognition, and the man, a tall, slender gentleman with thinning gray hair, smiled back.

"Hello, Miss Middlebury, how are you today?"

"Fine, Reverend, thanks, and yourself?"

"Well, well enough," he said, absently, and Louise immediately wondered why he sounded so tentative.

"I expect you're here to order your wreaths," she said, continuing to wrap branches and green wire together as she talked. "I doubt even you will be buying perennials today."

"That's right," he said. "We must have our fir wreaths every year. No one makes them like you do."

"You could have called it in," she said. "It's always nice to see you, of course, but it's a bit of a drive."

"I was in Colville anyway, and I thought I'd kill two birds."

Louise set down the wreath that she was working on, and pulled an order book and a pen from beneath the counter. "How many this year?"

"Twelve, I believe that's what I ordered last year. One for each door inside the church, two for the big outside doors, and two for my house."

She made some notes in her order book. "Delivered?"

"Please."

Louise consulted a calendar. "I can bring them up to you on next Monday afternoon. Is that soon enough?"

"Certainly. Do you need directions?"

She smiled. "No, I remember where you are. A shame it's winter, you have a lovely garden. I like to keep an eye on it, and I don't get out to Skipton often."

"Hardly anyone does." He smiled, and his face relaxed. The contrast made her realize how tense he had been before. "But thank you. Most of the flowers in the garden came from here, you know."

"You're one of my best customers, Reverend. Would you like to pay for the wreaths now, or when I deliver them?"

"Now would be fine."

She tapped a few buttons on the cash register, and Reverend Bradley took out his checkbook.

"Miss Middlebury, may I ask you a strange question?"

Louise looked up. Reverend Bradley was staring not at her, but at a slip of paper which he had evidently pulled out of his jacket pocket along with his checkbook. The tenseness in his expression was suddenly back, along with another emotion. On a different face, it might have been fear, but she had a hard time imagining anything so harsh disturbing the air of serenity that Reverend Bradley usually carried. She paused, and her fingers hung, poised above the buttons of the register.

"I just had a rather... odd experience. I mean..." He stumbled over the words, swallowed, and said, "I scarcely know where to start."

Louise looked at him, a little quizzically, but didn't respond.

He began again. "It's so peculiar. I don't know why it's bothering me so, but I feel I have to tell someone, if for no other reason to convince myself that I'm not losing my mind."

"That doesn't seem very likely, Reverend," Louise said, smiling in a way she hoped was reassuring.

"I don't know. I hope you're right. I've never had anything like this happen before." He took a deep breath. "Some weeks ago, a young man showed up in my church, before services on a Sunday morning. He claimed he was being pursued by people with some sort of intent to kill him, and asked for... I suppose one would call it asylum."

Louise's eyebrows rose. "My goodness. What did you do?"

"Well," he replied, and the color rose in his cheeks. "I was surprised, and I hesitated. The man decided, I suppose, that I didn't want to help him, so he left, but not before saying the most curious thing. As he left, he told me that if I ever saw him, I wasn't to believe anything he said."

"Wow."

Reverend Bradley nodded. "Odd, isn't it?"

"And have you seen him since?"

He nodded again. "Just this morning. In Colville Hardware."

"You're kidding! What did he say?"

"He told me that the man I ran into must have been his identical twin brother, who was mentally disturbed and whom he had not seen for ten years."

"Reverend, that is amazing."

"Yes, but Louise, don't you see..." Reverend Bradley leaned forward. "What about what he said, as he was leaving the church, the first time I saw him? He said I wasn't to trust him if I saw him again."

Louise didn't answer for a moment. "Did he say anything out of the ordinary? The second time, I mean?"

Reverend Bradley considered for a moment. "Other than the fairly strange story about his brother, no."

"And the first time? Did he tell you anything more about these people who were after him?"

"No. Just that he needed help, and that the police wouldn't have been able to help him. And that by not helping him, I was setting some kind of clockwork in motion."

"Wow," she said again. "Strange."

"Strange indeed. It's quite unsettled me."

"I can see why."

"I suppose I should simply forget it. He wasn't anxious to talk to me this morning. Quite the opposite, actually. In fact, that was odd in itself. He didn't act at all what I'd have expected on hearing news of his long-lost brother."

"Well, he said the brother was disturbed."

"True." Reverend Bradley didn't sound convinced.

"In any case," Louise said, "you shouldn't upset yourself about it. Whatever the story is, it's nothing you need to be involved in."

"I suppose you're right. I don't see anything I could do now, in any case."

"That's right." Louise reached out and touched the back of his hand. "On the other hand, I think if the brother—the disturbed one—shows up at your church again, I might call the police. If he's mentally disturbed, you never can be too careful."

"I told him this morning. The man in the hardware store, I mean. I said I'd call him if his brother showed up. He gave me his name and phone number." He showed her the slip of paper, which was still in his hand.

Louise looked at the paper and didn't respond for a moment. When she finally spoke, her voice was high and thin. "This is really giving me the creeps, Reverend."

Reverend Bradley frowned. "You know, Louise, I'm having the hardest time thinking of them as two separate people.

I'd swear, it was the same man. I'm sure of it, despite the fact that there were differences. He'd cut his hair, and he looked like he'd gained a couple of pounds, and was better dressed. But I'm so certain of it."

"Identical twins can fool you," Louise responded. "There was a pair of identical twin brothers in the high school I attended. They used to switch places in classes and take tests for each other if one had had time to study and the other hadn't. The teachers were none the wiser, so far as I ever heard."

"I suppose you could be right. But..." He paused, and then said again, "I was so sure."

Louise smiled. "Pretty disorienting, huh?"

Reverend Bradley attempted to return the smile. "Very." He returned his attention to his checkbook. "How much do I owe you?"

Louise finished entering the amount on the cash register. There was a ping, and the drawer popped open. "At twelve dollars each, plus tax, it comes to $155.28."

Reverend Bradley wrote the check, tore it out, and handed it to Louise. She pulled the receipt from the register, stapled it to a carbon-copy pull-out from her order book, and handed it to the Reverend.

"Thank you. Monday, then?"

Louise nodded. "Monday it is. Probably after four."

"That'd be fine. Sorry for bending your ear about my strange morning."

"No problem, Reverend. Glad to listen. I can see why you were shook up."

He carefully folded the receipt, put it inside his checkbook, and slipped it back into his jacket pocket. "Have a nice weekend."

"You too."

He walked to the door, which jingled as he pushed it open. There was a wash of cold air into the store, then the door closed.

Louise watched him through the window, her hands returning to twisting florist's wire around fir branches, knowing the movement without needing guidance from her eyes. She continued to watch him, her face expression-less, as he climbed into his car, started it, and backed out into the parking lot, and her gaze didn't waver until he made the right turn onto the highway and his car passed out of sight.

She set down the wreath she'd been working on, and reached for her telephone. She punched in the number and waited for a moment. There was a click, and a hello.

"Helene, this is Louise. You need to come down here as soon as you can. It looks like you didn't catch Stephen soon enough."

6

LUNAR ANOMALY MECHANISM: CALIBRATED AND ENGAGED

FRIDAY, December 4, 2015

KELLY DELAHANTY'S steps became progressively slower as she approached Professor Keith Sparlin's office door. She didn't find him intimidating—quite the opposite. He was one of those uncommon people who combined being highly intelligent and funny in a self-deprecating way, and she found his manner in front of his class charming and engaging. Still, she had never approached him on any subject other than neurophysiology. This was new ground.

She corrected herself. This *was* neurophysiology. This was a real-life neurophysiology experiment. Just because she was the subject didn't mean that it was any less appropriate for her to ask him what he thought.

Dr. Sparlin's door was covered with various comic strips and articles. The comic strips were mostly *The Far Side* and *Calvin and Hobbes*. The articles were mainly about the debate—which Sparlin himself always referred to as 'the so-called debate'—between evolution and creationism. He was something of a fanatic on the subject. Although an even-tempered, genial man on most topics, the subject of creationism raised his ire in a singular manner. Creationists, by and large, didn't take his class.

In the midst of the chaos of newspaper clippings on the door was a large sign, written in a scrawly cursive: "Dear Students: I am grading exams. I am BUSY. I will not tell you your grades, so don't bother asking. In fact, why don't you go away? Love, Keith Sparlin."

Kelly smiled a little, and before her rational mind could make her take the suggestion of the sign to heart, she raised her hand and knocked on the door.

"Yes?" came a voice from inside the office. Not a terribly pleased voice, she thought.

"Dr. Sparlin? It's Kelly Delahanty. From your neurophys class. I'm not here to ask about grades. I just need to talk to you. I know you're busy, I promise I won't take long."

The door was opened by a tall, slender man, with a shock of red curls and a long, narrow, foxy face. If he was actually displeased he hid it well. His smile was warm and genuine.

"What can I do for you, Kelly?" he said, motioning her toward a chair.

She sat down and took a deep breath. "I have a question, and I thought you'd be the best person to ask about it."

His gingery eyebrows raised a little, but he didn't say anything.

"It's a question about dreams," she said.

"Ah." His response was non-committal, and not exactly encouraging. She knew what his opinion was about people who put too much stock in dreams. He'd made that abundantly clear in class when they'd discussed the sleep cycle.

"I know we talked in class what was happening in the brain when people dream," she said, sitting in a chair he indicated with a gesture. "And you said that the whole idea of dream interpretation was pretty much nonsense. But... I have had..." She paused, cleared her throat nervously, and then continued. "I've had some dreams that really have bothered me. Actually, one dream, that I keep having over and over."

"Recurring dreams aren't uncommon," Dr. Sparlin said, sitting down at his own desk, and leaning back in his chair.

"I know. I've had others. This one's different, though. It's very disturbing, and I can't see any reason for it."

He smiled patiently. "Why don't you tell me about it."

That was all it took. The words came tumbling out.

Kelly had always dreamed vividly, in full technicolor and sensurround, but ever since her teenage years, her dreams had become stranger and more intense. Several of them had been strikingly precognitive. She had dreamed of watching a portrait of her grandmother crack and bleed four days before she died of a stroke. She had dreamed of trying to have a conversation with a friend of hers when they were both seniors in high school, but her friend's voice was inaudible over the noise of breaking glass, a sound that in her dream only she was to hear. The following weekend her friend had been involved in an automobile accident, in which the windshield had shattered. Her friend had escaped serious injury, but the doctor in the emergency room had counted over eighty small cuts on her face and arms.

The weird thing about her recent recurring dream was that there was no apparent reason for it. It always began innocently enough. She was in the backyard of the small house near Colville College that she shared with two other girls. She was wearing a heavy lined coat, and her breath fogged in the icy air. About a foot of snow scrunched under her feet, making that squeaky sound that snow only makes if the temperature is near zero. The only noise other than her own footsteps was one she couldn't place at first—a rhythmic, grating crunch, like someone biting into a very crisp apple, but much louder. She looked around, trying to find the source of the noise.

There was a hedge that separated her back yard from that of the neighbors' house, and when she looked in that direction, she saw where the sound was coming from. Old Mr. May, her neighbor, was standing on the other side of the hedgerow, and despite the weather was wearing a plaid short-sleeve shirt and shorts. If he was aware of the cold, he didn't give any sign of it. He was using a set of large clippers to cut the hedge, but as she looked, she saw he wasn't trimming it, he was mangling it, chopping through layers of snow, hacking deeply into the even lines of the shrubs, shredding the branches. There were fragments of cut twigs littered all over the ground, and Mr. May had flecks of bark and wood in his hair and on his clothing.

She went over to him. The first time she'd had the dream, she had gone unwarily, but each time afterwards she'd tried with increasing vigor to stop herself. Each time she'd failed. She walked stiffly across the yard as if someone else was operating her body, while her mind wailed, *Stop, stop, you know what he's going to do to you!*

"Aren't you cold, Mr. May?" she asked.

Only then did he look up at her, his expression frighteningly blank. She saw no sign either of recognition or emotion in his dark eyes. And at that point, he reached over the hedge, and with one snap of the clippers, cut Kelly's head off.

"It didn't hurt," she said to Dr. Sparlin. "It was totally painless. The last thing I remember about the dream is that Mr. May was dragging my head away, holding it by the hair. I could still see, so my view depended on which way my head turned as he dragged it. At one point, I could see back over the hedge, and my body was still standing there, headless. There was blood streaming from my neck, it was all over my jacket, but I was still standing up. At that point, I always wake up."

Keith didn't respond for a moment. Finally, he said, "Disturbing."

She nodded.

"You're the one who asked about precognitive dreams, aren't you? In class?"

She nodded again, feeling faintly embarrassed that he recalled her question.

"I'm assuming that you asked because you've had dreams that could be interpreted as precognitive."

"I've had dreams that it'd be hard to interpret any other way." She told him about her dreams of her grandmother and her friend in high school. Keith's eyebrows went up.

"Remarkable." His gaze moved away for a moment, toward the window, as if he were considering his words carefully.

"I'm not making this up," she said, a little defensively.

He looked back and smiled. "I'm not saying you did, Kelly. At the same time, you must realize that there have been thousands, possibly tens of thousands, of reports of precognitive dreams, but all of them—no exceptions— were reported after the event that the dream supposedly predicted had already happened. There is no recorded, verifiable case where a person reported a dream to a researcher or some other unbiased witness, and the event in question happened afterwards." He paused for a moment. "None that I'm aware of, in any case."

"Why would they report it before it came true?"

He nodded. "That's the difficulty, of course. Everyone has bad dreams. They only become precognitive after the fact. So in all the cases I've ever heard of, we have nothing to rely on but the dreamer's memory and veracity. As for veracity—well, there are a lot of liars out there. And we discussed in class what a plastic, and unreliable, thing memory actually is."

"I'm not making this up," she repeated.

"For myself, I don't think you are," he said. "But I suspect that the reason you came here was for advice of some kind, not just to tell me about a scary dream."

She leaned forward in her chair. "Every time I've had a precognitive dream, it's come true within a week or so. And each time, they don't come literally true. It's more like the dream is a symbol of what's going to happen. I don't think Mr. May is going to attack me with hedge clippers."

Keith held out his hand, palms up. "Kelly, I'm not a psychologist. You might be better off to..."

"I'm not going to a psychologist," she said firmly. "Whatever this dream is, it's..." She paused, looking for the words. "It's not about the way my brain works. It's coming from outside of me."

He smiled. "So why did you come to me? I'm not an expert in psychic phenomena. In fact, I'm sort of the resident skeptic around here."

"That's why," she said. "That's exactly why. You're not the kind of person who will immediately jump on some weird explanation for things, but you also know about dreams. I thought you could tell me if there's a reason to be concerned. And maybe tell me what I should do."

"Whew. That's a tall order." He leaned back, tipping his chair on two creaking wooden legs. For a moment, it was the only sound in the office. "What can you tell me about Mr. May?"

"I've only known him since I moved into this house in September. He's an old guy, probably seventy-five or so. He and his wife are really nice. They invited me over for lunch a couple of weekends ago. They putter around in their yard a lot, or at least they did before it snowed. He's a retired college professor. Math, I think. I don't know about Mrs. May. She's sweet, kind of grandmotherly. She plays the piano really well."

"And you've seen nothing, or heard nothing... that..." He trailed off.

Kelly smiled. "That'd lead me to believe that Mr. May was a serial killer? God, no. They're nice folks. And really quick mentally for their age. I remember my grandma got really senile when she was that age. My mom called it 'foggy.' She couldn't remember anything, and she'd kind of fade out during conversations. Mr. and Mrs. May are really alert and are pretty interesting to talk to. I guess they've traveled a bunch. When I was over having lunch with them they showed me some photographs they'd taken this past summer, on a trip to Greece."

"So, nothing at all odd about them?"

"Nothing."

Keith paused, considering. "Well... Like I said, Kelly, I'm no psychologist. But I do know that in my own personal experience, a lot of times fears are defused by facing them. Like we talked about in class, dreams are often oblique manifestations of strong emotions or fears we have. Sometimes the emotions or fears are ones we're not even completely aware of. I must say I'm a little at a loss to explain why you'd be having violent imagery surrounding a neighbor you've only met recently and so far had pleasant encounters with, but you may be resonating on some deeper level to something he said, or something you saw when you were in the house. Or maybe he reminds you of someone that you have negative emotions toward."

"What if it's precognitive?"

Keith looked at her, then looked away, as if unwilling to answer at first. "Kelly," he said, "I don't want you to take this personally. I simply don't believe in precognitive dreams."

"Dr. Sparlin," she said earnestly, "I've had them."

"I know," he said. "One of my demands when someone makes an extraordinary claim is to say, 'show me the mechanism.' This, to me, is one of the problems with psychic phenomena of all types. There's no known way that any of them could occur. Not so much as a single brain structure, a single neural firing pattern, a single synaptic pathway, that has ever been associated with people who have alleged psychic powers."

"No *known* way," Kelly said.

"You're right, of course," admitted Keith. "Magic is science we haven't understood yet, and all of that. Still, I can't commit to belief in something unless I can see how it works. Or at least, unambiguous proof that it *does* work. Anecdotal evidence simply isn't enough."

"But you can see why I'm scared," Kelly said.

"Of course! I'd be scared, too. The dream is disturbing enough by itself, not to mention your history of... um, precognition."

"But you don't think there's anything real that I should be scared about."

"Nothing I can see. Dreams are dreams, no more. They presumably serve some function, as most mammal species dream. Whether their function is to alert us to emotional states we weren't aware of or to help us consolidate memory, or whether it's just taking out the psychic trash, isn't really known."

"So I shouldn't call the police and warn them about Mr. May."

Keith laughed. "I'd say no. In fact, you may want to go over and see him. You might even tell him you'd had a disturbing dream about him, and that you wanted to make sure he didn't harbor any ill feelings toward you. If he's as smart and kind as you say, he'll probably give you a hug and a cup of tea and that'll be that."

Kelly looked dubious. "Maybe I should."

"Facing our fears is sometimes the best way to pull the plug on their power. I'm not saying that as a scientist. It's just been my personal experience."

She nodded.

Keith smiled wryly. "On the other hand, if he has a pair of hedge clippers on the kitchen counter, get the hell out of there."

7

Zodiac Dial: Calibrated and Engaged

Monday, December 7, 2015

Marcia Pacheco's fingers clicked out the last line of the document she was preparing, and in a smooth, quick movement, swung the mouse up and clicked on "Save As PDF." Her computer began to make the grumbling noises that signified that it was mulling over her request, noises that Marcia always thought sounded a little like a contented pig. It was a forty-three-page document, a scholarly paper by her boss, Professor Henry Larkin, chair of the Colville College Pre-Law Program. Professor Larkin—Marcia wondered if even his wife called him Henry—was a venerable figure around the College, the focus of both respect and puzzlement for staff and student alike. He had made a career as a trial lawyer, but at its height had given it all up to take a teaching position at Colville. Why a successful lawyer at the zenith of his career had preferred a modest position at a small, relatively obscure college was a mystery. His demeanor, which would have done a nine-teenth-century British nobleman proud, prevented anyone from asking him, but there was no doubt that he had been a significant prize for the college, and in the years since he had risen to the post of department chair. Under his able direction, the department regularly turned out students who were eagerly accepted into outstanding law schools, and Professor Larkin himself equally regularly produced scholarly papers expounding upon the finer points of jurisprudence.

Marcia also felt lucky that she had him for her boss. When, at the beginning of last school year, she had been in the middle of a nasty divorce, Professor Larkin had allowed her to take time off as needed and to work hours of amazing flexibility, and as long as the work got done, he acted as if nothing was wrong. Indeed, he acted as if the situation didn't exist. He never talked to her about the divorce, and actually, Marcia didn't want him to. One time she idly pictured him walking up and saying, "So, Ms. Pacheco, at what stage are your divorce proceedings? Might I do anything to help you?" and had blushed crimson at the thought of that refined and stately counte-nance even admitting that he knew she had a personal life. And given that the cause of the divorce was that Jeff Gaines had slept with virtually every female mutual friend they had, up to and including their next door neighbor's teenage daughter, there was no way she wanted even to bring it up. No way.

But Professor Larkin had known enough of what was happening to let her take whatever time she needed, and she vowed never to take advantage of it. When the divorce was final, Marcia threw a party and invited all of her friends that Jeff had not had sex with. She had given a brief thought of inviting Professor Larkin, but very quickly settled on writing a sincere thank-you note instead.

Which she sent by mail.

She was especially glad that her boss hadn't been there when, at the party's climax, she signed the paperwork to change her name from Marcia Gaines back to Marcia Pacheco, to the rousing applause of all of those assembled. Her best friend, Stacy Weinstein, had shouted over the tumult, "Halle-fucking-lujah. Next time, girl, find a guy who isn't hung like a baby hamster," causing three people to simultaneously spit their drinks all over the table.

So everything had worked out in the end, she supposed. She had done well with the settlement. Jeff was a general contractor and had a thriving business, knew he had been caught dead to rights, and her lawyer had gotten alimony from him without even trying hard. Her job wasn't the most interesting job in the world, but it was secure, paid her rent, and left a little over at the end of each month. It'd been over a year, and she felt like she was past the worst of the grief over her broken marriage.

But it was the Christmas season. She gave a moody stare at the document on her screen. She always felt worse at this time of year. No one is supposed to be alone at Christmas.

Marcia's only brother lived in Seattle, and she had visited him the previous year. She couldn't afford another ticket so soon. Both of their parents were dead. She supposed that she could wrangle an invitation from a friend, but that thought didn't exactly thrill her either.

Maybe she should ask Stacy what she was doing for the holidays. Stacy was Jewish, but happily celebrated any holidays she liked, and that included throwing parties and giving presents at Christmas times. Marcia closed Professor Larkin's paper, put her computer on sleep mode, took her purse from her desk, and stood. She was meeting Stacy for lunch. Maybe there would be an opportunity to bring it up without seeming like she was begging.

"So, Marsh, what's eating you?" Stacy asked around a bite of cheesecake.

"I'm fine," Marcia replied, smiling a little. Damn, this woman was a freaking mind reader. Comes from knowing someone since forever.

"Yeah, you're *fine*," Stacy said, giving her an appraising look. "You're in one of those, 'I feel pissy but I'm going to wait and see if anyone notices' moods. You know I hate those."

"You might be right, I guess."

"I might be. You're not pining away over Jeff again, are you?"

"God, no." Marcia took a sip of her coffee.

"Good," Stacy said firmly, gesturing with her fork. "I still say that the only thing wrong with your settlement was that you should have demanded that they surgically remove the part of him that committed the offense."

Marcia laughed. "You could do it with a pair of nail clippers."

"Yeah, honey," Stacy said. "That's the way." She took another bite of cheesecake. "So, then what's bothering you? Probably the holidays, I bet. Empty house, no tree, no nothing."

"Lady, you scare me sometimes. I swear you can read minds."

"Only yours. But you know," she said, leaning forward in her chair, "that reminds me of something. I've been meaning to tell you about this psychic I've been seeing. This woman is amazing."

"You're seeing a psychic?" Marcia didn't know whether to laugh. It was sometimes hard to know when Stacy was pulling her leg.

"Yeah!" Her voice was enthusiastic. "Judy, you know Judy? Girl in Accounts Receivable? She's been seeing her and told me I should try her out. So I figured, hell, it's only money, twenty bucks for an hour. I can afford one hour. If she's a fraud, I'm out a twenty, big deal. So I went. She's phenomenal."

Marcia gave her a skeptical look. "What did she tell you that was so amazing?"

"Everything!" Stacy made a sweeping arm gesture. "First, she starts out by telling me that most of my problems are due to the fact that my mother was hypercritical and disapproved of everything I did. I mean, right off the bat, like she was reading it from my biography or something. She was absolutely sure."

"Whose mother isn't critical? It's a pretty shrewd guess about anyone, don't you think?"

"No, wait. There's more. So she says, 'But now, your mother doesn't disapprove of you anymore.'"

"Stacy," Marcia said, trying not to smile, "your mother died ten years ago."

"I know! She said my mother was standing there with me, that she'd 'passed over.' But she was with me and she approved of me, that she didn't feel like she had to criticize me all the time anymore."

"Well, that's good, I guess. But it doesn't exactly prove anything..."

"Wait," said Stacy. "Then, she gets all serious, and says, 'It's interesting, your mother doesn't look anything like you. That's what started it, you know? When you were little, and you looked just like your dad, and you had your dad's personality. Your mom wanted a daughter who would be like her, and then she got you, and somehow you never understood each other. Your mom wanted a little blonde, blue-eyed girl, with a few freckles across her nose. You didn't even get your mom's nose, your mom had a regular ski-slope, didn't she?' And all the time, she's kind of looking over my shoulder, and her voice is sort of sad like she feels bad for what my mom and I went through."

"Jesus," said Marcia under her breath. "She said all that?" She stared at Stacy, who looked as if she were near tears. Stacy never cried.

"She said all that."

"Okay, that is phenomenal."

Stacy cleared her throat and pushed her glasses up onto the bridge of her nose. "Told you so."

"What's this woman's name?"

"Andrea Yarbrough. You ought to go see her, Marsh, you really ought to. She'd cure your doldrums, I just know it."

"I don't especially want to find out my parents are still lurking around," Marcia said.

"Well, that isn't all she said, of course. She's told me lots of other stuff. It's a hoot, much more fun than some counselor. Cheaper too."

———

Two days later, on a Wednesday evening, Marcia turned her car into a gravel driveway, past a mailbox that said "Yarbrough" and had a stenciled design of a row of ducks wearing sunhats and pinafores. The car crunched over the frozen gravel surface, and she braked to a stop underneath the bare gray branches of a huge sugar maple tree. There were no signs saying "Psychic" in the yard, or on the house. It looked like any other country house, with a screened-in front porch, a small garden, and a ramshackle barn in the back. Marcia got out of her car, her hands shaking a little, and walked up to the house. She pulled open the screen door, which creaked and grated, crossed the porch, and knocked on the front door.

She heard footsteps, echoing on what had to be a hardwood floor. An unaccountable fear suddenly sprang up in her, and an inner voice whispered, "Run! Run back to your car while there's still time! You can get away before she's seen you!" but she quelled it, and had achieved a somewhat satisfactory smile by the time the door opened.

"You must be Marcia." The woman holding the door open smiled broadly. "I'm Andrea. Please come in."

Marcia nodded wordlessly and followed her in. Truth be told, her first sight of Andrea Yarbrough had been so contrary to her expectations that she didn't know what to say. She had pictured the Hollywood image of a psychic— a tall, elegant woman, with flowing mauve robes, an olive complexion, and deep-set dark eyes.

It would be hard to find someone who was more opposite to that mental image than Andrea was. She was nearer fifty than forty, of medium height, and what probably had started out being big bones had turned into true fat. She had a pronounced double chin, and a plain, homely country face, framed with thinning, board-straight hair of an indeterminate shade of brown. A pair of bifocals sat crookedly on the end of her prominent nose.

Fortunately, Andrea didn't seem to want to stand in the doorway and engage in small talk, and led Marcia inside. The interior of the house was warm and spotlessly clean. The decor could have been copied directly from an issue of *Country Living*. An opening into a living room passed by, and Marcia caught a glimpse of lace antimacassars on chairs, and a mantelpiece covered with what her father had called "artsy-craftsy crapola" —wooden statues of animals painted in pastel colors, polished brass candle holders, ceramic statues of children with umbrellas and bookbags. A dimly-lit hallway had an assortment of family photographs and a large framed needlepoint demanding, in capital letters, that God Bless This Home. They passed through the kitchen, its immaculate tiled floor looking clean enough to serve food on. A small door opened to the right, and Andrea led the way through it, down two steps, and into a small, cozy study, with a wood stove, two chairs with thick cushions, and a desk with a litter of papers and books, the first sign of disorder Marcia had seen in the house.

Andrea turned, and gestured to a chair. Both women sat, and Andrea, still smiling warmly, said, "So, what brings you to me?"

Marcia didn't answer for a moment. That was a good question. What did bring her here? She stifled an impulse to say, "Lady, you're the psychic, you tell me!" Finally, she said, "My friend Stacy Weinstein said I should come, that you were really good and that I'd find out a lot about myself."

"Ah," Andrea said, nodding, a smile brightening her broad face. "Stacy. She's quite an interesting person, your friend Stacy."

"We've known each other since we were children."

Andrea nodded. The gesture said, "I already knew that, of course." "And what do you hope to find out today?"

"I don't know, really. Whatever you can tell me. I've been depressed a lot lately. I feel like... like there's something missing, or something I should be doing. My life feels pretty empty."

Another knowing nod. "A common enough problem," she said, her voice soothing. "Well, let's see. Let's see what we can do." She half-closed her eyes and sat for about a minute, breathing slowly and deeply.

Marcia's heart was pounding, and a tremor ran up her spine. She tried to fight down a sense of panic and shivered a little with the effort.

Andrea's eyes opened, and one eyebrow raised a little. "Dear," she said, "you really must relax. I don't bite, you know. You needn't worry, I'm not going to tell you anything alarming." She smiled again. "Here, give me your hands." Marcia reached out, still trembling a little, and her small hands were enveloped in Andrea's large, warm, rough ones. Andrea squeezed gently. "Concentrate on your breath, and relax."

Marcia took a breath, and let it out slowly, trying to let the panic drain from her. She quelled her trembling, and sat, her hands in Andrea's, waiting for the other woman to speak. Andrea's eyelids drooped again, and silence fell.

A minute, perhaps two, passed, before Andrea spoke, in a slow, deep voice. "You do miss your parents, don't you, dear? They're here beside you, both of them. They're smiling on you. You've done well. They're proud."

Marcia had been expecting something like this. It was similar to what Stacy had been told. She didn't respond.

"Your mother especially. She's proud of her little girl, staying firm in the storm. The storm..." Andrea's voice became a dreamy monotone, like someone talking in her sleep.

"What storm?" whispered Marcia.

"Your husband," she said. "He did wrong. He did wrong by my little girl. I'm not surprised, I never really liked him, you know. Not from the start. But you wouldn't hear of it, you wanted so badly for him to be true, but you knew from early days too, didn't you, early days..."

Marcia's eyes widened. She had spoken to no one of her suspicions of Jeff in the first years of her marriage. Especially her mother. Her mother had warned her, warned her only a few days after she'd announced their engagement that there was something about Jeff that couldn't be trusted. She had brushed it off and had never told anyone about the conversation, not even Stacy. Marcia's hands began to tremble again.

"But you did the right thing. You did it, right enough. You were too good for him, too good, I always said so..." Andrea's voice trailed away, and silence fell again. Marcia heard the ticking of a clock in another room, the soft murmur of the furnace turning on, a faint breath of wind and rustling leaves from outside.

Stacy must have told her about Jeff. That had to be it. The rest of it, about Marcia's mom knowing Jeff was a cheater, that had to be a shrewd guess. And since her mom was dead, there was no way she could verify the psychic's claim in any case. A laugh arose, unbidden, in her chest. The explanation, once she saw it, was so simplistic as to be funny.

But suddenly Andrea's brow wrinkled, in an expression of pain. She winced, and a ripple passed through the point where their hands connected. There was a startled look on her face, there for a moment and then gone just as quickly. Andrea didn't speak, but her grip on Marcia's hands tightened.

"What is it?" Marcia whispered.

"Marcia," she said, in a different voice, this one sounding old, creaking like a dry branch. "There are forces at work in your life. You must be careful."

"Careful of what?"

"Careful of who you trust. There are people out there who will try to hurt you. Soon. Steer clear of them."

"Who?" Her voice rose, the panic sliding its fingers around her heart again. "Who is it?"

Andrea didn't answer for a moment. She sat, her forehead creased as if in some kind of inner conflict. "Someone who speaks with the voice of God. He and his kind. They want to use you, you and what you can do for them. They are dangerous."

"What can I do?" Marcia's voice was a squeak. "I can't do anything, I'm just a typist!"

Andrea's face smoothed, and her smile returned, but her eyes remained half-closed. "You are capable of far more. You haven't realized it yet."

Somehow, the blissful expression frightened Marcia worse than the anguished look and dire predictions had. She pulled away, but Andrea didn't release her grip. She began to struggle, unable to articulate any words, and her chair scraped on the polished wood planks as she pushed backwards.

Andrea's eyes snapped open. She immediately released Marcia's hands, and her face became sympathetic, warm, almost apologetic. "Dear, it's all right, there's nothing to be scared of..."

Marcia shrank away from the other woman, cowering back against the soft upholstery. "Nothing to be scared of?" she said, her voice a thin gasp. "You said I was in danger, and now you tell me..."

Andrea shook her head. "I'm sorry, I should have held back. I saw..." She paused. "I see what may be. I don't always see clearly. Sometimes what I see doesn't come true, or isn't literally true."

"Then what good is it?"

Andrea didn't bristle at this question. It was obviously one she was used to hearing. She smiled. "Think of what I say as a guide. My trance was deeper today than usual, far deeper than I usually go during a first meeting. I saw a danger to you, and without thinking, I told you what I saw. I'm sorry if I scared you."

The panic was once again subsiding, but Marcia suddenly wanted more than anything else to get out of this house, and get away from Andrea Yarbrough. She stood up. "I'd better go."

Andrea remained seated, looking at her a little sadly. "Dear, please understand that I mean you no harm. I'm only... well, think of it like listening to the weather forecast. You may not like it, but the weather isn't the weatherman's fault."

Marcia fumbled in her pocketbook, pulled out a twenty, and dropped it on the desk. "I really have to go," she said, and suddenly felt that if she wasn't out of that house in under two minutes, she was going to cry, vomit, or both.

One of Andrea's rough hands clasped Marcia's for a moment, and then let go. "Promise me, that if you... meet someone, someone who is like the person I saw, you'll come back. I can help you."

Marcia recoiled, and turned and virtually ran from the room, her hip striking the corner of the desk. The tears started as she went down the hall, and past the living room, and through the front door. She jogged to her car and stifled a sob as she climbed into the front seat. She started the ignition, threw it into reverse, and the car lurched down the driveway. She caught a glimpse of Andrea Yarbrough's homely face in the living room window, watching her retreat with an expression like a grandmother worried about an errant granddaughter.

She'd only gotten a mile down the road when the combination of panic, relief, and crying forced her to pull over. She sat idling on the shoulder till the worst of the sobbing had passed, then eased her car back out onto the road.

By the time she got back to Colville, she had pushed aside most of the dark thoughts and passed the remainder of the drive trying to decide what to tell Stacy about her visit.

"At least I'll never have to see that woman again," Marcia said out loud. It was amazing how comforting that thought was. She smiled a little, her first smile since she'd pulled into Andrea's driveway.

"Never again. Never." Her body relaxed. She said it a little louder as if it were a mantra, and her smile widened. Once again, she felt like laughing. "Never again. Never."

8

L UNAR *ANOMALY MECHANISM: FIRST TURN*

KELLY LISTENED to the doorbell echo into silence, as she stood on the Mays' doorstep, wrapped in her winter jacket.

Just checking them out. No reason to be scared. It was only to verify that her first impression had been correct.

Really it was.

The thin noontime winter sunshine filtered down, not really warming anything, but better than the thick clouds of the previous two days. The handle turned, and the door swung open.

"Well, hello!" The smiling woman standing in the open door looked like an illustration of a grandmother from a children's book—white hair in a bun, rimless glasses that were a little askew, and an old-fashioned flowered dress. She stepped away from the door, made a gesture of welcome, and called, "Stanford, dear! It's Kelly Delahanty, from next door!"

Kelly stepped through the door and into a cozy, if somewhat untidy, living room. A moment later Stanford May entered the room from the other side, clad in a shabby cardigan and khaki trousers, drying his hands on a tea towel. He smiled broadly, and Kelly wondered again at the source of the dream that had so unsettled her. How could she ever have had violent images associated with this kind old gentleman? He was a tall man, with steel gray hair and an academic's slouch. His bespectacled eyes were a bit watery but were bordered by a fine tracery of smile lines.

Mr. May tossed the towel onto the back of a rocking chair, and said, "How are you today, Kelly?"

"I'm fine, Mr. May." She hesitated a moment, suddenly feeling embarrassed at taking her dream seriously. "I wanted to see how you folks were doing. I really enjoyed our last visit, and I'm on winter break now, and I thought perhaps I'd stop in. If it's a bad time..."

"Oh, dear me, no," he said. "We're delighted to see you."

"Can I get you some tea?" Mrs. May asked. "We were just tidying up after lunch, and have a kettle on."

"That would be great, thanks."

Mrs. May retreated to the kitchen, and Mr. May gestured to the sofa. Kelly took off her jacket and sat down, earning an aggrieved glance from a large tabby cat who had been draped on the arm of the couch. The cat silently dropped to the floor, walked a few paces away, and sat down with his back to Kelly, the message "We are not amused" rolling off him in waves.

Okay, now what? What should she say to them?

"I was telling a friend of mine about your travels," Kelly began, immediately aware of how lame it sounded.

Mr. May, however, smiled broadly. "Well, it's one of our favorite avocations, I must admit. We were afraid we'd bored you last time with all of our travel tales."

"No, not a bit," Kelly said. "I'm fascinated with travel myself. I've wanted to travel ever since my friend spent some time in Africa." She hesitated, trying to think of the most obscure country she could remember the name of. "In... Cameroon."

Mr. May's eyes lit up immediately. "Really, how very interesting! We were there some years ago." He turned toward the kitchen. "Dear, Kelly has a friend who has been to Cameroon."

"Indeed!" said Mrs. May, entering the room with a silver tray with tea and cookies. "It's quite a fascinating country. The capital, Yaoundé, is a positively dreadful place, all noise and dirt and corrupt government officials. But the countryside is exquisite. When we were there, was it ten years ago, Stanford, dear? More? We stayed in a fairly remote village for four weeks, immersing ourselves in the customs of the natives, and the music, and the wildlife." She set the tray down on the coffee table. "Where did your friend stay, dear?"

"Um," Kelly said, and helped herself to a cup of tea, taking a sip to stall for time even though the tea was still too hot to drink. "He didn't say."

"What I found the most fascinating," said Mrs. May, "was the connection with nature. So many people idealize the

Native Americans and their link with nature, but I'm sure you know that much of this was romanticized fiction. Not that I'm denigrating the Native Americans, mind you. I grew up in Nova Scotia, where the Native populations of Mi'kmaq and Maliseets are making great strides toward reclaiming their cultural identities."

Mr. May gestured with one hand. "Of course, dear. But I know exactly what you mean. Here in North America, even the Natives have hardly been able to maintain what you might call a pure culture. In the remote parts of west Africa—the parts that are still relatively untouched by the western European milieu—they still have that connection virtually intact. They're part of nature in a way we never could be. They don't see a dichotomy between themselves and the natural world, nor between the technological and the purely natural. It's all one thing. Our American idea of 'this is human, this is nature, this is technology,' is completely foreign to them. It's a point of view that is refreshingly basic."

Kelly nodded, thankful at least that the Mays hadn't pressed her for details about her imaginary friend's stay in Cameroon. "That's really fascinating," she said, taking a bite of a cookie.

"Well, dear," said Mrs. May, "I'm sure you didn't come here to listen to Stanford and I blather on about our travels again. We did far too much of that last time. What's going on in your life? Are you staying in town for the holidays?"

Kelly nodded. "My parents are out of the country, actually. They're like you—they travel a lot, and are spending the holidays in Provençe. And both of my roommates will be going home to be with their families. It will be the first holiday I've ever spent on my own."

"Ah, Provençe," said Mrs. May dreamily. "Provençe is a lovely part of the world, I'm sure your parents will have a great time. We once spent two wonderful weeks in Vaucluse. Of course, that was twenty years ago, but I can still remember the smell of the lavender fields. It carries for miles."

"The lavender won't be blooming in December, dear," said Mr. May.

"No, of course not. But it will still be lovely."

"Some quiet time will probably be good for you," said Mr. May. "Family holidays are nice, but I probably don't need to tell you that they can also be quite stressful."

"This semester has been stressful enough," said Kelly. "It's been my roughest thus far, academically. I did fine, but the workload was tremendous. Having some alone time, with no demands, will be a welcome change."

"I'm sure. You're a psychology student, aren't you?" Mrs. May finished her tea and set the cup down on the tray. "I think you said that you were aiming toward practice eventually?"

"Yes. I'm planning on focusing on clinical when I reach that point, but I'm only a junior. For right now I'm keeping my doors open."

"Wise," Mr. May said. "And psychology is a fascinating subject, fascinating. The human mind." He gestured toward her with his empty teacup. "A colleague of mine— biology professor, not math, which was my field before I retired, you know—she once said that the twentieth century was the century of the gene, the twenty-first will be the century of the brain. She said we know as little about how the brain works now as we did about how genes worked in 1900. A bit of an exaggeration, perhaps, but she has a point." He tapped his temple with a forefinger and winked. "So much going on up there in the brain, so many mysteries. The turning of the mental gears. It's hard to fathom."

Kelly looked up, suddenly wary. What did he mean by that? With an effort, she forced herself to consider the words at face value. He was doing no more than small talk. She, after all, had been the one who had told them on her previous visit that she was a psych major. What did she expect them to talk about?

So okay, then. She'd gotten her answer. They were perfectly nice, harmless people. Just like they appeared. Just like Dr. Sparlin said.

"Thanks for the tea and the conversation," she said, smiling. "I won't take up any more of your time. I just thought I might say hi, and see how you were doing."

"Well, it was very sweet of you," said Mrs. May.

On an impulse, Kelly said, "If you need anything—if there's snow and you need help shoveling the driveway— I'll be around, I'm glad to do it." She stood, and slipped on her jacket. The resident cat slunk past her and jumped back up onto the couch, stretched luxuriously, and curled back up in the spot where Kelly had been sitting.

"That's so kind!" said Mr. May. "I must say, we're in good enough shape for our age, but a bit of help shoveling would be greatly welcome. And if you need anything your- self, do come knocking." Mr. May got up and walked Kelly to the door. "We'll be around. Even if you should simply get lonely. Perhaps we can have you over for dinner one night before your classes start again?"

"Oh, you needn't do that," Kelly said.

"It's no problem, we'd love to," said Mrs. May, smiling, and again giving a quaint, birdlike cock of her head. "We'll give you a call sometime soon."

"Thank you so much. Again, I'm sorry to drop in unannounced. Thanks for the tea."

"Our pleasure," said Mr. May.

CRUNCH, crunch, crunch. The noise from the dark, snowy yard and Kelly turned her head, squinting into the night to try to figure out where it came from. Her booted feet squeaked in the dry snow, and still, the noise came, like some large animal chewing its meal.

The hedgerow shuddered, and there was a small snowstorm of debris from one spot.

Stop don't go there you know what

"Mr. May! What are you doing?" Her thoughts were shrieking, but her voice sounded pert and cheerful. It was as if she couldn't control either what she was saying or how she was saying it.

he'll do it he's going to kill me

"You're ruining your hedge!" she said, in her sweet, concerned neighbor voice.

help make me stop make me run away

But her feet were no more obedient to her will than her voice was. And the old man, clad once again in his incongruous shorts and plaid button-down shirt, turned to look at her. His face was expressionless, the smile-lines smoothed into a blank absence. He reached over the mangled bushes, and the hedge cutters flashed. She felt the skin and muscle cleave apart, but there was no pain. In slow motion, Kelly's head toppled backwards, falling into the snow. She could feel the flakes' icy touch on her forehead, the meltwater seeping into her hair. There was a tug, and she realized that Mr. May had her hair in his fist, and her head swung like a pendulum, her eyes registering different parts of the yard as it twisted and turned.

Let me go let me go put me back where I came from I'm not yours

She saw her decapitated body, still standing by the hedge.

At least I'll wake up now at least I'll wake up

But she didn't. Mr. May turned a corner and crossed the patio behind his house. There was a sound of a door opening, and a brush of warm air on her cheeks.

He set her head on a table and bent over to examine it. His eyes were still appallingly empty, so devoid of expression as to be barely human. He said, in a quiet, even voice, "Can you hear me?"

Don't answer don't talk to him you mustn't

But she did. "Yes," her rebellious voice said calmly. "I can hear you."

"Excellent."

He picked up her head again, and turned with it, allowing her eyes to sweep across the room. Right in front of them was a large, rectangular machine, with bronze gear wheels and lever arms and handles. In the middle was an empty space, and Mr. May put her head in the space, turning it around so that she was peering out, looking into the center of his chest. To the side there was a creaking noise as screws were tightened, metal teeth were engaged, pins were set. Then the entire device began to vibrate, ticking like a giant clockwork, and the machine drew energy from her, pulling life from her severed spinal cord.

Then from the shadows came Mrs. May, still wearing her flowered dress from the day's visit. She looked at Kelly, tilted her head to one side, and said, "Perhaps you'd like some tea, dear?" Then she gave a frown of mocking sympathy. "Oh, my, no, that wouldn't do, would it? Not in your present state. Wherever would you *put* it?" She *tsk*-ed under her breath and shook her head. "But in any case, you ought to relax. We've got some questions for you, and it may well take a while." She turned away from Kelly, and said, "Stanford, dear, turn on the machine, will you?"

KELLY WOKE UP, sure she had screamed out loud. She was drenched with sweat. The down comforter had slipped from her shoulders, and her pillow was on the floor. She sat upright, her heart slamming in her chest, and listened for sounds. Of course, even if she had shrieked, her roommates were already gone home for the holidays. She was alone in the house. She concentrated on slowing her breathing and finally regained some semblance of control over herself. Her digital clock read 1:26.

"It's a dream," she said, whispering to herself the words that everyone has said at least once, trying to escape the terrors of the night. "Only a dream."

She slipped out of bed, put her feet on the cool wood of her bedroom floor, and stood up. She walked to her bedroom window, which looked out into the side yard, and what she saw made her wish that her roommates were still there, that she could call her parents, that she was not completely and utterly alone.

It was snowing. Fine, powdery flakes were cascading down from clouds invisible in the darkness, passing through the beam of the streetlight, and settling in drifts on the side-walk and yard. There were at least six inches of new snow already, and it was still going strong.

Kelly looked over at the Mays' house, hazy through the curtains of snow, and it was only then that she saw that there was a light on, up on the second floor.

When have I ever seen anyone in that house up at 1:30 in the morning? Her mental voice sounded a little hysterical. *I've never seen a light on at their house after ten o'clock. What would they be doing up this late?*

She closed her eyes, trying to will herself to think of the Mays as she had seen them that afternoon—to remember the pleasant conversation, the tea, and cookies, and to erase the horrific images of the dream.

So one of them has insomnia. Stop being a frightened little girl. Dreams mean nothing. Forget it.

She opened her eyes.

The window in the Mays' house was dark.

It was three hours before she got back to sleep that night.

9

M AIN DRIVE WHEEL: SECOND TURN

THE SNOW WAS FLYING. The tiny dry flakes made a steady hissing noise as the incessant wind sculpted the drifts into fantastic shapes, and drove them across the road as fast as the plow could scrape them away. The snow had started in earnest in the late afternoon. There'd been a brief period of the sun around noon, but the clouds rolled in, driven ahead of a stiff north gale. The worst part of the storm was still to come, but the bitter wind, thin as a knife blade, was already picking up strength.

Reverend Bradley pulled back the curtains as the little German clock in his study pinged out five o'clock. The driveway was empty. Louise had said she'd be there by four with the wreaths for the church. Of course, the roads were probably terrible. He said a quick but fervent prayer for her safety and reproached himself for not calling her earlier to tell her not to bother with the delivery.

At fifteen after five, he heard the dull thud of a car door closing, the sound muffled by the distance and the snow. He rose from his chair and went to open the door.

Louise, bundled in what looked like at least three layers of heavy clothing, with a purple knit scarf, a bright red wool cap, and ski gloves, stood on the front step, her breath turning to ice crystals and whirling away on the wind into a darkness that could have been midnight. She smiled at him, seeming unfazed by the weather.

"I made it. Sorry, I'm late. I was following first a school bus, then a tractor trailer. Neither of them ever topped twenty miles per hour, not that I can blame them."

"Come in, Miss Middlebury, do come in and warm up. I have a fire going. Might I get you some tea?"

"Oh, no thank you, Reverend," she responded. "I've actually been quite toasty, my van has an excellent heater. All the extra clothing is mainly for the trip to and from the van."

Reverend Bradley took his own jacket from the back of a chair, and said, "I'll help you unload them. Most of them are for the church, as usual. You'll probably want to pull your van around into the church parking lot, it'll be a much shorter walk." He sat down and pulled on a pair of worn galoshes.

"Would you like a ride? I know it's only a short distance..."

Reverend Bradley held up his hand. "On a day like today, I'd be foolish to turn you down."

They walked to the van. Louise climbed into the driver's seat, and somewhat more slowly and stiffly, Reverend Bradley sat down on the passenger side. Louise started the van and turned around as she backed down the Reverend's driveway.

"I so dislike cold weather," she said. "I should have been born in the tropics."

Reverend Bradley smiled. "I must say I prefer the cold to the heat and humidity. I don't know how people live in the Deep South. They must positively melt in the summer. I'd be immobile for half the year."

"I suppose we're all made differently."

"God makes all types of folks, for all types of places," the Reverend said. "That's the beauty of the world. There's something for everyone, no matter what your tastes are."

"I suppose it would be boring if everyone was alike."

"Dreadfully."

Louise pulled into the empty church parking lot and rolled to a stop near the door. The lot hadn't been plowed, and the van left deep grooves in the smooth surface of the snow.

"Dear me," said Reverend Bradley, "I need to call Jay Powell tomorrow morning. He plows the parking lot for me. Usually, he does it without my even asking, but I'd guess he has his hands full today."

Reverend Bradley winced as he opened the van door and the wind slapped him full in the face, but he climbed down from the high seat, turned and slammed the door shut, and trudged to the back of the van. Louise was already pulling bags of wreaths out of the back.

"Here, may I take one?" Reverend Bradley offered.

They carried the bags toward the church. The Reverend unlocked the church door and it swung open, and a tornado of glittering snow crystals swirled into the foyer and vanished into the gloom. He flipped a switch, and the lights flickered and came on.

"There are only two more bags," Louise said. "I'll get them."

He stood in the foyer, rubbing his chilled hands together, thankful at least for being out of the wind. Louise soon returned with the last two bags.

"You can set them down in here," he said. "The Ministry and Oversight Committee found a few teenagers from the Sunday school who are willing to come down and hang them. They should be fine in here in the bags for a day or two, shouldn't they?"

"Oh, yes," Louise said. "It's quite cool in here. It's the heat and dry that really shortens their lives. No problem with that in older buildings."

Reverend Bradley nodded. "Did I pay you in full?" he asked. "I've misplaced my receipt."

"Yes, indeed, Reverend. You paid the day you came in and ordered them. Remember? We were talking about that odd man you met in the hardware store."

He nodded again. The odd man in the hardware store. He'd tried, unsuccessfully, to forget about him. It had been right about here where the whole bizarre affair had begun, that Sunday morning when he'd showed up in the church. No, he corrected himself. They weren't the same person. They were brothers. Twin brothers. The man at the hardware store said so.

But he still couldn't really make himself believe that.

Louise smiled at him. "Woolgathering, Reverend?"

Reverend Bradley looked up at her and grinned, a little sheepishly. "Sorry. I was just remembering the man I told you about. It still strikes me as so peculiar. I haven't really been able to let it go."

"I can understand that. It must have been upsetting."

"I am certain that they were the same man. The man in the church and the man in the hardware store. I know it's ridiculous, but I'm certain of it."

Louise shrugged. "Why does it matter?"

"It doesn't, I expect. I can't really say why it bothers me."

"You really should try to forget it."

"Actually, I've been toying with the idea of calling the phone number he gave me."

"Oh, Reverend Bradley, are you sure you want to do that?" Louise looked genuinely alarmed. "It might not be such a good idea."

"Why not?"

"You don't know this man. He says his brother was crazy. Perhaps he is, too. Identical twins, after all."

"He seemed normal enough."

"I daresay. But to be on the safe side. And why on earth do you want to talk to him, in any case? What more could he tell you than he already has?"

"I don't know. I simply feel compelled to call him. It's really rather extraordinary. I've never had anything affect me like this before."

Louise shook her head. "I wouldn't if I were you." She smiled. "I don't trust people very easily, I suppose. Not very nice of me, I'm afraid."

He made a *tsk*-ing noise, and frowned, and gave her a pat on the hand. "You are really a lovely person, and I've taken up enough time of yours with this ridiculous situation. You must get home before the roads get worse than they already are. It's pitch black already. Drive carefully, won't you?"

"Always do. Don't you worry about me. I've driven in worse than this. The main problem is the deer. Snowdrifts you can avoid—they don't suddenly run into your path."

She pulled open the door, letting in a fresh blast of frosty air, and Reverend Bradley switched off the lights and followed her, momentarily turning to relock the door.

"Want a ride?" asked Louise warmly.

"You head on home," the Reverend said. "I'll cut across the cemetery and be home and in front of the fire in no time." He pulled his coat around him, slipped his hands into his pockets, and trudged off through the snow and around the side of the church.

LOUISE RETURNED TO THE VAN, put the key in the ignition, and started up the motor. A welcome rush of warm air came from the heater, and she unwound her scarf and tossed it on the seat. She backed up into the middle of the empty parking lot, put the van in drive, and crept out toward the highway.

No one was approaching. There were no headlights in either direction. She pulled into the homebound lane, and gradually edged the van up toward thirty miles per hour. She glanced out of the passenger side window and faintly saw Reverend Bradley, hunched against the wind, coming out of the cemetery and into his own yard.

When the Reverend's house was lost to sight in the gathering darkness, she reached into the pocket of her overcoat and pulled out her cellphone. One hand on the wheel, one eye on the road, she punched in a number and put the phone to her ear.

"Helene, it's me… Yes, I did. And I didn't need to ask him, he brought it up with almost no prompting… I know, I know, but… Look, Helene, this isn't my fault. Don't get all snippy with me. It's Stephen's fault. I'm the one trying to clean up the mess… I know. Apology accepted, for what it's worth. But Helene, I haven't told you yet. Bradley says he's planning to call Stephen… No, I don't know when. He didn't say. I tried to talk him out of it. I don't know if it worked… I know… Yes, I know that too. You need to tell Stephen that… Sure, I'll call him. It's more your place than mine, but if you want me to… Yes, well, it's not a matter of fear. I'm not afraid of Stephen, for god's sake… I think he'll listen to you more than to me."

She listened for some time, and then gave a little laugh. "Good. Tell him that. If Bradley calls, he has to put him off. You know how Stephen is. He'll try to do something about it, and you know he'll make it worse. The less said the better."

Louise considered. "Probably the best thing would be for him to not answer the phone for the next few days, and if Bradley calls, let voicemail get it, then don't call back… Yes, you're probably right. But you could suggest it anyway… Helene, look. If he gives you a hard time, remind him that it's his fault that this happened. Well, the whole cockamamie twin story thing, anyway. I guess we couldn't have prevented or even foreseen what happened in the church. That's your husband's fault if it's anyone's… Yes, I know… Make sure he understands how important it is to tell Bradley nothing. Not one thing, nada. No more stupid embellishments that will make Bradley more curious. How about telling him to say, 'I don't want to discuss it with you,' and hanging up? How hard is that?… I know… Well, tell him… I know."

Louise looked at the snowy road, spooling away ahead of her, gray and white and black in the beam from her headlights. She smiled unpleasantly. "I have an idea. Maybe you should tell him the truth. It's probably occurred to him, but I don't think he really believes it. Not really."

After a moment, she laughed. "The truth that if we get any inkling that what he's doing is thwarting us in any way, Stephen's life expectancy will drop to about ten minutes."

10

Zodiac Wheel: First Turn

Friday, December 11, 2015, through Sunday, December 13, 2015

"Stacy, how are you?" said Andrea Yarbrough, a smile spreading across her broad face. "I thought that after my encounter with your friend, I might have lost you as a customer, too." She motioned Stacy to come inside her house.

"That's one of the things I wanted to talk to you about," said Stacy, following Andrea down the hall to her study. "Marcia was seriously freaked out."

"I could tell. That wasn't my intent. I hope you know that."

Stacy gave a dismissive wave of the hand. "Look, I've known Marsh since we were toddlers together. She's my best friend in the whole world. No one knows her better than I do. She has a tendency to overreact sometimes. I think she was scared of... well, not you, exactly, but what you said. The message."

"Oh, don't think I took it personally. It's not the first time this sort of thing has happened. I'm psychic, but that doesn't mean that I'm always going to see things that are nice."

Stacy considered. "What exactly did your warning mean, though? I'm really worried about Marcia. You said she was in danger."

Andrea pursed her lips. "I had to tell her."

"But what you said was so vague. Couldn't you have been more specific? All you did was scare the hell out of her, without giving her anything concrete to go on so she could avoid the danger you saw."

"I told her what I did see," Andrea responded. Her forehead wrinkled up, and she looked genuinely dismayed. "If I had seen more specifics, I would have told her that. Sometimes I see more clearly than others. Here, all I saw were vague forebodings. Like seeing a line of black clouds on the horizon when the sun's still shining overhead."

"What exactly did you tell her?" Stacy's voice was sharp.

Andrea raised one eyebrow slightly. "Stacy, I don't know if it's really appropriate for me to say."

"Look, Andrea, I'm not mad at you. I'm not mad at anyone. I'm concerned for the welfare of my oldest and best friend. I know it's prying, and it's entirely your right to refuse to tell me. But if your concern is really for Marcia's safety, you should know that I'm going to do what it takes to protect her. You'll have to take my word for it that I only want to know what you saw because I care about her." She paused a moment, and then said, "I would die to save her, you know."

Andrea was silent for a moment. "Well, I don't know…"

"It depends on whether you really want to help me help Marcia," Stacy interjected.

"I suppose that's what it all comes to," said Andrea. "But it feels a little like I'm handing you her diary to read. What I saw…" She hesitated, her brow creasing as she struggled to remember. "I saw a direct danger to her. Someone who was trying to exploit her, use her, and whose concern for her person was far less than his desire for power."

"You said it was a priest or something."

"Definitely, someone who saw himself as a man of God. A minister, a priest, someone of that sort. Elderly."

"Someone she knows?"

"I don't think so. Or not yet. Someone she will meet."

"What does this person want with her?"

"I'm not sure. It has to do with control, though. Something that Marcia can do, something that this person can use to control others."

"Marcia? What can Marcia do that anyone could possibly use?"

Andrea smiled faintly. "You don't have much faith in your friend," she said.

"It's not that. Look, I love her dearly, but I also know her probably better than anyone on earth. She's smart, sweet, and has a heart of pure gold. But as far as having any kind of unusual talent that someone can use—unless this priest guy is looking for a good typist, I don't know what he could possibly want with her."

"You perhaps don't know her as well as you think you do," Andrea said. "Everyone has abilities that they don't suspect, and in fact, they may never develop them unless they're in the right situation to do so. Many people go to their graves with psychic abilities they never realized."

Stacy looked unconvinced.

"Trust me. I saw in your friend an energy, something that is absolutely unique. A power source. I'm not entirely certain. But I do know that she has abilities that would be useful for someone who knew how to tap into them."

"So she should just avoid priests and whatever?" Stacy's voice was peevish. "Look, I do believe you or I wouldn't be here. But you've got to give me more specifics."

If Andrea was annoyed by Stacy's brusqueness, she didn't show it. "I've told you what I could. I can tell you that the religious figure, whoever he is, he gives the appearance of being holy. Of being harmless, even. He isn't what he seems. Other than that, I really don't know any more." She frowned. "Stacy, what you really need to do is to convince Marcia to come back to me. I can only do so much long distance. In order to gain more information, I really need to be in proximity with someone, or ideally, in physical contact with them. It is a limitation of my own ability."

"I don't know if she would."

"You said you wanted to help her. To protect her."

"I do."

"Then get her to come back here. Either with you or on her own. If you want more information, if you want her to be safe, you need me."

TWO DAYS LATER, Marcia Pacheco was sitting in the passenger seat of Stacy's car. The previous evening another snowstorm had blown through the area, and although the roads had been plowed, there was still a thick, uneven layer of grimy snow on the blacktop. A tornado of fine flakes followed in the wake of the car.

"I really don't want to do this, Stace," said Marcia glumly, looking out of the side window at the drifts and the bare, leafless trees sliding past.

"I know."

"What possible good can it do? I'm not even sure I believed her."

"For not believing her, you sure were scared."

Marcia gave Stacy a sour look. "*The Babadook* scared me. It wasn't because I believed it."

"Yeah, but there's more to this, honey. And I anyhow, I believe her. Andrea knows stuff. I'm only trying to find out more information. If you're in danger, I want to know how, and how we can avoid it or prevent it."

"Fine. Whatever." Marcia looked back out of the window.

"Oh, 'fine, whatever,' yourself," Stacy said. "Look, do this for me, okay?"

"I am. I'm in the car, right?"

"Yeah, well, cooperate. See if she can find out more. If you block her or get all defensive, you'll interfere with her ability to see."

"So all of a sudden, you're an expert on psychics?"

STACY PULLED into Andrea's snow-covered driveway, the tires making hardly a sound. They emerged into the bitterly cold wind, their boots squeaking as they walked through the foot-deep drifts.

Andrea was waiting at the door, and in spite of her fear, the warm, cozy interior was welcoming. It was a relief to be out of the wind. Andrea reached out and took one of Marcia's mittened hands, and said, "Dear, thanks for coming back. I know you're scared. There's no reason to be. You're safe here. But it did take some courage to return, and I'm glad you did." She smiled. "May I take your coats?"

Marcia attempted a weak smile in return, and after shedding their winter wear, Andrea turned and led them to her study.

"You do know that Stacy came here to talk to me about you," Andrea said, once the three were seated in chairs in the small, untidy back room.

Marcia nodded.

"You're angry at her for doing that?"

"No," Marcia said. "Well, not really angry, so much. I was irritated at first, but I know she did it because she's concerned for me."

"That's right. And she asked me what I thought she should do. My feeling is that I didn't get enough information the first time, that we needed to probe deeper. I still get this sense of a danger to you, but it's unfocused. We need to find out more."

"You said there was a priest or someone who was trying to hurt me."

Andrea frowned and shook her head. "It's not to hurt you, at least not in the usual sense. But psychic hurt. To use you. He wants some kind of power that you have." She looked at Marcia, sympathy evident in her homely face. "That can be worse, you know. Worse than being physically hurt."

"Who is he?" asked Marcia, suppressing a shudder.

"That's what we're going to try to find out. With your permission, of course."

Marcia looked over at Stacy, who was watching, tight-lipped, her expression taut with worry.

"Okay," Marcia said. "I guess it's okay. There's nothing harmful about finding out more information, I suppose."

"That's it exactly," Andrea said. "Think of it as reading the newspaper. You may read something you don't like, but it can't directly hurt you. There's nothing to be afraid of."

As with the previous time, Andrea reached out and took Marcia's small, cool hands in her large, warm, rough ones, and closed her eyes. The room went completely silent for a minute, two minutes, three.

"It's still there," Andrea said, her voice slow and a little slurred as if she were talking in her sleep.

"What is?" whispered Marcia, a tremor passing through her whole body.

"The darkness. In the distance, but closer now. He's still out there, waiting for you."

"Who is he?"

Andrea didn't respond, but her grip tightened slightly. Marcia had to force herself not to pull back, not to yank her hands out of the older woman's, not to jump up and run for the door. With an effort, she slowed down her breathing and waited.

"He's a minister. An older man, thin, with white hair and glasses. But he's also something else."

"What do you mean?"

"He will contact you. It will appear to be by accident, but it isn't. He already knows about you, knows what you can do. He's already seeking you out."

"What can I do? Why is he looking for me?"

Andrea's eyes moved beneath her closed lids. "You're like a battery. An energy source."

"What does that mean?"

"You have an internal power." The psychic's voice became softer, fading almost to inaudibility. Suddenly the room felt warmer, as if a down blanket had been wrapped around reality. Marcia's eyes drooped. "You're the channel. When the planets and stars align, the power will flow through you. Then others will be able to tap into that power, to make things happen."

"What things? I don't understand what you mean."

"Whatever they want."

Stacy's voice suddenly cut across the drowsy, soporific atmosphere, her voice sharp with anxiety. "You've got to be more specific. Who is this man who is hunting her?"

Andrea and Marcia both started, and Andrea's eyelids fluttered briefly and then closed again.

"He looks harmless," she said, in the same sleepy voice. "He's not."

"Who is he?" said Marcia, feeling the anxiety creeping back into her.

"I don't know his name. You'll know when you meet him."

"What should I do if I do meet him?"

"There is no if. It will happen. When you meet him, you should come back to me immediately. I can protect you. But you must come here right away. On the first meeting, nothing will happen. By the second one..."

"What?"

Andrea didn't open her eyes, and her voice was steady. "By the second turn of the wheel, it will be too late."

11

Main Drive Wheel: Third Turn: Locked With Zodiac Wheel and Engaged

Monday, December 14, 2015

The bright blue van, with the logo of a happy little bird with a flower in its mouth and the words "Robin's Nest Nursery and Florist" written in flowing script underneath, pulled into the parking lot of the Blue Heron Organic Foods Market. The lot had only been plowed once and had not been salted at all, the owners of the Blue Heron not considering road salt sufficiently organic, and the van's wheels scrunched through the ridged ice and grimy snow and came to a halt.

Louise pulled her scarf more tightly around her neck and exited the van. Even though the sun was out, the light was weak and warmed nothing. She went through the entrance and into the relaxed warmth of the store.

The Blue Heron's customers that day were the typical odd assortment that frequents organic food markets—aging hippies, young mothers trying to do the right thing by their families, college professors of nutrition and health science who knew what horrors lurked on the shelves of big box grocery stores, idealists of all ages and all walks of life. Louise, with her layers of rough, warm garments, her flyaway brown hair, and work-hardened hands, fit right in, and no one gave her a second glance as she walked to the back of the store.

She caught up with him in the produce section, as he was unpacking boxes of lettuce.

"Stephen," she said in a low voice.

Stephen Calhoun turned, and for a moment, looked alarmed, but he recovered just as quickly. He smiled broadly and continued his work. "Louise," he said, in an amiable voice, "nice to see you."

Louise smiled, but the smile never reached her eyes. "I'm sure it is."

"What brings you here?"

"You know damn well what brings me here," she said. "And we need to talk. Now."

Stephen continued to smile and set down the crate of lettuce. Without answering, he walked down the aisle toward the front of the store. "Deanna," he said, to a woman who was cashiering, "I'm taking my break now. If Jay is looking for me, tell him I'll be back in ten."

The cashier nodded, and Stephen and Louise went out of the store and into the icy parking lot.

"Into my van," said Louise, gesturing.

"Why?" said Stephen warily.

"Don't be an ass. It's cold out here."

"Oh."

Louise climbed into the driver's side, and a moment later, Stephen got into the passenger side. Both pulled the doors shut. Louise looked over at Stephen, but he wouldn't meet her eye.

"Helene is pissed," said Louise.

"Why? All I did was..."

"She told you not to talk to him. She told you if he called, you should refuse to talk to him. I told you not to talk to him. All you had to do was listen, Stephen."

"I figured he'd be more suspicious if I suddenly told him I didn't want to talk."

"He's already suspicious. But he doesn't know anything. Yet. But if you keep the way you're going, he's going to find out. Andrea's seen him. He is a threat, even if you're too damned stupid to see it."

"Andrea doesn't know what she sees."

"She knows that she saw him."

"That woman is a carnival sideshow psychic, no more."

Louise's hand moved faster than a striking snake and grabbed Stephen's shirt front. There was a sad little ripping sound as some internal seam tore, but Stephen didn't resist. He looked terrified. Had Reverend Bradley seen him at that moment, he would have had no doubt that Stephen Calhoun had been the man in the church.

"Look, you idiot," Louise hissed. "Andrea is more important than you are. If I were in charge, you'd be long gone. Understand? Helene thinks you're still useful, but right now you look like one serious liability to me."

"You were singing a different tune when you met me at the airport this summer."

"That's because you did what you were supposed to do, and came back home like a good soldier. But since then, you've done nothing to help us. You hear me? Nothing. Helene's only rationale for not getting rid of you is that it's too risky to have a fourth murder, close to home. Me, I'm not so sure. We don't have time for dead weight, and we have other flunkies who can swing a heavy object and who know when to keep their mouths shut. You, Stephen, are nothing more than a disposable errand boy. So you know what you do? You follow orders. Do you understand me? You follow the fucking orders, no questions asked. Or I'll put more pressure on Helene to see things my way."

Stephen swallowed convulsively once, twice, and then gasped out, "Okay, Louise. Okay. I get it. Let me go."

Louise released his shirt front with an irritated little gesture and leaned back in her seat. "Andrea thinks that old reverend is a real threat. You've got to stop trying to fix things. The more you talk, the more suspicious he gets. He's not stupid, you know. I know the guy. He gives the impression of being a helpless little old man. Don't be fooled by that."

"What did Andrea see?"

Louise looked at Stephen sidelong. "Why should I tell you?"

Stephen straightened out his shirt and gave Louise a look with a hint of defiance in it. "I'm in, Louise. You may not like me, but I'm in until Helene says I'm out."

"If Helene says you're out, you'll be dead."

"Maybe." His voice quavered slightly, then steadied. "But until that time, I'm in, and you need to tell me what Andrea saw."

"You? In? You're light years from the inner circle. Helene likes you as an hired hand, for some reason, and I'm goddamned if I see why. Don't flatter yourself."

"You think your own position is secure, Louise. Did it ever occur to you that maybe somewhere, there are people who are saying the same thing about you? Don't be surprised if some day you find yourself in the bullseye."

That point hit home. "They know they can trust me," she said, her voice in a flat monotone.

"Sure. Keep telling yourself that. Remember Helene saying, the last time she met with us, 'We're all gears in the machine. Any of us could be replaced.' Except herself, of course." Stephen gave a dry, mirthless laugh. "They don't care about any of us, not really. But I'm still one of the gears, whether you like it or not. So tell me what Andrea saw."

"Fine." Louise looked out of the window for a moment, and then back at Stephen. "But if you do anything to fuck things up further, I hope Helene has you skinned alive." She paused. "Andrea thinks she's found someone who could be the power source. Someone who has the capacity for what we're trying to do."

"Who is he?"

"She. Her name is Marcia something. Some woman who's a secretary up at the college. She has no idea of what she can do, or what's going on. But Andrea, as usual, was right on target. Marcia's friend was one of Andrea's clients, and Andrea picked up on it during a reading with the friend."

"Picked up on what?"

"That Marcia was important. The usual vague stuff, but accurate as always. So Andrea asked the friend about her and found out that Marcia had some kind of messy personal life thing. I don't know the details. Anyhow, Andrea gave the friend a nudge in the direction of suggesting that Marcia should come in for a reading, and she did."

"What happened?"

"Well, it confirmed what Andrea already knew, that Marcia was the power source. Off the scale. But during the reading, Andrea kept getting the picture of someone interfering, someone who could ruin everything."

"Reverend Bradley."

"Your friend and mine, Reverend Morris Bradley."

"Ruining things how?"

"No idea. We're hoping that if Andrea can scare Marcia badly enough, she'll be able to maneuver her into a position where we can connect her to the Mechanism. I mean really hook her in, more or less permanently. We think that it will amplify what we've already been able to do. But for right now, all we know is that Bradley is a danger. He needs to be kept out of the picture as much as possible. And you, Stephen, need to pull your head out of your ass and listen to people who are smarter than you. Stop talking to Bradley. Don't answer the phone for a few days. And don't return his calls if he leaves a message."

"I didn't really tell him anything..."

"Like I said, the man is smart. And you are not. You're telling him things whether you think you are or not. So leave him completely alone."

"If we leave him alone, how will we stop him from interfering, like Andrea saw?"

Louise gave him an exasperated glance. "I said you leave him alone. I didn't say that *we* were going to leave him alone."

"Oh."

"What Andrea saw is that somehow, Bradley will meet Marcia, the power source, and the result of the meeting is that he will try to stop her from linking up with us. That must not happen. Andrea thinks that the first meeting is inevitable, but she's told Marcia that she's in danger, from a priest or a religious person, and if she meets such a person she's to come and tell her, that Andrea will protect her."

Stephen gave a bray of laughter. "That's brilliant."

"It's still risky," Louise said sourly. "I guess Marcia was pretty freaked out the first time Andrea saw her, and it took some doing to get her to come back. We debated having Andrea tell her Bradley's name outright, but decided that keeping it vague and mystical-sounding would work better to scare her. Anyway, it's all set up now. All we have to do is to sit back, and not do anything too awfully stupid, and she should come to us when the time is right."

"Fine. I'll leave Bradley alone."

"You'd better."

"I've got to get back to work," Stephen said. It sounded like a plea for dismissal.

"Go ahead. Just remember what I told you. And don't even dream of trying to double-cross us, like you did in October. You're in too deep ever to have a chance of getting out alive."

He nodded, and opened the door, and stepped out of the van.

Louise watched him as he retreated into the grocery store, her face inscrutable. She sat for a moment, watching the store front, and then started the van, pulled out, and drove off back toward her shop.

As LOUISE WAS DRIVING toward her florist's shop on the south end of Colville, she passed an old Nissan station wagon heading the opposite direction. She always prided herself on her keen observational ability, but this time, preoccupied with thoughts about her meeting with Stephen, she didn't even look at the driver. Reverend Bradley saw her, however, in her bright blue van, and gave her a small wave, but she didn't respond.

Reverend Bradley quickly returned to his own thoughts and his own preoccupations. His last conversation with Stephen Calhoun had been profoundly unsettling. On an impulse, he had called Stephen, to ask him if he'd heard anything from his twin brother. There hadn't been anyone home, but he'd left a message, and much to his amazement, Stephen had called him back that evening. The exchange itself had not revealed any new information, nor solved anything of the mystery of the man in the church and his supposed identical twin. Stephen had been friendly, breezy even, and had again encouraged Reverend Bradley to call back if he should ever see "David" (Reverend Bradley always mentally put quotation marks around the name, as if David was Stephen's imaginary friend). There was nothing obviously suspicious about the conversation, but Reverend Bradley was more than ever convinced that Stephen was lying.

And why? Why would a man tell a false story about having an identical twin brother to a total stranger? And further, if the twin story was a lie, that would, of course, mean that Stephen actually *had* been the man in the church on that strange Sunday morning, now almost two months ago. For the hundredth time, Reverend Bradley's mind returned to the last words the man spoke: "If you ever run into me again, don't believe a single thing I say."

Reverend Bradley shuddered. "Well, I've got to resolve this one way or another," he said aloud. "I've got to settle my mind about it." It was the determination to reach closure on this odd episode that had made him that morning call up an old friend whom he had not seen in almost five years, and make an appointment to have lunch with him. It'd be nice to see him, of course, but more importantly, it would give him an opportunity to ask him what he thought of this strange episode.

In years now very long past, Reverend Bradley had gone to college with Henry Larkin, now head of the Colville College Pre-Law program, and Bradley still considered Larkin the smartest and most practical man he had ever met. They had kept in touch throughout their careers, and after twenty years of each of them being in various locations around the northeast, they had ended up living only thirty miles from each other. If anyone could help him think things through in a logical fashion, it was Henry Larkin.

Parking at Colville College was always dicey, but Reverend Bradley found that his humble petitionary prayer not to have too far to walk on icy sidewalks in the chill wind had been unexpectedly answered. He pulled into a recently vacated metered parking space right in front of the pre-law building, which more amazingly still, had forty-five minutes on the meter. Giving a quick word of thanks for this unforeseen bounty, he walked into the building and up the single flight of stairs to Henry's office. He'd never met Henry at the college before, and had to do a bit of searching to find the office, tucked into a back corner at the end of the hall. The secretary, a pleasant-looking young woman with neatly cropped dark hair and brown eyes, looked up as he entered the room.

"Can I help you?"

"I have an appointment to see Henry Larkin."

"May I tell him who's here?"

"Morris Bradley."

She picked up the phone, punched in the extension, and said, "Professor Larkin? Morris Bradley is here to see you."

She replaced the receiver, and a moment later, Professor Larkin emerged from his inner sanctum, shook hands with his old friend, and inclined his head slightly in a quaint, old-fashioned gesture. "Morris, how nice to see you."

Reverend Bradley smiled, and said, "It's been a while, Henry. How have you been?"

"Well, thank you. Quite well." Professor Larkin looked over at his secretary. "Marcia, I'll be back by one-thirty or so."

Marcia Pacheco smiled, and said, "Have a nice lunch, sir."

12

L

unar Anomaly Mechanism: Second Turn

Wednesday, December 16, 2015

"Would you care for some wine, dear?" said Mrs. May.

Kelly hesitated. "I'm not twenty-one," she said, and the statement ended on a question mark, but the implication was there. If she was to be offered some, she wouldn't turn it down.

And indeed, Mrs. May smiled, and said, "Oh, it's the holidays. And you must be close to twenty-one, anyway, right?"

"Only three months till my birthday," Kelly said, and Mrs. May said, "Well, then," and filled her glass with a red wine so dark that it looked almost black. *Like the wine-dark seas in Homer*, she thought absently.

Mr. May cut into his slice of roast beef, and said, "I'm so glad that you could come to dinner tonight."

"Me too," Kelly said.

Mr. May raised his glass. "Here's to new friends and good neighbors."

Kelly followed suit and drank a large sip of the wine. It was as rich as its color, with a spicy overtone, like pepper and cinnamon. She smiled. The good conversation, good food, and now the good wine had erased the last of her misgivings about the Mays. She had not had the dream in over a week since that horrible evening following her last visit with them.

Her thoughts slipped back, as she set her wine glass down and glanced around the spotlessly clean dining room. Three days ago, she had run into Mr. May while getting the mail, and had offered to help him shovel the snow from his driveway. He cheerfully accepted, and they spent two hours, made pleasant despite the work by a conversation which had touched on literature, history, travel, and even sports—it turned out that both Kelly and Mr. May were college hockey fans. She came in afterwards for hot cocoa, and returned home later that afternoon with a dinner invitation and the pleasure of a fear put to rest. She had a momentary pang of apprehension as she prepared for bed that night, but she slept soundly. Her only dream had been a familiar one, a recurrent dream of long standing. She was wandering up and down the aisles of a clock shop, an old and dusty room filled with hundreds of swinging pendulums and turning keys and rotating pointers. The place was filled with the sounds of ticking, from the dry, insect-like clicks of small bedside clocks to the *basso profundo* of tall grandfather clocks. A broad, curtained window looked out on a snow-covered street, empty, illuminated only by a halo of light from a single street lamp. She turned back to the clocks, and only then saw that it was nearly midnight. This knowledge filled her with panic. She ran toward the door, but before she could get there, every chime, bell, and gong in the room began to toll out twelve o'clock, a deafening cacophony of sound that made her clap her hands over her ears. The noise echoed, vibrating the walls and floor. At that moment she realized that there was someone with her in the shop, someone she needed to talk to, but the sound was so loud that it was physically painful, so loud that she could think of nothing else. Then the deafening din began to feed back on the machines that were creating it, pulling them into a death spiral. Glass fronts shattered, shards of glass bursting out and tinkling onto the floor. Carefully-painted brass faces cracked asunder. Wooden cases splintered, spilling bronze gears and wheels and pins in a cascade of ruin. And finally, as the last pieces spun rattling on the tiles, silence fell, and she woke, tangled in her bedsheets.

Kelly had been through this dream dozens of times. It had always left her shaken, lying in bed with her heart pounding and her ears ringing.

Now, in comparison with her recent nightmares, it was positively comforting. She sat in bed, pulled the blankets around her, and smiled. Her quixotic brain was finally settling back into normality.

Kelly had called Dr. Sparlin the day of her dinner with the Mays. He wasn't in, but she left a message saying that she was finally convinced of what Dr. Sparlin had told her, that dreams, in general, were nothing more than taking out the psychological trash, and more specifically, that she was reading too much into her dream about the Mays. Why this particular piece of neural refuse involved a harmless elderly couple was one of those inexplicable filigrees of the unconscious mind. She had ended by saying that she was looking forward to dinner with the Mays that evening, and thanked him for his steady, rational reassurance the previous week, and went to her neighbors' house without a qualm.

And so the meal passed with nothing but pleasant conversation, and excellent food and drink.

Dessert was a home-made pound cake, something Kelly hadn't had since her grandmother died six years previous. As Mrs. May set the sliced cake, crumbling and fragrant, on the table, she turned to Kelly and said, "You were starting to tell us about your trip to England earlier, dear, but we got sidetracked. Do tell us all about it."

Kelly smiled. "Well, compared to your travels, it wasn't much," she said. "I spent three weeks in the UK this past summer. I've always been attracted to England, for some reason, but not the tourist places like London and Dover and Blackpool. I actually didn't even hit London on the way in. I flew into Manchester, got a BritRail pass, and went from there."

"Quite a coincidence," Mr. May said. "We were in Britain last summer ourselves. But we spent most of our time in London, so our paths wouldn't have crossed."

Mrs. May served slices of the cake to each of them and sat down. "I would love to go back again. Perhaps head up into the north. Go rambling. That's what the English call hiking, isn't it, Stanford?"

"I do believe," said Mr. May.

"I've loved stories of England since I was a child," said Kelly. "*Narnia*, of course, and *The Wind in the Willows*. And *Watership Down*." She took a bite of the cake, which was as delicious as it smelled.

"Yes, indeed," said Mrs. May. "There's something so... so old about the place."

"Exactly!" said Kelly. "When I was in Glastonbury, for example. I mean, there's the inevitable tourist stuff, sort of like Salem, Massachusetts. But you still have the feeling that there's something underneath all the trappings. Something real, not just the silly hype."

"I felt that, too," said Mrs. May. "About Rievaulx Abbey, particularly, although I agree with you about Glastonbury. Rievaulx is somehow a holy place. One gets the feeling that the abbey was built on the site because the land was holy, not the other way round."

"There are energies in some places," said Mr. May. "You've heard of ley lines, I'm sure."

"I've heard the term," said Kelly.

"They're like lines of force, but psychic force, not any kind of physical energy that you could measure with a piece of hardware. They say that Glastonbury is the intersection point of dozens, possibly hundreds, of ley lines. The highest concentration of any spot in the world."

"Oh, I doubt that's true, darling," said Mrs. May. "I'd bet in the unexplored parts of the world, there are places even stronger than Glastonbury."

"You may well be right."

"When we were in Australia, for example. There were places on the Cape York Peninsula that felt like a volcano to me. Not a real volcano, you understand, but a mental one. A psychic hotspot." She considered. "I've never understood the deal with Ayers Rock, however. I'm sure the Aborigines have their reasons, but it didn't really speak to me."

Mr. May nodded. "It's not always the obvious places which have it," he observed.

"Indeed not."

"You get the impression that the ley lines, or the powerful places, are somehow completely independent of anything people do."

"Of course," said Mrs. May. "It's the most we can do simply to tap into it. To create a bridge between the energy and ourselves. Controlling it is quite, quite impossible. Out of the question."

Both of the Mays looked over at Kelly. Increasingly, she found herself feeling disconnected from the conversation, like a child listening to a philosophical discourse between adults. She knew that what was being said was perfectly understandable, but she couldn't quite make sense of it. She was sure that she had just heard Mrs. May say something about building a bridge using straight lines that were forced out when you turned on the tap, but that couldn't be correct.

"Are you quite all right, dear?" said Mrs. May.

"You look flushed," said Mr. May.

"I'm fine," said Kelly, and the words came out in a syrupy, slurred drone without any inflection.

"I do believe the wine has gone to her head," said Mrs. May. "Perhaps you should lie down, dear."

"Maybe so," Kelly said, amazed to hear her words come out in that odd voice, so unlike her own.

Mr. May stood up, and walked to her, and helped her to her feet. She didn't feel any fear. Somehow, whatever it was that was affecting her had diminished her ability to feel anything. She knew that she'd been drugged, but the realization carried no emotional weight. Was it the cake? Or the wine? The wine, she thought. Anything in the cake wouldn't have had time to affect her yet. It seemed like a pointless thing to worry about, anyhow. The whole world was slipping underwater, and what she was seeing and hearing came from a tremendous distance. She looked over at Mrs. May, who was watching her curiously, her head cocked to one side.

Mr. May maneuvered Kelly to the sofa, once again evicting the resident cat. Kelly hardly registered it. As she was lowered down onto the cushions, she felt she was sinking into them, or that they were rising up and padding everything around her. Mr. May turned away from her, and said to his wife, who was still seated at the table, "Helene, will you get the poor child a blanket?"

That was the last thing that Kelly Delahanty heard for quite some time.

KEITH SPARLIN DIDN'T GET HOME until after nine that evening, following a day of Christmas shopping, a stiff workout at the gym, and dinner with his girlfriend followed by a highly satisfactory workout of a different sort in her apartment afterwards. He tossed his jacket on the back of his sofa, went into the kitchen and rummaged around in his fridge until he found a beer, and pressed the "messages" button on his answering machine.

The first message was from his mother, reminding him that his sister and brother-and-law and their new baby were going to be coming down for Christmas, and not to forget to buy a present for the baby. Keith sighed deeply and deleted it, but not before making a note on the phone pad saying, "present, baby." The second was a reminder from the local police department that he had agreed to donate to their Christmas charity, and could they expect his check soon? They sure hoped so.

The third message was Kelly's. Keith listened to her, his face expressionless, as she thanked him for his reassurance and described her certainty that the Mays were as harmless as they appeared and that she was having dinner with them that evening.

Keith stood there quietly for several moments after the message ended, then picked up his bottle of beer and went into the living room, and plopped down into the old recliner in the corner.

Shouldn't he feel glad that she took his advice? She'd been afraid because of what, a dream? A pointless dream.

But truth be told, he didn't feel glad. At all. The message, despite its cheerful content, had left him feeling subtly disturbed. Maybe he should call her, and find out how dinner was? Just to see. Immediately he chided himself. Was he really succumbing to the nonsense about precognitive dreams?

Of course not. Still, it wouldn't hurt to call. To say happy holidays, and thank her for calling.

He returned to the kitchen and pulled the phone book out from under a stack of unopened mail. There was a K. Delahanty on Prospect Street, north of the college. He dialed the number.

Four rings, and voicemail picked up. A female voice, not Kelly's, said, "Hi! You've reached the home of Maria Alessandro, Kelly Delahanty, and Angela Cho. We can't come to the phone right now, but please leave a brief message and we'll get right back to you." And three voices chimed together, "Merry Christmas!" The machine beeped.

Keith started to hang up, then changed his mind. "Kelly," he said. "It's Keith... Dr. Sparlin. I was glad to get your call, sorry I couldn't return it earlier. Hope all went well with your dinner. I'll be in town 'til Christmas Eve, call me if you want to."

He hung up, still feeling a vague disquiet that would not be quelled by any rational argument.

He returned to his armchair and turned on the television. *It's a Wonderful Life* was on. It was a classic he'd seen way too many times, but it was reassuring tonight.

I'll call her again tomorrow morning, just in case, he thought, taking a sip of beer and putting up the foot rest. *I shouldn't worry. She'll be there, of course. But I'll call anyhow.*

Just in case.

13

Zodiac Wheel, Locked With Lunar Anomaly Mechanism and Main Drive Wheel: Calibrated and Engaged

Friday, December 18, 2015

"It's already happened," said Andrea Yarbrough, her forehead creasing. "I've seen it. I don't know how it happened, but she met him, and she didn't get in contact with me."

Helene May sat in a chair in her upstairs study, her hands interlaced in her lap. Her dress, pale dove gray with a print of tiny roses, and her fuzzy pink sweater accentuated her grandmotherly appearance. "You said that she had assured you she would come back to you if she met him, Andrea, dear," she said. "Do have some tea," she added, gesturing

at a tray with cups, a china teapot, and a plate full of
cookies sitting on a folding table in the middle of the room.

Andrea ran her hands through her hair in a gesture of
dismay. "No, thank you," she responded. "And Marcia did
say she would come back if she saw him."

"It was always risky," said Mr. May. "We were relying on
her to come back to you, rather than the more direct
means of your going to her."

"It was the only way," said Mrs. May. "It wasn't like with
the girl. The girl's parents and roommates are away, and
school's out of session. She won't be missed, not for some
time at least. Not till it won't matter anymore. Marcia has
her friend looking out for her, and a regular job. If she
vanished, an alarm would be raised within twenty-four
hours."

"I don't see that it matters," said Louise Middlebury. "We
still have time to find her and get control of her."

"How much time?" said Mr. May.

"Well, that depends on what you mean, doesn't it, dear?"
said Mrs. May. "If what Andrea saw is correct, and we
have no reason to believe it isn't, then we may already be
too late."

"What the hell does that mean?" said Louise sharply.

"What I saw," said Andrea, "is that if she meets the
Reverend a second time, she will be beyond our grasp."

"And that will happen when?" asked Louise.

"There's no way to tell," said Andrea. "I don't even know
when the first meeting happened, but I'm sure it did. She

met with the old Reverend somehow. I only saw it after it had already happened."

Mrs. May's lips tightened until they were a thin line. "We must act quickly, then. You're certain of what you've seen?"

"Helene," said Andrea, her broad, plain face turning pale, "you know that I can never be a hundred percent certain..."

Mrs. May nodded, but the tightness around her mouth didn't diminish. "I'm well aware of your limitations, Andrea. I want you to be well aware of how critical Marcia is to our plans. So once again, I'm asking you if you're certain of what you've seen."

"All I know," Andrea replied, in a quiet voice, "is that if Marcia comes into contact with the Reverend twice, she will come under their influence, and I probably will lose any access I have to her." She swallowed. "I can't see it very clearly. I don't know how it will happen. But if it does, we've lost her as a potential ally."

"Ally is the wrong word," said Louise.

"It doesn't matter," said Mrs. May, with an impatient wave of her hand. "All we know is, Andrea has never been wrong before. She doesn't see everything, and sometimes doesn't see it very clearly, but what she sees has never been wrong. We must assume if Andrea has seen that Marcia has met the old Reverend, it has happened."

"Perhaps Andrea should call her, and tell her that somehow, she met him without knowing it, and she needs to put herself under our care immediately," said Louise.

"That approach has its merits," said Mr. May, flicking a cookie crumb from his rumpled cardigan. "There is a possibility, of course, that fear may freeze Marcia into immobility. Don't forget that, by Andrea's reports, the woman is almost as afraid of Andrea herself as she is of meeting Reverend Bradley."

"And we mustn't discount the influence of her friend, Stacy," said Andrea. "I think she's as likely to go running to Stacy as to me. And if that happens, I can't be responsible for the outcome." She glanced nervously over at Mrs. May.

"And we still don't know how or where she met Reverend Bradley the first time?" asked Mrs. May.

"I haven't been able to see it," said Andrea. "All I know is that this morning, I got a clear vision, the clearest I've had in some time. I saw Marcia speaking with Reverend Bradley. I couldn't see the room, or hear what they were saying. I am certain that they've already met. And for some reason, she didn't get in contact with me as she promised she would."

"What will the circumstances of the next meeting be?" asked Mr. May.

"I don't know," said Andrea. "My glimpses of the future are never as solid as my glimpses of the present and the past."

"Hell of a lot of good..." Louise began, but Mrs. May made a slight gesture with one hand, and Louise fell silent.

"We are well aware of what Andrea can and cannot do, and we also know full well that her gifts have been useful to us before. We will get nowhere by falling into mutual criticisms. We all play our roles, you know."

"I notice that Stephen isn't here, though," said Louise, chuckling grimly. Andrea glanced over at her in alarm but said nothing.

"Could we use the girl's ability to get more information?" asked Mr. May.

"Kelly can only look forward," said Mrs. May. "At least, so far as we know. That is, perhaps, the best idea yet."

"I don't see her usefulness to us," said Andrea petulantly.

"Stepping on toes, eh?" said Louise.

Andrea flushed crimson.

"You haven't been seeing all that clearly yourself, Andrea, dear," said Mrs. May. "We need all the help we can get."

"It isn't that we needed Kelly's help," said Mr. May. "It was more that she was a danger. She was seeing more and more. We couldn't take the chance that she might find out more about our plans, and then somehow make contact with the other side. We tried to stop her dreams from our end, but what we did had no effect. And perhaps her forward-looking ability may turn out to be an asset, especially if we can amplify it."

"Which brings us back to the issue at hand," said Mrs. May. "Amplification. We must secure Marcia's help. Soon. And with, or without, her consent."

"Could Marcia's friend be of use?" asked Louise. "She's been helpful so far. Without meaning to be, of course."

"I don't know," said Andrea. "In my last meeting with her, she was suspicious. She's very protective of Marcia."

"Perhaps we could use that," said Mrs. May. "Is there any way to induce her to perceive the danger to Marcia as imminent?"

"Again, it's risky," said Andrea. "Stacy's definitely a mother hen type. She'd be more likely to take matters into her own hands, and try to help Marcia herself."

"If it backfired, it could make our situation worse," said Louise. "She could just as easily begin interfering with us in an effort to protect her friend."

"We could deal with that," said Mr. May grimly. "No one would be protecting Stacy, after all."

Mrs. May reached out and patted her husband's hand. "Not yet, dear. Not yet. And if we did... ah, dispose of the friend, who knows what effect that may have on Marcia's ability? It's well known that psychic abilities of all types are highly responsive to emotional stresses. Her power might vanish entirely, especially if she knew that we were responsible."

"There's no reason that she would if it was done carefully," said Mr. May. "We took care of necessities this past summer without any particular difficulty."

"No," said Mrs. May. "Categorically no. At least at the moment. Such measures may become unavoidable. But not yet."

The doorbell rang, and everyone in the assembled group started. Mrs. May looked at the others, and said, "No need for alarm. But we're not done here yet." She stood, gave a brief tug at her pink wool sweater to straighten it, and walked to the door of her study, opened it, and disappeared down the stairs.

"MAY I HELP YOU?" said Mrs. May to the man at the door.

"Hi. I'm wondering if you might know where Kelly Delahanty is. I thought she'd be at home. She called me a couple of days ago, but I've tried calling her back. She wasn't there and hasn't returned my calls."

Mrs. May's forehead creased with worry. "Oh, dear me, I don't know. Kelly is such a sweet girl, I hope nothing is wrong."

"She told me that she was having dinner with you earlier this week. Did she mention anything about going away afterwards?"

Mrs. May paused. "Well, yes, now that you mention it, I believe that she may have mentioned something about going to visit family. But I'm afraid I don't know any more than that."

"It is the holidays," he admitted. "I guess it's the season for visiting."

Mrs. May looked visibly relieved. "Yes," she said. "But I'll keep an eye out. Would you like me to have her call you when I see her next? I'd be happy to pass along a message, Mr....?"

"Sparlin. Keith Sparlin."

"Mr. Sparlin. I'd be glad to tell her you came by. Of course," she added, "she may not be back until after Christmas. You know how family visits go."

Keith nodded. "But thanks for passing along the message. I'd like to be able to put my mind at ease."

"Perhaps I could take your phone number?" said Mrs. May. "That way I could call you as soon as I see her return."

"Certainly," said Keith. He reached into his jacket pocket. "I'm sorry, I don't have anything to write with, or on."

"It's no problem. Just a moment." Mrs. May stepped into her living room, and returned with a pen and a small notepad, with a corner design of a small, smiling rabbit hugging a bouquet of flowers.

Keith took the pad, a flicker of a smile crossing his face. "I really appreciate it."

"It's no problem," said Mrs. May. "Kelly really is a dear person, I can understand your concern."

"Thanks again," said Keith. "Happy holidays to you and your family."

"And the same to you."

After the door closed, Mrs. May stood to stare at the slip of paper in her hand for almost a minute. Then, her face expressionless, she walked across the room, down the hall, and back up the stairs.

She opened the door into the study. All eyes turned to her. She held up the slip of paper in her right hand, and said, her voice grim, "We have a problem."

14

MAIN DRIVE WHEEL: FOURTH TURN

LORD GOD, prayed Reverend Bradley silently, *I ask You humbly for solace.*

He knelt on a small cushion in his study, where he usually performed his afternoon devotions. Today's prayers were purely petitionary, not a usual thing for a man who normally wanted and needed so little to be content.

I am weak. None knows that better than You. But my weakness is interfering with my doing Your will and serving Your people. I ask You for help, to let go of this obsession and focus on Your service.

Reverend Bradley's mind slipped back to four days previous, to his last attempt to put the odd occurrences of the past weeks behind him.

The meeting with his friend Henry Larkin had been both helpful and unhelpful. Henry's opinion was strikingly like

Louise's. There were only two possibilities, Henry had said. One was that Stephen Calhoun did indeed have a twin brother, in which case the whole series of encounters and telephone calls was an odd set of coincidences, but nothing to be unduly concerned about. The brother obviously needed mental help, but Reverend Bradley was not a psychiatrist and could probably do little in that regard. In the phone conversations about the situation, Stephen himself was almost breezy about the possibility, not what you'd expect from someone whose disturbed identical twin brother had resurfaced after ten years' absence, but there was nothing criminal about a lack of care toward a missing relative.

The other possibility, of course, was that there was no twin brother, and the man in the church had been Stephen. If so, Stephen was lying, and was clearly either deeply disturbed himself, or was covering up for something, probably something illegal.

"In either case," Henry had said, his voice taking on an oratorical quality more suited to the courtroom, "there is every reason not to further entangle yourself in this matter. This man Calhoun is either in the first instance someone who cares little about his own brother, or in the second a liar or worse. You have nothing to gain, and nothing to contribute, to this situation by continuing your involvement." Henry took a sip of his after-lunch coffee, and said, in a more conversational tone, "You're not a young man, Morris. I know you have a strong do-good instinct, and I don't mean to denigrate that. But if this Calhoun is involved in something illicit, you are in no place or condition to interfere."

"You're older than I am, Henry," Reverend Bradley said.

"Yes, and I'm not getting myself involved with whatever mentally disturbed individuals happen to cross my path," Henry replied, one bushy eyebrow raised.

"So, basically, you're advising me to forget about it."

"Essentially." Henry set down his coffee cup. "Honestly, Morris, you should know that no one has a stronger sense of justice than I do. But even if Calhoun is involved in something wrong, you have no indication of what it might be. He certainly is making no efforts to hide from you, which would argue against his being connected to something illegal."

"True."

"So, then, yes. Yes, I'm advising you to forget about it. Go back to looking after the errant members of your church flock. Concern yourself with them. Or, at the very least, spend more of your time visiting with old friends. It's been years since Jeanine and I have had you over for dinner."

So the conversation had passed on to other things, and in the four days since, Reverend Bradley had done his best to follow his friend's advice. Each day he prayed for release from what was worrying at him, and each day his prayer had not been answered.

Lord, he prayed, trying to ignore the dull ache in his aging knees, *I ask You only for the strength to let this go. You know that I have no desire but to do Your will, and dear Lord, this is interfering with my ability to do that.*

Then a thought popped into his head, unbidden, and his eyes snapped open. What if this was God's will? What if he was becoming obsessed with Stephen because that was what God wanted him to do?

As that alarming thought passed through his mind, the telephone rang. Normally Reverend Bradley let voicemail pick it up if someone called during his prayers, but today he stood, straightening out his legs with some difficulty, and went to his desk and picked up the receiver.

"Hello?" he said.

"Reverend Bradley?" came a voice. He recognized it immediately, although there was a different timbre to the voice now, and he felt as if the temperature in the room had dropped twenty degrees. A thought, *He's back! It's the man in the church!* ricocheted through his brain, followed by a quieter, but more alarming certainty that he should hang up now, that this was the watershed moment, his last chance to break the chain.

Perhaps it is God's will, Reverend Bradley thought. *Either way, I have to find out.* And he said, "Stephen. What is it?"

"We need to meet," Stephen said, his voice hoarse and quiet.

"Why?"

"I don't want to take the time to tell you over the phone. If they realize I'm talking to you, they'll come after me, and my apartment is the first place they'll look."

"Who?"

"I'll tell you when I see you. Can you come into Colville today?"

"I could. But you could come out here..."

"Too risky. They'd know."

Reverend Bradley swallowed. "Is this about your brother?"

Stephen didn't answer for a moment. When he did, his voice was even more hushed. "Forget about that. Just come to Colville. You know the Old Mill Trail, near Quincy Falls?"

"Yes," said Reverend Bradley. "But the trail is closed for the winter, and in any case, I don't think I could hike it. My knees…"

"I'm not asking you to hike it. The whole point is that there won't be anyone there. Meet me in the parking area at the trailhead. In an hour."

"I suppose I can," began Reverend Bradley, "but can't you tell me why…"

The line went dead.

REVEREND BRADLEY DONNED his winter coat, gloves, and scarf, all the time considering in wonder whether Stephen's call had been some kind of oblique answer to his prayer. He gave only a cursory thought to his own safety. Was this a trap? Henry would certainly advise him against going. Perhaps he should give Henry a call, and tell him what had happened, in case something went wrong?

He went to the telephone, and paused, with his hand on the receiver. No, not Henry. Henry was a dear friend, but he was also someone who didn't appreciate finding out that his advice had been ignored. Perhaps he'd tell Henry afterwards, but calling him up and saying that he was doing the exact opposite of what he had been counseled to do was too much like thumbing his nose in Henry's direction.

Who else could he call? Purely as a precaution, of course. And then a thought occurred to him.

Louise. She knew about the situation, and her shop was close to Quincy Falls. If anything did go wrong, he knew he could count on Louise to get hold of the police quickly.

Reverend Bradley picked up the phone book and looked up the number for Robin's Nest Florist. He dialed the number.

It rang four times, and a recorded voice said, "Hi. This is Louise from Robin's Nest. I'm off on a delivery, but will be reopening at four o'clock this afternoon. Please leave a short message, and a phone number where you can be reached, and I'll get back to you as soon as possible. Have a lovely day." The machine beeped.

Reverend Bradley began, "Hello, Miss Middlebury...?" but then paused. He had the dislike, common in people of his generation, of talking to machines. "This is Morris Bradley. I'm not sure if you're the right person to tell this to, but as I'd already spoken to you about it, I thought of you. I've received another call from the man I saw in the church, the man who calls himself Stephen Calhoun. He wants to meet with me in the parking lot near the trailhead for Quincy Falls. I have agreed to meet him, but I thought it was too risky to go there without anyone knowing. I don't know what this is all about, but I have a feeling I'm about to find out. If there's a… um, a problem, if something should happen to me, then you'll know to contact the police. I'll call you later if everything is all right." He cleared his throat, a little embarrassed at how theatrical it all sounded. "I'm sure I'll be fine, but anyway. Thanks. I'll speak with you soon."

He hung up the phone.

———

THE DRIVE to Quincy Falls was uneventful. The swirling flurries of the past few days had slackened to a flake or two, and the roads were clear. A mile before the southern outskirts of Colville, there was a sign with the words "Quincy Falls/ Old Mill Trail/ Dalton Pond" and an arrow pointing to the right. He turned that way, onto a narrow road that had been plowed only half-heartedly. The road wound up a small hill, turned back south around a dense stand of bare sugar maple trees, and vanished from sight.

The parking area for the Old Mill hiking trail was about five miles into the hills, along Quincy Creek. It had been a favorite picnic spot for Reverend Bradley and his family when his children were young, and he knew it well, although he'd never driven on the road in winter. The further along he went, the worse the drifts became, but he saw that at least one car had been there before him. There was a fresh pair of tire tracks through the snow, recently enough to still be clean and sharp despite the wind's continual resculpturing. His heart pounding slightly, he continued up the road, underneath the eaves of the trees, all the while praying that he had made the right decision. "God, let me have done Your will," he said fervently. "I'm not asking to be safe. I'm only asking, as Your Son did, for Thy will to be done."

There was a battered brown Toyota in the snow-covered parking area, its engine still running. Reverend Bradley pulled his own car up next to it and looked over. Stephen Calhoun was sitting in the driver's seat, and looked over at him, and then gestured with one hand for the Reverend to join him.

Swallowing hard, Reverend Bradley adjusted his scarf around his neck, and shut off his motor. He exited his own car, and opened the passenger door of Stephen's, climbed in, and sat down, pulling the door shut behind him.

"Why..." began Reverend Bradley, and suddenly found his mind whirling with a hundred questions. Choosing one was like trying to catch one particular snowflake in a blizzard.

"I'll explain," said Stephen, and looked over at him, his eyes wide and dark. "But you must understand. You can't let them know I've told you. I'll be killed if you do. And probably you will be as well. But I had to warn you, so at least you have a chance against them."

"But who are they?"

"A group of... very bad people. They've got me snared. They're trying to catch another person, an innocent person, and use her too. You've got to try to stop them."

"How can I stop them? I don't even know who they are or what they're trying to do."

"There are four of them here in Colville, and probably two dozen more in other places. The two leaders are Professor May and his wife. He used to teach math at Colville College."

Reverend Bradley shook his head. "I've never heard of them."

"What they're trying to do is simple enough," said Stephen. "They found out about a mechanism, a thing that was used in ancient times to channel power, and to alter time. They want to rebuild it. Charge it. Use it."

"What does that mean?"

"Just what it sounds like," said Stephen, an edge of exasperation in his voice. "The Mays have traveled all over the place. They know more about this kind of thing than anyone. This machine… it's called the Antikythera Mechanism. I guess it was something that the ancient Greeks knew about. The first one was destroyed, sent to the bottom of the Mediterranean, something like two thousand years ago, most likely because it was so dangerous. It was a sort of hybrid thing, half machine, half organic. It used power that it channeled from a human source. Pulled psychic energy from whoever was hooked up to it, like a flashlight uses a battery. Given the proper charge, it was one of the most powerful devices humanity has ever created. Anyone who could tap into it, they'd be able to accomplish pretty much anything they wanted."

"How do you know about this?"

"They told me some. I got into this more or less by accident, because I knew Professor May from when I was a college student. I ran into him when I was out of work and about to get thrown out of my apartment, and was in some other legal trouble. I was in a tailspin. And he asked me if I wanted a job, a lucrative job. If I accepted, he'd get me out of my troubles. All of them. So I accepted." His expression was bleak, hopeless. He looked out of the window, and added, "My only excuse is that I was desperate."

"What was the job?"

"Hit man."

Reverend Bradley goggled at him and did not respond.

He laughed, but there was no mirth in it. "I don't look the part, do I? You're looking at a double murderer. I took care of people that the Mays thought was getting too close to finding out what they were doing. If the police found out about me, I could be extradited to two different countries, and would probably spend the rest of my life in jail. The Mays have me over a barrel."

"Why did you come to me?"

"Because someone has to stop them. I can't be part of doing what they're trying to do any longer. I'll probably be dead soon, but it doesn't matter. My days were numbered from the moment I killed a guy named Armand Soileau in London this summer. I only wish I'd realized sooner."

Reverend Bradley looked at him in sudden comprehension. "You tried to get out in October. If I'd helped you then…"

Again, there was a dry, humorless laugh. "Don't beat yourself up for that, Reverend. Honestly, there was nothing you could have done at that point. It was already too late. All I did was to rope you into this mess, and put your life at risk as well as mine."

"What can I do now? I don't see how I could possibly be a threat to them."

"I don't know the details. They don't trust me enough to tell me much. But you're a danger to them, for some reason. They were clear about that. They consider you to be the biggest threat to their plans. But it has to be soon. They've almost completed reassembling the Mechanism, using plans I stole from Soileau. Professor May wants to activate the device on the winter solstice. That's important for some reason. Don't ask me why."

"What do they think that this device can do for them?"

"I think Professor May sees himself becoming some kind of high priest or something. I don't know. He's an odd one, and has big plans, plans he doesn't talk about much. Mrs. May, well, she's a lot more straightforward. Practical. None of this supernatural hocus-pocus for her. I know what she wants."

"Which is...?"

"Immortality."

"She can't really believe..." began Reverend Bradley, shocked.

"Oh, she does. It's in all the old legends. All of the immortal figures, they're all connected with psychic amplifiers, and messing around with the idea of time. Merlin, Nuada Silver-Arm, Taliesin the Bard, Aesculapias, Iktomi of the Lakota."

Reverend Bradley frowned and shook his head. "But none of those… personages… none of them were real."

"So you say."

"You can't mean to tell me that we are to take mythological figures as reality."

"Says the man who believes that the Bible is literally the Word of God."

Reverend Bradley didn't answer for a moment. "I… I hardly see how that's that same thing."

"You wouldn't, of course. It's only mythology if you're talking about other people's beliefs. But all of this is beside the point. Whatever you think about the old legends, the Mays, and what they're trying to do, are very real. As is the device they're constructing."

"I… I need some time to think about what you've said," Bradley said in a weak voice.

Stephen gave an annoyed snort. "You're wasting time. You know I'm telling you the truth."

"Yes," the Reverend said, his voice dropping to a low monotone. "Yes, I believe that you are."

"Then it's up to you to do something about it. Stop them."

"There's one thing I don't understand, though. Why are you suddenly switching sides? Wouldn't you be safer trying to lie low, not make waves, hope for the best?"

"I'm surprised that a religious man asks that question. I finally show traces of a conscience, and you ask why?"

The comment hit home. Reverend Bradley didn't answer for a moment. "I suppose," he finally said, "that I've always considered matters of conscience in a purely theoretical way. When it comes down to telling a man who is sitting in front of you to do something that will be likely to get him killed by evil men and women, it's not as easy to be certain of oneself."

"Compassion versus righteousness, eh, Reverend?"

"Yes. That's it exactly."

Stephen patted Bradley on the shoulder. "Well, don't get too worked up on my behalf. I'm not a good enough man that you should waste your sympathy on me. I killed two people, remember?"

"I remember. Our Lord forgave a thief while He Himself was hanging from a cross."

"I'd like to have your convictions. It must be comforting." He shook his head. "But it's too late in any case. I'm on a short tether. I've been downgraded from hit man to flunky, and none of them trust me. Especially one of them, who'd like nothing better than to see me dead. They keep tabs on me using a psychic woman. Fortunately, she's not very good. If she was better I wouldn't have even dared to call you today. That's another thing they're hoping to accomplish, to increase her psychic power using this energy. Think of what you could do, if you had a real psychic on your side. Not one of these card-reading charlatans who puts out a placard on the street."

Reverend Bradley nodded, stunned into silence.

"The whole thing scared the hell out of me. So two months ago, I ran. I tried to get away from them. That's when I met you in the church. I should have given you more of a chance, but I was terrified. The psychic figured out where I was, and they caught me the same day I talked to you and made me come back. They said if I ran again, they'd hunt me down and kill me." He swallowed. "They'd do it, too. The Mays and this woman friend of theirs they've let in on the secret. She's their strong arm. If anyone will be the one to kill me, it'll be her. As for the psychic, I think she's scared too, but she's a weakling." He paused. "Anyhow, I was completely freaked out when I ran into you at the hardware store, so I made up the story about a twin brother. I expect you knew I was lying."

"I did have my suspicions."

"And now, apparently they've found someone who they say can make the power source amplify, far beyond anything I could have done. So if I stay with them, I'm done for." Stephen looked up at him imploringly. "At least now that I've told you, there's a chance."

"But what on earth can I do?"

"The psychic. She saw that you were going to meet this woman, the one who can act as the energy source. And she said that if you met her twice, somehow that would lead to them failing in what they were trying to do." He paused. "Her name is Marcia."

Reverend Bradley shook his head, and turned his hands palm upward. "I don't know anyone named Marcia."

"You haven't met anyone recently with that name...?"

"Not that I know of."

"It's got to happen soon," he said. "The Mays want to have everything set up for the winter solstice. There's some kind of magical significance of that, I don't know what. That's what, like three days away?"

Reverend Bradley nodded.

"So it's going to happen soon." Stephen reached out and touched Reverend Bradley's arm. "I have to go now. They may already know what I've done, but the longer we stay here, the more likely it is that they'll find out. Look out for a woman named Marcia. If you meet her, you've got to connect with her, and let her know the danger she's in."

His gaze dropped to his hands, which were resting in his lap. "Look, at this point, I don't care much what happens to me. I'm kind of screwed no matter which way this goes. But I'm scared to think of what these people will do with their power if they can access it. You religious always talk about evil. I wonder if you've ever really met it."

"I don't..." said Reverend Bradley quietly, and paused. He swallowed. "I don't really think I have."

"Well, when you meet the Mays, that's it. That's the real thing."

15

F IXED INPUT CROWN GEAR: CALIBRATED AND LOCKED WITH LUNAR ANOMALY MECHANISM

"Do you really think it's necessary to wait for the solstice, dear?" Mrs. May said to her husband. He was seated in a rocking chair in their living room, following his wife with his gaze as she puttered about, dusting tables and straightening knick-knacks.

"It is the best way. The proper rituals must be observed."

"Well, I know, dear. You hardly need to tell me that. But with Sparlin snooping about, and Reverend Bradley still in a position to cause problems, we might be well advised to proceed. I am speaking purely from a practical standpoint, you understand."

"If we begin making excuses and cutting corners regarding protocol, we risk causing our own enterprise to fail," Mr. May said, his watery blue eyes expressionless.

"Now, that's not what I meant, and I believe you know that. But consider, dear, that we may only have two options. Should we move forward now, we risk the Mechanism not being at its full capacity, an eventuality we are not even certain would cause problems. If we wait, we take the far greater risk of mischief by Bradley or Sparlin or both. It is the lesser of two evils, doesn't it?"

Stanford May laughed, but his slack face still showed little expression. "Perhaps you are right."

"Let us ask our colleague this evening. Our dinner plans are still on, are they not?"

"As far as I know. He said that he was working on several refinements to the Mechanism that he could not interrupt, but would be done by five. He said that he would meet us at six at Arcangeli's, or call if he was delayed. We can speak with him about our options."

Mrs. May set down her dusting cloth and sat in an antique wooden chair across from her husband. "I wonder," she said, "if we are perhaps putting too much faith in his understanding of the Mechanism."

"He knows more about it than anyone else in the world, or at least anyone who is likely to be willing to cooperate."

"I don't mean the technical details. I mean what is going on beneath the surface, behind all of the gears and wheels and pins." Her eyes glittered. "I'm speaking of what is really driving the Mechanism."

"I know. And you may be right." He considered for a moment. "It's a pity about Soileau. He would have been ideal."

"I don't think that would have proven true." Mrs. May pursed her lips. "He was an arrogant man. I don't think he would have taken orders well. And we would have been unwise to trust someone who was as fond of alcohol as the late Dr. Soileau. Had he been more moderate with his imbibing, and his tendency to speak at inopportune times, we might not have been forced into putting him out of the way, not to mention other inconveniences."

"Do you regret Verhoeven?" Mr. May said.

"I?" Mrs. May put one hand to her chest. "It was not solely my decision, you might recall."

"She could have been useful as well."

"Entirely the wrong personality type, I think. From what we knew of her, at least. Brilliant mind, quick to piece together what she sees and hears. Not the type to be tempted by money or power, and hardly… hardly the sort who would have been easily cowed. She showed great defiance, there at the end. She almost escaped."

"She did. But only almost. For that, at least, we have Stephen to thank." Mr. May looked at his wife, one eyebrow raised. "Dr. Verhoeven was on the verge of uncovering what we were doing. Do you think it possible that she may have alerted others?"

"Who, dear? We know she tried to contact Metaxas, but who else do you think she would have spoken to? It's been four months since Stephen killed her. We would have heard by now, had information gotten out. We are quite safe, I assure you. You're not losing your own nerve, are you?"

"Not at all."

"Good. Because soon it will come down to the point. We mustn't have our own equanimity upset by either fear or over-eagerness."

Stanford May smiled. "No. And perhaps you are right. We will discuss this evening what our best course of action is. If the decision is to go forward, I will acquiesce." His smile widened, his mouth stretching into what could have been mistaken for a rictus of pain. "I am as delighted as you are the fruition of all of our hard work." He stood, and still grinning, motioned toward the stairs. "Shall we dress for dinner?"

THEY BOTH CHANGED into nicer clothes, Mr. May in a navy suit with a pale blue silk tie, and Mrs. May in a rose-colored dress, with a cream-colored ruffle-fronted blouse that could have come straight from a vintage clothing store. She put a shell-pink hat on top of her head, and looked in the mirror this way and that, tucking an errant strand of her white hair underneath the edge before straightening her sleeves and heading toward the bedroom door.

"I'll feed our guest," Mr. May said. "But we shouldn't dawdle if we want to be there by six."

"Very well, dear."

They were headed toward the front door fifteen minutes later, Mrs. May with her handbag looped around the crook of her right arm when the telephone rang.

"Oh, my," Mrs. May said, her brow wrinkling.

"I'll get it," Mr. May said. He went up to the telephone and looked at the caller ID display. "It's Louise Middlebury."

"Whatever can she want?"

"Shall I answer it?"

Mrs. May thought for a moment and shook her head. "Whatever Louise wants can wait," she said. "Our dinner engagement is the most pressing concern. If it's important, she'll call back."

"Very well." Mr. May walked away from the telephone as it rang for the fifth time, and then stopped. He paused for a moment and watched the display until it turned dark. "She didn't leave a message."

"It must not have been critical, then," Mrs. May said, her voice cheerful. "Shall we?"

THEY ARRIVED at Arcangeli's Italian Restaurant as six sharp. The hostess smiled in recognition at the two of them, and said, "The other member of your party has just arrived, Professor May. Please come with me."

They followed her toward the back of the restaurant, past framed oil paintings of Italian pastoral scenes, faux-marble Roman statuary, and a wide mural depicting naked people picking grapes. Mrs. May had always disapproved of the naked grape-pickers and wondered why you wouldn't put some clothes on if you were working in a vineyard. It wasn't proper. But her disapproval did not stop her from enjoying Arcangeli's fine cuisine and excellent wine list, and it certainly was the only appropriate place to take their colleague.

They arrived at the table, where a tall, slender man with curly black hair and small rectangular steel-framed glasses sat, an open bottle and three glasses of rich red wine in front of him. He stood when he saw them approach, and reached out a slender, manicured hand to shake Mr. May's large, coarse ones, and gave Mrs. May a neat little bow.

"My dear Metaxas," Mr. May said. "A pleasure to see you again."

"The pleasure is mine, Professor May," he said. "I took the liberty of ordering a bottle of wine for us to share. It is a 2011 Aglianico from Molettieri. One of my personal favorites. I think you will find it an interesting vintage."

They sat. Dinner was ordered. Gnocchi with pesto for Mr. May, seared scallops with linguine and Romano cheese for Mrs. May, wild mushroom risotto for Dr. Metaxas. Mrs. May kept up a stream of small talk while dinner was being eaten. Her husband, used to her ability to function on many levels at once, let it pass, only occasionally responding to a comment about the weather or politics or what book she was currently reading with a noncommittal "Huh" or "Really?" or "That's interesting." Dr. Metaxas, on the other hand, appeared to become more impatient as the evening progressed, and the food and bottle of wine disappeared.

Finally, he said, "Mrs. May, I apologize for my impoliteness, but all of this talk is hardly to the point."

"Oh, no, you're quite right, Dr. Metaxas. I apologize. I can be a silly, garrulous old woman at times, and you must forgive me my foible of chattering on so."

Mr. May looked down into his empty dinner plate and smiled.

Dr. Metaxas inclined his head slightly. "I was discourteous to say so. But the evening wears on, and we have not discussed the issues we must address. You wish to essay a, what is the word? A trial run, prior to the solstice? I was given to understand that to activate the Mechanism prior to that was inadvisable."

"Your research has been more in depth than mine, Metaxas," Mr. May said. "I cannot say that I know with any certainty what would happen should we try connecting the power source earlier than planned."

Mrs. May took a sip of her wine. "This evening I was discussing with Stanford the dual risks of activating the Mechanism early, and the potential for interference by two troublemakers who have become involved."

"There is no possibility of simply taking care of the troublemakers?" Metaxas said.

"It has gone beyond that," Mrs. May said. "The two prime movers have connected with others. Should one of them meet with an unfortunate accident, it would be immediately suspicious."

"You took no such precautions with Soileau, I note," Metaxas said.

"With Soileau, it was easy enough to eliminate him and cast suspicion about. He was a man who made enemies easily, both in the academic world and in his personal life. Did you know that at the time of his death, he had a wife, not to mention three mistresses, all of whom were mutually unaware of the others' existence, and two of whom were themselves married?"

"I was aware of his improprieties, yes," Metaxas said, an expression of distaste on his refined face.

"It was more difficult with Dr. Verhoeven, I believe," Mrs. May said. "We would have let her be if she hadn't begun to make rather unfortunate inquiries into our business. But our colleague who was in charge of eliminating her made it look like an accident—an unlucky pedestrian struck by a falling piece of masonry dislodged from the top of an old building. There were no questions asked, especially when it was seen that the entire façade of the building was in a highly unstable and unsafe condition."

"But again, this gets us no closer to deciding how to proceed," Metaxas said. "I still have work to do, which means a half-hour's drive back, and at least three hours of labor before I can rest. Especially if you intend to move forward earlier than planned."

"I know Stanford disagrees with me," Mrs. May said, "but I think we must do so. One of our enemies, in particular, is a real threat. I have hope, however, that if we can achieve full activation of the Mechanism, soon, he will not be able to stand in our way."

"You have procured the power source, then?"

"With luck, tomorrow."

"Then I must be ready by tomorrow afternoon at the latest."

"Yes," Mrs. May said, her plump face creasing in concern. "My apologies to you once again, my dear Dr. Metaxas. If we have exceeded your capacity for work, please do say so.

It would be unfortunate to have to delay on that account, but if you must…" She stopped, her eyebrows drawing together in an expression of concern.

"No, Mrs. May, there is no need for worry. All will be in order. Simply procure the woman, and let me know when you plan to arrive." He gave her an icy smile. "The Mechanism will be ready for you."

16

Z*ODIAC WHEEL: SECOND TURN*
MAIN DRIVE WHEEL: FIFTH TURN

S*ATURDAY*, December 19, 2015

S*TACY* W*EINSTEIN* *WOKE* up on Saturday morning at six-thirty, and couldn't get back to sleep. Her mother used to say that as a teenager she got up at the crack of noon, and her sleeping habits had changed little since her teen years. Weekends were a time to wake up slowly, maybe have a cup of coffee, and probably return to bed for a dozy hour or two, before getting up for good.

This morning, however, she was restless and uncomfortable. She'd had uneasy dreams, and had gradually risen to a waking state that was no less disturbed. She'd tried sitting in bed and watching some television, but all that was on were Looney Tunes and some televangelist with a loud suit and big hair demanding that she accept Jay-sus as her personal Say-viah.

She clicked off the television, lay back, and closed her eyes.

Twenty minutes later, she was still awake. Why couldn't she sleep? She always could sleep.

Stacy sighed heavily and sat up. It was Marcia, of course. She was brooding over Marcia. Andrea's dire warnings had scared them both. Strangely, even though it was Marcia who had initially freaked out more about their last visit to the psychic, Stacy was the one who was shaken on some deeper level.

Marcia called faithfully to give her daily status reports. No, she hadn't run into any priests or monks or whatever that day. Yes, she was sure. Yes, of course, she'd tell her if she saw one. No, she wasn't planning on having a sudden desire to take in a mass or to go to a revival. Yes, she was taking this seriously, of course, she was taking this seriously.

But it still bothered Stacy. She wasn't simply worried by the predictions of danger—Stacy found herself questioning the psychic herself. Andrea hadn't told them all she knew, Stacy was sure of it. But why? If Andrea was concerned for Marcia's security, why wouldn't she give them all the information she had?

But there was something else, something besides Stacy's vague misgivings about Andrea. There was something else more concrete that was bothering her, and she couldn't identify it. There was some practical aspect of this, something simple but elusive, that they were both missing.

She swung her legs out of bed. The faux-wood flooring was cold under her bare feet. She found her slippers— thick fuzzy black ones, with wicked-looking suede bear claws protruding from the front— pulled them on, and padded into the kitchen to put on the coffee.

A priest. A priest or a monk or something. Should be obvious. No missing that, with their typical attire, the black clothing, collar, or robes or whatever...

That was when it struck her, with a suddenness that made her spill a scoop full of coffee grounds all over the counter and floor.

"Stupid!" Stacy said out loud. "God, how stupid!"

Why would he necessarily be wearing religious attire? Ministers did other things. They worked in the garden, they went to the grocery store, they walked the dog, they mowed the lawn. It wasn't like priests cleaned their gutters while wearing their church robes, for heaven's sake. Why had they both assumed that they'd be able to tell who he was by what he was wearing?

She crossed the kitchen and reached for the phone, her hand shaking. She punched in a few numbers, hissed "Dammit," hung up, and redialed.

The phone rang only twice before a sleepy but irritated voice, said, "Hello?"

"Marsh? It's Stacy. Sorry if I woke you up."

"You didn't. What's wrong?"

"Marsh, I just realized something. The priest guy. He wouldn't necessarily be wearing clothes that identified who he was. You could have met him and not known it."

There was a long pause. "Stacy, what the hell is going on here?"

"What do you mean?"

"I just got a call from Andrea Yarbrough, who did wake me up. She said the exact same thing and told me that somehow, I'd already met the guy once. She said she wants me to come over to her house immediately."

Stacy's jaw dropped. "Get out of here!"

"No, really. I swear. I only now got off the phone with her."

"When?"

"Five minutes ago."

"What are you gonna do?"

"Beats the hell out of me." There was a pause, and Marcia added, a little reluctantly, "Stace, I'm not sure about her."

"Yeah," said Stacy. "Me neither."

"Really?" Marcia's voice sounded surprised. "I thought you thought she was the bomb."

"Well, I did. I mean, she's good at what she does. But there's something... I'm not sure about her motives. I suddenly realized that I was scared, scared for you, but kind of scared *of* Andrea."

"I'm not scared of her, not really," said Marcia. "She doesn't appear dangerous. But I don't trust her. I'm not entirely sure why, but there's something else going on here."

"Agreed. But this reverend guy. Do you really think you've met him already?"

"Andrea asked me that too," said Marcia.

The anxiety came surging back in waves. "What did you tell her?"

"Well, there's only one person I can think of who it might be. A few days ago some old friend of Professor Larkin's came to meet him for lunch. He was probably seventy or so, seemed like a nice enough guy. Didn't say he was a minister, but he could have been."

"What did Andrea say when you told her that?"

"She said that was him," said Marcia.

"God," said Stacy. "I wonder if she's sure?"

"She's a psychic, Stace."

"Yeah, but still. Could you ask your boss if his friend is a priest?"

"I suppose. But it'd have to wait till Monday. No way am I calling Professor Larkin at home."

"Wait," said Stacy, a little breathlessly. "Do you remember his name?"

There was a pause. "Yes, I think so. His first name was Morris. I remember thinking about Morris the Cat. His last name was, like, Bradford or something. Morris Bradford. I think that's right."

Stacy picked up her telephone book and began to flip through the pages. "I'm looking it up. Let's see... Bradford. A. J. Bradford. Theo Bradford. That's all." She continued to run her finger down the page. "Wait! Marsh! I found it. Right here. Bradley, Morris, Rev. He lives in Skipton."

"That's it. Morris Bradley."

Stacy shivered a little. "So Andrea was right. You did already meet him."

"I guess so."

"Look, Marsh. This is all giving me a hell of a case of the willies. You wanna meet at the Colville Bakery for breakfast and talk?"

"I don't know. I told Andrea I'd come right down."

"The hell with Andrea. Don't call her back, or at least not yet. Look, girl, I'm creeped out, but I think Andrea was right on one account—you're in danger. I just don't know if it's from this reverend guy or from Andrea herself."

FORTY-FIVE MINUTES LATER, Stacy and Marcia were sitting at a small table in the corner of Colville Bakery, eating black currant scones and sipping coffee.

"Andrea's gonna wonder what happened to me," said Marcia.

"Let her wonder."

"I can't not call her back."

"That's true," said Stacy, leaning back in her chair. "At some point, you've got to talk to her. But you can't go down to her house. Especially not alone."

"What do you think she's going to do?"

"I don't know. But whatever it is, she can cool her heels for a while. If she really is on the up-and-up, it won't hurt her to wait. I can protect you as well as she can."

"Protect me from what? We still don't know what the danger is, except that it's somehow linked with this Reverend Bradford guy."

"Bradley," said Stacy.

"Bradley. Whatever."

Stacy took a sip of her coffee. "Say, Marsh, I have a good idea."

"Uh-oh. Coming from you, that phrase always makes me cringe a little."

"Nah, nothing to worry about. What if I drive up to Skipton and check out the Reverend? You could stay at my place. Call Andrea if you feel like you have to. Tell her you came down with the stomach flu or the creeping crud or whatever, and you can't make it. Tell her you'll bolt your doors, won't answer the phone, and will come down as soon as you feel better. I'll go check out our Reverend, see if his story checks out, and report back what I find out."

"Andrea said he'd look harmless, but that he wasn't."

"Yeah, well, I think I'll be able to tell if the guy's some kind of psycho," Stacy said. "Give me some credit, here. And in any case, Andrea said that the danger was to you, not to me. I'll simply be collecting information."

"What are you going to ask him?"

"I'll figure that out on the way."

"You better be careful."

"Well, I can defend myself against some old minister guy." She set down her cup. "And in any case, it's better than you walking into Andrea's house by yourself, saying, okay, here I am."

"You're probably right."

"Damn skippy I'm right."

"So I'll call her and tell her I'm sick, and you go down and see if you can figure out about Reverend Bradford."

"Bradley."

"Bradley. Whatever."

* * *

A HALF HOUR LATER, they were sitting at the kitchen table in Stacy's apartment. Marcia had wrapped herself in Stacy's bathrobe and put on her slippers. "Look," she said, "if I'm gonna call in sick, I gotta look the part. An actor I'm not."

She dialed the number for Andrea Yarbrough, then looked up at Stacy, and screwed her face up into a passable imitation of nausea. Stacy put her hand over her mouth to stifle a laugh.

"Hi, Andrea, it's Marcia." Marcia's voice was low and hoarse.

"Marcia," said Andrea, "I thought you'd be here by now."

"I know," said Marcia. "I'm sorry. I'm sick. I got up after we talked, and had a light breakfast, and then I started throwing up."

"Oh, dear," said Andrea. "I'm so sorry. Would you like me to come pick you up?"

Marcia's eyebrows shot up. She hadn't anticipated that one. "Oh, no, no," she said hurriedly. "I'd puke all over your car. I'm sure it's a twenty-four-hour bug. I'll be better tomorrow. I'll be okay. I'll come down to your place tomorrow if I'm feeling up to it."

"I'm concerned about your safety, Marcia," said Andrea. "You'd be safer with me."

"I feel too sick to move," said Marcia, her voice dropping even lower. "It was a major effort just to call you. Look, I'll lock the door. I won't even answer the phone. How much danger can I be in?"

"Well, I don't know," said Andrea. "I still think you'd be better off here. But if you're really that sick..."

"I've got to go!" said Marcia, in a panicked voice. "Oh, god, I'm gonna throw up..." She made several very convincing retching noises, slammed down the receiver, and looked up at Stacy, smiling a little sheepishly.

Stacy grinned at her. "Nicely done, Marsh. Girl, you da man. Now let's see if I can be as convincing an actress as you are." She held out her hand for the phone and punched in a number.

"Hello?" came a voice. A mild, gentle voice, she thought, hardly someone who sounded dangerous. But voices, like appearances, could deceive.

"Hello, Reverend Bradley?" said Stacy.

"Speaking."

"Hi, my name is Stacy... um, Johnson. I'm going to be moving to Skipton in a few weeks, and I'd like to talk to you about joining your church." It was Marcia's turn to snicker softly. Stacy deliberately avoided making eye contact with her.

"Well, that'd be lovely," said Reverend Bradley. "I'd be delighted to meet you. Where are you moving from?"

"California," Stacy replied.

"So far away," said Reverend Bradley. "You're finding the winter here a bit trying, I'd expect."

"It's not so bad," she said breezily.

"Where in Skipton will you be living? I don't think I know of anyone who's selling a house."

Stacy's eyes widened a bit, but she answered smoothly. "We're staying with some friends in Colville for now. We're hoping to buy in Skipton within a few months. We are so taken with it, it's a sweet little town, and we'd like to get acquainted with the church right away."

"I understand. When would you like to come up to visit?"

"I was hoping that perhaps today sometime... I know it's short notice."

"It's not a problem. Would eleven o'clock work?"

"That's ideal," said Stacy.

"I expect you know where the church is?"

"Well," Stacy hedged. "We drove past it once."

"It's right on the main highway. About a hundred yards past the village signpost. My house is right before it, set back from the road a bit. You'll see the church before you see the house. Just knock on the door and I'll take you in to see the church, and we can chat a bit."

"Sounds good. I'll see you in an hour or so."

After saying goodbye to Reverend Bradley, Stacy looked over at Marcia and took a deep breath. "Well, it's done. I'm going up at eleven."

"Stacy *Johnson?*" Marcia asked, smirking.

"It was the best I could do at the moment. Stacy Weinstein sounded too Long-Island-Jew."

"You are a Long Island Jew."

"Yes, well, I couldn't let him know that, now could I? Not too many Long Island Jews join evangelical Christian churches in small towns in upstate New York. And man, that is a small town. He wanted to know whose house I was buying."

At five till eleven, Stacy pulled her little blue Geo Prizm into Reverend Bradley's long gravel driveway and pulled to a stop by the garage. She looked over, and the front door opened a bit, and a smiling man with silver hair leaned out and waved. She wiggled her fingers in return, got out of her car, pulled her coat tighter around her, and walked carefully down the snowy sidewalk to the front step.

"Ms. Johnson? Do come in. I'm Morris Bradley."

She shook his outstretched hand. "Please. Stacy," she said and stepped into the foyer of his house. It was orderly, spotlessly clean, and modestly furnished. She couldn't imagine a less alarming place.

"Stacy it is, then. Come in and sit down," said Reverend Bradley. "I have tea on. I expect you'd like to sit for a moment and warm up. We can chat for a bit before we head over to the church."

"That'd be great," said Stacy, taking off her coat and draping it over a chair back. Reverend Bradley retreated to his kitchen and returned with a teapot and two mugs, which he set on the coffee table.

"Do sit down," he said. She took a seat on the sofa. "What brings you and your family to a remote place like Skipton?"

She had spent the half-hour drive planning her answer to this question, and it flowed from her effortlessly. "My husband, Jim, he's a free-lance writer. We lived in California, but it was so expensive to live there, and ever since Jim turned free-lance, well, you know, we can more or less live anywhere, what with the internet and all. We came here last summer to visit, and fell in love with it."

"I expect it was a good bit more inviting in summer than it is now," said Reverend Bradley.

"Oh, the cold doesn't bother me that much. It's a beautiful place."

"It is that." He poured her a mug full of steaming tea, and one for himself. "Any children?"

"None yet."

He smiled and nodded. "Now, you had asked about joining our church. What church do you belong to currently?"

This was also one she'd rehearsed. "Well, Jim and I have both been away from the church for some time, and have been feeling like we'd like to get back to our relationship with God."

Reverend Bradley nodded again, evidently pleased. "That's wonderful. God always treasures his lost lambs returning to the fold. It's interesting that you chose our tiny church, though. I'm curious, I must say, as to how you found us, and why you'd want to join us rather than some larger congregation in Colville."

"Well, you come recommended," said Stacy.

"Indeed! By whom?"

"A mutual friend," said Stacy, watching his face closely. "Her name is Marcia."

The mug dropped from Reverend Bradley's hand and struck the corner of the coffee table, cracking a chunk out of the side. Hot tea splattered the floor.

"Dear me," said Reverend Bradley in a hoarse voice, staring at the broken pieces of ceramic and the dark stain on the floor. "How clumsy of me." He picked up a couple of the larger pieces and dabbed ineffectually at the carpet with a napkin.

"Here, let me help," said Stacy, and took several napkins and began to mop up the spilled tea.

Reverend Bradley watched her in silence for almost a minute. Finally, as if he had made a decision, he cleared his throat. "You're not really here to ask about church membership, are you?" he said.

Stacy looked up at him, her eyes narrowing. "No. But Reverend Bradley, how on earth would you know that?"

"Merciful heavens," he said, and he slumped back into his chair.

Stacy stood up. "What do you know about Marcia?" she demanded. "What is your connection to her?"

The reverend looked up at her helplessly. "None. None whatsoever. I don't know her at all. But somehow, I've gotten tangled up in some sort of... business with her."

"What sort of business?"

"I don't quite understand it," he said. "But I'll tell you what I know." He recounted his encounters with Stephen, culminating with the meeting in the car the previous day. His method of discourse was meandering, and Stacy waited politely and silently for him to finish, simultaneously giving thanks that she wasn't actually considering joining his church. His sermons, she thought, must be something to endure.

"The psychic," said Stacy thoughtfully. "Yes. It makes a little more sense now. She tried to get Marcia to go see her this morning."

"She mustn't do that!" said Reverend Bradley with some vehemence.

"You believe Stephen, then?"

"Well," he hesitated, "yes, I think I do. I mean, it's all quite fantastic. I can say that I believe that Stephen believes. And that means that somehow, these people do mean Marcia harm, whether it's by supernatural means or otherwise."

"Agreed."

Reverend Bradley considered. "You must understand, Ms. Johnson. I don't mean your friend any harm."

"I think I know that now," Stacy said. "And by the way. My name's Weinstein. And I won't be joining your church, sorry." She gave him a sheepish grin. "My rabbi would be pissed."

17

L*UNAR ANOMALY MECHANISM: THIRD TURN*

S*TACY* W*EINSTEIN* WASN'T the only one who was restless on that chilly gray morning. Keith Sparlin woke up early the same day. He came to consciousness slowly, pulling himself up out of fragments of a dream into fragments of waking, and finally rolled over and looked at his alarm clock. It said 6:23. A night owl by nature, it wasn't a time of day that Keith usually saw. This close to the solstice it looked like night anyway, barely the faintest light on the eastern horizon presaging a sunrise that was still a good hour away.

Keith sat up, the quilt slipping off his bare shoulders, and rubbed his eyes. He knew his own body well enough to be certain that further sleep wasn't likely, so he got up, stretched, yawned, picked up his robe from the foot of the bed and pulled it on, and went into the kitchen to start a pot of coffee.

An hour later, showered, shaved, dressed, and working on his second cup of coffee, he considered his misgivings about Kelly's sudden absence.

She's gone to visit family, he thought. *The Mays said so. It's the holidays. There's nothing unusual in that.*

What was unusual was that she hadn't mentioned it. Her telephone message had mentioned dinner with the Mays, and thanked him for his reassurance, but she hadn't said anything about going away the following day.

But honestly, why would she? She was a student, not his best friend. Why should she tell him what her holiday plans were?

But there was no way around it. It didn't seem right. There was nothing concrete, but the whole thing felt wrong. That characterization bothered Keith no end. He was a man who was innately distrustful of his own feelings. He always knew that they had a singular way of misleading. It was why he had been attracted to science very early on. In science, there was fact, certainty, measurability.

But something had drawn him into neuroscience, that most human and intangible of sciences. It was the search for meaning in the shifting sands of human consciousness. It was a need to make sense of the alignment between physical reality and perception, to find something concrete and measurable in a realm that otherwise contained nothing but chaos.

But he still didn't trust his own feelings. Rationally, there was no reason to be concerned for Kelly. So: feelings be damned. Kelly was away with family, celebrating the holiday, and more power to her. The Mays were a nice old couple with no reason to lie. He stood, picked up his coffee cup and cereal bowl, and went into the kitchen to wash up.

AND AT EIGHT O'CLOCK, he called Kelly's house again. The voicemail, with its cheerful message, picked up after four rings. He set down the receiver, picked up his keys, jacket, gloves, and a knit wool cap, and stalked out of his apartment, feeling vaguely foolish, but also knowing that he would not be able to sit still until he'd paid another visit to Kelly's house, and to the Mays.

THE NEIGHBORHOOD NORTH of the college where Kelly lived was still and quiet as Keith drove up to Kelly's house. The house itself was dark and showed no signs of habitation. He pulled up to the curb and got out, his booted feet leaving deep indentations in sidewalks which had not been shoveled for several days. The snow itself had stopped, and a weak and watery sun shone down from a pearly gray sky, but the temperature was probably hovering around zero. There were no footprints in the new snow on the front doorstep. No one had come there since his last visit day before yesterday.

He went up to the door and knocked, and as he expected, there was no answer. Going around to the side of the house, he passed the garage. He rubbed the frost from the front window and peered in. A red compact, of some make and model indistinguishable in the gloom, sat in one bay. The other was empty. He didn't know what kind of car Kelly drove in any case. He peered around, not even sure what he was looking for, and slowly walked around the back of the house.

A voice, muffled by Keith's stocking cap and the fresh snow, called out, "I don't think they're home."

Keith looked up, startled out of his reverie. Peering over a low point in the hedge between Kelly's yard and the Mays' was an old man, well-wrapped in a thick jacket and a fur cap, carrying a bag of birdseed.

"Do you know when Kelly might be home?" Keith said, walking over to the hedge.

"I believe she's away for the holidays," the old man said.

"I need to get in touch with her. Do you happen to know who she's visiting?"

"I'm sorry, I don't. Is it an emergency?"

"Not really. I just would like to get a hold of her. I thought you might know where she was."

The old man shook his head. "All I know is that she's away visiting family. Out of state, it sounded like, but I really don't know for sure. She asked my wife and me if we'd watch the house while she was gone."

Keith nodded. "I spoke to your wife day before yesterday. I was hoping Kelly might be back by now."

The old man gave a shake of his head. "I don't think she'll be back till after Christmas. That was the impression she gave, at least, but she didn't mention specific plans."

Keith thanked him and reached a gloved hand over the hedge to shake the man's hand. "I'm Keith Sparlin. I gave my name and number to your wife when we spoke. If you could let me know when she comes back, or tell her to call me if you see her, I'd really appreciate it."

The old man smiled. "Stanford May. I'd be glad to."

———

MR. MAY STOOD, his breath fogging in the icy air, scattering birdseed around his back yard until the sound of Keith's car receded into the gentle background noise of a Saturday morning in winter. Then he walked back to the house, carelessly dropping the bag of seed onto a snow-covered picnic table, and went inside.

"He's still snooping around," he said to his wife while pulling off his coat, hat, and scarf.

"He'll be trouble yet," said Mrs. May, her hands deep in a sink of warm sudsy water, washing up the breakfast dishes. "I knew Louise was wrong about him. I can tell by the look on his face. He's not just a boyfriend or a college friend. He suspects something."

"Andrea didn't see any harm in him either. She told you that you were overreacting."

"I'm aware of that," said Mrs. May. "And I was perfectly willing to consider that point of view when he had only visited here once. This is the second time he has come, which would point to his having less innocent motives."

"Should we have Louise keep an eye on him?"

Mrs. May considered. "Probably. But first, we should get more information on him. If he is a danger, we can act more quickly. If he is only a curious but casual friend, we can rest easier."

"Information from Andrea?"

Mrs. May shook her head. "No, I think it's time that we induce Kelly to tell us what she knows about her gallant friend." She dried her hands on a pastel-colored tea towel and lifted a brass key from a ring hanging on the side of the cupboard. She gave Mr. May a faint smile and walked toward the cellar door.

She unlocked the door and pulled it open. Its well-oiled hinges moved noiselessly. She descended the stairs, holding onto the wooden railing.

The cellar had been partially finished. It had cement walls, but a spotlessly clean linoleum floor. It was lit by a fixture with a single bulb and two small windows just above ground level which were partially obscured by bushes. A bathroom was half-visible through a partly closed door in the far wall. A brass bed sat in the middle of the main room. An unkempt pile of quilts on the mattress was the only untidy note in the cellar.

Kelly Delahanty sat in an overstuffed chair next to the bed. Her right wrist was handcuffed to the bed frame. Her face was pale and unsmiling as she watched the Mays approaching.

"When are you going to let me go?" she asked, her voice weak.

"Now, Kelly, dear," said Mrs. May, sitting primly on the edge of the bed, "you know we've been through this before."

"I don't understand what you want with me."

"We want information," Mr. May said. "Which we've also told you before."

"Stanford, darling," said Mrs. May. "Don't, or you'll upset the poor child again, and what use would that be? None whatsoever." She smiled at Kelly in a grandmotherly way. "Kelly, we need you. You could be our eyes and ears. Like... like an advance scout!" She brightened. "You remember Jill in *The Chronicles of Narnia*? You said you liked those books, didn't you, dear? Jill was such a help to them all, because she had such good eyesight and hearing, and she became their scout. Now you," and she reached out and touched Kelly's cuffed hand, "you have a different kind of sight. But it could be helpful all the same."

"I can't make the dreams come," she said wearily. "I told you that."

"Perhaps you're not trying hard enough."

Kelly's eyes registered a brief angry flash. "How can you try to dream something? That's just stupid."

Mrs. May's smile vanished. "Now, dear, don't become cross with me. I don't wish to become cross with you. We both shouldn't like that, now should we?" She patted Kelly's hand, but there was no affection in the caress, and Kelly jerked her hand away as far as she could. The chain rattled against the brass posts of the bed, and Kelly looked away.

"Perhaps we should start with something other than your dreams. What about your friend, Keith? Perhaps you could tell us about him?"

Kelly looked up at her warily. "What about him?"

"What... what kind of a friend is he, dear?"

"Why is that important?"

"Oh, now never you mind why. Tell me who he is, dear."

"Who my friends are is none of your goddamned business."

Mrs. May stared at her impassively for a moment, and then reached out and took Kelly's left hand in hers. Kelly flinched, but Mrs. May's grip was tighter than her age would have predicted. "Oh, my dear," Mrs. May said, in the same calm voice as before, "I do believe that whatever is my business is my business, and you don't know nearly enough to tell me what that is. And I'll ignore your use of highly unladylike language. For the moment. Now, dear, tell me who Keith is. As I said before, I have no wish to become cross."

"Go to hell."

Mrs. May's grip tightened, and her nails dug into the back of Kelly's hand. Kelly winced and struggled, but between the old woman's viselike clasp on her left hand, and the steel chain on her right, there was little room for Kelly to fight back.

"That's very unbecoming, Kelly," said Mrs. May. "Perhaps if you cooperate with us, you would find your stay here less unpleasant."

"The only thing I'll tell you is if I dream that you both are dead!" Kelly spat. The nails dug in deeper, and scarlet welled up around the crescents cut into Kelly's fair skin.

"Dear me," sighed Mrs. May, her voice dropping even lower. "Perhaps I should start you off. His name is Keith Sparlin. He lives at 356 Banks Road, Apartment 5." Kelly's eyes widened. "He is an employee of the college and works as a lecturer in the biology department. You see? We know who he is and where he lives, and it would be child's play to take care of him if you don't cooperate. So, my dear, why don't you tell us why he has such an interest in you. Perhaps what you tell us will convince us that he's harmless, and there will be no need to have any further unpleasantness on his account."

"Don't you hurt him," Kelly said, her voice thin. "Don't you dare."

"If you'll cooperate, perhaps there'll be no need to."

Kelly writhed, and a trickle of blood slithered down the back of her hand and splattered onto the immaculate linoleum. She bit her lip and looked away, and finally said in a trembling voice, "He's... a friend. Just a friend. We were introduced by a mutual acquaintance. I think he's got a crush on me. I told him I wasn't interested in him, but he keeps following me around."

The grip didn't loosen. "You haven't told him about your dreams?"

Kelly's lip pulled back in a snarl. "You think I'm crazy? Why would I tell him that? My best friends don't know about my dreams."

Mrs. May sat there, her gaze mild, still clutching Kelly's bleeding hand. "Oh, my dear," she said. "I do think you're lying, I honestly do." She looked up. "Don't you, Stanford?"

"I think it's likely," said Mr. May grimly.

Mrs. May released Kelly's hand suddenly. Kelly gave a small, quickly-stifled sob, and clenched her hand into a fist and then flexed the fingers painfully.

"But I suppose that we'll have to accept your veracity for the time being. I do hope you're telling the truth. It would

be so unfortunate for both yourself, and for your friend
Keith, if you weren't."

LATER THAT DAY, after being fed a light lunch, Kelly slipped
from the chair back into the bed and lay flat on the
mattress. The Mays had left the cellar soon after their visit
that morning, and she had for a while heard them
bumping about upstairs, but she hadn't heard any sounds
for almost an hour. They were either gone, or napping, or
had gone out of earshot into the upper floor of the house.

She cried a little, thinking back on the last three days. The
first day, after waking from her drugged sleep, she had tried
screaming for help, but all that had done was bring Mr.
May running down the stairs, and he had tied a gag across
her mouth. This was so uncomfortable that she had acquiesced when they said that they'd only leave her ungagged if
she promised not to raise a racket. For the next day, they
had treated her fairly kindly, feeding her regularly and
providing her with an assortment of comforters and
pillows, as well as offering her reading material.

The evening of the second day of her captivity, Mrs. May
had asked her about her dreams. Kelly met this request
with a stony silence, but it was clear that the Mays already
knew a good deal about them. How they knew about them
at all was beyond guessing, but after her refusal to tell them
more, their manner changed. They became threatening, at
first vaguely, and then more directly, culminating in the
painful encounter that morning.

What on earth could they want with Keith? What, in fact,
did they want with her? It was likely that it had something

to do with her gift of precognition, but the Mays were very careful about giving her any information. However much she tried, she always felt like, in every conversation with them, they got far more from her than she got from them.

Her left hand ached, and there were four semicircular patches of dried blood on the back of it. Her right wrist was chafed raw from the handcuff. Despite her discomfort, she slipped into an uneasy sleep.

She had only slept for a moment when there was a noise. Her eyes snapped open, and she jerked her arm, making the chain rattle against the brass bars. The dark cellar was brighter than before. Half sitting up, she looked toward the foot of her bed.

Standing there, bathed in a faint radiance, was Keith Sparlin. The first thing she noticed about him was that he was shirtless, but he seemed not to be self-conscious about his lack of clothing. He looked at her with a stern pity in his green eyes. As she stared at him, speechless with shock, a ripple passed through his body, and he raised his arms, palms upward toward her, and a pair of wings unfolded from his shoulders. Strong, brown-feathered eagle's wings. He crouched, and then gave a great leap over the bed, catching her around the waist. The warmth of his bare skin pressed against her face. The great wings gave a tremendous beat, and the overstuffed chair blew over with a crash. To Kelly's alarm, he flew straight at the wall. The chain around her wrist parted as if it were made of putty. The concrete wall burst asunder, and they were out of the Mays' house. Together they rose up into the frosty air.

A noise beneath them made Keith turn. He gave a quiver of his wings, just enough to stay aloft. They hung there, suspended, maybe two hundred feet off the ground. Both he and Kelly turned their heads toward the source of the sound. Far below them, looking small with the distance, was Mrs. May. In her hands was a heavy wooden bow. Her round, apple-dumpling face now looked old, impossibly old, carved of rough stone, as implacable and dangerous and inhuman as the craggy face of the Oracle of Delphi. Kelly tried to cry out a warning, but she was unable to make a sound.

With a barely audible twang, she shot an arrow into the air, and it struck Keith in the chest, below his left nipple. They were thrown backward, and tumbled from the air, the icy wind whistling in Kelly's ears as they fell, fell, fell, finally crashing in ruin into a snowy clearing in a forest.

Kelly gasped, the air knocked from her lungs. Fresh snow powdered her face. She saw Mrs. May walking toward them, her face grim, but she hardly spared her a glance. She rolled over, lifting Keith's body, feeling the blade of the arrow protruding from his back, watching his chest laboring to rise. She sobbed, unable to say a word, trying to will him to live, trying to help him breathe, but his eyes clouded, and his head fell back. His red curls lay against the snow, and a trickle of scarlet came from the corner of his mouth. The great eagle wings gave a shudder and were still.

And Kelly woke up alone, drenched with sweat, in the dim cellar of the Mays' house. She was still cuffed to the bed, and her hands still ached.

It was the most miserable moment of her entire life.

18

Z*ODIAC WHEEL: THIRD TURN*

LUNAR ANOMALY MECHANISM: FOURTH TURN

FIXED INPUT CROWN GEAR: PIVOT SET, LOCKED IN PLACE

STACY HAD BEEN INFATUATED with psychics and the supernatural since she was a teen. She read her horoscope faithfully and had participated in many a party featuring Tarot readings and Ouija board sessions. Still, it had all been play. Even Andrea's amazing hits regarding Stacy's mother had been filed under the heading "this is really cool." Cool, she thought grimly, but not serious.

This stuff, though, involving Marcia and Reverend Bradley —this was serious.

She left Reverend Bradley's house at about 11:30, and spent the half-hour's drive home pondering what he had told her. Stacy considered herself an excellent judge of character, and for the most part, she was right. She had an uncanny ability to spot little cues and gestures that meant "I'm lying." Scanning her memory of their conversation, her first conclusion was that Reverend Bradley was being honest. Every word out of his mouth had the clarity and sincerity that only comes from being absolutely truthful. The problem was, that led to one inescapable conclusion—Andrea was lying.

But about what? Surely she hadn't lied about everything. Her psychic read of Stacy had been eerily correct, so unless she was an outstanding guesser, she did have some psychic ability. Her advice had been good. She had found out about Marcia more or less by accident. Stacy had mentioned her "friend who is depressed" in one of their sessions, and Andrea had, completely offhand, suggested that perhaps Marcia might want to see her. Andrea's concern for "Stacy's friend" had at first all appeared to be completely aboveboard, completely sincere.

It wasn't until Marcia actually did see Andrea that the pressure started, along with the whole story about Marcia being in danger. So, Stacy reasoned, the first meeting was by accident, but during that meeting, Andrea had discovered something about Marcia that she realized was important to...

To what? What exactly were these people trying to do? Reverend Bradley had mentioned machines that could alter time, and people being channelers and amplifiers and sensitives, all of which—despite Stacy's toying with the supernatural—had been pretty farfetched.

Of course, it didn't really matter. If Marcia was some kind of critical person to them, they were not going to accomplish whatever it was. Marcia was out of their reach and would stay that way. She pulled into her parking space, set the parking brake, and turned the motor off, her face set in a defiant scowl.

They'd better stay away from her. They'd just better.

Stacy trotted up the stairs, eager to tell Marcia about her encounter with Reverend Bradley.

The first inkling she had that something was wrong was when she turned her key in the lock and didn't hear the usual click of the deadbolt sliding back. The door was already unlocked, despite her certainty that she'd locked it when she left. A little chill down her backbone.

"Marcia?"

No response. She called again, went into the kitchen, then out to her bedroom and bathroom.

The apartment was empty.

She went through the whole apartment again, despite there being nowhere she could be that Stacy hadn't already checked. No Marcia. There was no note, nothing. The counters were bare. There was nothing attached to the refrigerator by a magnet. There was nothing on the end table.

She sat down on her sofa, then immediately stood up again, went back into the kitchen, and rechecked the counter for notes again.

Nothing.

She picked up the telephone and punched in Marcia's number. No answer.

No way would Marcia have left without leaving a note. No way. There was something very wrong here.

She stood for a moment, staring at the bare counters as if she could will a note to appear, a hint, a clue as to where her friend was. And then she picked up the telephone again, tucked it between ear and shoulder, flipped through the phone book, and dialed a number.

"Hello, Reverend Bradley? It's Stacy, Stacy Weinstein. Marcia's gone."

"Gone?" Reverend Bradley said. "Gone home?" Something in his voice made it clear that he knew this wasn't true.

"No, she didn't go home. I called. They got her." Her voice caught. She cleared her throat and went on steadily. "I don't know how they found her, but they did."

"They found her through you, though, didn't they? Isn't that what you told me?"

"Of course, you're right," Stacy said. "Andrea knew my name. She'd know where to look."

"I think… I think it's essential that she be found, quickly."

"Yes. You're right about that, too. We've got to find her."

"Perhaps it might be best, Ms. Weinstein, if I made the trip into Colville. There is only so much I can do from here." He paused. "Not that I am entirely sure what I would do from there, either. But it might be time to marshal our forces, as it were."

"Yes, I think that's a good idea. I'll be here." She gave Reverend Bradley brief directions for how to find her apartment and hung up. And then she sat down on the kitchen floor and began to cry, but it was tears of anger.

"If they hurt her, I'll kill them," she said, through clenched teeth. "I'll kill every one of them."

———

Marcia Pacheco sat in the back of the Mays' car, wedged between Andrea Yarbrough and Stanford May. Mrs. May, wrapped in a fur-lined beige suede coat, with a pink felt cloche hat perched on her head, drove their 1992 blue Buick down the highway, heading south from Colville.

"Untie my hands," Marcia said.

"Now, dear," Mrs. May responded. "You realize that we wouldn't have had to tie you if you hadn't struggled so in the first place. I hate to put it this way, but we simply can't trust you not to do something foolish. And at this point, you are too important to risk injuring."

"Cutting off the circulation to both hands isn't injuring me?"

"Not enough to reduce your utility to us, no."

"What are you going to do with me?"

Mrs. May smiled. "Don't worry about that, my dear. All in due time."

"I'm not your dear," Marcia said.

But Mrs. May wouldn't rise to that bait.

Marcia looked over at Andrea Yarbrough. She looked petrified. It was hardly the triumphant expression she expected to see, given how easily Marcia had fallen for their ruse. Mrs. May had knocked on Stacy's apartment door that morning, shortly after Stacy left to meet with

Reverend Bradley. When Marcia said, "Yes?" and looked through the peephole, she saw a white-haired grandma type, wearing an absurd magenta hat, and looking fretful.

"Can someone help me?" Mrs. May said. "My husband has fallen in the parking lot and hit his head on the curb. He's unconscious!"

Without thinking, Marcia opened the door and found herself pinned by a completely conscious, and amazingly strong, Stanford May. She was hustled down the stairs by Mr. May and Andrea Yarbrough, with one of Mr. May's hands clamped over her mouth to keep her from calling for help.

It had all been absurdly easy.

Stacy's going to wring my neck, Marcia thought miserably. *All I had to do was to stay silent and keep the door locked. And I didn't do either one.*

The drive proceeded in silence for another twenty minutes, and then Mrs. May turned onto a side road toward the town of Lamont, a little village in the sparsely-populated hill country south of Colville.

Two more turns, and a drive of perhaps ten miles during which Marcia did not see a single house, took them onto a dirt road that wasn't so much a dead end as that it simply petered out, becoming a pair of ruts in the snow. Mrs. May drove her old car, bumping and creaking, alongside a rusted pole barn that was the only building in sight, and braked to a stop behind a sleek gray Mazda that was the only other sign of habitation.

"And here we are!" she said in a cheerful voice. "Allow me to point out, Ms. Pacheco, that you are currently in the middle of nowhere. You are several miles from the nearest house, even if you should be lucky enough to strike off in the right direction, which the odds are very much against. Not only that, but the temperature is at the moment about ten degrees Fahrenheit, and regrettably, we did not think to bring along a jacket for you. Running away would be inadvisable. I doubt very much whether you would survive such an attempt."

Marcia shuddered, not so much from the cold as from the saccharine voice Mrs. May had just used to describe her likelihood of freezing to death, alone in the woods.

Still, she was probably right. Marcia frantically considered whether she had other options, realized she didn't, and allowed herself to be conducted out of the car and toward the pole barn. With a metallic creak, the door slid open to admit them, and they passed inside into a dimly-lit, and marginally warmer, space with a dirt floor and cobwebby metal beams overhead.

Standing inside the door was a tall, slender man, with dark, curly hair and small, rectangular steel-rimmed glasses, wearing a black wool jacket cut in an elegant European style. He gave Mrs. May a little bow, acknowledged Mr. May with a nod of the head, and paid no attention whatsoever to the other two.

"Dr. Metaxas," Mrs. May said, her breath fogging in the cold air. "I trust that you have progressed far enough that we are ready to try our little experiment? Our hand was forced, and we had to take action, as you no doubt have figured out from the presence of Ms. Pacheco a little earlier than we had anticipated."

"It is of no consequence," Metaxas said. His voice was cool, courteous, and had an accent that was somewhere between that of the English intelligentsia and continental aristocracy. "The Mechanism is ready to test. I might have to make some fine adjustments, but I think we may risk a trial."

"But my dear Dr. Metaxas," Mrs. May said, "what if you're wrong? It would be so unfortunate to cause damage to the mechanism because we were overeager."

"Forgive me, Mrs. May, but you said that your acquisition of the woman was necessitated by circumstance and that therefore the test needed to be run as soon as possible. Perhaps I have misunderstood you."

"Not at all. It is more that I would not want to supersede your greater expertise in these matters."

Marcia looked at the man's face. A chilly smile crossed his lips. Two more opposite physical types would have been hard to find—Dr. Metaxas, thin and wiry and dark, and Mrs. May, plump and round and white-haired. But despite the differences, there was a common ground between them that was not shared by anyone else in the room, even by Mr. May. Georgios Metaxas and Helene May were cut from the same cloth, and even though they seemed to argue, they understood each other completely. They were part of an inner circle that excluded everyone else present, and perhaps excluded most of the rest of humanity.

Metaxas turned away toward a rectangular shape, covered with a piece of rough canvas, that stood in the center of the pole barn. "Come, then," he said, and pulled back the canvas.

"Oh, my," Mrs. May said reverently, looking up at what had been behind the cloth. "You have indeed made progress."

"It is a pity that Soileau is not here to appreciate what we have done. He, of all people, would have been thrilled."

"You know as well as I do that he was too much of a risk."

"I am aware of all that. We discussed it at length last night."

"You were the one who brought Dr. Soileau up, my dear Dr. Metaxas."

"I merely said that he would have been impressed. You know that I approve of your actions in July. There is no need to discuss this."

"As you wish, of course." She turned toward the other three, who had been, for a time, forgotten. Marcia looked at the contraption in front of her. It looked like some kind of ancient timekeeping device—a maze of interlocking gears, pins, and dials, with several different pointers, and inscriptions in Greek. It sat inside a steel frame with glass sides. A pair of narrow bronze cylinders of uncertain purpose extended from the front, like handlebars.

"You even transcribed the writing on the dials in the original Koine Greek," Mrs. May said, examining the face of the Mechanism. "Your attention to detail is remarkable."

He gave her another stiff bow. "I thought it best to reproduce the original as faithfully as possible. We are not, as you know, creating a simple mechanical device here. When you deal with an intersection between the natural, the technological, and the supernatural, it is essential to take nothing for granted."

"Certainly," she said.

"Then if you please," he said, gesturing at the Mechanism.

Mrs. May turned toward Marcia, who had been listening to the entire exchange wide-eyed, and wondering if there would be a chance of escape before they used her. That was what this was about, of course—use. She was not human to them, but a mere source of energy for powering this device. Toward what end?

There was no way to tell.

"Marcia, dear, you need to step forward, and put your hands on the posts coming from the front of the Mechanism."

"My… my hands are tied," she said, and only then realized that her teeth were chattering.

"Silly me," Mrs. May said, chuckling. "Stanford, darling, did you bring your pocket knife?"

"Of course," Mr. May said, and retrieved a knife from his pants pocket. He slit the cord that bound Marcia's wrists, and for a moment she stood there, rubbing her hands, trying to reestablish feeling in them.

"Enough dawdling, dear," she said. "Grasp the posts. A nice solid grip, please. And don't let go until we've told you to."

"She will not be able to," Metaxas said, flashing a row of perfectly straight teeth in a smile that held not a hint of warmth.

Marcia didn't move.

"Oh, now, dear. You are only prolonging the agony. We are quite able to force your compliance. Leap off the diving board or be thrown. It is entirely your decision."

Marcia still hesitated, only for a moment, but it was enough. Stanford May and Dr. Metaxas flanked her and pushed her toward the machine. Her arms were pulled forward, and her hands pressed down toward the bronze bars. May and Metaxas, she noticed, were careful not to touch the bars themselves.

She thought, as an electric bolt of fear surged through her, *It's alive. The Mechanism is alive.*

That was the last conscious thought she had for quite some time.

But the people watching Marcia Pacheco were transfixed by what was happening. Marcia's head tipped back, her eyes wide open and staring, her backbone arched like a bow. Her entire body shuddered, like a woman in the throes of a powerful orgasm. From her mouth came an inarticulate moan, whether of terror or pain was impossible to tell.

And the Mechanism began to move.

With a tinny, musical creaking, the gears turned. The needles, pointing at a pair of spiral inscriptions on the face of the machine, jittered forward, then settled into a slow, graceful rotation. There was a thrumming sound, from deep in the innards of the Mechanism—a powerful sound, almost organic in its resonance, like a voice that is too deep to be heard, or the beating of a giant heart.

Then, with the suddenness of a lightning flash, there was a soundless explosion. All of the people in the room, with the exception of Marcia, saw it clearly. It was an aura, an expanding bubble of radiance, a shimmering shock wave of light. It was over almost before anyone registered it.

Marcia let go of the handles and dropped to the floor, insensate.

But the others felt a change as the wavefront passed through them. And in each, it manifested differently.

Georgios Metaxas felt like someone had revved the engine of his mind. His thoughts had taken wing. There were changes that needed to be made in the Mechanism, he could see that now. How could he have not realized it sooner? He had been so simpleminded, so coarse in his fashioning of the Mechanism. There was much to do. Refinements, ways to focus the Mechanism's energy, ways to harness it to do… things. What things would become apparent later, he knew. All he had to do was to think about it, and it would reveal itself to him.

For Stanford May, it felt like all the world's powers had become accessible to him. He looked around, and what he saw were not objects and people. He saw energies, tools that were fit to his hand. Words went through his mind, in a voice completely foreign to him, chanting as if from a great distance:

And immediately I was in the spirit: and, behold, a throne was set in heaven, and one sat on the throne. And he that sat was to look upon like jasper and sardonyx: and there was a rainbow round about the throne, in sight like unto an emerald. And round about the throne were four and twenty seats: and upon the seats, I saw four and twenty elders sitting, clothed in white raiment; and they had on their heads crowns of gold. And out of the throne proceeded lightnings and thunderings and voices: and there were seven lamps of fire burning before the throne, which are the seven Spirits of God. And before the throne, there was a sea of glass like unto crystal: and in the midst of the throne, and round about the throne were four beasts full of eyes before and behind. And the first beast was like a lion, and the second beast like a calf, and the third beast had a face as a man, and the fourth beast was like a flying eagle. And the four beasts had each of them six wings about him; and they were full of eyes within: and they rest not day and night, saying, Holy, holy, holy, Lord God Almighty, which was, and is, and is to come. And those beasts gave glory and honor and thanks to him that sat on the throne, who liveth for ever and ever.

Mrs. May, of all of them, understood best what was happening. She felt the power enter her and received it gratefully. She knew that just from what she had taken that moment, her life span had been lengthened, perhaps as much as doubled. There was a vigor flowing through her that she had not experienced for decades. She also knew, knew without a hint of uncertainty, that she had only experienced a fraction of what the Mechanism could do. With it, she could live forever, or as long as the Earth itself was alive. Perhaps longer. Who knew what the boundaries really were? Had anyone ever tried them? There had been hints of people who had hungered for immortality—the Comte de St. Germain, Nicolas Flamel, Qin Shi Huang. All had failed.

Until now.

If Helene May understood the Mechanism the best, Andrea understood it least. All she knew was that her psychic powers had been amplified. More than amplified—clarified. She had the sudden realization that all her life, she'd been looking through a fogged window, and that the Mechanism had wiped it clean. She saw what was happening around her, heard the triumphant thoughts of her three co-conspirators as they recognized their gifts, heard the thin, keening wail that was all Marcia Pacheco's mind was capable of. She knew, from afar, that Stacy Weinstein and Reverend Bradley were preparing to fight them.

Then, from nearer at hand, she felt a familiar presence. Again, it was with frightening clarity, but still recognizable as a thought-pattern she'd heard before.

And it was terrified. No, worse—it was in that region that is beyond terror, and had crossed into the realm of near collapse. She heard a breathless string of words, in a whining panic:

Maybe if I run far away run far away they won't find me, this time, they won't find me I have to get away I have to God help me God help me.

"Stephen?" she said aloud, and her heart raced as the exhilaration of her increased psychic ability dimmed before the screaming horror that Stephen Calhoun was experiencing.

Mrs. May whirled around toward her, her plump face for once wearing a completely unambiguous expression. "What is it, Andrea?" she said. "What have you seen?"

Andrea stared back at Mrs. May. The saliva seemed to have dried up in her mouth. Would they kill Stephen Calhoun for running away again?

But to resist them, to lie—she couldn't do that. The personal risk was too great. Especially given that she didn't know what the Mechanism had done to the Mays and Dr. Metaxas. Maybe they'd see that she was lying, kill her as well as Stephen.

They hated Stephen anyway, she rationalized. Mrs. May had been waiting for some time for an opportunity to be rid of him. *It's not my fault*, she thought.

It's not my fault he ran.

"It's Stephen," Andrea said, her voice thin and shaky. "I hear him."

"Where is he?" Mr. May said.

"I don't know." This was true enough. "But I think he's running away."

"Is he?" Mrs. May said, her eyes narrowing.

"It is of no consequence," Mr. May said. "He is nothing. We have the Mechanism working. We can take care of Stephen whenever we need to. Let him run. What can he do? If he goes to the authorities, he seals his own fate. He knows this."

"What if he tries to contact the other side again?"

"He wouldn't dare," Mr. May said.

"You are so certain, dear?"

"If he did, we would know. We have Andrea, remember? With her improved sight, he would be a fool to try it."

Andrea relaxed a little. Maybe it was going to be all right. Maybe she wasn't going to become an accomplice to a murder.

Mrs. May considered. "Perhaps. Perhaps he isn't worth our time. Not at the moment." She smiled. "But if he transgresses again, we will finish him. Let him run away, to the ends of the Earth if he wishes. The Mechanism knows no boundaries of space. If he does not realize this, the more fool he."

19

L UNAR ANOMALY MECHANISM: FIFTH TURN
ZODIAC WHEEL: FOURTH TURN

How COULD every fact of a situation add up, and yet the answer not feel right?

Keith had been wrestling all morning with that question. He came back from his visit to Kelly's house feeling profoundly unsettled. At about ten-thirty he called his girl-friend and bowed out of a last-minute Christmas shopping expedition—not that he was upset about an opportunity to avoid shopping, an activity he frankly loathed. He gave the excuse that he had to deal with something that had come up having to do with the college. It was pretty vague and wasn't the whole truth. But he rationalized that it wasn't exactly a lie, either. He figured that he'd think a bit about the situation with Kelly, and try to let go of it. There was clearly nothing concrete to be suspicious about. Nothing about this was grounded in reality. It was all nerves.

Nerves, he could deal with. And after he had, he could kick back for a few hours.

Dealing with it turned out to be impossible. Instead of spending the morning relaxing and reading, he'd spent it fretting. He hated fretting even worse than shopping. He went over every piece of his two short conversations with the Mays, and there was nothing to point explicitly to their knowing what had happened to Kelly, and yet he was sure somehow that they did know.

He hung around in his apartment, drinking coffee and pondering, until about lunch time. He fixed himself a sandwich, sat down at his table, and glanced outside. There was a smooth pall of gray clouds hanging over the ever-present snow and slush. Not an inviting day, especially given that he'd already gone out once. But after he had eaten his lunch and put the dishes in the sink to attend to later, he headed out one more time to see if he could obtain more information from the Mays.

THERE WAS no answer to his knock.

Keith had decided, on the drive over, to meet whichever of the Mays answered the door with a smile and a triumphant statement that they shouldn't worry anymore, that Kelly had come to visit him and that everything was all right. If they really were simply kindly neighbors, they would be relieved. If there was something unpleasant going on, and they had a hand in it, Keith doubted that they'd have the presence of mind not to betray some quick puzzlement as to how that could possibly be true.

He stood on their front step, shifting from foot to foot from a combination of cold and nerves, waiting for someone to come to the door. Nothing happened. He knocked again and then rang the doorbell.

Nothing.

He was embarrassed that he felt some measure of relief at their absence. Spending days thinking about the Mays, especially considering the content of Kelly's dreams about them, had colored his impression of them. Honestly, they gave him the creeps, for no obvious reason. This relief was tinged with disappointment, however, at having no further information about Kelly's whereabouts, and the Mays' part, if any, in her disappearance.

Keith walked back down the sidewalk toward his car and pulled his keys out of his jacket pocket. He was in the act of reaching for his door handle when he glanced back at the Mays' house, and stopped for a moment, considering.

There was no one home, either here or at Kelly's house. The next house further down the block was shielded from view by a thick hedge. There was no reason he shouldn't take a quick walk around the Mays' house before he left. Perhaps he'd find something that might be useful.

What do you think you'll find? he thought as he walked slowly back up the sidewalk. A bloody pair of garden shears? A person-sized mound, freshly dug, in the back yard? Mr. and Mrs. May looked like storybook grandparents. Kelly was right. It was hard to imagine less likely candidates for any kind of wrongdoing.

He went back up to the front door, cupped his hands around his eyes, and peered through the window. He could see a neat little foyer, a narrow slice of what was probably the living room, and further back, a shiny linoleum floor and a bit of spotless counter that could only be the kitchen.

He went around the right side of the house, which faced the side of Kelly's house. There was a thick growth of lilac, now bare and leafless, lining the side of the house. There was a small window in one corner that was a little too high to peer into conveniently, but a quick jump-and-glance confirmed that it was a bathroom. Further on, a somewhat larger window, mostly obscured by ruffly curtains, belonged to what appeared to be a small bedroom.

Around the back, there was a deck and several more windows. The first one had curtains that matched the previous one and clearly belonged to the same room. Keith passed the picnic table, looking forlorn and forgotten in the snow. That was when he noticed the first thing that was out of place—the bag of birdseed that Mr. May had been carrying earlier that morning was sitting crumpled in the layer of snow on top of the table. In this place where everything was neat, where everything was just-so, it stuck out in a way that was somehow ominous.

Up on the deck, there were two small windows that looked into an immaculate kitchen. He went back down the two stairs off the deck into the back yard and continued his perimeter of the house. Two more windows, also curtained, looked into a second bedroom.

Keith stopped for a moment and looked up. Higher up were several more windows. Obviously, there was a second floor to the house. No way to reach those without a ladder, and that would be too conspicuous even if he'd had a ladder handy. He turned toward the far side of the house, ready to walk back toward his car, with no further information than he had come with.

That was when he noticed the two small windows, partially obscured by a neat foundation planting, a bit above ground level. Basement windows.

Keith got down on his hands and knees in the snow and peered into the window nearest the deck. Unlike everything else in and around the house, this window hadn't been cleaned in a while and was crusted with dirty snow. He rubbed at it with the sleeve of his jacket, clearing a small circle to look through.

The basement had little light. Even with the overcast skies, it was bright enough outside that he could only see vague shapes in the interior.

Then one of the shapes moved. He heard a scream of, "Dr. Sparlin!" then a rattle and a grating crash from inside.

There was a suspended moment when he was frozen to the spot, speechless, then he shouted, "Kelly?"

Her voice half choked by sobbing, she yelled back, "You've got to help me. They have me chained up down here. They might be back soon, you've got to hurry!"

Keith snapped out of his daze and looked around frantically for something to use to break the window. There were rocks that had been used to edge the garden. A couple of the larger ones protruded from the layer of snow, but they were frozen to the ground and impossible to pick up.

Keith shouted, "I'll be right back!" and he ran to a small shed in the back corner of the yard. Fortunately the Mays, like many residents of Colville, didn't lock up garden sheds, and he pulled the latch and swung it open.

Inside were a number of garden tools. He picked up a small hand axe, and jogged back to the window.

He struck the window with the back side of the axe, and the glass shattered. He used it to knock the remaining shards out of the frame and stuck his head through the opening.

Kelly was standing next to a brass bed frame and a large armchair, which had overturned and was lying on its back. She was sobbing hysterically and looking up at him as if she could hardly believe what she was seeing.

Keith pulled his head back, and then slipped his feet into the opening. With some difficulty, he squeezed through the window, his thick jacket scraping against the metal frame. As he dropped to the floor, he mumbled, "Good thing I have a skinny ass," and then ran over to where Kelly was standing, the chain of the handcuffs still connecting her to the bed frame.

He felt the pipes of the frame, and weighed the heft of the axe in his hand. It was a fairly lightweight frame, but he doubted the axe would be able to do more than dent the brass.

"Do you know where the key to the handcuffs is?" he asked.

Kelly shook her head.

"Tools," he said. "Have you seen where they have any tools?"

Kelly took a great, hitching breath, and got control of herself enough to say, "I think there might be a utility room over there." She pointed to a door in one of the walls. "He went into it once. Mr. May did. I saw a work bench or something."

Keith ran over to the door, and opened it. It was indeed a utility room, with a neat workbench and a variety of tools hanging from pegs. Including, hallelujah and praise be, a hack saw.

Keith grabbed the hacksaw from its peg, and ran back to where Kelly was still standing, shaking uncontrollably. While it was tempting to try to saw through the chain, it was made of steel, and would undoubtedly be more resistant to cutting. He began to saw at the brass rail of the bed frame, and was relieved to see the saw biting quickly into the metal.

Within a minute the saw had cut a slot in the rail. He tossed the saw onto the bed, and tried to pull on the rail to bend it and widen the cut.

The rail wouldn't bend.

"Shit!" Keith said, under his breath, and picked up the saw again.

Kelly said, "Hurry!" as he began to make a second cut near the first.

The saw grated its way through the metal, and soon there was a snap, followed by the clink of a piece of the rail hitting the floor. Kelly slipped the loop of the handcuffs through the opening.

"The basement door is locked," she said breathlessly. "We'll have to climb out of the window."

They ran to the window, their shoes scrunching on the broken glass. "You first," said Keith. Kelly reached up to the frame, and hoisted herself up. Keith lifted her foot to give her leverage. She slipped through the frame and out into the snow. Keith followed, with Kelly tugging on his arm to help him as he squeezed his way through.

"Come on!" she said urgently, and they half-jogged toward the side of the house. And that's when they heard a car braking to a stop at the front of the Mays' house, and doors opening and closing.

Keith said, "Oh, fuck," and grabbed Kelly's arm and pulled her to the house. Kelly began to cry again, softly this time, but her whole body was shaking.

There was the sound of footsteps in the snow, coming up the walk toward the Mays' front door. Keith waited for the sound of the front door opening, but instead there was a knock. He peered around the corner, and said, "Wait here."

Kelly rubbed her sleeve across her eyes, and hissed defiantly, "Like hell."

Together they crept along the wall of the house, with Keith in the lead. As they reached the front corner, they could hear voices.

"There's no one home," said a female voice.

"That may be best," answered a quiet male voice. "I still don't think this... um, frontal assault is the best idea in any case."

"Look. They kidnapped my best friend. I'm going to confront them."

"We don't know that for sure. We only have Stephen Calhoun's word for that, and who knows how truthful he was?"

"It's all we have to go on. Andrea wasn't home, and we have to do something. Whether Stephen was telling the whole truth or not, the Mays are in it somehow, from what he said. We can't not respond."

"I don't mean that we shouldn't respond, I simply think it might be best to respond carefully."

"Now that we're here, I'm going to have a look around the place. They might have Marcia here."

Keith half turned toward Kelly, and simultaneously both of them mouthed, "Marcia?"

And as Keith was turning back, ready to look cautiously around the corner of the house to see who these strange visitors were, he found himself face to face, and only about five inches away, from a furious Stacy Weinstein.

"Who the hell are you?" demanded Stacy, looking him right in the eye.

"Look, we don't have time for this," said Keith. "We have to get out of here."

Reverend Bradley appeared around the corner, and stood there staring at them, his face creased with incomprehension. Stacy, however, took in Kelly's tear-streaked face and muddy, wet clothing, and the handcuff dangling from her wrist, and said, "God. I think we need to talk to you two."

Keith swallowed, and nodded mutely.

"Where?"

"Anywhere but here," he said. "They kidnapped Kelly. We're not sure why."

Kelly hitched a sob, but kept her control. She said urgently, "We've got to go! What if they come back?"

"Look, honey," said Stacy, "I don't care who these people are, but if they show up now, they'll be dealing with me. You're not the only one they've kidnapped."

"Come on," said Keith. "We can go to my apartment. Do you know where the Collingswood Apartments are? On Banks Road?"

"Yes."

"I'm in number 5. Meet us there."

The four of them split, Kelly following Keith to his car, and Stacy and Reverend Bradley heading toward Stacy's. Engines were hurriedly started, and both cars pulled out and down the street, and turned right at the corner and out of sight.

Moments later, an aging blue Buick turned the corner on the other end of the block, and pulled up toward the Mays' house, and turned into the driveway. The automatic garage door sprang into life, creaked its way open, and the car vanished into the gloom of the garage.

The door gave a reluctant groan and reversed course, dropping downward like a theater curtain at the end of a performance.

20

ALL CALIBRATED WHEELS ENGAGED: FIRST COMPLETE REVOLUTION

THE MAYS' car was headed north, back toward Colville. Once again, Helene May was driving. All four occupants were silent during the first half of the ride, each lost in thought about what had happened when the Mechanism had been activated. Marcia was still exhausted, but was beginning to come back to herself. She knew without a doubt, however, that if they hooked her up to that thing again, without a time to rest, it would suck the life from her, leave her nothing but a desiccated husk.

The idea had little emotion attached to it. At least if she died, they'd have to find a different power source. Maybe that would delay them long enough for Stacy to find them, stop them from whatever it is they're trying to do.

But what exactly they were trying to do still wasn't obvious. Dr. Metaxas had stayed behind, saying that he had some modifications he needed to make. His expression was one of barely-contained excitement. It looked incongruous on that elegant, controlled countenance. Neither he nor the Mays had anything more to say about their ultimate goal.

But it wasn't good, she was certain of that.

They had just passed Louise's nursery, on the southern end of Colville, when Andrea suddenly spoke up, almost involuntarily.

"Helene..." she said hoarsely. "Kelly. Someone's taking Kelly."

Mrs. May started out of her reverie, and turned toward Andrea. "You're certain?"

Andrea swallowed and nodded. "I can see it. Clearly. It's a young man with curly red hair. He's broken a window and is climbing inside."

Mrs. May's lips narrowed until they nearly disappeared. "Sparlin. We must stop him."

"I think..." said Andrea, and then paused. "Um, I think it may be too late. We won't arrive in time."

Mrs. May didn't respond. Andrea caught a glimpse of her face in the rear-view mirror. It was tight with fury. Her eyes glittered like chips of quartz.

"She's right, Helene," Mr. May said. "Even if we hit all the traffic lights green, we're still a good fifteen minutes from home. They'll be gone by then."

Mrs. May brought both hands down on the steering wheel, and gave a strangled sound of rage.

"We'll find them," Mr. May said. "Don't worry. With the Mechanism functional, we'll find them. Kelly is less important than she was."

"They would dare to get in our way," Mrs. May growled, lips curling. "Oh, no, no, my dears, that is unacceptable. They must not be allowed to escape."

"We should, perhaps, inform Louise. She has proven useful in the past in these sorts of matters."

"Yes," Mrs. May said, but her voice sounded tentative.

"You don't trust Louise?" Mr. May said.

"Not entirely. But then," she added, and gave a little laugh, "I don't trust anyone entirely. Yes. Call Louise."

Mr. May got out his cell phone and turned it on. His eyebrows rose. Instead of dialing Louise's number, he saw the message, "You have three missed calls."

All were from the same familiar telephone number.

"Interesting," he said. "It appears that Louise tried, more than once, to call us. We must have been out of cell phone range."

Mr. May dialed the numbers to access his voicemail, and sat, listening, for a moment. He looked over toward his wife, and Andrea recognized apprehension in his face.

He's scared of her, too, Andrea thought, with some amazement. *Who is this person I've allied myself with?*

"Dear," Mr. May said, as he ended the connection to voicemail, "I believe we have another problem."

"Yes?" Mrs. May said, her voice taut with barely-submerged anger.

"Louise said that yesterday, she received a message from Morris Bradley. He told her that he had been called to a meeting with Stephen, and he wanted her to know about it in case… something happened to him."

"And why didn't Louise call us yesterday?" she said. She was no longer making any attempt to control her rage. "We might have done something!"

"She said that she did and that we did not answer either our home phone or cellphone." Mr. May gave his wife a steady look.

Mrs. May was not quelled by the implication, which Mr. May left unstated. "She could have left a message on voicemail."

"She said you told her months ago that voicemail is never secure, and to avoid doing that unless absolutely necessary."

"And this, this situation doesn't qualify as an absolute necessity?" Mrs. May was nearly shouting again.

"It probably doesn't matter. It was too late by that time in any case. There was nothing that we, or anyone, could have done at that point to stop the meeting. When she wasn't able to get a hold of us, she did the best she could. She went herself yesterday afternoon to try to find Stephen, but he had already fled from his apartment. The damage is done. But when this morning she was again unsuccessful at reaching us, she realized that she had to chance leaving a voicemail, rather than delay further."

"That fool! That witless fool!"

"Helene," Mr. May began, "It is hardly her fault. She called us last night. It must have been the call we ignored as we were leaving for dinner. You didn't want to answer the phone. You said our meeting with Metaxas was more important. And remember, Louise has always been one of our most stalwart…"

Mrs. May's sudden swerve was so unexpected that both Marcia and Andrea cried out with alarm. Mr. May was jerked to the side, and the back of his head bounced off the headrest. A driver behind her honked his horn, and a window was rolled down to reveal a left hand flipping her off.

Mrs. May was aware of none of this. Her vision was fogged with scarlet. No, they must'nt be allowed to interfere. It was not to be tolerated. She knew that soon, very soon, she would not need the Mechanism to pull down the powers of heaven on the heads of her enemies, but she was not at that stage, yet. She was still at a point where she could be stopped.

But she must not be. Must not.

Her hands gripped the steering wheel so tightly that it seemed she would break the plastic asunder. Her face was white, except for two spots of high color on her cheeks. She couldn't manage any words, but from her chest came a low rumbling growl.

"Dear," Mr. May said soothingly, "perhaps I should drive."

She didn't respond, but stared straight ahead, her whole body trembling.

He set the parking brake, then got out of the car and circled in front of it. He opened the door, unfastened her seatbelt. Gently, as one would deal with a savage animal, he urged her to slide over into the passenger seat. Amazingly, she allowed herself to be moved.

Once she was over on the right of the front seat, he got behind the wheel and maneuvered his way out into traffic. Mrs. May didn't put on her seatbelt, but that was hardly the most pressing issue.

"We can return to the Mechanism this afternoon," he said, softly. "Once Ms. Pacheco has recovered sufficiently. Then we can deal with them. We can deal with them all."

Mrs. May didn't respond, but continued to stare out the window.

They arrived at the house fifteen minutes later. Several sets of footprints in the snow proved the accuracy of Andrea's vision. They followed the trail into the backyard. The broken basement window, with the axe lying next to it, confirmed the fact of Kelly's rescue. Mrs. May still looked furious, but had restored her self-control enough to speak.

"How dare they," she hissed. Mr. May put a hand on her arm, which she shook off with angrily. "How dare they! They will pay. All of them. But especially Sparlin. And Stephen."

"We'll take care of them," Mr. May said.

"Did you get a hold of Louise?"

"Yes. She said she would come right over."

"Did you discuss her transgression with her?"

"I didn't think it was the time to do so."

"You may be right. There will be time for that, later when I ascertain if she is still loyal to us."

"Louise hardly showed disloyalty by her actions. We can't afford to lose more allies, Helene."

Mrs. May rounded on her husband. "I can do this by myself if need be," she snarled. "Alone. All I need is the power source. Even Metaxas will be expendable soon."

They brought Marcia into the house and into a bedroom on the second floor, which Mr. May locked from the outside. Louise arrived twenty minutes later, and her lined face was creased with worry.

"I was concerned when I couldn't reach you," she said.

"Not concerned enough to keep trying, however," Mrs. May said. Her voice was once again modulated, saccharine, a little condescending.

"I did keep trying."

"You dropped the ball, dear. That is all. At a time when dropping the ball could well be fatal to our enterprise. But we shall discuss it later. The question now is to determine what steps we need to take. There are three separate problems that need to be dealt with. First, we have Bradley, and what he knows, what Stephen may have told him."

"Stephen doesn't know that much," Louise said.

"He knows enough. We don't know what he told Bradley, and therefore, what information the enemies may have access to. We need to stop Bradley, and soon. Then there is the issue of Sparlin and Kelly Delahanty."

"Do you think that now is the right time for revenge?" Mr. May asked.

"They, too, could interfere. Perhaps not in as great a way as Bradley. But still, they're a danger."

"Kelly may go to the authorities, and lodge charges of kidnapping against us," Louise said.

"That would be unfortunate," Mr. May admitted.

"I am less worried about the police than I am about what mischief Sparlin could cause if he and Bradley joined forces. The secular authorities we can take care of."

"I don't see how," Louise said.

"No, dear, I'm quite sure you don't," Mrs. May said, in a sweet voice. "But last, we have Stephen himself. We have waited too long in this matter. Stephen must be liquidated."

"No question there," Mr. May said. "But in regards to Bradley. Could the Mechanism do anything against him? I mean, directly? He is, insofar as I understand, protected."

"Because he's religious, you mean?" Louise said, and her smile looked a little incredulous.

"No," Mrs. May scoffed. "Hardly that. Because of who he is. He is at least as strong as Ms. Pacheco. Were he… shall we say, corruptible… he would have been a better choice for the power source than Ms. Pacheco is. But that was quite out of the question. Still, I think it might not be best to deal with Bradley directly."

"What do you have in mind?" Mr. May asked.

"Perhaps a show of force. Bradley will take the meaning immediately, especially now that Stephen has given him some clue about what is happening. Maybe it's for the best that Stephen did what he did." Her smile evaporated. "Not that it changes the outcome, from his perspective. We still need to eliminate Stephen, and soon. Before the day is out, I think."

"Meaning another trip to the Mechanism," Mr. May said.

"Yes. Unfortunate to have to drive all that way twice in one day, but I see no other option. Louise, this time, you should come along. And since last time we left the house unguarded, our enemies took advantage of our absence, I think we should leave someone here to stand guard, as it were."

"Who?" Andrea said, but she already knew the answer.

"Why, you, dear. I believe that you have already received your little gift from the Mechanism." She gave a grand-motherly smile at Andrea, who swallowed and did not smile in return.

"Do you think Ms. Pacheco is capable of another encounter so soon?" Mr. May said.

"Not immediately. You are quite right. We will give her a time to rest. But by mid-afternoon at the latest, we must try again. It would be nice to have a longer respite, but I fear that there is no alternative." She turned once again to Andrea. "Andrea and Louise, would you go up and check on Ms. Pacheco's well-being? I hope that she is sound asleep by now. If not, perhaps we should administer a sedative of some kind to help her recuperate, and also to make her more pliant when the time comes."

"Would a sedative interfere with what the Mechanism can get from her?" Mr. May said.

"I doubt that. I think the Mechanism is unlikely to be hindered by a simple thing like that. Perhaps a call to

Metaxas might clear up that point, however, if you are concerned. For now… Andrea, Louise? Please check on our guest."

The two women rose and left the living room, heading toward a staircase that led to the second story. Neither spoke until they reached the landing, turned, and headed toward the closed door of the bedroom where Marcia Pacheco had been imprisoned.

Andrea leaned toward Louise, and said in a whisper, "Louise, I've been thinking… I know that they were right when they said that this thing they're trying to create, that it's powerful. I know what it can do, I felt it. But did they think of... I'm not sure how to say it. Did they consider that it might not be good? I mean, there are all kinds of power."

Louise turned the key in the lock, and looked at Andrea, her weatherbeaten face grim. "You know, Andrea," she said, "I think that somehow, the question of good or evil never even entered the discussion."

21

All Calibrated Wheels Engaged: Second Complete Revolution

"We should call the police," said Stacy firmly.

"I'm not going home until we do," said Kelly, the handcuff still dangling from her wrist.

"I'm not sure that's the best approach," said Reverend Bradley hesitantly. "After all, we're dealing with supernatural forces."

"Supernatural, my ass," said Stacy. "Begging your pardon for my language, Reverend. But these weirdos kidnapped two people. If that's not a reason to call the police, then what is?"

"Well..." said Reverend Bradley, making a small, apologetic gesture, "you're right, of course. But there is a difference. They are not simple lawbreakers. They have allied themselves with a power. It will protect them, I suspect, from any kind of interference from the... um, enforcers of earthly law."

Keith smiled slightly. "I'll beg your pardon as well, Reverend. But I don't believe in that sort of thing. The Mays are probably psychopaths, but they're not somehow linked to anything beyond a misguided greed for the ordinary sort of power."

Reverend Bradley turned his palms upward. "I'm sorry, Mr. Sparlin, but I haven't any other way to explain it to you. What Stephen told me squares with all the facts we have. And you know," he added, "there are other forces at work in the world besides the scientific type, even if you wouldn't be able to detect them in your laboratory."

"Mr. May said the same thing," said Kelly with a shudder. "In almost exactly those words."

"The trouble is," continued the Reverend, "the distinctions between natural and artificial, human and non-human, good and evil, don't necessarily line up as you might expect. Many people are confused about this. Strychnine, for example, is perfectly natural, but it can kill you."

"Good and evil are human constructs," said Keith firmly. "Value judgments with no independent reality. I flatly refuse to believe that strychnine is evil because it could kill me if I swallowed it."

"That isn't what I was getting at," said the Reverend. "And I think you know that. I wasn't saying that strychnine was evil. Simply that the concepts of 'good' and 'natural' don't overlap, or at least not completely. As far as your point, however, I understand what you are saying. Unfortunately,

I also believe that you are dangerously wrong. Good and evil do have an independent existence. Or, rather, they are real external influences on our minds as conscious beings. My point is that what the Mays are trying to do is to combine the powers that are natural with those that are created, to blur the lines between man and machine."

"Even if you're right," Keith said, "what's the difference between that and an artificial heart? Or a prosthetic limb?"

Reverend Bradley shook his head. "You mistake me. Like anything, such a device can be used for good or evil. But here…" He stopped, and looked up at Keith, and shrugged slightly. "They are using this fusion to access a power that is most certainly evil. But I'm guessing that you probably think that's all a lot of nonsense."

"It doesn't really matter if I believe it," Keith said. "As long as we stop the Mays from hurting anyone else."

"And if the philosophy lecture is over for today," said Stacy, quivering with impatience, "can we please get on the horn to the police and do something?"

"I agree," said Kelly.

"I think it's three against one," said Keith. "Sorry, Reverend."

Reverend Bradley shrugged again. "Go ahead. I don't suppose it could do any harm. From what Stephen told me, they don't intend to hurt Marcia directly, simply use her. We certainly have evidence of their wrongdoing," he gestured at Kelly, "and perhaps we could convince the police to search the house."

"Exactly," said Stacy.

"We'll have to hope that they won't do anything rash," said Keith, standing up and walking toward the kitchen. "If they get desperate, who knows what they'll do? I don't want put Marcia at additional risk."

"I'm more worried about the police, actually," added Reverend Bradley softly, but by that time Keith was already on the phone calling 911.

OFFICERS TODD SHARDLOW and Anna Markelz were at Keith's door fifteen minutes later.

"You're accusing your neighbors of kidnapping?" Officer Shardlow said to Kelly, looking at her handcuffed wrist with interest.

She nodded. "Helene and Stanford May. I'm at 141 Prospect Street, so I suppose they're 143."

Officer Markelz made a notation on a clipboard, and said, "Why don't you tell us exactly what happened."

Kelly described having dinner at the Mays' house, and the sensation of being drugged, and the events of the next two days, during her confinement in the Mays' basement. She also told them how Keith had rescued her.

"How did you know she was there?" asked Officer Markelz.

"Intuition, I suppose," said Keith. Reverend Bradley raised an eyebrow but said nothing.

"And you," said Officer Shardlow to Stacy, "you believe they may have kidnapped your friend as well."

Stacy nodded. "They must have. She was missing from my apartment this morning."

"Do you have any evidence of this? Was there a sign of a struggle?"

"No," Stacy admitted.

"But you still think they kidnapped her."

"Well," said Stacy, and hesitated. "There's what Reverend Bradley knows." She looked over at the Reverend.

The two police officers looked at the Reverend expectantly. Reverend Bradley cleared his throat, and recounted his meeting with Stephen. Sensing the skepticism of his audience, he downplayed the supernatural aspect of the conversation as much as he could, but it was impossible for it not to come out.

"So, let me get this straight," said Officer Shardlow, his brow wrinkling from a combination of confusion and disbelief, "they kidnapped this Ms. Pacheco because they believed she could help them power some kind of psychic machine they're building?"

Reverend Bradley gave an apologetic smile. "I know it sounds ridiculous."

"You got that right," said Markelz.

"But still," interjected Keith, "the Mays believe it. Whether it's true or not is immaterial, if they're acting on that belief and hurting people in the process."

Shardlow nodded. "That's true. Well, we'll call it in, and check it out. We'll let you know what we find out." He gestured at Kelly's handcuffed wrist. "You'll have to get a pair of bolt cutters to get out of those things."

AT THE MAYS' house, Mr. and Mrs. May, Andrea, and Louise were all seated at the dinner table, preparing to eat a belated lunch, when Andrea spoke suddenly.

"Um," she began, then stopped. Her face blanched, and she looked up from the tray of little sandwiches that Helene had prepared, and from which she was about to pick up a triangle with liverwurst and cream cheese.

Three faces turned toward her, with questioning eyes.

"What is it?" said Helene.

"Helene," said Andrea, "there are two police officers. A man and a woman. They... Kelly and the others. They've called the police. They're on their way here. The police, I mean." Andrea stood, the legs of her chair scraping on the linoleum. Her face showed clear signs of panic. "We should get out of here. Get Marcia to a safe place."

"You worry over nothing," Helene responded.

"But it's the police," Andrea said, and then added, with a baffled tone, "Isn't there anything that bothers you?"

"Only one person concerns me. Bradley. The others are nothing. The police are nothing. Let them come. You will see."

"You're confident," Louise observed and took a bite of a turkey sandwich with avocado.

"I have reason to be." Helene considered. Finally she said to Andrea, "Sit down, Andrea, dear. I believe that the Mechanism has given us this much, that faced with a... shall we say, unenlightened adversary, we will have no problem. In any case, if you are correct, and I have no reason to believe that you are not, we will see. For now, we will simply wait and let them come."

Andrea slowly sat down, but her forehead was beaded with sweat, and her eyes were still wide with anxiety.

"When they arrive," Helene said, "we will let them in. Let them look at what they wish. It will come to nothing."

"What about the damaged window in the basement?" Mr. May said. "It will certainly lend credence to Kelly's claim of having been held against her will, and then escaping."

"There is no time to remedy that." She smiled. "I begin to understand why the Mechanism was destroyed the first time. It gives a clarity of purpose that to lesser minds would be quite terrifying." She gave a coy smile to Andrea. "But it does reduce the need for you to worry, Andrea, dear. I am quite certain that we are in no danger whatsoever from the secular authorities."

Twenty minutes later, there was a knock on the door. Mr. and Mrs. May exchanged glances. "If they come in here, be friendly but say as little as you can," Mr. May said to Louise and Andrea, who were still seated at the dinner table. He looked intently at Andrea. "Especially you."

Mrs. May went to the door and opened it.

Officers Shardlow and Markelz were standing on the front doorstep.

"Can I help you?" said Mrs. May, smiling sweetly.

Officer Shardlow stared at her, a little incredulously. "Are you Helene May?"

Mrs. May nodded. "Yes, sir, I am. What can I do for you?"

Shardlow looked over at Markelz for a moment, and then back at Mrs. May. "Um... I have a complaint against you and your husband, that you... um, unlawfully detained your neighbor, Kelly Delahanty, for two days. She claims that you kept her locked in the basement."

Mrs. May's brow creased. "Oh, poor Kelly. She has such an imagination, it quite carries her away sometimes. I'm afraid that this isn't the first time this sort of thing has happened." She shook her head. "It is the first time she has involved the police, however."

"Well," said Markelz, "we also have another complaint against you, that you kidnapped a second woman, a Marcia Pacheco, this morning, from the apartment of her friend, Stacy Weinstein."

"Kelly told you that, too, I would surmise," said Mrs. May sorrowfully.

"No," Shardlow said.

"Oh," said Mrs. May, dismay sounding in her voice. "Oh, dear. Well, I'm sorry, officers, but I don't know anyone with those names. Who is this complaint coming from, if I may ask?"

"The friend," Markelz said. "Weinstein. And I should mention that Kelly had a handcuff hanging from one wrist. It did look suspicious."

"Oh," Mrs. May said again. "Yes, well, unfortunately that there's that boyfriend of hers. Keith Sparlin. I believe they have these," her nose wrinkled up in distaste, "games they play. You understand. This sort of thing has become all too commonplace in recent months. Movies and such trash."

"I don't know about that," Shardlow said. "But you can see how it bolsters their claim."

"Of course," said Mrs. May.

"Perhaps we might take a look around your house?" Markelz said.

Shardlow nodded. He looked uneasy, shifting his weight from foot to foot. He consulted his clipboard as if he'd forgotten something, and finally tucked it under his arm. "Yes. Maybe we could take a look around."

"Of course," Mrs. May said. "Please come in and feel free to look anywhere you'd like."

The two officers went into the living room and glanced around. They went back into the kitchen, followed by Mrs. May.

Mr. May stood. "Good afternoon, officers. I'm Stanford May. What can we do for you?"

"Don't let us interrupt your lunch," said Markelz. "We're simply here to ask a couple of questions. There's been a complaint from your neighbor, and your wife has said that we could take a quick look through your house if that's okay."

"Of course," Mr. May said.

Andrea and Louise said nothing and the two officers took little notice of them.

"Do you have a basement?" Shardlow said as they exited the kitchen.

"We do," said Mrs. May. "We don't use it much, as it's rather damp and uninviting."

"May we take a look?"

"Of course." She went back into the kitchen, and unhooked the key, and led them to the door. Andrea watched them, her eyes widening. Mrs. May's hand trembled visibly as the key turned in the lock and she opened the door, but it was the only thing that might have betrayed any nervousness. Markelz and Shardlow walked down the stairs, followed by Mrs. May.

The basement was icy cold, and a chilly breeze came in through the broken window. A thin dusting of snow lay on the floor beneath, partially covering the broken glass. The officers both stared at the shattered pane, taking in its meaning immediately, but somehow not able to believe what they were seeing. Markelz walked over to the brass bed, with its cut railing. Splinters of brass littered the floor, and the small section of rail that Keith had cut out that morning still lay next to one leg. She reached down, frowning, and ran her finger along the jagged edge, winced, and straightened up. Her face had a look of shock.

"Shardlow…" she said, and then stopped.

"I see it," her partner said, his voice hoarse.

Together, they turned toward Mrs. May, who was standing with her hands behind her back, her pudgy face wearing a benevolent smile.

"Mrs. May," Markelz said, "can you explain this?"

"Yes, of course I can," Mrs. May said. "Simply put, I was lying earlier. Kelly Delahanty is quite correct. My husband and I, with the assistance of the two women you saw in the kitchen, did kidnap Kelly and keep her here against her will. Keith Sparlin apparently rescued her earlier today by cutting the bed frame, although you can see that I have only the evidence before you, and their version of the story, to go by. I was not here at the time."

"And Marcia Pacheco?" said Shardlow.

"She's locked in a bedroom upstairs," Mrs. May said cheerfully. "A bit tired out, but otherwise unharmed. We kidnapped her as well, you see."

The two officers' eyes met, for a moment, and then they looked back toward this matronly, rosy-cheeked woman who could not possibly be saying what she sounded as if she were saying.

"I…" Shardlow began. Then he stopped, swallowed, and said, "You're under arrest. You have the right to remain silent…"

The corner of Mrs. May's eyes crinkled into a hundred fine lines, and she gave a merry laugh. "Come now, officer, there's no need for all of that."

Shardlow stopped in the middle of the Miranda rights that five minutes ago, he had no idea he'd need to use. "What… what do you mean?"

"What I mean is that I am most certainly not under arrest. I'm not going anywhere. And you both will leave, and let Keith Sparlin and Kelly Delahanty and the others know that despite their rather outlandish claims, my husband and I are completely innocent of wrongdoing."

"But you just said…"

"Precisely. What I said happened, and what you will tell them, are two entirely different things."

Shardlow evidently had had enough. He pulled out his gun and leveled it at Mrs. May. "You have admitted to a crime," he said. "I told you that you were under arrest. You need to come with me. Now."

"I will do no such thing."

"Ma'am, don't make this any worse than it already is."

"You have no idea how bad it already is," Mrs. May said. "But not for me." She glanced down at the gun, and Shardlow's arm bent at the elbow, pulled by a force he was powerless to resist until the barrel was pressed to his chin.

"Now, Officer Shardlow, I think you see that the danger here is not to me and my husband. Do I make myself clear?"

Markelz pulled her gun as well, in a swift, sure movement that was not nearly swift enough.

"My dear Officer Markelz," Mrs. May said. "You'll have to do better than that." And now Markelz also pivoted, moving with no conscious volition, until her gun was pointing at her partner's belly. "You appear, Officer Shardlow, to be in a situation that I believe they call 'between the devil and the deep blue sea.'"

Anna Markelz tried without success to move her arm away from its deadly aim on her partner, but it seemed to have been turned into carven stone. "How…" she said, through a clenched jaw that didn't want to open, "how are you doing this?"

"Magic," Mrs. May said, wiggling her fingers, her eyes twinkling.

"That's impossible."

"You can see for yourself that it isn't. I could give you more information, but that wouldn't be helpful for me, and it would be decidedly unhealthy for the two of you."

"You can't think you'll get away with this," Markelz said.

Mrs. May pursed her lips. "But that is exactly what I do think. Now, you have a choice. If you put the nasty guns away, we can go upstairs, and I think you will find yourselves realizing that there was nothing of interest down in the basement. The visit to our house will be a regrettable waste of time, and you will go back and inform Ms. Delahanty and her boyfriend about your findings."

"And if we don't?"

"Then it will be my duty to see to it that you and your partner both have an unfortunate accident. You came down here and were acting erratically. You, Officer Markelz, were having some kind of argument with your partner, that had begun before you arrived. I don't know about what, but it sounded serious. Then, down here in the basement, you two began to fight. I panicked, ran up the stairs to call 911, and as I did so, shots rang out. I came back down to find that you'd killed your partner and then yourself."

"What about the evidence?" Markelz ground out. "The bed frame? The window? The call from Delahanty and Sparlin?"

"I assure you that we can take care of those details before anyone is the wiser. And if the fates smile upon us, Kelly and her friends will be taken care of as well, soon enough that we will have nothing more to fear from their accusations. I appreciate your concern, Officer, but really, it is your well-being that is the most at risk, here." Mrs. May smiled again. "So let us proceed then, shall we?"

Markelz's index finger tightened on the trigger. Her forearm was trembling with the strain, but her muscles would only obey the will of this elderly woman was watching them both with an expression that was a strange amalgam of mild amusement and supreme confidence. Shardlow's eyes rolled in their sockets, but he was unable to utter a word.

"Okay, okay!" Markelz said, her voice high and desperate. "Stop! Don't hurt him!"

"You've made your decision, then? Oh, I'm so relieved. I do hate the sight of blood, and it's such a dreadful mess to clean up. Let's call it settled, then."

With only a little lift of her eyebrow, she released the two police officers. Markelz's finger relaxed, and her gun hand dropped to her side. Shardlow's gun swiveled downward as well, his arms nerveless, his chest heaving. Where the barrel was pushed against his chin there was a ring-shaped indentation from the pressure.

They stood, blinking, looking at each other, for nearly a minute. There was silence in the chilly basement, except for the sound of the wind hissing past the broken window.

"Perhaps we should go upstairs now," Mrs. May said, "since you didn't find anything of note."

Markelz frowned, as if she were going to say something, but then holstered her gun, turned and went back toward the stairs, moving like a marionette. Shardlow followed suit, only once looking back at Mrs. May with a perplexed expression.

As they passed Mr. May, Louise, and Andrea, still sitting in the kitchen, Mrs. May said, in a conversational tone, "I told the officers about Kelly's unfortunate mental lapses."

"Yes," Mr. May said. "A pity. So young. But they say schizophrenia often strikes people in their late teen years."

"You should…" Shardlow started, and then cleared his throat and went on in a stronger voice. "You should probably fix that broken window down in the basement. You're losing a lot of heat right there. Cost you a fortune."

"Keeping up with the repairs in old houses," Mr. May said. "It's a full-time job."

"I'm sorry you had to come all this way for nothing," Mrs. May said. "Would you like a sandwich or a cup of tea?"

"No, thank you, ma'am. And it wasn't a problem. We have to check out all complaints."

"I understand completely. Don't be too hard on Kelly. It only occupied a few minutes of our time. I feel more pity than anger, and I wouldn't want her to suffer more than she already is."

"But a charge of kidnapping…" Markelz began.

Mrs. May held up her hand. "I know. You do what you must, but if it comes to it, we'll not press charges, or whatever the terminology is. Please consider her age and her… her condition."

"If that's what you want," Markelz said.

"It is. It most certainly is."

"Very well then," Shardlow said. "Good day to all of you."

He and Markelz went down the hall, Mrs. May following. As they were donning their jackets in the foyer, Shardlow said, "Hey, Markelz. Your finger's bleeding."

She looked at her hand. The finger she had rubbed across the cut surface of the bed frame had a bead of bright red blood on the tip.

"How'd you do that?" Shardlow said.

"There must have been a rough spot on that old bed frame," Markelz said. "Didn't realize I'd broken the skin."

"Might I get you a bandage and some disinfectant?" said Mrs. May.

"No, ma'am, that's all right," Markelz said. "There are some in the squad car. We won't trouble you further." They went out the front door, and down the sidewalk. Mrs. May watched them go.

SHARDLOW GOT into the squad car behind the steering wheel, and Markelz climbed into the passenger side.

"Kidnapping," Shardlow said to his partner, shaking his head. "Can you imagine?"

Markelz wrapped a bandage around her finger. "Not in a million years. I bet the worst thing she ever did was gossip at a church social."

"Call it in, will you?" Shardlow said. Markelz nodded and unhooked the intercom phone. "What a fucking waste of time."

"We had to check it out," Markelz said.

"I guess. But like hell that woman kidnapped anyone," said Shardlow, shaking his head again. "She reminds me of my grandmother."

22

A ll Calibrated Wheels Engaged: Third Complete Revolution

It was a little before three in the afternoon that Mr. May went to wake Marcia. Despite her situation, she had fallen deeply asleep as soon as she'd lain down on the bed and didn't hear the key turning in the lock, shutting her in. She wasn't aware of Andrea and Louise checking on her, only a half hour earlier. If she had any dreams, she couldn't remember them.

Her recollection of what had happened when she grasped the handles of the Mechanism was blurred at best. She was aware of a sensation like an electric current. She could feel the muscles in her upper body spasm. Then a power swept through her, throwing her mind about like a rowboat being tossed by high waves. The Mechanism was alive, she could sense that. It was drawing energy from her, pulling it down from the base of her skull, through her neck and shoulders, down her arms, and into the bronze handgrips of the Mechanism. She could feel its power laughing at her.

It was a sound like the roar of a tornado.

That was the last thing she remembered. She had no idea how she'd gotten back to Colville. She was dimly aware of being bundled up the stairs of the Mays' house, and into a bed that felt supremely comfortable. The next thing she knew, Mr. May was shaking her by the shoulder.

"Ms. Pacheco," he said, "you need to come with me."

"Why?" Marcia said.

"You are wanted at the Mechanism."

This made her snap to attention. "I can't," she said. "I can't do that again."

"I am afraid that you have no choice."

"It might kill me."

Mr. May looked down at her for a moment, his blue eyes wide, the corners of his mouth sagging a little. "Yes," he said. "It might."

He grasped her upper arm and pulled her to her feet, and then with surprising strength, guided her out of the room, down the hall, and downstairs to the first floor. Mrs. May already had her coat on, and Louise was wrapping a scarf around her neck.

"Why are you doing this to me?" Marcia said. She was dangerously near tears. Her bodily fatigue, combined with her fear, were leaving her with little energy to fight them.

"Oh, dear, believe me," Mrs. May said, "if anyone else could do what you can do, we would not need to use you this way. But our friend Andrea has assured us that you are the best choice. You must understand, what we are trying to accomplish will take some sacrifices."

"Never yours, of course," Marcia said.

Mrs. May's expression became peevish for a moment, and then the disapproval was swallowed up by sweet condescension once again. "My dear Ms. Pacheco, you have no idea what I've sacrificed to accomplish this. No idea whatsoever. This is the culmination of thirty years of study, travel, and risk."

"You signed up for that. I didn't."

"We all play a role, Ms. Pacheco. We all play a role. But you will not delay the inevitable by trying to draw me into a discussion of my motives. It is time to go. We have much to accomplish this afternoon."

Mr. May again took Marcia's upper arm, and Louise held the other one with one work-toughened hand. "You should know," Marcia said, "I will do everything I can to stop you." She hoped it sounded more threatening than she felt.

But Mrs. May gave her a beatific smile. "I believe that in the current parlance, the appropriate response is, 'Knock yourself out.' Shall we go?"

As they were walking toward the door, Mrs. May turned to Andrea, who was still seated at the dinner table. "Andrea, dear," she called back, "it may be that Bradley or Sparlin will show up. This is one of the reasons we are leaving you here. With your heightened abilities, you'll likely sense them approaching. My recommendation is that you do not answer the door if they knock. Simply wait, and listen to their thoughts. Remember everything you hear. It may be useful later." She smiled as she pulled on a fuzzy glove. "When we eliminate them both."

They exited the front door, and Andrea heard them lock it behind them.

———

THE DRIVE back to Lamont was, for the most part, silent. Louise was naturally taciturn. Marcia, for all of her fear and her brave talk, found herself fighting to stay awake. Mr. May drove this time, and Mrs. May sat in the passenger seat, a chubby Mrs. Claus figure that smiled at passersby and once gave a little wave to a family with young children who were crossing the street near one of south Colville's many strip malls, carrying bags laden with wrapped Christmas presents.

She's like a layer cake that's frosting over poison, Louise thought. *Why am I willing to help these people?*

But she knew why—it was because they were the first people, perhaps ever in her life, who had included her, who had trusted her with a position of power. Louise had been orphaned at age eight by an automobile accident that had killed both of her parents and left her hospitalized with grave injuries for a month and a half afterwards. She recovered, with physical therapy regained her strength, and went to live with an aunt in Colville for the remainder of her childhood. Her injuries had delayed her schooling, and she felt left behind for the rest of her years in public school. The aunt was a cold, distant woman who always treated Louise like an outsider. She wasn't trusted with a key to the house until she was a senior in high school, and even then had to hang it from a hook in the kitchen when she got home. Forgetting it in her pocket or backpack earned a severe reprimand.

She'd left that home as soon as possible, but a part of her never recovered. She hadn't been thought trustworthy, and as a result, she never trusted. She didn't trust the Mays, either, of course. But she did respect power and authority, and she recognized in Mrs. May someone who might one day change the world. Survival had been the critical thing when she was a child, and it was the critical thing now. Here, survival was a matter of choosing the right allies.

It was nearly four when they arrived back at the pole barn. Metaxas's car was still parked outside. The wind had picked up, a cutting north wind that found its way beneath jackets and hats. Marcia, still coatless as a way to insure that she wouldn't flee, was chilled to the bone by the time they got inside the pole barn and out of the wind.

Georgios Metaxas looked elated when they came inside.

"I have finished the refinements I needed to make," he said, a smile flitting across his narrow face. "I believe that you will find the Mechanism's operation to be quite satisfactory."

"It was satisfactory before, my dear Dr. Metaxas," Mrs. May said. "But I have bigger ideas in mind for this evening." She motioned to Louise and Mr. May. "Bring the woman."

Marcia's last thought was a feeble, half-amused, *I don't have a name anymore? I'm just 'the woman?'* before her hands were forced down on the bronze handles, and once more the electric jolt of the Mechanism's powering up surged through her body and mind.

Louise hadn't been there the first time the Mechanism was activated, but she had been thoroughly briefed on its operation. She thought she was prepared for what was going to happen. But when Marcia's body went rigid, her eyes staring sightlessly at the ceiling, the tendons standing out in her neck, Louise thought, *It's like watching someone being executed in the electric chair.*

Her gorge rose, and she had to will herself not to vomit.

But then there was the soundless bubble of light, even more, radiant this time, that flashed forth as the gears in the Mechanism turned and creaked. All of the horror and nausea was gone in an instant. Energy surged through her. Her muscles felt were as taut as bowstrings. She had, in the last couple of years, found herself recognizing signs of aging. Hefting around potted shrubs and fifty-pound sacks of topsoil weren't as easy as it had been.

Now, she felt as if she could have tucked Mr. and Mrs. May under each arm, and run back to Colville without breaking a sweat. Her strength and energy were inexhaustible.

As before, the connection was broken suddenly, like someone flipping a switch. Marcia collapsed to the dirt floor, this time completely unconscious. The gears in the Mechanism slowly wound down and stopped. Only then did Louise look over at Mrs. May. Her face was shining, as if with some sort of inner light, but it was light that gave no warmth, as inaccessible as the aurora borealis.

"I believe the time has come," she said, and she smiled at each of the people standing in the chilly dimness of the barn in turn. "We need a show of power. Bradley and his friends should have a demonstration of what we, and the Mechanism, are capable of."

"What do you have in mind, Helene?" Stanford May said, looking at his wife with a distant expression that had, Louise thought, a trace of apprehension in it.

"An unequivocal message," Mrs. May said. "Something that says, 'perhaps you should reconsider your decision to fight us.'"

She took a deep breath and closed her eyes. Her plump face relaxed, and her expression became almost cherubic in its innocence. Louise, who had been distracted for a moment by the sudden gift of physical strength, felt a resurgence of her fear toward this woman. What devastation would she accomplish, with whatever newfound power the Mechanism had gifted her?

There was no time to question her, much less to consider whether it might be best to try to stop her. Only moments later, Helene May opened her eyes, and lifted them upwards, raising her hands as well in a gesture of benediction.

"It is done," she said.

23

SUPERIOR PLANET MECHANISM LOCKED AND ENGAGED

FAY KALIVODA HAD WORKED for WDNY Television, Channel 5 News, for four years. Her usual coverage was the local news. She rarely got even as far as Syracuse to cover a story, let alone Albany. News about state government was given to Steve de Forest, who'd been there for seven years, and anything that took reporters further afield, especially if it required travel to a vacation spot like Lake Placid, were given to silver-haired Dean McManus, who had seniority over the entire rest of the news crew.

God knows I don't envy Steve having to cover monumentally boring stories about what bills are on the agenda in the State Assembly, Fay thought with a mental sigh, as she pulled her car into the parking lot of the television station on what would turn out to be her last day on the job. But a paid business trip, even an overnighter, would be a nice diversion from local news, which was often even more boring. She had thought many times about asking her boss if there was any chance of this. The producer, a five-foot-tall, chain-smoking seventy-something from Mobile, Alabama named Ruth Vanlandingham, didn't exactly invite such questions, and Fay was not the most self-confident person in the world. Each time she'd pictured herself walking into Mrs. Vanlandingham's office, clearing her throat, and saying, "Ma'am, I really think I'm ready to try something a little more challenging, don't you?" her heart had thudded violently in her chest, and she'd found something pressing that had to be attended to right then. More often, she daydreamed about one day being hard at the work in the newsroom, and looking up to see Mrs. Vanlandingham staring at her, her blue eyes glittering. "Miss Kalivoda, ah've been watching you," Mrs. Vanlandingham would say in her smoke-roughened southern drawl. "Ah think you have the makings of a grade-A repawta. Ah've got an assignment for you that maht just let us see if mah assessment of youah skills is justified." And she'd be sent to do investigative reporting on Corruption In High Places.

Of course, Mrs. Vanlandingham knew who she was. She hadn't gotten to be producer by being unaware of who her staff members were. Fay, however, had yet to do anything to distinguish herself. Except in her daydreams, in which she was a Reporter of Exceptional Courage. Daydreams, of course, counted as little for Mrs. Vanlandingham as they did for most bosses, and as a result, she seldom got to cover anything more exciting than Colville city politics, house fires, and the occasional weather-related event.

It wasn't that Fay disliked her job, really. She had to admit that she'd enjoyed standing in the flying snow the previous

February during a blizzard that brought the entire region to a standstill for three days. She'd watched the footage afterward, and thought that the purple wool scarf she had been wearing at the time had really made the story. The way it curled and snapped in the wind had been quite effective. On the other hand, she was beginning to wonder what the point of it all was. Purple scarf or no, no one had really needed her to report that there was a blizzard in progress. Anyone in a house with windows knew as much about the blizzard as she did. The one actual fact she had reported that night—that over 5,600 residents in the Colville area were without power, but that it was expected to be restored by daybreak—had caused the cameraman to quip that the people who needed to know what she'd said couldn't find out about it because they had no power. The comment had stung, especially when she said, "Well, I have to report on my story," and he responded that he didn't give a flying fuck about her story, he just wanted to get out of the damn wind and get somewhere warm.

She was finally having to admit to herself that she was bored with her job. "Fay Kalivoda, News Reporter" had seemed so glamorous at first, but the reality had turned out to be one dull small town story after another, day after day, year after year. Talented Young Reporter Pursuing The Story had become Bored Young Reporter Putting In Her Shift And Then Going Home.

So on mornings she didn't daydream about being noticed by her boss, she fervently wished for something exciting to happen that day. Something really, truly, unusual and exciting that she could cover. Something that would make the audience (and Mrs. Vanlandingham) sit up and notice. Something that would cause a stir. And every day there were more stories of municipal government, more house fires, and more weather.

And then the afternoon of December 19 rolled around— her last day as a reporter—the day her wish came true.

She heard the sirens before the dispatcher called her, screaming up Grant Street, so she knew that something had happened. A serious automobile accident or maybe, please God no, another house fire. But the when the dispatcher called, ten minutes afterward, he had sounded mystified as to what exactly it was Fay was being sent out to report.

"It's some kind of... I don't know, an accident or something. Several bystanders called it in. I guess there was a wreck or something on the bridge over Carlisle Inlet."

"A wreck or something?" Fay had said, already standing up from her desk and beginning to pull on her jacket. "What does that mean?"

"I don't know. They were kind of incoherent. But it sounded big. You better get out there."

Her heart beat a little faster, but she tried to suppress it. One shouldn't get one's hopes up, only to be dashed. "On my way," she said and hung up.

THE TRAFFIC BACKUP began about two miles from the bridge.

Josh, the cameraman, sitting in the passenger seat, looked out of the window and rolled his eyes. "Whatever it is, it's blocked both lanes. There's almost no one coming the other direction."

"Well, let's see if we can get a little closer," Fay said. Josh was an irritable ex-hippie with a long blond ponytail and a habit of blaming any inconvenience on whoever happened to be nearest. Fay, ever the pleaser, immediately tried to forestall being the target of his ire by nosing her car around onto the shoulder and seeing if she could slip up and past the jam. It wasn't a legal move, but hey, they were a Reporter And Her Cameraman On The Way To An Important Story. She got a nasty look and a couple of horns honked at her, and a lot of good it did. She got only about five cars up before she was halted by a line of people who'd had the same idea, but had gotten no further than a block before being thwarted by the same unseen obstacle that had brought everyone else to a dead stop. Josh gave an annoyed sidelong glance at Fay, which she pretended to ignore, and she pulled her car into the only available exit from the road, which was the parking lot of Hennen's Ice Cream Store.

"Dessert first?" asked Josh sourly.

Fay turned off her motor and began pulling on gloves and a wool hat. "No," she said, trying to make her voice as conciliatory as she could. "We're going to have to walk."

"Fuck that," Josh said. "It's freezing. And we're still a good mile and a half away from the bridge."

"Well, we're not getting there in the car. It's on foot or not at all."

Josh swore again, but got out and pulled his camera bag out of the back seat. Fay was already trudging through the dirty snow along the edge of Route 12, past the idling line of cars, more from a desire not to meet Josh's eyes than any real urgency about reaching their destination.

"Don't those idiots realize they should give up and turn around?" Josh asked, gesturing at the stopped vehicles.

"Most of them don't have room to turn," Fay said. "And it's one-way. What can they do?"

"Walk, I guess," Josh observed. Fay elected not to respond to that.

It took over a half hour to reach the crest of the hill where Route 12 turned and started its sweeping curve downhill toward the inlet. The Carlisle Inlet Bridge, a graceful, arched structure that had been part of a highway project three years previous, leapt across the inlet at its narrowest point, where the road curved again and continued to wind its way up the west edge of the lake toward the village of Guildford, fifteen miles north.

Except the bridge was gone. Fay stopped. She stared, and then blinked, trying to figure out what she was looking at. Josh bumped into her, started to say, "Watch out!" but the word caught in mid-throat.

"Holy shit," Fay said under her breath. "Where's the bridge?"

Josh shook his head and swallowed. "I..." he began and stopped. This was beyond even his finding someone to blame. "Jesus. I don't know."

Fay's mind was spinning. Terrorists, she thought. A terrorist bombing of a bridge in Colville. Who would bomb Colville? But then a louder voice in her mind over-rode the first: This was it. This was the Big Story. The one she'd been waiting for.

The drivers here had turned their motors off. It was obvious to them that they would be stuck in place for a while. The two continued their walk along the road's shoulder, approaching the space where the bridge once was. Closer still, the line of cars was ever so slightly out of skew, as if they had been jounced out of place. These drivers were out of their cars, talking in small clusters and in quiet voices. Fay and Josh walked past them, and the people momentarily turned stunned, uncomprehending faces toward them. The cars which had been nearest to the inlet were scattered like toys. A maroon Toyota truck was lying on its back, its door hanging open at an odd angle. A tall, sandy-haired young man sat in the snow next to it, dazed, his face covered with blood, and a woman with a gash on her forehead was trying to wrap a blanket around his shoulders. Fay looked over at Josh, her mouth slightly open, her eyes wide. Josh looked back at her, and then glanced around, shrugged in hopeless puzzlement, and simply said, "Jesus."

Fay and Josh came up to the edge of the inlet.

The Inlet Bridge lay in ruins. Pieces of concrete and twisted iron beams were scattered along the shore, and in places there were smaller pieces on the ice. The main ice sheet over the Inlet was shattered, the water showing like a dark gash underneath. Chunks of ice were tipped crazily on edge, harsh, jagged gray-white edges sticking upward like teeth. There were at least two cars in the Inlet itself. One was nose down, protruding from the water between two slabs of ice, and the other was on the far shore, upside down, smashed flat beneath a twelve-foot section of roadway.

"Holy shit," Fay said again.

Josh turned toward her, his face pale. "Jesus, Fay, how are you going to report this?"

"I..." She stopped, swallowed, and tried to get a hold of herself. "We need to talk to some of these people. Then I need to call the newsroom."

Fay looked around at the knots of people, trying to find someone who might know what had happened here. Before she could decide who to approach first, the woman with the cut forehead straightened up and began to walk toward them. She looked composed and calm, but she wasn't wearing a jacket, and her gray sweatshirt was freckled with blood.

Fay went out to meet her. "Are you okay?" she asked.

The woman nodded. "I'm all right except for this cut, which isn't bad. Better than some."

"Did you see what happened?" Fay asked, trying to keep the tremor out of her voice. "I'm a reporter for WDNY. What happened here?"

"Hell if I know," the woman said. "Maybe an earthquake or something. I was in the blue Honda." She gestured toward a small blue car, its windshield shattered, sitting on the shoulder of the road. "I was almost to the bridge when something picked my car up and knocked it off the road. When the shaking stopped, I looked out and the bridge was gone. Broken up, I mean." She brushed a lock of hair out of her face, and shivered. "I keep thinking, I was in a hurry, and I was so pissed because the light changed just as I reached the intersection at Grant Street. If the light had been green, I'd have been fifteen seconds ahead of where I was, I might be..." Her words caught in her throat, and she swallowed, glancing out at the car in the inlet, its rear bumper protruding from the dark water.

Fay nodded.

A heavyset man came up, carrying a Yorkshire terrier who was wearing a pink knit sweater.

"You a reporter?" he asked, in a heavy Brooklyn accent.

"WDNY News," Fay said.

"I saw it happen," he said. "Well, I saw the bridge go, but I don't know why it went. It wasn't no earthquake. I was walking my dog, and suddenly I heard a screeching sound. Like a high squeal, like someone hitting a bad note on a violin. Then it felt like the pressure dropped. You know how your ears pop when you go up in a plane? Like that. And you couldn't hear nothing for a few seconds. Then there was a huge boom, and a crunching noise. Like someone smashing a bunch of crackers. Like that. And there was dust and rocks and stuff flying. And when I could see again, the bridge was gone."

At this point a red-haired girl, about thirteen years old, joined them. She looked unharmed, but had gently in tow a woman who was probably her mother, and who had the vague, wide-eyed expression of a person in a state of complete mental shock. "I saw it too," the girl said. "We were a couple of cars back from that lady," she gestured toward the woman with the cut forehead, "and my mom rear-ended the guy in front of us. I thought it might be an earthquake, so of course I jumped out of the car."

Fay nodded at this piece of inscrutable teenage reasoning.

"And the guy with the dog is right. It was raining gravel and dust and stuff. But I saw something weird, right before the bridge fell. I was looking ahead and I saw it."

"What did you see?" Fay asked.

"The clouds," she said and pointed into the featureless gray sky. "The bridge fell because of a piece of cloud that came down. I saw it, just for a second, I saw the shape of it. It looked like a huge fist."

24

A *ssembly Complete: Entire Mechanism Active: First Turn*

KEITH SPARLIN WAS PACING around in his apartment like a caged lion, the same as he had been doing since the two police officers left almost an hour earlier. They had accomplished only one thing during that time—Keith went to find the groundskeeper of his apartment complex, who provided him with a bolt cutter to free Kelly from what was left of the Mays' handcuffs.

There was nothing else to do but wait, frustrating though that was. Keith hated forced inaction, but Reverend Bradley repeatedly urged them not to act rashly. They had discussed and re-discussed what their course of action should be, and afterwards had discussed it yet again. None of this had brought them to within hailing distance of a solution.

"I suppose we at least have to wait until the police return," Stacy said. "But I want to do something now. Anything is better than sitting here."

"Amen," Keith said under his breath.

"I'm afraid sending those police officers will all come to nothing," Reverend Bradley replied. "They're up against something that they won't be able to recognize, much less fight. There are powers at work here that are quite beyond any sort of... um, ordinary law."

"So what do you propose to do?" Keith demanded. "You're awfully good at pointing out how defenseless we are, and not so good at proposing any real solutions yourself."

Reverend Bradley shrugged apologetically. "All I'm telling you is the truth. You can't fight supernatural forces by natural means."

Stacy rolled her eyes. "Oh, my god, let's not get all bogged down in philosophy again. You two talk way too much."

"No, wait, Stacy," Keith said, holding up a hand. "I want an answer. Reverend, meaning no disrespect, because you seem like a nice guy and you have your heart in the right place, but what exactly do you mean by supernatural? The word literally means 'above nature.' There is nothing above nature. We don't understand all of nature, but whatever this is does follow natural laws, and we should be able to fight it based on those laws."

Reverend Bradley shook his head. "I can't explain it to you because you're starting from a position of disbelief. There are some things above, or beyond, or outside of nature. What the Mays are trying to do might be one of them, but the point is that we don't know. And our one constant ally is God, who is beyond nature. If you go against the supernatural, and you have only knowledge of natural law as your guide and your shield, you will be about as defenseless as a kitten trying to stop a hurricane." He shook his head. "I'm sorry. You also seem like a good person. But your disbelief is going to disarm you. If we do eventually... um, mount a frontal assault on these people, you should be the last person to lead it."

"Well, for what it's worth, I don't really believe in God, either," Stacy said.

"You haven't made your disbelief in God into a religion," Reverend Bradley said. "I rather think that Mr. Sparlin has."

Keith ignored the last statement. He had heard it from many critics of his position in the battle between science and religion, and he declined to be baited. "So you're proposing that the three of you are better equipped to fight these people than I am?"

"I'm sorry," Reverend Bradley said again. "But yes, that's exactly what I'm saying."

Keith snorted.

"Well, we should decide what to do," Stacy said. "One way or the other."

"One way in which Mr. Sparlin is correct," said Reverend Bradley, "is that we shouldn't act until we find out what happens to the police officers."

"What happens to them?" Kelly said. "What do you mean, what happens to them?"

"I have a bad feeling," said Reverend Bradley, "that the Mays and their cronies are in far less danger than the officers themselves."

"And then what?" asked Keith. "The police officers return unless the Mays have turned them into frogs or whatever you're claiming they'll do. Then what do we do?"

"It will come to our facing down the forces of evil," Reverend Bradley said. "On some level I've known ever since Stephen Calhoun told me about their plans, but I'm sure of it now. We will have to be the ones to defeat the Mays, when the time comes. I don't know how, and I don't know when, but I believe that to be our task. We need to find them, induce them to release Marcia, and destroy the evil Mechanism they have created. With that, the Mays will be, if not defeated, at least weakened and exposed. We must trust in God and wait for the right time to do this. But that is what I believe it will come to."

Keith shook his head. "Give me a baseball bat, or better yet, a gun, and I think I'd be better off than you, with all your reliance on God's protection."

Reverend Bradley smiled. "A kitten with a gun is still a kitten."

About twenty minutes later, there was a knock on the door. Keith opened it to find Officers Markelz and Shardlow, looking at him with an expression of mixed distaste and annoyance. Kelly looked up eagerly from where she was seated on the couch.

"What did you find out?" she asked. "Did you arrest them?"

Shardlow's face clouded. He looked completely exasperated. Markelz made a small gesture with her hand, and she was the one who responded.

"Well, no," she said. "There was no evidence of what you claimed. We searched the house and questioned Mr. and Mrs. May. Your accusation was totally unfounded."

Kelly opened her mouth, and then closed it again without saying anything. Her cheeks reddened. Reverend Bradley sighed, and got up and walked over to the dinner table, where he sat down heavily in a chair.

"How can that be?" asked Keith.

Markelz ignored him, and continued to speak to Kelly. "In fact, Miss Delahanty, they would have had reasonable grounds for making a complaint against you for false accusation, and only out of kindness did they decide not to do this. Apparently this sort of thing has happened before?"

Kelly started to speak, but Keith interrupted her before she could begin. "Now, wait a moment. I'm the one who freed her from the basement. I'm the one who got her free from being chained to the bed. Didn't you see the broken window? Didn't you see the bed with the cut railing? They couldn't have hidden that, not that fast."

Shardlow, in the background, muttered, "I'll bet you chain her to the bed, ya perv," but Markelz again gestured for him to let her respond, and he fell silent.

"Yeah, there was a bed in the basement," said Officer Markelz. "It had some damage, okay, but it was an old bed frame. There was no evidence whatsoever that what you claimed happened. The Mays certainly didn't hold anyone against their will, not Miss Delahanty here, and not anyone else. There was no evidence of any wrongdoing. None."

"That's impossible," said Keith. "That's flat-out impossible."

Reverend Bradley said nothing, but his brow creased, and he looked out of the window and into the blank gray sky.

"Mr. Sparlin," Officer Markelz said, her voice rising in annoyance. "I wouldn't push this if I were you."

"What about my friend?" Stacy asked. "What about Marcia? Did you look for her?"

"There was no one in the house except the Mays and two friends of theirs."

"You're sure?"

Markelz' eyes flashed. "Now, look. I've tried to be patient. I think we've wasted about as much time on this as it warrants. Do you think we wouldn't have responded if there had been someone being held against her will in that house? Do you think we wouldn't have arrested the Mays if there was any evidence of what you're saying? Like I said, be glad we're not citing you for making a false accusation. You and your boyfriend both. I suggest you leave the Mays alone. Next time, I'll make sure that you do receive a citation."

With a suddenness that made them all jump, the walkie-talkie on both officers' belts went off. Shardlow was the first to respond. Keith, who was closest to the two officers, heard the words, "all officers within range, report to Carlisle Inlet Bridge. Massive accident being reported."

"We have actual police work to do," Markelz said, straightening her jacket with an impatient gesture. "You know, like helping people who actually have real needs? We're going to mark your complaint against the Mays as resolved, and I suggest you don't pursue it any further."

The two officers turned, Shardlow giving Keith one last disgusted glance. As they walked off down the hall, Keith overheard Shardlow muttering, "... fuckin' pervs wanted us to arrest my goddamn grandmother, for chrissake."

Keith shut the door.

"At least they didn't harm either officer," said Reverend Bradley. "God be praised for that."

"Don't even start with me," said Keith. "You can't really believe..."

"Actually," said Reverend Bradley, "I do believe. That's the difference between us. And I can see things that you don't because of it."

"What do we do now?" said Stacy. "We can't give up on Marcia and let the Mays do whatever they want."

"Of course not," said Reverend Bradley. "But it is as I suspected—the ordinary police will be powerless against them. As I said earlier, I believe, as frightening as this prospect may be, that it is up to the four of us."

"What can we do?" asked Kelly. She was still sitting, pale and defeated, on the couch. "Look at us."

Reverend Bradley cleared his throat. "I think it is wise to keep in mind the adage that all things are possible with God."

"Your certainty that your superstitious beliefs are eternal truth is your blind spot," snarled Keith.

"Your faith in natural law is yours," retorted Reverend Bradley, with an edge to his voice that was the closest to exasperation that any of them had yet heard from him.

"My faith in science won't get us all killed," Keith said.

"I hope you're right. But when you are before this infernal machine that the Mays have created," Reverend Bradley said, "I doubt that science will be much of a shield."

25

Entire Mechanism Active: Second Turn

Andrea Yarbrough had never been so scared in her life.

She had joined the Mays and been apprised of their strange plans five months previous, and to be honest, it had never seemed particularly real to her. Violence of any kind never had seemed real, as far back as she could remember. Even news reports had sounded like fiction, like some exciting thing you'd read about. Not real people suffering and dying, and certainly not anyone deliberately hurting or killing someone else.

She had grown up as the youngest child, and only girl, in a rural farming family with a distant father and a sweet, conventional, and highly overprotective mother, and between her parents and her three tough, muscular, farm-boy older brothers trying to keep their baby sister from experiencing the bumps and dents of life, she had had a remarkably placid childhood. She married shortly out of high school. She and her husband never had children, and while they had talked for a while about seeing a doctor to find out why, they finally let the matter drop. Life proceeded in its even track until she was widowed three years previous at the young age of 45.

When George, her husband, dropped dead of a heart attack while repairing his tractor, it had been the first real experience with hardship to enter her life. Once her grief began to subside, she responded to life with her characteristic attitude that everything would work out fine, and that the world was basically a nice place where being nice meant that you'd win. And for a while, it appeared that she was right.

Andrea had been vaguely psychic since her teenage years, but her Christian and God-fearing parents would never have approved of, nor even understood, their daughter's odd gift. Out of nothing more than an obscure sense of morality she had never used her second sight to cheat, or gain an advantage over others, but her friends quickly figured out that she had an uncanny knack for picking up on what was bothering them, and that she sometimes had access to knowledge that wasn't coming to her in any conventional fashion. When, five years earlier, she asked her eldest brother when he'd last had a physical, and had pushed him to go get one soon, it had been because of a feeling of cold whenever her eyes passed across his midsection. His subsequent diagnosis with very early stage colon cancer, and the three year treatment that left him cancer free, was labeled "nothing short of a miracle" by her sister-in-law, and had already become a family legend.

Still, she had misses. Big ones. There was no inkling, not the slightest twinge, of George's impending heart attack and death. She hadn't seen her mother's last illness coming, either. Her ability was like a television with a faulty antenna. The picture came and went, and sometimes all you saw were hints of shapes, so vague as to be hardly there at all.

After George's death, however, it had been enough to make a living. The house was paid for, there were no children to look after or worry about, and her own needs were few. It had been her sister-in-law who had suggested that she advertise as a psychic.

"You know you can do it," Ann had said. "You know about people. You saved David's life, after all."

Andrea had been hesitant, but something led her to put out some fliers in a few places in Colville. As much to her surprise as anyone's, it worked. A few months after she did her first psychic reading for a woman who had seen her advertisement, she was becoming well known as someone who did have vision, however incomplete or indistinct it sometimes was.

Then she met the Mays.

It had felt like chance, the typical sort of friend-of-a-friend thing that brings counselors and psychics much of their business, and often from the same customers. She had sensed that the Mays were different right from the beginning, but that blur in her sight prevented her from having any real recognition of how different they were.

They were charming, articulate, even funny. Mr. May had heard about her from a former colleague, he told her, a member of the Colville College math department with whom he had kept in touch and who knew his interest in the paranormal.

"She told me that you were the real deal," Mr. May had said to her, and the compliment brought a flush to her cheeks.

They had asked her to do a reading for them, tell them what she could, just as a "cold session."

"To prove to us that Stanford's friend was right about you," said Mrs. May, with an ingratiating smile.

Andrea hated being under pressure, but she did what she could. Apparently, it was enough. She correctly told Mrs. May that she had been raised an only child after the death of a sister in infancy, and that she saw her, much younger, in a small home near the ocean. She heard French being spoken, she said, and it sounded like a prayer.

"I was raised in Nova Scotia," said Mrs. May, smiling in a satisfied way. "My family is French Canadian, and they were devoutly Roman Catholic. And you're quite right about Adele's death. She died when she was two weeks old. Premature. They couldn't do much about premies in those days."

Andrea smiled, relieved that everything was working. It was never a sure thing. When she told Mr. May she had a clear picture of him, somewhere exotic, it had been the final nail.

"It looks like one of those National Geographic specials, with palm trees and tropical plants," she had said, "and some kind of big gray stone pyramid behind it. There's a carving of a face. Not human. An animal face, with long pointed teeth in an open mouth."

Mr. May looked over at his wife, and nodded slightly. "I believe you're seeing me in central Belize, last winter," he said. "The Jaguar Temple at Lamanai."

And that was when they told her about their plan to create a channel for psychic force, using a technology that they'd found out about on one of their travels, a technology that had been lost to humanity for over two thousand years.

Had she ever heard of the Antikythera Mechanism, they asked her? She said she hadn't.

"It is an artifact that was recovered from a shipwreck in the Mediterranean Sea," Mr. May explained. "Discovered in 1901, but over two millennia old. The pieces that were recovered were fragmentary, and were thought to be gears from an ancient astronomical calendar."

Andrea simply nodded. She couldn't imagine how a calendar could have gears, but she didn't say that.

"Further research, conducted by archaeologists at the University of Antwerp and the University of London, demonstrated that the Mechanism was not simply a device for calculating planetary positions and the timing of eclipses. It was far more than that. It was a machine that, if activated at the right time, would act as an amplifier."

"An amplifier?" Andrea said. "Like, for sound?"

"No, dear, not for sound," Mrs. May said, and Andrea reddened a little in embarrassment. "For psychic energy."

"We would like to try to rebuild the Mechanism," Mr. May said. "But there are people who will try to stop us. Two of the archaeologists who were researching the Mechanism were murdered earlier this year."

"Murdered?" Andrea said. "That's horrible."

"It is. And we are undertaking no small risk ourselves. This is why we need you."

"We would like to ask you to join us, to be our eyes and ears," Mrs. May said.

"Why do you want to do this?" asked Andrea, her eyes wide with wonder, and not a little flattered at being asked.

"Our lives have become so unnatural," said Mr. May. "We believe that it is time that humans connect the forces of technology to the forces of nature. We have to relink the two, close the circle, merge technology with humanity so as to exceed the capabilities of both. You as a psychic must realize that this is true."

Honestly, it had never occurred to Andrea, but she nodded and said, "Of course."

And so she had agreed to help them. At first, it didn't affect her life much at all—occasional calls, updates, sometimes questions.

"We are looking for someone who can act as a psychic battery for this technology," Mrs. May told her once, about three months previous. "Just as a computer runs on electricity, this machine needs a power source as well, only a human one. You see all sorts of people with all sorts of abilities. Be on the watch for anyone who might be able to help us in this way. This is why we need you and your abilities. You'll be able to identify this person when he or she comes along. You'll see a different energy in them, and we need you to tell us."

And so Marcia had stumbled into Andrea's life, and her capacity was so overwhelming that even Andrea, with her dim sight, had recognized it immediately. She also got a clear picture of Reverend Bradley, and saw him trying to interfere with her plans, and the Mays.

This panicked and angered Andrea. More than any time in her life, her connection to the Mays' plot had made her feel essential. She was like a character in a book. For the first time, she felt like something special, something secret, depended on her. She didn't really stop to think about the Mays' motives, nor anything else except how good it was to be in an inner circle. When she was with the Mays—even when she talked to them on the telephone—she felt indispensable.

We would like you to be our eyes and ears.

Even when she found out that the Mays had kidnapped Kelly, and that they were planning on kidnapping Marcia, she was still able to convince herself that everything was fine. The feelings of importance, of finally belonging, were so much more critical. And she still never really could fathom that the Mays might hurt someone along the way.

That perception had completely collapsed that morning.

What Andrea was seeing had little to do with her cozy world, in which nice people won. Before this morning, she had been able to maintain her part in this plot by casting it as some kind of suspense novel. None of it seemed real. It was all a grand, secret story, like the fantasies she liked to read when she was a child.

Now that her vision had cleared, the veil had been torn away. When she looked at Stanford May, she saw a strange and dark labyrinth of magic, all hidden from view beneath a prosaic, academic veneer. In high school she had once picked up a book of short stories by H. P. Lovecraft. She hadn't finished it—none of the stories had happy endings, and she couldn't bear that—but she had gleaned one word from her reading of Lovecraft's prose. *Eldritch.* She'd had to look it up, and it came back to her now, after all those years. Mr. May had an eldritch soul, full of twists and turns, staircases leading nowhere, doors opening onto stone walls, trapdoors gaping into unfathomable spaces beneath. He was a man whose mind was filled with robes and orbs and scepters, whose vision of his place in the world was as high priest, master magician, grand wizard. His mind had expanded like mist. He was so lost in his delusions that anything that remained of the original Stanford May was virtually inaccessible.

Mrs. May was a different story. There were no tortuous passageways there. She was solid steel, ice cold, and rock solid. Others might change, but not Helene May. She knew what she wanted, and God help anyone who thought they could thwart her. She would stop at nothing, Andrea knew, to achieve the power she was seeking. If that power commanded her to slaughter every one of her friends and associates, Helene May would do it without a second thought. Yes, she could appear to be kind. The appearance could even be convincing for a while. But it was like a drift of soft snow on a metal fence post in the depth of January. Brush aside the softness, and what was underneath was so cold it could burn your skin.

And the others. She was picking up information whether she wanted to or not. Marcia was frightened, and weary to the bone, but more than anything she was furious at having been kidnapped and used. Earlier, Andrea had felt the waves of anger pounding against her, even though she was in the kitchen and Marcia was upstairs. Nearer at hand, she had also sensed Louise's uncertainty—a new thing. She knew that Louise despised her, and this rejection made her ache even though she didn't find Louise all that likable. Andrea, fundamentally, wanted nothing more than to be needed, stroked, made to feel comfortable and welcome. There was a great deal of the golden retriever in her personality. But now, Andrea was picking up a subtle loss of confidence, and she realized that even Louise had not been ready for what had happened that day, nor for the way Helene May had turned on her in the matter over the failed telephone call. Andrea heard Louise think, *That woman is psychotic!* But then Louise was able, somehow, to return her mind to other channels, to accept that Helene might be dangerous, but she was still to be obeyed rather than thwarted.

And Andrea had also heard the two police officers' internal voices, and had felt rather than heard it die down into confused and garbled chatter. What had happened there? It was Mrs. May's doing, she knew that, but how? Had the Mechanism given Helene May the power to alter people's thoughts, control their actions?

Now there was a terrifying idea.

But it was no better when she was away from Louise and the Mays. Further afield, Andrea was being bombarded by background speech, from people in nearby houses, even people driving by. It formed a ceaseless murmur in her brain, like a radio turned on low. If she tried, she could focus on specific thoughts, like tuning into one voice in a crowded room. She heard a woman mulling over what to have for dinner. She heard what sounded like a teenager thinking angry thoughts about his father. Once, very clearly, she heard a male voice saying, "man, she's so hot, and I need to get laid so bad!" and had quickly turned her attention away, blushing.

And, not to put too fine a point on it, she didn't like it. Her previous visions had mostly been soft-edged, wrapped in cotton. That was fine with her. These voices were sharp and clear, and many of them were simply not nice. Andrea didn't think she could deal with a world where so many people weren't nice. She sat at the table in the Mays kitchen, vaguely wondering how on earth she would be able to get away from all of this and get back to her comfortable, predictable life. Her nice life.

When the police had been escorted from the house, and Mr. and Mrs. May had discussed returning to the Mechanism with Louise that day, leaving Andrea behind and alone, a wild hope surged in her heart. She was careful not to let it show in her face. Who knew what the Mechanism had given Stanford and Helene May? Were they now able to read thoughts, too? She wouldn't have been surprised. She controlled her mind, and with some difficulty, turned it into other channels. They seemed to take forever to retrieve Marcia from the bedroom, put on coats and hats and gloves, and then go. But finally they were ready.

Then Mrs. May had turned, right as they were leaving, and had given her final instructions to wait for Bradley and Sprain, and listen to their thoughts. The door opened, then closed.

After they left, Andrea remained sitting at the dinner table, breathing hard, until she heard the car engine start, the outside garage door opener's creaky growl begin and end, and the noise of the engine retreat down the street.

Finally, she stood, looking around her as if still afraid that the Mays would jump out of the shadows.

How long should she wait? It would be foolish to leave immediately. What if one of them forgot something, and came back only to find Andrea gone? They'd know what had happened immediately, she was certain of that. And if all went well, she'd have a good bit of time to spare before they came home. She decided to give it a solid half-hour before she left, to be on the safe side.

It may have been the longest half-hour of her life. She spent it teetering on the edge, knowing what she had to do, but terrified of doing it. The whole tangled skein of ugliness in which she had become enmeshed was not going to be undone without some pain, she knew that.

So she waited, watching the clock's hands slowly measuring out the minutes, hoping that some other solution would present itself.

None did.

No part of Andrea's character was naturally combative. She detested confrontation. But for the first time, she had come to the conclusion that there was no choice but to betray the Mays and help the people she had come to think of as "the good guys." This idea simultaneously attracted and terrified her. Wasn't such a betrayal why the Mays were now talking about killing Stephen Calhoun?

She had always thought of herself as a good person. The fact that sustaining this opinion of herself would require her to act on her conscience even if it meant putting herself in danger came as something of an epiphany. Part of her had known from the beginning that the Mays were exactly what her God-fearing parents had meant when they talked about evil, but the excitement of being part of something Big and Secret (she always mentally capitalized these words when she thought about the Mays' plans) had mostly silenced this inner voice. After seeing the Mays' treatment of Marcia, and hearing of their plans to kill Reverend Bradley and Keith Sparlin, she knew she couldn't continue in her alliance with them.

It was just as she made the decision that she had let enough time pass, that acting was not going to get any easier by further delay, that she heard the sirens start.

Her ears perked up, and she turned her head toward the front of the house. Of course, there was nothing to be seen from there. But she felt a weird energy… The noise was still far in the distance, somewhere away in the direction of central Colville. She listened for a moment, and heard other sirens following. Whatever it was must be big. Accident of some kind, most likely.

She gave a mental shrug. Whatever it was didn't concern her. Her only concern now was getting out of there. Andrea walked to the kitchen counter, the sound of her own footsteps in the silence increasing her fear to near panic. She reached for the phone book and flipped the pages, her fingers trembling and fumbling as she found the right section. Then she picked up the handset and dialed the number.

A male voice said, "Hello?"

"Is this…" Andrea's voice squeaked, and she cleared her throat and continued. "Is this Keith Sparlin?"

"Yes." There was wariness in the voice.

"This is Andrea Yarbrough."

An angry noise came from the other end of the line.

"Wait," Andrea said, desperately. "Don't hang up. Please. I know I've helped them but I have to stop. You have to listen to me. I don't want to help them any more. I want to help you." Andrea suddenly found herself on the edge of tears. She was not someone who cried easily, but the tidal wave of emotion was trying to find an outlet any way it could. Her vision blurred, she blinked a few times, and got control of herself.

"Why should I believe you?" Keith's voice came, accusatory, hostile.

Andrea heard a voice in the background saying, "Who is it?" and then Keith's muffled voice as he pulled away from the receiver and said, "Andrea Yarbrough."

There was a sudden outburst, from which Andrea could only hear one clear voice, which sounded like Stacy's, saying, "Let me talk to her!" but Keith's voice came back on.

"What do you want?"

"Look, you don't have much time," Andrea said. "There's things I need to tell you quickly. The Mays left me at their house but I'm going to leave in a moment before they get back. I had to tell you before I get caught. Louise and Marcia and Mr. and Mrs. May have gone back to where the machine is. It needs to be recharged or something. You need to catch them and stop them before it gets its power back."

There was a moment of silence, and then Keith repeated, quietly, "Why should we believe you?"

"You have to," said Andrea, desperation sounding in her voice. "You simply have to. I know you probably won't believe this, but I'm so sorry for what I did, for helping the Mays with their machine. I know that won't mean much to you, that you're still mad at me. You're right to be."

"Okay. Apology noted. But how does that help us?"

"You need to see if you can find out more about this thing, this machine. And stop them from doing… whatever it is they're doing." In her own ears her words sounded weak, pathetic, unbelievable even though she knew she was speaking the truth.

"How can we stop them?"

"I don't know for sure. But they want to finish what they're trying to do on the solstice. That's what, day after tomorrow? I know that it's got to be done before then. At that point, they'll have the full power of the Mechanism. After that, it'll be too late."

"Do you know where this thing is?"

"Yes. I've been there a couple of times. It's out in the middle of nowhere. Near Lamont. You take Highway 12 south, then you take a right on Moore's Corners Road. You'll see the sign for Lamont. About five miles further along, take a left at a flashing light. I don't remember what the name of the road is, but it's the only light. When that road ends in a 'T,' take a right, and follow it all the way to the end. There's a pole barn. That's where they are."

"But what…"

Terror brought a whine to Andrea's voice. "I can't talk any more. I don't know when they'll get back. I've got to get away from here. I've got to leave now." The tears welled up and slid down Andrea's cheeks, and she wiped them away with the back of her hand. "I'm so scared," she added, realizing how pitiful it sounded but unable to stop herself from saying it.

"Look," said Keith, "you can come over here. We'll protect you." There was another angry outburst from the other people in Keith's apartment, but he continued. "My apartment is at 356 Banks Road. The Collingswood Apartments, number 5. We'll leave someone here to let you in. I'll go and see if I can catch them."

Relief overwhelmed Andrea. She hadn't realized how pleasant it would be simply to be believed by people who were what her long-dead mother would have called 'good.' "I know where that is. I'll come over now."

She hung up the phone, and walked quickly to the door. She opened it, stepped out into the cold, and closed it quietly behind her.

She half expected to see the Mays' car pulling into the driveway, but the street was empty. She trotted down the sidewalk as fast as her weight and the ice and snow would allow, got into her dented little Toyota Corolla, and drove off.

"Thank God," she said, over and over, as she pulled out onto the beautifully anonymous stream of traffic on the Colville highway. "I did it. I've escaped."

26

Eⁿᵗⁱʳᵉ Mᴇᴄʜᴀɴɪsᴍ Aᴄᴛɪᴠᴇ: Tʜɪʀᴅ Tᴜʀɴ

"Now ʟᴏᴏᴋ," said Keith.

"No, you look," said Stacy, giving her head an imperious shake. "I am not staying here sitting on my ass and letting you play the hero. If we know where they're bringing Marcia, I'm going."

"We shouldn't risk it," Keith said. "I should go alone."

"That sounds awfully noble," Stacy said.

"As I've said," Reverend Bradley said, "I'm the one who should go. And alone. The rest of you will be in too much danger."

"Now that's the least sensible thing I've heard all day," Stacy said.

"What makes logical sense," Keith said, "is that Reverend Bradley and Kelly stay here and wait for Andrea to show. I'm going after the Mays, and if we don't stop yapping endlessly, we'll miss our chance. Stacy, you can come or stay, as you please." He was already pulling on his jacket. "But I'd really rather you stay."

"Tough shit," Stacy said. "I'm going."

"I don't expect this to change your mind," Reverend Bradley said quietly, "but of all of us, you're the one who is in the most danger."

Keith frowned at the older man, and it looked, for a moment, as if he were going to argue with him, that a chink had formed in his certainty. Finally he said, "I can't in good conscience let you come along."

"And nothing I can say will stop you from doing this?"

Keith gestured with one hand. "You saw what happened when we tried to get the police to do something. It's up to us."

"Exactly," Reverend Bradley said. "That's it exactly. You saw what happened to those two police officers. You think anything with an earthly power could have done that? Anything that you can explain with your scientific rationalism?"

But the chink had closed. Keith answered that with nothing more than an exasperated look, and went to into his bedroom. He returned a moment later with a small handgun, which he slipped into his jacket pocket.

"I don't think that will help you," Reverend Bradley said.

"Don't start with me."

Stacy looked at him with a raised eyebrow. "You don't strike me as the licensed-to-carry type."

Keith's face relaxed, and he allowed himself a little smile. "I did my doctorate at UC Berkeley. My apartment was in a rough neighborhood. It was prudent then. In Colville, it hasn't been so necessary." His smile vanished. "Until now."

"Are you willing to use it?" Kelly asked.

"I'll defend myself, yes. I'll defend Stacy. I'm not going unarmed, that's for sure."

"Even with a gun, you are unarmed," Reverend Bradley said quietly, but no one seemed to hear him.

"Lock this door," Keith said, "and do not open it unless you're certain who's behind it." He turned and walked out. Stacy followed, buttoning her coat as she went.

The door closed.

Reverend Bradley said, to no one in particular, "I think I'll pray for them." He got up off the couch, and lowered himself into a kneeling position.

Kelly, sitting in an armchair, looked at him with curiosity. "Do you really believe that will help?"

"I really do."

"I wouldn't know who I was praying to," she said.

Reverend Bradley smiled at her, and realized it was the first time he had smiled that day. "Although there are many members of my church who would no doubt disagree, I doubt that matters to God. I've always thought that our insistence on finding a name for God probably gets in the way of our really knowing him. It's like a scientist who finds out the scientific name of a plant and thinks that means he knows the plant." His smile turned wistful. "Gardeners know better."

Kelly shook her head. "What if God doesn't exist?"

Reverend Bradley looked at her quizzically. "Don't you think the more important question is, 'what if He does?'"

WHEN REVEREND BRADLEY opened his eyes, his devotions finished for the time being, Kelly was asleep. He looked at her with pity for the frailty of youth. Weak where they thought themselves the strongest, and strongest in part of themselves they usually didn't even acknowledge.

He stood, massaging his knees into a grudging acceptance of the daily abuse he put them to, and walked around Keith's apartment. A five-tiered bookshelf stood near Keith's desk, lined with an eclectic variety of texts, novels, magazines, and notebooks. One title caught his eye: Richard Dawkins' *The God Delusion*. Smiling slightly, he pulled the book off the shelf, went back to the couch, and sat down to read.

KELLY WAS DREAMING AGAIN.

It was her dream of being in the clock shop. It started out the same way—her wandering in the shop, the ticking of the clocks, the darkened window, her panicked awareness that the clocks were about to strike the hour of midnight. She realized again that she wasn't alone in the room. But for the first time in her memory, she could see the person who was in the clock shop with her as more than a shadow. Standing near the door was a tall figure, wearing a coarse brown monk's robe with the hood pulled over the face. A rope belt was knotted around the waist.

As the mechanisms began to turn, activating the bells, chimes, and gongs, the monk-figure stretched out gnarled hands and reached toward the largest clock, a huge grand-father clock with an ornate painted face, and a grand, heavy pendulum swinging on the end of a wooden rod. It had a giant bronze key still sticking in the keyhole below the clock's face, large enough that it would have taken two hands to turn it.

And the monk did just that. He clasped the key as the gong began to sound.

Kelly clapped her hands over her ears. But she watched the monk, whose body was shuddering as the clocks struck the hour, each of the twelve strokes making the man's arms vibrate like a plucked guitar string. But somehow, his hands were sending the vibrations back into the clock's inner workings, reflecting the sound back to its source.

"You're the one who destroys them!" she shouted out, as the clock's front shattered, and the cascade of wheels, gears, springs, and fragments of wood and bronze and glass exploded into the air.

Kelly straightened up in the chair with a gasp. It was dark out. Reverend Bradley had just turned on the television, and he looked over at her apologetically.

"Sorry," he said. "I didn't mean to wake you."

"You didn't," said Kelly, willing her heart to slow down and her sense of panic to dissipate—a skill she'd learned from years of having bad dreams. "How long was I asleep?"

"About two hours."

"Have they returned?"

Reverend Bradley looked sorrowful. "No," he said. "No word at all."

Then Kelly looked past Reverend Bradley at the television screen, and her eyes widened. "Turn it up," she said. "Look."

Reverend Bradley complied, and the voice of Fay Kalivoda rose to audibility.

"... two hours ago. There has been some speculation that it was the result of a strategically placed bomb," she said. Fay was standing in front of an ill-defined scene of searchlights, broken blocks of masonry, and official-looking people stepping into and out of focus behind her. "Demolitions experts are on the scene, already trying to ascertain the cause of the bridge's collapse. There are scattered reports from several people who witnessed it happen that immediately prior to the collapse, there was something from the clouds, some sort of atmospheric disturbance, that may have contributed to the bridge's failure."

The scene switched to Andy Weissner, the evening news anchor, who was wearing an impeccably tailored suit and an equally well-fitting frown, suitable for any tragic occasion.

"What sort of disturbance do these witnesses describe?"

It was back to Fay, and for a split second, Kelly thought she caught a slight wince in the reporter's expression, as if she'd said more, or something different, than she'd intended. She continued on smoothly, however. "It's important to keep in mind that these are the recollections of people who have just seen something emotionally over-whelming. But several independent witnesses describe a pattern of wind and clouds above the bridge right before it collapsed, which may point to some kind of atmospheric weather phenomenon having had a role. At this point, however, the experts aren't talking, and anything along those lines is pure speculation."

The anchor sounded just as glad to leave this aspect of the story behind. "Fay, can you tell us how many are confirmed dead?"

"Four confirmed, Andy," she said. "But there may be more found once the town gets cranes in here to remove some of the bigger blocks of roadway from the inlet."

Back to Andy. "Well, we'll pray that doesn't happen," he said. "Thank you, Fay."

"Thanks, Andy."

"That was Fay Kalivoda, at the scene of the collapse of the Carlisle Inlet Bridge. We'll bring you more on that story later. Now, we go to Albany, where Steve de Forest..."

Reverend Bradley turned the volume back down, his face ashen. "This," he said. "This was their doing."

Kelly frowned at him. "How do you know?"

"I know," he said. "Sometimes I simply know. The bridge was only built three years ago. How could it simply collapse like that?"

"The reporter. She said a bomb..."

"It wasn't a bomb."

"How can you be sure?"

"I'm sure."

Kelly looked out of the window, into the gloom. "If they could do this..." She faltered and fell silent.

"Yes," Reverend Bradley said. "It's up to us to stop them."

"Maybe Dr. Sparlin and Stacy..."

"Perhaps," Reverend Bradley said, but he didn't sound convinced.

"What if they don't come back?"

"Then, as I said," he replied, "it's up to us. We put our lives in God's hands every day. So we do it once again, and then we try to stop them."

27

E*ntire Mechanism Active: Fourth Turn*

A*NDREA* Y*ARBROUGH WAS STUCK* in traffic.

Upon leaving the Mays' house, and realizing that she had successfully avoided getting caught, her mood had been buoyant. Turning the corner out of the Mays' neighborhood onto Grant Street, her heart bounded in a sense of exhilaration unlike anything she had ever known. The approval of one's own conscience, especially in a situation which had put her at no small risk, was heady stuff.

Her exalted mood began to evaporate when she hit the first slowdown, about a mile east of where Fay Kalivoda and her cameraman had abandoned their car in the parking lot of Hennen's Ice Cream Store. She could hear the annoyed thoughts of other drivers around her, bits and pieces fading in and fading out, like someone scanning through radio stations.

"... now I'll be late for dinner..."

"... fucking trains... must be a fucking train... they always..."

"... wreck, must be a bad one, hope no one's..."

"... wonder if I can turn around and somehow find my way..."

It was the thoughts of the people coming the other way that upset her more. They were few, and within minutes, there were no more cars from that direction. But as those few passed her, she caught more disturbing words.

"... must have been a hell of a crash... heard the sound from a mile away..."

"... Jesus, I won't sleep tonight after this..."

And most frighteningly, the last woman who passed her, her face twisted with anguish: "... it could have been me, I shouldn't be alive..."

Andrea had planned to turn north on Route 12, go past Colville High School, turn on Cascade Avenue, and then climb in a sweeping curve toward Foxcroft, the wealthy north end of Colville that was the bedroom community for Colville College and the local hospital. Keith's apartment complex was just south of the actual village boundary of Foxcroft, on a hill overlooking Carlisle Lake.

Taking this route, however, was beginning to look impossible. Andrea was sitting on Grant Street, five cars back from the stoplight that would have let her onto Route 12. Both directions on Route 12 were at a dead stop. The stoplight plodded on through its changes, red, green, yellow, red, green, yellow, and no one moved.

Another person might have honked her horn, or gotten out and talked to the drivers, to see if she could get them to pull up slightly, turn around, and try to find another route.

It never occurred to her. People were thinking their thoughts, lost in their frustrations at late appointments, late dinners, and negligent traffic cops, and sat there, sat there as if nothing was odd about all this, as if this was simply another minor inconvenience in an otherwise normal day, as if there was no machine capable of channeling a power that, if it found her, would kill her as blithely as someone might kill a fly.

Andrea's fear spilled over into panic. She shut off the motor, and got out of her car.

There was a foot of dirty snow on the side of the road. She stumbled through it, filling her shoes with grimy ice. The person behind her saw her leave, and blew his horn, gesturing at her angrily, and mouthing words. Andrea didn't hear the words but heard his thoughts, *get back here you stupid bitch where are you going when the traffic starts moving your car will be in the way get back here...*

She looked around, frantically, trying to see where she could go that might be safe. The only buildings on Grant Street were low-rent duplexes, most of which looked as if they were either unoccupied or else no one was home. None had lights on. Even in this fairly questionable part of town, she might have knocked on a door, just to have someone, anyone, say, "Oh, come in, warm up, you can sit for a while." But in the fading light of late afternoon, the buildings looked like hollow shells, not only empty but probably haunted.

What a word that was. Haunted. It was a terrifying word. In those empty, dark windows, she saw shadows, only half-human, with lidless eyes, watching her, feeding on her panic. She knew there was nothing there—she could feel that there was nothing there—but it didn't quell her fear nor stop her from seeing the shadows. She shuffled down the sidewalk toward the corner of Grant and Route 12, and turned the corner and began to walk north.

How far was it to Keith's apartment? Maybe four, five miles? She wasn't sure, but it couldn't be more than that. Even accounting for her weight and the hill that faced her, it would take her no more than a couple of hours to get there. Then she'd be safe. When she realized that not only were Keith and Stacy at the apartment, but Reverend Bradley was, too, her relief had been instantaneous and overwhelming. She knew from hearing Helene May talk that Reverend Bradley was the only individual that was able to stand up to the power the Mays had called up, although she didn't understand why. She had wondered if it was because he was a Christian, but somehow that didn't seem right. She herself was a fairly regular church attender, and considered herself a believer, but the power that had flashed outward from the Mechanism certainly hadn't hesitated to sweep through her. So it must be something else. Anyway, the simple fact of Bradley's presence would be a protection. Once there, she planned to stay at his side like a well-trained puppy. But first, she had to get there.

Walking appeared to be the only choice. So she walked.

Three-quarters of a mile later, chilled to the bone and nearly worn out, she turned the corner onto Cascade. By this time the traffic had begun to move. Slowly, but steadily, the jam was breaking up, but it seemed to be because people were abandoning their idea of staying on Route 12 and were veering off onto other paths. She squinted into the distance. She was still hearing bits and pieces of people's thoughts, about bridges smashed to bits, people dying, people injured. It honestly never occurred to her that it was anything more than a serious accident, perhaps one involving several cars, like the ones the news announcers always called "multi-car pile-ups on the Interstate." She sensed that the power in the Mays' machine was huge, and malevolent. If asked, she would have certainly agreed that it was capable of a calamity like this.

But that explanation never entered her mind.

She turned on Cascade Avenue, past Arcangeli's Italian Restaurant, and down the sidewalk in front of increasingly nice and well-kept houses. It occurred to her she could stop, ask for help, especially now that she was in a more congenial neighborhood, but she didn't, exhausted and cold though she was. The idea of Keith Sparlin's apartment, and the protection of Reverend Bradley's presence, was magnetic. She knew that if she stopped, even if she was in someone's house, she was vulnerable.

After all, she thought, *they're planning on using the Mechanism to kill Stephen. I've got to keep going or they'll get me, they'll kill me too. They'll know what I've done, and they'll eliminate me. Wasn't that the word they'd used?*

She shuddered and walked a little faster.

Cascade Avenue went east for five blocks, and then crossed Cascade Creek on a long bridge with a low rail. Cascade Creek had been named for its series of waterfalls, the first ones on the Colville College campus, and several more in the city of Colville itself—its scenic gorge had been photographed countless times. Andrea, never an outdoorsy type, had seen it before, but always from a car's window.

She walked onto the bridge, and looked over the railing. The near side had a shallow drop, no more than ten vertical feet and perhaps twenty wide, but beyond that shelf of snow-covered rock there was a second plunge of sixty feet to the floor of the gorge and the frozen surface of the creek itself.

Andrea didn't like heights. She looked behind her, at the lit windows with their Christmas decorations, looked at the bridge ahead, and then told herself that she needed to keep going.

"The people in those houses can't protect you," she said aloud, her breath fogging in the still cold air. "Bradley can."

She walked a little further, out over the part of the span that arched across the gorge.

And that was when she felt the Mechanism reawaken.

They had somehow gotten the machine restarted. They had tapped into that source of energy, somehow brought that evil power back to wakefulness...

... and merciful heavens no, it was aware of her.

Its fingers reached out and touched her, like a brush of a feather across her cheek. She stopped, her heart pounding, clutching the bridge railing. It touched her again, inquisitive, like a little child playing with an insect that it's about to dismember.

She felt its amusement, its utter lack of empathy for her fear. And she knew that it recognized her intent, that she was even now seeking to betray it to its enemies.

That was when she realized something—it wasn't the Mechanism by itself. What she was feeling was Helene May. Helene was acting through the Mechanism, that was certain, but the malign intelligence that was even now reaching toward her was not the product of gears and wheels and pins. It came from a human being. The Mechanism had amplified that awareness, expanded it beyond what anyone could imagine. But behind the force that was now toying with her was not the cold metal wheels of a machine, but the harmless, grandmotherly face of Helene May.

Andrea took one step forward.

The gentle touch brushed past her again, then with horrifying suddenness it wrapped around her, twisted between her legs, surrounded her. Its pull was inexorable, and she knew she was going to be drawn over the side. Her breath was coming in thin, whistling gasps, but she couldn't articulate a word, couldn't scream for help. She flailed her arms, trying to grab for the railing, and missed by inches—not that it probably would have done her any good had she caught it.

She was swept over the edge, held out at an impossible angle, only her toes touching the sidewalk. Anyone who saw her would have wondered how she was doing it, somehow leaning out over the precipice, balanced like the world's fattest gymnast. Andrea was making terrified, animal noises, looking down at the frozen creek bed, sixty feet below her.

She heard Helene May's soft, amused voice, just behind her left ear... "... goodbye, Andrea..." and the force holding her let go. Now she did scream, her body flipping up over the railing, then hurtling downward into the snowy gorge.

Marion Mason, a seventy-year-old widow who owned the house nearest to the gorge, heard Andrea scream, and was out on the bridge in thirty seconds. She couldn't see very well, but was fit and healthy could still hear as clearly as she did when she was twenty. She peered down into the gorge, looking this way and that, but in the fading light she couldn't see to the bottom. From the way the footprints ended, and the spot where snow was scraped off the railing, she was sure someone had gone over the edge. Her mouth set in a grim line, she trotted off back to her house to call the police.

As she reached the end of the bridge, something stroked her cheek. It was like being brushed by a cat's tail. It circled her face, grazed her neck, and then slipped upward into the evening sky.

As the sensation disappeared, she was certain that for a moment she heard the sound of laughter.

28

E*NTIRE MECHANISM ACTIVE: FIFTH TURN*

FAY'S EYES kept returning to the bit of the car she could see, poking out from underneath the fallen block of masonry on the far side of the inlet.

A fist. A piece of cloud came down... it looked like a huge fist.

She looked around her. Ambulances had finally arrived. The tall young man with the cut on his forehead had been taken away, and two or three others with injuries varying from bumps and bruises to shock were attended to. People who had cars still in driving condition were escorted by police the wrong way down Route 12, until they could turn off onto a side street and find their way home.

Emergency crews were still working, now by artificial light, to remove wrecked cars. The car in the water still sat there, mostly submerged, its outline ghostly in the fading light.

As she talked to more people who had witnessed the bridge collapse, her sense of unease about the cause deepened. Her first thought—that it had been a bomb of some kind—didn't fit what people had seen, nor what the scene looked like afterwards. There was little debris on the land on either side of the inlet. The pieces of concrete looked like they had fallen straight down, the steel rebar and I-beams sheared off as cleanly as if they had been cut with a knife. Some of the witnesses, mainly ones who hadn't seen the cloud curl up and punch the bridge into the cold waters of the inlet, had suggested that it had been an earthquake. This made sense given how the nearby cars had been shaken and tossed around, but if it was an earthquake big enough to knock down the bridge, why hadn't it flattened the entire city of Colville?

Josh, the cameraman, was becoming increasingly restless as Fay went from person to person, trying to find someone who could clear up what had happened.

"Look," he said, his exasperation coming through loud and clear, "you've already talked to everyone who saw it happen. You talked to some of them twice. I should have been heading home an hour ago. I got a date tonight if you care."

"I don't," said Fay, in a distracted way, and walked toward some workers who were winching one of the cars out of the ditch.

"Fuck you, Kalivoda," he called after her. "What can those guys tell you that you haven't already heard?"

By the time Fay gave her live report for the five o'clock news, all of the witnesses and most of the workers had gone home, and Fay had no better answers regarding what had caused the bridge to fall than she had when she first arrived. Even the police were baffled. Once the report was completed, even she had to admit that there was no further reason to stay there.

"Thank god," Josh said with bitter emphasis, and they began the hike to the car.

Back in the studio, Andy Weissner, who had anchored the news that night, greeted her with a scowl.

"Fay, what the hell was that stuff about something coming out of the clouds?"

Joe McGill, the newsman who had the desk next to Fay's, chuckled. "UFOs," he said. "Aliens. Call Giorgio Tsoukalos."

Fay set down her purse and jacket. "All I said was what the witnesses told me," she said, not meeting Weissner's eyes. "Isn't that why they call it 'reporting'?"

McGill snickered again, but Weissner froze him with a glare. McGill began to flip through the papers he was holding with exaggerated attention.

"Look," Weissner said. "It's hard enough to do a story when we don't know the details. I realize that you've got to say more than 'the bridge fell down,' but throwing in wild speculation means that every End Times fruitcake in upstate New York will be calling in with signs that the apocalypse is upon us. Reporting doesn't mean quoting what every wacko happens to say."

"They weren't wackos," Fay said. "I'm not talking about one or two shell-shocked drunks. These were normal, intelligent people, who saw something weird happen."

Weissner rolled his eyes upward. "Normal, intelligent people don't see things coming out of clouds and knocking down bridges," he said. "Maybe these people were in shock. Maybe they hit their head on the windshield of their car. Maybe they were wackos in disguise. I dunno. But don't start talking supernatural crap on live air. Not while I'm anchoring."

He turned on his heel and strode away.

McGill looked at her sidelong, as the door swung shut behind Weissner. "You really shouldn't piss him off, you know. Andy and Mrs. Vanlandingham are in bed together. Along with Dean McManus and one or two others."

Fay wrinkled up her nose. "Now there's a mental picture I didn't need."

"Andy says a good word about you in Mrs. V.'s ear, your game piece moves forward. Andy hints you're unstable or unreliable, and you're back to go, honey. Do not collect two hundred dollars."

Fay sighed. "It's 'go to jail, go directly to jail' not 'back to go.' And I'm not your honey."

McGill shook his head. "You don't know good advice when you hear it."

Suddenly Fay grabbed her purse and jacket from her desk. "Okay, fine, Joe," she said. "When I need advice on whose ass to kiss, I know who to ask."

She walked out of the office.

ON THE WAY to her car, she tried to maintain her feeling of self-righteousness, but it began to leak away almost immediately, and by the time she pulled out onto Morris Street her anger had given way to a feeling of profound foolishness. Joe had been right. She had embarrassed herself on live TV, in front of the news anchor, and likely in front of her boss, who had not missed the five o'clock news in twelve years. Joe, for all of his chauvinistic sneer, had called it correctly. She had set her game piece back to the beginning. If what she wanted was to succeed in this career—to become the Next Great Investigative News Reporter—she hadn't done herself any favors that day.

FORTUNATELY, getting from the station office to her apartment didn't require her to take Route 12, and she pulled into her parking space just after 7:30. She unlocked her door, and walked into her darkened apartment, tossed her coat and purse onto the couch. Her cat padded silently out of her bedroom as she switched on the light, rubbed against her leg, and meowed piteously.

"Just a minute," she said. "Give me a chance to take my shoes off, already."

The cat looked at her, yellow eyes narrowing as if considering whether her request was reasonable.

She pulled off her shoes, briefly massaged each foot, and walked into the kitchen.

While she was retrieving the bag of kitty chow from the kitchen cabinet, the phone rang.

Fay sighed heavily and set down the bag of cat food, eliciting another pathetic meow from the cat, who was watching her every motion and knew what it meant when the bag was set aside before the chow was dispensed. Fay picked up the receiver.

"Hello?"

"Is this Fay Kalivoda?"

"Speaking."

"Are you the woman who did the report on the Inlet Bridge?"

Fay closed her eyes. Great. Andy had been right, and the wackos were coming out of the woodwork. "Yes, it is."

"I have some information that might be of interest to you."

"Go ahead."

"I know who is responsible for the bridge collapse. It's a group of people. Or rather, a power that is acting through them."

"What on earth does that mean?"

There was a pause. Fay thought she could hear someone crying in the background, a long, low, despairing sound. "It means that it's up to a few people to try and stop him. We don't have much time, and we need help. It seemed from your news report that you witnessed, or saw people who witnessed, what happened today and that you might be in a position to help us."

"How could I help?" Fay said. "Even assuming you're right."

"You're a reporter. You can warn people. Let people in power know what is happening."

Fay sighed. "I'm not in much of a position to do that at the moment."

"Why not?"

"Look," Fay said. "My boss is mad at me, everyone's mad at me, and I have no reason to believe that you have any better idea than I do about what happened today."

"I assure you that I do."

"Who is this?"

There was a pause. "My name is Morris Bradley. And I can tell you that if you knew what I know, you would do everything in your power to help us."

She shivered slightly. "What do you know?"

"The people who did this are named Helene and Stanford May. They are willing to kill innocent people to accomplish their ends. And what the Mechanism they are using has called up is something that some of us would call a demon."

"Like, the devil?" Fay felt incredulity rising in her, but something in the man's voice made him impossible to dismiss entirely.

"What name you give it is unimportant. But you talked to people who witnessed what it can do."

Fay hesitated for a moment, and then said, "Yes. Yes, I did."

"Then you understand."

"No," Fay said and rubbed her hand over her eyes. "No, I'm not sure I understand at all. Can you… can you give me more details, here?"

Bradley hesitated. "I could. But you need to realize something. We are running out of time. We—the people who know about this—are a very small number of quite ordinary people. It is entirely possible that we may fail to stop the Mays and their allies. If we do, we need someone who is willing to make what we have found out public. To warn people, and to give someone else a chance to defeat them."

Fay didn't answer for a moment. Competing thoughts were rushing through her mind: *Don't get involved. If you throw your lot in with these crazies, you'll lose your job. There can't be anything to this, right? He's got to be a loony, one of the End Times wackos that Andy Weissner was talking about. But… but…*

A kid saw a piece of the cloud, shaped like a fist, come down from the sky and destroy the bridge.

Then one final thought sealed the deal: she'd been waiting for her entire career for a really big story, for a chance to make a difference. If she turned her back on this now, she'd be back to reporting on house fires and blizzards, kissing Mrs. Vanlandingham's ass, not to mention the equally unappealing posteriors of people like Andy Weissner. Is that what she wanted?

And Fay said, "Okay, fine. I'm in." But simultaneously, a voice inside her head shouted, *What are you doing? What this man is telling you is insane!*

But the relief was clear in Reverend Bradley's voice. "I will tell you what I know. The Mays are trying to rebuild something called the Antikythera Mechanism. Archaeologists found it in a shipwreck from over two millennia ago, and they thought it was some kind of timekeeping device. But it's more than that. It's a channel for psychic power. It draws energy from a person, and then strengthens it, amplifies it, and can allow others to accomplish things through it."

"Things? What sorts of things?"

"You saw one of them."

"The bridge collapse…" Fay stopped, her mouth hanging open a little.

"That was done through the power of the Mechanism. They have found a woman whom they can use as a sort of battery to activate the Mechanism. They kidnapped her and are holding her hostage. I fear that they will use her until her store of energy is gone."

"Kill her, in other words."

"Yes. They have killed others, including two archaeologists who were doing research to find out what the Mechanism could do."

Fay swallowed. "What are they trying to accomplish?"

"That's not completely clear. My… um, my informant, he told me that he thought that Mr. May wants power, and Mrs. May wants personal immortality."

"The Mechanism could do that?"

"You see that I have no way of answering that for certain. But yes, I think that given what we have already seen it do, it could."

"I'm supposed to get people to believe this?"

"Doing so might well save many lives."

"Like I said, my credibility is not at an all-time high right now. And this isn't exactly the most believable story I've ever heard."

"Do you know of another one that fits what you saw today? And what people told you they saw?"

Fay didn't answer. Her confidence was leaking away like water from a cracked dish. She felt a sudden desperation to get off the phone. Play it safe. Find a way to get this man, with his quiet, patient voice, to hang up and never call her again.

"This power is not done with killing," Reverend Bradley said. "It must be stopped. But first, people must be warned. No one of us will be believed as you will, as a news reporter would be."

"I don't think I believe you myself."

"Then how do you explain what you, and the people you interviewed, saw at the bridge?"

"I don't know."

The man paused, then seemed to make a decision to take a different tack. "Miss Kalivoda, why did you become a reporter?"

Fay scowled. "I know where you're going with this. Commitment to the truth, making sure people are informed, and all that sort of thing."

"Am I wrong?"

That point hit home. But the resistance in her was rising fast. "Look, I can't do what you want me to do. I might be able to help you myself, but there's no way I can go on tele-vision and say what you want me to say."

Bradley did not respond for a moment. "Can't? Or won't?"

"Both." Fay had the sense of a door closing, of an oppor-tunity that she was turning her back on, an opportunity that might well be the most important thing she'd ever done. But then she thought about going up to Andy Weissner and saying, "I need to get on the air and warn people about a magic machine that sucks out people's souls and destroys bridges!" Her face reddened at the very thought.

She couldn't do that. There was no way in the world.

Bradley, too, seemed to realize that some watershed moment had passed, perhaps beyond recall. He simply said, "Very well." His voice sounded sad, but there was no trace of recrimination or anger in it. In the background, the disconsolate crying continued. "We all do what we are able."

"Yes," Fay said. "We do."

And she hung up the phone.

29

E CLIPSE POINTER DISENGAGED FROM MAIN DRIVE WHEEL

Drive. Drive as fast as you dare. But be careful. The roads are snowy, and there'll be cops out. No sense driving so fast that you get pulled over, or end up hitting black ice and plowing your car into a telephone pole.

Stephen Calhoun held onto the steering wheel of his battered brown Toyota Yaris, his knuckles white, his arms rigid. The radio was on low, playing some angry-sounding music, maybe Linkin Park or the Stone Temple Pilots, but Stephen barely registered it. It intruded on his consciousness little more than the intermittent *thwap-thwap* of the windshield wipers, pushing away the snow and the dirty spray flung up from the highway surface by passing cars.

His mind kept up a continual monologue of instructions to himself.

Keep going. You can drive all night. Get somewhere where they can't find you. Even if they know you told Bradley about what they were doing, they can't hurt you if they don't know where you are. And maybe Bradley will be able to stop them, destroy the Mechanism, and then you'll be safe. You can come home, back to your apartment and your job, and you won't have to be afraid of Louise or the Mays ever again.

He crossed into the state of Pennsylvania at a little before seven o'clock. It was pitch dark, with a frigid wind blowing swirls of snowflakes across the road, pushing drifts into the southbound lane, drifts he sometimes didn't see until right before he hit them. He'd had a couple of near misses with losing control of his car, but so far had made good time heading south, aiming toward…

… where? He had no idea. Anywhere. He wanted to be somewhere that the Mays couldn't see, somewhere that Andrea couldn't spy on him and rat him out, somewhere safe. And warm. He wondered idly how long it'd take before he'd notice it warming up. Pennsylvania, so far, looked just as cold as New York was. And the terrain was becoming hilly, the countryside wrinkling up into folded hills covered by rank upon rank of leafless trees. The traffic, which had picked up as he neared the city of Binghamton, was now down to a car or two passing him every ten minutes or so. In between, there was nothing but the snow, the wind, the sound of the windshield wipers, the radio (the station itself was breaking up into static), and his own thoughts.

He'd done what he could. The only thing he could do. He couldn't stop them, not him by himself. Louise had been waiting for an excuse to kill him. If she thought he'd betrayed them, she'd have done it. Better to leave it all in Reverend Bradley's hands, and then get the hell out. Because the Mays couldn't really win, could they? They couldn't really take over the world, or whatever it was they were trying to do. Someone would stop them. If not Reverend Bradley, then… someone.

When Stephen was approached by Mr. May, that spring, he'd been at the end of his tether. Allying himself with them felt like a game at first. It made him feel tough, edgy, fierce, not a down-and-out college dropout with a history of DWI, no job prospects, no life, and no future. What did it matter if he killed a few people, if it got him in with a group that could see to it that he was taken care of, that would look after him?

That would make certain that no one, ever, thought of him as a nobody again?

It had all been simple enough. His first target had been a pompous professor in London. Mr. May's comment was that it was "regrettable" that Dr. Soileau had squandered his knowledge in drink and womanizing and loose talk, but he was getting out of hand and had to be silenced. That was the way Mr. May always talked. It was never "killed" or "murdered." It was "silenced" or "eliminated" or "liqui-dated." All of which made Stephen's job feel more excit-ing, not simply the actions of a common thug.

"Silencing" Dr. Soileau had been child's play. Stephen's heart was pounding in his ribcage so hard he thought it must be audible, but the guy was dead drunk in his office, lolling in his desk chair, his shirt untucked and partly open. He barely looked up as Stephen walked in, and frowned at him in complete incomprehension as Stephen picked up a heavy marble statue in one gloved hand. It was a bust of some longhaired dude Stephen didn't offhand recognize. Soileau slurred, "Hey, who're you?" just as Stephen brought the weight down on his head.

The impact made a sickening crunch, and Soileau flopped sideways in his chair and came to rest on his back, his fat legs sticking up in the air. He was dead before he landed, Stephen knew that. The dent in the top of his head was considerable, and there was a lot of blood. Stephen tossed the bloodied marble statue to the floor, and calmly, unhurriedly walked out of the building without anyone seeing him.

The whole incident had taken less than five minutes.

He'd had a moment of fear, though, when the morning after the murder he saw that Mrs. May was keeping an eye on him. Never one to leave anything to chance, that woman, and suspicious as hell that he'd cut and run. She'd not been watching only him, though. She made a point of colliding with that other archaeologist—Lise Verhoeven— while getting on to the Tube. Then she put on a big show of being an innocent fluffy-minded old woman. Verhoeven was evidently taken in by her ruse and ignored her completely.

He, on the other hand, had been completely unnerved to know that the Mays didn't trust him. Worse, Verhoeven herself showed every evidence of being onto him. She certainly had a suspicious look on her face when she glanced in his direction. Hoping to deflect her attention, he chatted up the cute redhead in the seat next to his, and fortunately the woman didn't just give him the hairy eyeball and look away. Sexier than hell, and that British accent was a knockout. Too bad he didn't have time to ask her if she'd like to have a drink later.

Business before pleasure.

And it had worked. When he looked over, Verhoeven was watching someone else, a nerdy-looking professor type wearing clothes that went out of style in 1950. At least that was one less thing to worry about. After all, what did Verhoeven have to be suspicious of? He wasn't stalking *her* with murder in mind.

Yet.

Those orders came later, delivered by cellphone five days after Dr. Soileau's murder. He was told that Lise Verhoeven, the pretty young archeologist he had seen on the Tube, had also become "troublesome." He was to leave for Antwerp immediately to deal with the threat. At first, Mr. May said, they'd thought that they could ignore Dr. Verhoeven, but she had put some pressure on "one of our allies" to provide more information on details of the Antikythera Mechanism that Soileau had taken to his grave. This nameless "ally" was of the opinion that Dr. Verhoeven was getting too close to discovering their plans, and spoiling the whole thing.

"Regrettably," Mr. May said, "Dr. Verhoeven will also have to be eliminated. Watch her movements, Stephen, and use whatever means seems prudent to make sure she is taken care of."

So Stephen had flown to Belgium.

It took him almost a week to formulate a plan. During that time he followed her, watched her every move. He found himself having some reluctance to kill her, or certainly more than had troubled him about murdering Soileau. Soileau had been a boor and a jackass, but Lise Verhoeven was young, cultured, and beautiful. He pictured himself striking her in the head with a heavy object, as he had Soileau, thought about her large gray eyes staring up at him in terror as he brought his arm downward and crushed her skull, and the unpleasant thought occurred to him: *I can't do this. It's wrong.*

But he couldn't very well tell Mr. May that. If Mr. May had still pretended that he was concerned about Stephen's well-being, Mrs. May had been less equivocal. If Stephen disobeyed orders, she said, it was a matter of a simple phone call to the appropriate authorities, and he would be arrested for Armand Soileau's murder. He hadn't been as careful as he'd thought not to leave any traces, Mrs. May implied. That evidence, she said, would be kept in safe-keeping, and would not "cause trouble"—as long as Stephen was a good soldier and followed orders.

He discovered the means for killing Lise Verhoeven quite by accident. He was tailing her one morning as she went to a little café for lunch, something she did almost every day. On her way back to the University, she walked past an ancient stone-fronted building that housed artists' studios. Lise seemed that day to realize she was being followed— she turned suddenly, looking right at him. He ducked into a doorway, but not before he saw Lise turn and walk toward him, a determined look on her face.

He panicked, and ran into the building and up the creaking staircase. He passed three landings with signs written in Dutch, a language of which he understood noth-ing. He ended on the third floor, opening a door from the top landing into a long hallway, wood-floored, with glass-fronted doors and a smell of dust and mildew and old books.

Would she follow him up this far? She certainly had looked like she knew what he was up to, and was ready to put a stop to it. He reached the end of the hall, and saw a narrow doorway, slightly ajar, with a sign that said: "Dak Toegang" and an up arrow.

He bolted through the door, shutting it behind him, and ran up the stairs. It turned once, twice, and ended in a doorway that opened out onto the roof.

He shut the door behind him and walked out onto the flat, slate-covered roof. After getting his bearings, he went to the edge that overlooked the street and looked down. In the distance, nearly two blocks away, he saw Lise Verhoeven's back. As he watched, she gave a curious glance behind her and then kept walking.

He laughed aloud. She hadn't followed him after all! He leaned on the edge of the low wall that surrounded the roof's edge, and then jerked back as a piece of the masonry shifted under his hand.

That was when the idea came to him.

But how long would it be before Dr. Verhoeven passed this way again? She liked the little café, he knew that, but to walk right in front of the old building with the rotten façade—that might take a while.

Fate, however, took a hand. It was after only three days of staking out the roof, sitting in the early August sunshine and watching for her to be in the right place before he got his chance.

He'd only get one, he knew that. A near miss and she'd be spooked, and his task would become much harder to accomplish. The timing would have to be perfect.

He spotted her that afternoon, walking out of the café with her briefcase, as neat and elegant as always. His heart hammered with the same pulse-pounding exhilaration he'd felt before murdering Soileau as he pried loose a piece of the stonework, a chunk that probably weighed a good ten kilograms. He watched her approach. Waiting… waiting…

He pushed the piece of rock over the edge.

She heard the grating noise of its coming dislodged and looked upwards. She didn't recognize what it was until it was too late. The stone struck her full in the face.

Lise Verhoeven was killed instantly.

Stephen realized that once people saw what had happened, the police would be up on the roof post-haste. At that point, he could be anywhere but there. He ran to the door, descended the stairs as quietly as he could, and had made it down one additional flight of stairs before he heard the sound of footsteps coming up toward him.

He sprinted down the second-floor hallway and ducked into a men's room, which was, fortunately, unoccupied. Afterwards, he simply waited for forty-five minutes or so, at which point the hue and cry had subsided. Then he walked down the stairs and out of the building, as nonchalantly as he could manage.

There was still a scarlet stain on the sidewalk, but Dr. Verhoeven's body had already been removed. The police standing nearby didn't even glance his way.

After that, Stephen returned to the United States. He thought that there'd be more opportunity for international travel, more opportunity to participate in Liquidating and Silencing and Eliminating, a vocation that he thought he could very quickly find himself enjoying. But back in New York, he'd found that the only thing he was expected to do was to stay quiet and out of the way. The Mays were standoffish with him. To them, he was simply a tool to be used at need, and to be set aside until then. Louise, on the other hand, bullied him directly, reminding him every chance she had that he needed to shut up and let his betters take care of things, or he'd find himself up on murder charges in not one, but two different countries.

But it wasn't until October that he began to realize that murder charges were the least of his worries.

He was privy to conversations, and overheard others, and he gradually came to realize two things: that what the Mays were trying to do was potentially horrific; and that once his usefulness to them was over, they would have no issues whatsoever with killing him. Stephen had overheard a conversation between Louise and the Mays in which his name had come up, together with phrases like "the regrettable lack of imagination and intelligence" and "not really the type we can trust long-term" and "sooner or later, there will be some culling that will be necessary." This had precipitated his flight to Morris Bradley's church. Why he had stopped there, he wasn't certain. The place had simply felt like a sanctuary.

But it hadn't worked out that way. Having nowhere else to go, he'd returned to Colville, and forthwith been recaptured by Louise, who'd told him that if it were her, she'd kill him right there, but the Mays told her not to because they still thought he'd have some use. Terrified, he'd played along for another month until the opportunity arose to talk to Bradley again. The Mays were afraid of Bradley, he

knew that and that by itself must mean something, something good.

So he'd called Morris Bradley, and spilled his guts to him.

The feeling of relief had been extremely short-lived. After
his betrayal, Stephen had panicked. He returned to his
apartment, but after a half-hour of fretting and watching
out of the window, he realized that it was only a matter of
time before Louise came to get him. And then he'd die.
That they wouldn't realize what he'd done was a possibility
that never even occurred to him. Of course, they'd know.
The Mays always knew.

So he fled. He grabbed a few of his belongings, ran down
the stairs leaving his apartment unlocked behind him,
jumped into his car, and drove off. He headed south, out
of New York. His ultimate destination was only a vague
concern. Maybe he'd go down to Georgia, to the coast.
He'd heard Savannah was nice. It certainly would be
warmer than this miserable climate.

The snow was falling harder now. The road rose, fell, rose
again, always climbing higher than it descended. Long
drifts intersected the lane, like white fingers reaching in
toward him out of the darkness.

When the first tentative tremor occurred, he barely noticed
it. It felt as if he had struck a pothole — certainly a possibility on this highway out in the deep country. The car
jolted, skidded a little on the slick pavement, and then once
again, he was moving smoothly forward into the icy
darkness.

The second one, however, was stronger, and he knew at
that moment that he was not going to escape, that his
thoughts of the South and Savannah and maybe one day

coming home to Colville were not going to be realized. This was Helene May he felt, her hand stretching out toward him. His heart gave a painful little flutter of fear, but he kept driving. There was nothing else he could do.

The third one bounced the entire back end of the car up off the surface of the highway, and for a moment, Stephen thought he was going to lose control, end his life in a snow-covered ditch. The car stuttered as if it had suddenly lurched forward into an empty pocket of space. The sensation was over before he was aware of it, but he braced for the next one, his face tightening, mouth twisting into a grimace of terror.

He saw this one coming. The lines of space around him twisted. The road warped, folding like a sheet snapping in a high wind. The bare trees on both sides of the highway reared high in the air, without disturbing the snow layered on the branches and trunks. The air pressure dropped, and his ears popped.

Then the bent fabric of the universe that surrounded him sprang closed, falling onto Stephen Calhoun's car like a tripped mousetrap.

He had time for only a single stifled yell, cut off short.

Nearby, a deer jumped out from the underbrush and sprinted away, its white tail erect. After that, there was silence. The snow resumed blowing on a north wind, spreading drifts across a now-empty highway in central Pennsylvania.

30

E*ntire Mechanism Active: Sixth Turn*

Conversation in the car between Stacy and Keith was light, almost offhand. Keith was driving, his right hand on the wheel, his left elbow resting on the window frame of the door. The traffic was terrible. At first, it was going at a crawl, but as soon as they passed where Route 7 and Route 12 crossed, things smoothed out. There was some sort of mess over west on Route 12, but given the icy weather of the previous few days, an accident wasn't unlikely. Keith had a passing thought, *Didn't those cops get a call about a big accident, right before they left?* But their upcoming confrontation with the Mays pushed any consideration of traffic problems out his mind.

"How long have you and Marcia known each other?" Keith asked.

Stacy laughed. "Literally forever. We were crib mates. My parents and Marcia's used to leave us with the same babysitter when they'd go golfing. That we both ended up in Colville, though, is a coincidence. We were born and raised in Plainview, on Long Island. I came here to go to school, and Marsh married that asshole Jeff Gaines, who was born and raised here. So we reconnected a few years ago. We'd always kept in touch, though."

"You care about her a great deal," Keith said. It was not a question.

"Damn straight. She's the sister I never had. That's a cliché, but it's exactly true. I'd die for her."

Keith didn't respond.

Stacy smiled a little. "You're thinking right now, damn fool woman is gonna get her chance in about a half hour."

"I don't know," he said. "I honestly don't know what we're up against."

"Maybe you should have let Bradley come along."

Keith snorted. "An old man like that? If the Mays can do half of what Stephen Calhoun claims, they'd slice him to ribbons. If he didn't have a heart attack."

"I don't know," Stacy said. "I think there's more to Bradley than there seems."

"Nothing I've seen. I mean, he's a nice enough old guy, but nice won't do you any good with these people."

"I'm not talking about nice. I don't really know what I mean. I certainly don't mean religious. It's something deeper than that." Stacy shrugged. "Well, it's a moot point.

It's up to us." She turned toward him. "How do you know Kelly? Girlfriend?"

Keith shook his head. "No. Former student. I'm a professor at Colville College."

"You don't look old enough."

"Thanks. I am, actually." He grinned, a little ruefully. "I do have a girlfriend, though, who is probably wondering why I've been ignoring her for the last couple of days. She wouldn't believe it if I told her what I've gotten myself involved in."

"What's her name?" Stacy asked. "I mean... maybe you should let someone know who to contact. If... you know. If something happens." She turned away, looking out of the window at the box stores and strip malls of south Colville sliding past in a wash of multicolored signs.

"A little late now, as we're in this together," Keith said, his face turning suddenly serious. "But if something happens, her name is Linda Wheeler. She's in the phone book." He paused. "Who should I tell... who should I contact for you?" He sounded embarrassed.

"My brother Matt. Matt Weinstein. He still lives in Plainview."

"Okay."

Stacy smiled a little. "But nothing's gonna happen, right?"

"Right."

"Like my dad always said, I'd rather be an optimist who is wrong than a pessimist who is right."

"Words to live by." A green sign saying "Lamont 18 miles" loomed up in the darkness, as they left the city of Colville behind. "Well, here we go."

THE DIRECTIONS WERE IMPECCABLE. The roads were not. The weather had taken a nasty turn, with flying snow, and gusts of the wind that shook Keith's car as it jolted over ice-filled potholes, and eventually, stone-hard ruts in a dirt road.

They finally braked to a halt beside a rusted pole barn, where two cars already sat, their tops covered with new snow. The place had an eerie, surreal appearance, and for the first time, a flutter of misgiving rippled across his skin. Had he really done the right thing to tell Bradley not to come with them?

No. He forced his jitteriness back. Now was not the time to start being suggestible. Bradley was old, frail, and didn't know what he was doing. And in any case, if he'd really been inclined, he could have followed them in his own car. Instead, he was probably on his knees, praying right now.

For all the good that would do.

"Are you still okay with facing these people?" he said to Stacy. "They're probably psychopaths. We don't know how far they'll go to protect themselves."

"They want psycho, wait till they see me if I find out they hurt Marcia. I'll go so psycho on their asses that they won't know what hit them."

Keith laughed. "Okay, then," he said. "Into the breach."

They opened their doors. A frigid wind slapped them full on, scattering ice crystals over the seat of Keith's car. Stacy's scarf snapped behind her like a whip as they struggled their way against the gale toward the door of the pole barn.

Keith reached out a gloved hand and pulled the sliding door open.

In the room were five people. And Keith's first thought upon seeing them was, *This is who we were afraid of?*

Mrs. May was nearest to him, wearing her fur-lined jacket and absurd magenta hat. She looked every bit the frumpy retired professor's wife that she was, and about as threatening as the Fairy Godmother from *Cinderella*. Beside her was her husband, dressed in tweed and with his academic's slouch. There were two others standing, whom neither Stacy nor Keith recognized. A little to one side, in jeans and a heavy sweatshirt, was a rugged looking woman with a lined face and flyaway brown hair streaked with gray, who was watching the whole scene with weary, suspicious eyes. And a further away was a tall, elegant middle-aged man, wearing a jacket with a European cut, with curly black hair and small steel-rimmed glasses.

None of them looked like they'd stand a chance against Keith in a fistfight. And the idea that they were going to fight back with some kind of magic spell was patently ridiculous. Maybe this wasn't as hopeless as he'd thought.

"Welcome," Mrs. May said, holding her hands out toward them, palms upward. "We've been expecting you. Now that you see our creation, what do you think of it?" She gestured toward a rectangular structure behind them.

It looked like the innards of a giant clock. Well over six feet tall, it stood within a steel frame, but the workings were made of bronze. It wasn't moving, but stood at the ready, gears interlocked, pointers set, needing only a source of energy to make it go.

"Impressive," Keith said. "Some kind of fancy jack-in-the-box?"

"Oh, Mr. Sparlin," Mrs. May said, "when you see what jumps out of this, you'll be startled, I promise you."

But Stacy wasn't looking at the Mechanism. She noticed that there was a fifth person in the room, a woman who was lying on the floor beneath two cylindrical bronze handles that protruded from the front of the Mechanism, and who was barely visible in the gloom, and Stacy was staring at the prone figure, wide-eyed.

"Marcia?" Stacy said, in a strangled voice, and took a step forward.

Mrs. May held up one hand. "Stop," she said. "Stop where you are. It is uncertain whether we need Ms. Pacheco's assistance any longer, but it's premature to allow you to go to her."

"So, really, what is that machine?" Keith said. "Let's see it do its tricks."

"You're a scientist," Mr. May said. "You figure it out." The tall man with the glasses gave him a frosty smile.

"And where is dear Reverend Bradley?" Mrs. May said. "We were hoping that he would come along."

"I told him to stay home," Keith said.

Mrs. May pursed her lips. "Foolish of you," she said. "Although perhaps fortunate for him, and for our little enterprise. He might have been able to do something… something unfortunate, here. But you two?" She gave a tittering laugh.

The misgiving Keith had felt earlier rushed back into his consciousness. Had Bradley recognized something that he had missed?

"No," said Marcia, weakly, interrupting his thoughts. She was trying to struggle to her feet, and had pushed herself into a sitting position, but was unable to do more than to lean forward, the fingers of both hands pressing into the dusty ground. "Please. Don't hurt them."

Mrs. May smiled at Keith, her eyes glittering. "They should have minded their own business, then." She fixed Keith with a triumphant gaze. "How dare you break into my house. I said I'd deal with you, and I will."

Keith drew his gun on her. "Give it your best."

Mrs. May's eyebrows went up, and then, unexpectedly, she began laughing. "Oh, my, Mr. Sparlin," she said. "You do show some spunk. I honestly didn't expect this."

"Then release Marcia Pacheco, and we'll leave."

"My word. Stanford, dear, I'm so dreadfully intimidated. Whatever shall I do?" She turned back toward Keith. "Mr. Sparlin, have you ever killed someone with that nasty little gun you're pointing at me?"

"No," Keith said, and then added, "Not yet."

"So you've never murdered anyone."

Keith didn't respond. A cold like ice crystals formed in the middle of his chest. Stephen had been right. If evil existed, if it was a force with an external reality as Morris Bradley believed, then Helene May was its embodiment.

"If you haven't murdered anyone, you might want to be advised that I have," she said. "This evening I dealt with both Andrea Yarbrough and Stephen Calhoun." Her voice rose, and behind it was a sound like thunder. "Woe to thee that spoilest, and thou wast not spoiled; and dealest treacherously, and they dealt not treacherously with thee. When thou shalt cease to spoil, thou shalt be spoiled; and when thou shalt make an end to deal treacherously, they shall deal treacherously with thee."

"You had them killed?" Stacy said, her voice thin.

"Had them killed?" Mrs. May said. "Hardly. I did it myself. Which of the two of you would like to be next?"

Keith thought, *This is it. Stop them now, or not at all.* He tightened his finger on the trigger. But as he did so, the rugged-looking woman on the left, who had yet to speak a word, gave a little motion with one hand, like someone flicking a piece of lint away from a sleeve. His gun jerked out of his hand. It arced through the air and landed with a thud in the shadows.

Mrs. May laughed again, a wild, triumphant sound. Mr. May's expression was eager, and the other two onlookers were smirking. A boiling rage built inside Keith, a rage he hadn't felt since seeing a friend of his being pushed around and ridiculed in middle school.

Playground bullies. That's all the Mays were. Whether they could do magic didn't matter. They were playground bullies who had learned how to do it bigger and better.

And he launched himself at Mrs. May.

Stacy shrieked, "No!"

His upraised fists never landed. Mrs. May, still smiling, met his attack by reaching up and grabbing Keith's face with both hands. There was a horrible sizzling sound, like an electrical discharge, and Keith's body went rigid, his back arched, his fingers splayed out, his head thrown back.

His last thought was, *Dear god, Bradley was right… how could that be?*

Mrs. May's brow furrowed, just a little. She looked like a woman trying to understand something perplexing. A thin play of light, like distant lightning, danced across Keith's body. Then with a careless, casual motion, she tossed Keith away, and he flew through the air, struck a wall, and slid to the ground. He lay there, eyes open and sightless, staring up at the ceiling.

"No," cried Stacy again, and then Mrs. May turned toward her, smoke curling from her hands, and took a step forward.

"Stop!" cried Marcia. Her voice was still weak, but it cut through the cold air in the dusty pole barn. Mr. May and the other two looked over at her. She had stood, swaying slightly, but not wanting to touch the Mechanism for support.

"Don't hurt her," Marcia said, her voice catching in a sob. "I promise. I'll do anything you want. I won't fight you anymore. Just don't hurt her."

Mrs. May didn't respond. Her eyes had never left Stacy's, and her hands were still raised, curled into claws.

Mr. May raised one eyebrow. "After what she's seen..."

But Mrs. May dropped her arms to her side. "No," she said, and her voice had returned to its previous condescending tone. "Perhaps it's best, Stanford, dear. Let's let her go. She can warn Bradley what he's facing. And let them know their friend Keith is dead. It is only," she smiled a little, "fitting."

"Marcia..." Stacy began, looking past the Mays at her friend, who was still in shadow, a ghostly whitish radiance flowing from her.

"Go," Marcia said. "I'll be all right."

"If you hurt her..." Stacy said, looking right into Mrs. May's eyes.

"Oh, my dear," said Mrs. May, "it's not Marcia or I who is in danger of being hurt. Now, scat. I suggest you follow your friend's advice and go before we change our minds."

Stacy turned, and went back toward the door. She heard Marcia call after her, "Stacy… I'm sorry. I'm sorry I got you involved in this." But she didn't turn. If she had, she would have been compelled to act—attack the Mays, as Keith Sparlin had, and probably die as he had.

She went through the door, closing it behind her. She found suddenly that she was crying. She walked to Keith's car, but only then realized that the keys were in Keith's jacket pocket. She thought again about him lying crumpled on the dirt floor of the pole barn, thought about the gentle and humorous conversation they'd had, and she began to cry harder.

She couldn't go back in and ask for the keys. Would they let her go a second time? She couldn't risk it. Now, knowing what she knew, she had to get back to Reverend Bradley, warn him and the others, tell them what had happened to Keith.

She walked back up the dirt road, pulling her jacket around her, stumbling on the ice-filled ruts. The rags of clouds had gathered together into a shroud, and the road-side was obscured in the shadows. The snow was falling faster now, spinning snowflakes into her face, dusting her shoulders with ice crystals.

A half-hour later, chilled to the bone, she arrived back at the first paved road, the one that led to the village of Lamont. It was another twenty minutes before she saw headlights in the distance, heading back toward Highway 12, the way she needed to go. She walked a little further, considering what she should do, then finally decided to ignore the advice of her long-dead mother and try hitch-hiking. Despite Mrs. Weinstein's frequent horror stories about what happened to hitchhikers—it had been a partic-ular obsession with her—and notwithstanding her bedrag-gled appearance and tear-streaked face, she stuck her thumb out. The car slowed to a stop, and a friendly voice said, "Hey, you need some help?"

"Yes," Stacy said.

"Then get in. You could freeze to death on a night like tonight."

"I thought I was going to." She sat down and looked over at the man, who was a balding, heavy-set fellow of perhaps fifty, wearing a thick fur-lined coat and a knitted scarf. He didn't look dangerous, whatever Stacy's mother would have thought of him.

"Car trouble?" he asked, as she got settled in.

"Something like that."

"Where are you heading?"

She told him where Keith's apartment was, and he said, "Wow. That's only about a half-mile out of my way. I'm heading up toward Foxcroft. My son's girlfriend is in labor. The first grandkid, you know?"

"Congratulations. And thanks for the lift."

"I'm thrilled to be a grandpa. And it's no problem, I'll drop you off. They said the baby wasn't imminent, so it's not like I'll miss the big event by giving you a ride."

He was as good as his word, and best of all, he seemed to sense that Stacy wasn't in the mood for conversation. The half-hour ride progressed mostly in silence.

"Hope everything's okay," he said, as he let her off in the apartment parking lot.

"Me, too," Stacy said, as she got out. "Congrats on the new arrival. And thanks for the lift."

"Not a problem."

Stacy walked to the door of Keith's apartment and knocked. *I will not start bawling again*, she thought. *I will not start bawling again.* But by the time she heard Reverend Bradley's voice, and she was being let inside, she was already crying.

He looked at her with concern on his kindly face, but there was something about his expression that gave Stacy the impression that he already knew what she was going to say.

Kelly came up behind him, and watched her, mute, her eyes wide with horror.

"They... they killed Keith," Stacy said. "I couldn't stop them. I couldn't help Marcia, and now Keith is dead..." The rest of the story tumbled from her, and she described their drive to the pole barn, and the fight before the Mechanism, and the way Mrs. May had described her murder of Andrea Yarbrough and Stephen Calhoun.

Kelly began to sob. Reverend Bradley listened somberly.

"I should have stopped him," he said.

"I don't think you could have," Stacy said, wiping her face with the back of one hand. "He was determined."

"I should have tried harder. God forgive me my weakness, but I let that boy go to his death. Andrea, too. We could have warned her."

"Blaming yourself won't accomplish anything," Stacy said. "But can we do anything to stop them? You don't understand what they did."

Reverend Bradley straightened up. "Stephen told Keith that this Mechanism has been built once before, but that it was destroyed, sunk in the ocean."

"So?" Stacy said. "That was two millennia ago."

"That means it can be destroyed. We need to find out how."

"We don't have time!" Stacy said. "Who knows what they'll do?"

"Only God knows," said Reverend Bradley. "We need information so that we don't rush in headlong and do no more good than Keith."

Kelly looked up, her chest still hitching with sobs. "It's not fair that he died."

"No," Reverend Bradley said. "It's not. And we'll mourn him later. For now, we have to finish this. If we must die, we must die, but I'll not let his death be for nothing." He paused. "We should find out as much about what we're facing as we can, first. Perhaps that woman Kelly and I saw on television could tell us more about what happened today."

"The reporter, you mean?" Kelly said.

Reverend Bradley nodded. "Didn't you get the impression that she knew more than she was saying? That the anchorman cut her off?"

Kelly nodded. "Her name was Fay. Fay Kaliboda or Kalivoda, I think."

"You have quite a memory," Reverend Bradley said. "If she's in the telephone book, we'll call her. Perhaps she can help. Whether or not, there's no more we can do tonight. Tomorrow is Sunday, and I have my services to conduct."

Stacy looked at him sharply but said nothing.

"My duties are what my duties are," he said. "The current situation doesn't exempt me from them. But afterwards, I will call my friend Henry, who works at the college. He may be able to get us access to the library archives, even though it's Sunday." He paused. "And we should try to see if there are others who might help us. I have one friend, someone I contacted right when all of this was beginning.

She might very well be able to help us. A strong person, physically and mentally."

"Who?" Stacy asked.

"She owns a nursery I go to frequently, but we've become friends over the years. Her name is Louise. Louise Middlebury."

31

E*NTIRE* M*ECHANISM* A*CTIVE:* S*EVENTH* T*URN*

N*IGHT THOUGHTS*, Saturday into Sunday, December 19-20, 2015

F*AY* K*ALIVODA* COULDN'T SLEEP.

She lay curled up on her side, her down comforter snug around her shoulders, listening to the soft hiss of snow against her window. She glanced over at her clock, which showed a few minutes before one in the morning, and tried for what felt like the hundredth time to will herself to relax into a doze.

She kept hearing the voices of the previous day, echoing as if her skull was a struck bell.

Don't start talking supernatural crap on live air. Not when I'm anchoring.

I saw something weird, right before the bridge fell. I was looking ahead and I saw it.

Andy hints you're unstable or unreliable, and you're back to go, honey.

Suddenly I heard a screeching sound. Like a high squeal, like someone hitting a bad note on a violin.

They will use her until her store of energy is gone.

Normal, intelligent people don't see things coming out of clouds and knocking down bridges.

This power will kill again. It must be stopped.

She recalled the last voice, the patient, slightly sad voice of the man who had called this evening. Wait, now it's last evening, she thought sourly, and I'm still not asleep.

His was a perfectly reasonable voice, she remembered, even if much of what he said had sounded insane.

My name is Morris Bradley. And I can tell you that if you knew what I know, you would do everything in your power to help us… Archaeologists found it in a shipwreck from over two millennia ago, and they thought it was some kind of timekeeping device. But it's more than that. It's a channel for psychic power.

FAY ROLLED OVER, and stretched a little, trying to relax her stiff limbs. "Well, Morris Bradley," she said, "you certainly have a weird imagination. And a lot of gall, calling me at home."

There was something there, though, something in what he'd told her, and she realized that it was this something which was keeping her awake. What had he said? Some blather about evil spirits, some demon knocking the bridge down, something about it killing again if it wasn't stopped. It sounded like the apocalyptic bad dream of someone obsessed with the fight between good and evil.

And that was when it came to her, at 1:03 AM, with such a start that she sat up in bed, her eyes open wide.

It had been one of those unsolved crime shows, focusing on odd murders, ones where the killers had left no evidence, where there was no motive. And there had been something… something about an archaeologist in London…

Fay swung her legs out of bed, barely noticing the chill when her bare feet touched the slick, cold hardwood floor. She unhooked her robe from her closet, slipped it on, padded out into her living room, and went over to her desk, switched on the lamp. Her squint was almost a wince, and she looked away until her eyes adjusted. Then she turned on her computer.

What had Morris Bradley called it? The Anti-something Mechanism. He had told her the name, but her memory stubbornly refused to give it back to her. Something that the archaeologists had brought up from a shipwreck. It had struck a chord when he'd mentioned it, but she hadn't been able to piece together why. Now, she remembered a man with a British accent talking about an unsolved murder.

She opened up a browser window, and typed in "shipwreck mechanism murder anti…" And the Google auto-fill function put in the rest:

Antikythera.

That was it. She clicked on it and waited while the search engine did its magic.

The first hit was from a webpage called "Modern Murder Mysteries." The clip beneath the website address said: "…**murder** of an archaeologist who… **Antikythera Mechanism**, an ancient timekeeping device… found in a Mediterranean **shipwreck** over a hundred years ago…"

She clicked on the link.

The page was a summary of an episode of a British television series. The host, one Philip Dawson, looked at her from the screen, his face in an eerie half-light, one eyebrow raised in an expression clearly intended to be mysterious. The episode was called "Murder by Clockwork," and was a sensationalized account of the death of one Armand Soileau, a prominent archaeologist at Birkbeck, University of London. He was the world's expert on ancient time-keeping devices, the writer said. And, from the tone, he sounded as if he had also been a bit of an asshole. In July, Soileau gave a talk on the Antikythera Mechanism, a mysterious find from a Greek shipwreck, and later that evening he was murdered in his office, hit over the head with a heavy object.

The next bit of the page included some salacious details about Soileau's sex life, with regards to which his motto apparently was "Plenty and often and with whoever is will-ing." But his wife and his various mistresses, and his mistresses' husbands were all accounted for at the time of his murder. An attempt by police to follow up this line of investigation, considering the possibility of collusion between more than one of the wronged parties, or perhaps even murder for hire, led nowhere.

Then there was a section giving details of Soileau's impe-rious behavior towards his colleagues, especially those who were working on research related to his. One, a Lise Verhoeven of Belgium, was said to have had "heated words" with Soileau the night of his death, and might have been a suspect…

… except that she was killed herself three weeks later in an apparent freak accident. And the whole thing took a further sinister turn when a colleague of Soileau's who was a specialist in ancient bronzes, one Georgios Metaxas, took an unexpected year-long sabbatical and had not been seen since.

Then there was a paragraph that went into vague allusions to supernatural forces and the mystical function of time, and that there were allegations that the sinking of the original Mechanism had not been an accident. There were whisperings amongst the community of researchers, the writer said, whisperings attached to no name because no one wanted to end up dead, like Soileau and Verhoeven. The Antikythera Mechanism was not an antiquated clock, it was an amplifier of psychic energy. But time did play a role, the writer claimed. His sources hinted that a rebuilt Mechanism would have its full strength realized on the winter solstice. Perhaps somewhere there were people trying to reconstruct the knowledge that Soileau and Verhoeven had taken to their graves, for who knew what dark purpose.

The webpage ended with a series of questions. Why would anyone kill two ivory-tower academics who were doing nothing more exciting than researching a two-thousand-year-old clockwork? Was the original Antikythera Mechanism merely a timepiece, or something more? Was Soileau killed not because of his knowledge of the Mechanism, but because of one of his romantic entanglements? If so, was Verhoeven's death simply an accident?

Would anyone ever find out who killed the two archaeolo-gists? And where was Georgios Metaxas?

A shudder twanged its way up her spine. She knew how Bradley would answer those questions. It was all of a piece, this murder mystery, Bradley's vague warnings about psychic amplifiers and women who could be used to charge a machine with energy, and the very real collapse of the Inlet Bridge.

But if all of that was real, then she had to do something about it. This went beyond her duties as a reporter. The facts and allegations that now clicked together in her mind like the pieces of a jigsaw puzzle were beginning to fashion themselves into a picture that was terrifying.

Helene and Stanford May. Those were the names. If Bradley was right, they were the ones behind this. Behind all of it. And, perhaps, behind other things, other evils that she had yet to link up.

Fay shivered again. Perhaps tomorrow, she'd see if she could find Morris Bradley, and give him a call. Maybe he could tell her more, explain all of this.

But perhaps I don't want to know, came the sudden thought. She had the sense of being at a watershed point, a place where she could still turn back, still retreat into her bed and curl up under her down comforter. She could perhaps even sleep. But first, she had to know if what she was considering was even possible.

She switched on the kitchen light and went to the counter. She picked up her telephone directory, flipped it to the "B" section.

There it was. Bradley, Morris, Rev. Skipton.

Reverend? she thought with some surprise.

She stood in the kitchen, staring at the directory open on the counter. That was when she knew that the watershed had been passed, that she had no choice but to call Morris Bradley, to leave the comfort of her secure world and venture off into tangled, dark places where little rural villages contained evil machines and malevolent spirits knocked down bridges and killed innocent people.

At least call him tomorrow morning, she thought, in one last, desperate attempt to stop herself from going down the road on which her feet had already taken the first steps. She glanced at the clock on her stove, which read 1:46, and thought, *It's the middle of the night. I'd wake him up.* But by that time, her hand was already on the telephone.

                                  32

Entire Mechanism Active: Eighth Turn

The last thing Reverend Bradley did before he left Keith Sparlin's apartment that night was to call the police.

This was, for him, dicey business. He knew he was obliged to report that Keith was dead, even though there was nothing that the police could do about it. The action felt vaguely illicit. He hadn't actually seen Mrs. May murder Keith, wasn't even there in the pole barn at the time, but he couldn't ask Stacy to be the one to call. So, he would have to lie to the police, or at the very least be evasive.

Such a small fabrication as this would probably have come naturally in someone else's mouth. It did not to Morris Bradley. He first thought to question whether he could do it at all, and then if he could do it convincingly. Then he wondered briefly if it was proper to pray for the strength to tell a falsehood. He said a brief and unhappy prayer instead that God would understand that he was doing it for the greater good, and dialed the phone.

The 911 operator picked up almost immediately.

"I want to report a... a dead body," Reverend Bradley said.

"Please give me your name, sir," the operator said.

"Um. No, I don't think I'll do that. But you must see to it. There's a body of a man, down near the village of Lamont. Off of Morris Corners Road."

"Sir, you should know that we have a caller identification system, and I know what phone number this call is being placed from. So please identify yourself."

This possibility had not occurred to Reverend Bradley, and his heart beat a little faster. "Take Morris Corners to the flashing light, then turn left, go to the end of the road, and turn right. Keep going until you see a pole barn. He may appear to have died of natural causes. He did not."

And he hung up.

"We should go home," he said to Kelly and Stacy. "I suspect the police will be here shortly. They were able to identify the telephone number from which I placed the call, and I suspect they'll send someone out to check. I'd prefer not to be here when they arrive."

This suggestion was met with unanimous approval. All of them had been through far too much that day to be sanguine about the prospect of being questioned by the police again. They exited Keith's apartment, locking the door behind them.

"Kelly, you're spending the night in my apartment," Stacy said with some authority as she unlocked her car door.

"You don't need to ask me twice," Kelly said. "I wouldn't be able to sleep, there next to the Mays' house."

"I think we should all lock our doors securely tonight, in any case," Reverend Bradley said, and climbed into his car. "I'll be in touch tomorrow," he said, and then closed the door.

"THAT OLD MAN HAS GUTS," Kelly said, as they were driving back to Stacy's apartment.

"Wouldn't think it, to look at him," Stacy said. "But you're right. I'm glad he's on our side."

There was a brief silence. "I can't believe Dr. Sparlin is gone," Kelly said, her voice cracking a little.

"I only met him today," Stacy said. "But I saw what you liked about him." She glanced over at Kelly. The girl looked exhausted, which was no surprise. It was a wonder she was coherent.

Then Kelly turned to face Stacy. A streetlight caught the angles of Kelly's face, and suddenly she looked fierce, ancient and fierce like a statue of Athena. "We've got to stop them," she said, and at that time and in that light, Stacy could have believed that it was possible. The girl looked like she was invincible. Then the streetlight swept away behind them, and the form of Kelly's face returned to the tired, young face of a college student, the heraldic clarity sliding back into the soft dimness of night.

"We'll do what we can," Stacy said. "We won't let Keith have died for nothing. And I'll get Marcia away from them or die trying." She started to add that now, having seen what the Mays could do, the latter was far more likely. Then she recalled the power in Kelly's face for that instant, and the unguessed authority in Reverend Bradley, and as she turned into the driveway of her apartment complex, the thought occurred to her that perhaps they might have some hope after all.

No sense saying that either, of course. Neither optimism nor pessimism was a good gamble. Best to let what happens, happen, and to do what they had to do.

When they walked into the dark apartment, the digital clock on the bookcase in Stacy's living room read a little after eleven. Stacy got Kelly settled on her pull-out couch, and the girl was asleep before Stacy left the room. Stacy herself felt completely done in, and undressed quickly, slipped under the covers, and was out in five minutes.

STACY SLEPT WITH HARDLY A TWITCH, sunk deep in the dark ocean of sleep that is both a comfort and an escape. For Kelly, however, there was little rest. By the time Stacy was asleep in the next room, Kelly was already dreaming.

It was her same dream, the dream of the clock shop. The ticking was deafening, the dials and pendulums and wooden frames and glass fronts gray and silver and black in the dim light. And there was the figure of the monk, hooded and cowled, just as the clocks struck midnight, the long-fingered hands clasping the great key in the largest of the clocks, the ruinous noise of the gongs and chimes. But now, it wasn't a key, it was two bronze bars protruding from the front of the clock, two metal cylinders like long, slender handles. And the monk had seized them with an unbreakable grasp, the vibrations making him shudder as if an electric current was traveling up his arms. But once again, he held on, and the clocks exploded in chaos all around her. The bars in his hands snapped loose, fell to the floor. And he turned toward her, and pulled the hood back, and it was Reverend Bradley, his lined face ancient and serene. Somehow, she realized that she had known it was him, from the first time the monk had appeared in her dream. Perhaps, in some unfathomable way, before she even knew Bradley himself. And he said to her, in a deep, steady voice: "Now you know what you must do. You know what we all must do." Then the vision went dark, and she slipped into some realm of sleep that dreams cannot touch.

THE TELEPHONE RANG at seven in the morning. Kelly startled awake, her heart throbbing in her chest, then she pulled herself out of bed, went into the kitchen, and picked up the receiver.

"Hello?" she said, her voice creaking sleepily.

"Kelly," came the answer. "This is Morris Bradley. It is time. Wake Stacy. We have to act now, or I fear that something terrible will happen."

"I know," Kelly said.

There was a pause. "You dreamed it," he said. "Last night."

"Yes," Kelly said. "They are planning something today. It may be our last chance. And it will take all of us."

"I received some information last night," Reverend Bradley said. "The Mechanism that the Mays have rebuilt

— they apparently killed two archaeologists this summer who were researching it. It was to stop them from interfering."

"Who told you this?"

"The reporter. The woman I called last night. She said that what it appears to do is to amplify each person's ability, taking what each can do and make it somehow more powerful." He paused. "Think of what such a machine could do in the hands of someone like Helene May."

Kelly said, "Holy shit."

Reverend Bradley let the vulgarity pass. "And there's something about the timing that is important. When the Mechanism is activated on the winter solstice, it will give whoever controls it power beyond anything we could deal with."

"That's tomorrow."

"It is."

"So it's now or never?"

"Yes."

"What can we do?"

"We need to try, once and for all, to destroy it. The reporter—Fay Kalivoda—has said she will join us. I believe she understands the urgency and wishes to help us, although she did take some persuading. The Lord knows," he added, "we need all the allies we can find. I believe that the greater the number of good people we can bring to bear on this evil, the greater our chance of success. Its power is limited only by the strength of the people who oppose it."

Kelly suspected that Reverend Bradley was thinking of Keith. "Why should we fare any better?" she asked.

"Because we believe," Reverend Bradley said.

"In God?" Kelly said. "Because I don't."

"Not in God necessarily, but in something," Reverend Bradley said. "In love. In each other. In ourselves. In the power of good to defeat the inherent weakness of evil. Or in God," he added, a little guiltily. "I'm sounding terribly unorthodox. That, on top of missing services this morning. But it's what killed Keith, I'm sure of it. In the end, he couldn't defeat it because some part of him still didn't believe that its existence was possible."

THERE WERE two other calls Reverend Bradley had to make, once he hung up with Kelly.

The first was to Lee Fredericks, the deacon, whom he asked to run services this morning. Lee wasn't thrilled by the idea, that much was clear in his voice. Still, Reverend Bradley reminded him that he had been the pastor of the church in Skipton for over thirty years, and he could recall only two other times he had missed Sunday services, so neither the deacon nor his congregation had any real reason to complain. Grudgingly, Lee had to admit that was true and agreed to perform that morning's service.

The second call was to Louise Middlebury.

Louise picked the phone up on the second ring.

"Miss Middlebury, I'm sorry if I woke you," Reverend Bradley said, although Louise's "hello" had sounded clear and wide awake. "This is Morris Bradley."

"You didn't wake me," she said. "What can I do for you, Reverend?"

"You may recall about two weeks ago, the matter of the man I met in the hardware store. I believe I told you about it. And perhaps you got my message a couple of days ago, that I had decided to meet him."

"Yes," Louise began and then stopped. There was something guarded in her voice, which Reverend Bradley took to indicate skepticism.

"The explanation turns out to be far more complex than what either of us had suspected. I will ask you to please suspend your disbelief for a moment because I'm afraid what I'm going to tell you is nearly beyond my own ability to believe."

Reverend Bradley proceeded to lay out the events of the preceding days, in detail, ending with Keith Sparlin's death and the call in the early hours of the morning from Fay Kalivoda.

"So, you see, Miss Middlebury," he concluded. "This power, this Mechanism, can only be destroyed if it is confronted by enough people who are strong and united and willing to risk their lives. It may be that some of us will die, but perhaps one of us will be able to stop it before it kills more innocent people. I would face it, even alone, but others standing with me would be a stronger instrument of God's will, that we might strike down this evil creation."

He ended, on what he hoped was an exhortation worthy of a hallelujah, not that he exactly expected it from her. The practical side of him actually expected some sort of accusation that he was out of his mind. What happened was neither. The silence extended out for several seconds.

"Miss Middlebury?" Reverend Bradley said.

"I'm here," she responded.

"I must reassure you that I haven't lost my senses."

There was another long pause.

"I believe you," she finally said.

He closed his eyes. "Thank you, Lord," he said, under his breath. "Will you help us, then? I have always thought of you as a strong person. You seem to me to have great personal power, and although we do not know each other so very well, I feel you would be a good person to have as an ally." He paused for a moment. "I must emphasize that it would be at no little risk to your safety, perhaps your life. If you decline, I understand completely."

Louise said, "It isn't that," and then stopped again.

"What, then?" Reverend Bradley said.

"I..." she began, and then took a deep breath. "I shouldn't say anything. You mentioned danger. Well, just talking to you..." and once again she stumbled to a halt.

His heart gave an uneven little flutter, and there was a sudden opening of horror in his mind, as comprehension dawned on him. The silence stretched out again, taut as a guitar string.

"You're one of them, aren't you?" he asked, his mouth dry as dust.

"Reverend," Louise said quickly. "I won't tell them you called. Look, for myself, I like you. You're a nice guy, and I don't want you to get hurt. Stay away from them. Don't try to stop them. If you leave them alone, they'll forget about you. For now, at least, and maybe you can leave town. What they've got planned..." she stopped again, the words catching in her throat.

"Miss Middlebury, how can you help people like them?" Reverend Bradley said, the revulsion clear in his voice.

She didn't answer for a moment. "I... I don't know," she said. "It was years ago. I was the first, the first one they brought in. I was their confidant, their bodyguard, part of the innermost inner circle. I had no real friends. I have no real friends. It gave me a cause."

"But the cause is evil!"

Louise's voice sounded bleak, hopeless. "Better than no cause. Better than no purpose. Better an evil pattern than no pattern at all."

"You can't mean that."

"Look, Reverend Bradley," she said, "stay away. Forget about them. They plan to destroy most of Colville. Starting with the churches this morning. Stay out of Colville, stay in your house, tend your plants, read your books. Maybe they'll forget about you."

"You must know that I can't do that."

"They'd kill me if they knew I'd spoken with you. Just like they killed Stephen and Andrea."

"So they are both dead. Stacy was right."

"You had to know that it was likely."

"Yes," he said. "But I cannot go home and let them harm anyone else."

"You can't stop them."

"I will try. I must go." He paused, swallowed. "I must tell you, Miss Middlebury. Louise. It isn't too late to change sides. By warning me, you have already begun to do so. God will help you. I can't promise you safety for your body, but your soul is in God's hands. Help us."

"It's far too late for me," Louise said. "You don't understand. Stephen and Andrea thought they could switch sides. Look what happened to them." And she hung up.

Reverend Bradley set the receiver down gently. His heart was pounding, and he was sweating. He had to focus his will to keep his knees from buckling.

They were planning on attacking the churches. Sunday morning—what better way to kill large numbers of people, to attract attention? The destruction of the bridge had only been a trial run, a flexing of the machine's muscles. This morning was the real thing. It couldn't have picked a better target.

Would Louise betray him? His mind was spinning wildly, frantic that at the last moment he had made a fatal misstep. Why would God have allowed him to make such a terrible mistake as trusting her?

Then he realized something worse. He had called Louise, left a message on her voicemail, letting her know about his meeting with Stephen Calhoun. He had therefore been, all unwittingly, the cause of that unfortunate young man's death.

He willed himself to calm down. Perhaps she wouldn't tell them he'd called. To do so would inevitably bring up the question of what she had told him, and he had no doubt that she was correct in saying that the Mays would kill her if they thought she'd told him too much of their plans. It might be that they would find out whether she told him in either case. Evidently Andrea at least had been found out somehow, and they'd killed her. But regardless, he had to act this morning. He hoped earnestly that Louise wouldn't be harmed because he had chosen to call her, but the dice were thrown. He couldn't help that now.

He looked at the clock. He had arranged to meet Fay, Stacy, and Kelly at the Mays' house in forty-five minutes. That would allow him just enough time to get there. Perhaps they could catch the Mays unawares, although he had little enough hope of that.

He donned his coat and gloves, settled a hat on his head, and opened his door. The realization occurred to him that it might be the last time that he saw his little house, where he'd raised his children, where he'd lived happily with his wife, where he'd overseen the needs of his congregation, where he'd served his God. The thought passed through his mind quickly, leaving behind a curious feeling, almost of hopefulness. He'd never had any real doubt of his own final destination, but if he died today, he felt certain, and with no trace of either pride or self-pity, that God would welcome him into heaven. He said a brief prayer for the strength to complete the task that lay before him.

He closed the door, leaving it unlocked as always, and walked to his car. He smiled slightly. That was what the likes of the Mays didn't understand. Either way, good will win. Perhaps Reverend Bradley and his friends would succeed in stopping this thing. In that case, praise be God. Perhaps they might fail, perhaps he himself might die. This life on earth was such a small thing, really, and regardless of what happened, they were all in God's hands. Evil never conquers completely, nor for long. What stronger position to enter battle, knowing that either way, their cause would ultimately triumph?

He started his car, and backed out of his driveway, the faint smile still on his lips. At that moment, the thought that he might pass the gates today, be united with the God he'd served all his life and reunited with the wife that he still missed with a grief so deep as to be almost physical, seemed like not such a bad outcome.

33

Entire Mechanism Active: Final Turn

"There's no one home," Kelly said.

Reverend Bradley, Fay, Stacy, and Kelly were standing in front of the Mays' house, Stacy peering into the dark window that ran along the side of the front door.

"When did Louise say that they were planning to strike?" Stacy asked.

"She didn't," Reverend Bradley said. "However, most church services start at nine or ten o'clock. I would guess that somewhere around that time would be the best time to... um, maximize the destruction of life."

"It's ten after eight now," Fay said.

"They're with the machine," said Kelly. "It has to be. Andrea said that they had to bring Marcia back to the machine yesterday, to re-energize it or something. Wouldn't it make sense that knowing that, they would bring her there ahead of time now?"

"Of course," Reverend Bradley said. "They wouldn't make the same mistake twice."

"Let's go," Stacy said, turning and heading back toward the cars.

"We should all go together," Reverend Bradley said.

"No. Let's take at least two cars. I'm not getting stranded out there again and having to walk back. We can leave one car here. With luck," she added grimly, "the Mays won't be coming back here, and we can come back to pick up the car in peace."

They took Reverend Bradley's and Stacy's car. Fay left her car sitting by the curbside and rode with Reverend Bradley.

"This still is beyond my comprehension," Fay told him, as they pulled out onto the highway, heading south toward Quincy Falls Road.

"It's beyond all of our comprehension," said the Reverend.

"Could a machine really channel psychic power?"

"Apparently. The writer of the website you found clearly thought so. And it's consistent with everything else we've experienced."

She didn't respond for a moment. Finally, she said, "I'm terrified."

"That's a reasonable response to confronting evil."

"I don't mean that I want to stay behind," she said. "I feel like this may be the first time in my life I've done something important."

Reverend Bradley smiled. "I will pray that it's the first of many."

———

THE MAYS' old Buick was once again parked next to the pole barn, and Dr. Metaxas's sleek gray vehicle next to it. Reverend Bradley pulled behind the Mays' car, and a few moments later, Stacy parked next to him. Doors opened, and they gathered together behind Reverend Bradley's car, pulling coats around them. The wind had kicked up, and it was bitterly cold, the coldest it had yet been that winter. The sky was a pearly gray, flat and undramatic, and the sun's position could hardly be seen behind the layers of clouds.

"I feel like we're totally alone," Fay said.

"We are," Stacy said, pulling on wool gloves.

"We're never alone," Reverend Bradley contradicted.

"It must be nice to believe that," Stacy said. "Right now, all we have is each other. And our anger."

"Whatever we each have, let it be enough," Reverend Bradley said, and walked forward. "Pray to whatever you find comfort in, and stay together. Let's go."

"I feel like I'm reliving last night," said Stacy quietly. No one heard her but Kelly.

They moved slowly toward the pole barn, Reverend Bradley in front, with the wind blowing into their faces and down their necks and up their sleeves however tightly they cinched up their jackets.

"It must have been horrible," Kelly said.

"I hope Bradley knows what he's doing," Stacy replied.

"I think he does. And I think you're wrong about our being alone."

"What do you mean? Are you a sudden convert?"

"No," Kelly said. "If I ever do become a Christian—not that that's likely—it won't be Bradley's sort. I don't have the certainty to be a fundamentalist. No, it's not God. I have the feeling that this place is full of ghosts. Don't you feel them, watching us?"

"No," said Stacy flatly.

"I do."

"Friendly?"

"Not sure." Kelly looked around and shuddered. "Indifferent, I'd say. And old. Very old."

"I wonder what Andrea would say," Stacy said, then added, in a bleak voice, "But Andrea's dead. They got her."

"And we're walking right in, unarmed, and giving them a chance to do the same to us." Kelly stopped, looking ahead, watching Reverend Bradley reach out a gloved hand to pull open the sliding door of the pole barn. "What do you think our chances are?"

"If I were a betting type, I'd put my money on the Mays and company."

"But you're here."

"I can't abandon Marcia."

"I guess we each have a reason for doing this, something that keeps us connected. Maybe protected."

"I hope so."

"Me too."

There was a grating creak as the metal sliding door opened. Kelly's heart rate accelerated. She had escaped one prison, and now was walking freely into another one, with the same jailers. But then she thought, *It's different. Reverend Bradley's here. Remember your dream. If anyone can stop them, it's him.*

"Well, I do believe that the cavalry has arrived," Mrs. May said, her voice full of high good humor, as she saw the four enter.

In the room were five people, each of whom shimmered with an internal luminance, and each with a different color. Kelly looked at each, in turn, wondering if what she was seeing was real.

To the right, and nearest to them, was a tall, wiry man whom Kelly had never seen before. He had the air of a court vizier, an advisor to kings, a man who knew everyone and everything and would not hesitate to use that knowledge to make the marionettes dance. His angular face sparkled with a bluish iridescence that reflected from the square lenses of his glasses, making his eyes invisible.

To the left was a rawboned woman with a tough, weather-beaten face, but whose stance suggested tremendous power. She looked as if she could lift mountains, as if a careless movement of one hand would knock down a stone wall. About her face flickered a scarlet light, like firelight.

Between them stood two figures that at first were unrecognizable. Enthroned royalty, images of a god and goddess of old, statues of demonic entities before which our ancestors might have slit the throats of human sacrifices. They did not look human. Then Kelly blinked, once, twice, and she realized that the two figures were Stanford and Helene May.

Mr. May no longer looked like the genial and slightly vague retired professor he was. Here he was an initiate, a holder of arcane secret knowledge, a wizard robed in purple, with the silver light of stars dancing across his face. Mrs. May gave forth a gold radiance, flashing like lightning. Her face was as far removed from the grandmotherly air she habitually wore as one could imagine, and Kelly realized that her façade had all along been a mask, an appearance she had adopted as easily as someone slipping on a Halloween costume. The real Helene May was immortal, an Isis, an Artemis, stern and pitiless and unreachable. The original of the Mother Goddess of Çatalhöyük might have been such a one.

Behind them was a fifth figure, crumpled to the ground, a shimmering white light playing across her prone form. She lay at the feet of a towering machine, built of bronze gears and wheels in a steel frame. And although it had no obvious energy source, the gears were turning, teeth meshing, pointers turning past mystical symbols and inscriptions in Greek. As Kelly watched, Marcia Pacheco lifted her head to look at her, her face as smooth and luminous as an alabaster Aphrodite. She began slowly to struggle to her feet, her arms and legs trembling with the effort.

Kelly looked at Reverend Bradley. *Is he seeing the same thing I am?* He looked calm, unmoved by the crazy light and godlike demeanor of their adversaries. He turned his eyes toward one of them, the hieratic figure of Mr. May, whom Kelly only now saw was holding a drawn pistol—presumably Keith's gun, that had been so woefully inadequate to protect him the previous evening.

"I wouldn't have thought you'd stoop to using such a prosaic weapon," Reverend Bradley observed.

Mr. May gave him a mirthless smile. Mrs. May said, "We use all of the tools we have at hand. Be they mechanical or otherwise."

"Is that what you want, Miss Middlebury?" Reverend Bradley said, turning toward Louise. "To be nothing more than a tool in the hands of these people?"

"I think you'll find that your attempt at wheedling Louise will prove unsuccessful," Mrs. May said. "You need have no doubts about her loyalty. In fact, I think we might have a demonstration of this." She smiled at her husband. "Stanford, dear, will you give Louise Mr. Sparlin's gun?"

Mr. May gave her a quizzical look but handed the gun to Louise, who took it, a little uncertainly.

"You're planning to have her kill us," Stacy said.

"You've left us with no other options," Mrs. May said. "Am I correct, Louise?"

Reverend Bradley looked at Louise with stern pity. "Miss Middlebury," he said, "are you so certain of what you are doing that you are willing to murder us on their orders? You look out of character holding a gun."

"You don't know me," she said.

"I think I know you better than you know yourself. You won't kill us."

Louise gave a grim laugh. "If that's what your faith is telling you, you should think again."

Mrs. May gestured at Fay. "What is your name, dear?"

"Fay," she said, her voice trembling a little. "Fay Kalivoda."

"What a lovely name! It's Czech, isn't it?"

"Yes."

"Recent immigrants, your family?"

"My father's parents were from Prague."

"Oh, Prague! What a glorious city! Have you been there?"

"No."

Mrs. May shook her head. "A pity you'll never have a chance to. But of course, you should never have chosen to interfere with affairs that have nothing to do with you. I am sorry. But Louise, will you do me the favor of killing Miss Kalivoda? Quickly, please. One shot. We don't want her to suffer."

Fay's eyes grew huge. She looked from Louise to Reverend Bradley, to the smiling figure of Mrs. May. She opened her mouth, but no words came out.

Louise looked at Mrs. May uncertainly. "Is this necessary?"

"Quite necessary, dear. You need to do as I ask. The price of meddling is death. Kill Miss Kalivoda."

"Louise," Reverend Bradley said. His eyes had never left hers. "You know that this is wrong."

"She may well know that," Mrs. May said, a scoffing tone entering her voice, "but that will not stop her from doing it."

"I believe it will. Louise, think carefully. You are standing on the brink of a cliff. Everything that has gone before, you can still turn back from. But if you do this, there will be no turning back. It will be irrevocable."

Mrs. May rounded on Reverend Bradley. "Oh, my dear Reverend," she said, "you don't know what has gone before, with our friend Louise. That Rubicon was crossed long ago. This would just be the final filigree, the coda that brings the concerto to its end." She turned toward Louise, who was still holding the gun, its barrel pointing uncertainly at no one. "Am I right, Louise? You know it's too late for you."

That was when Marcia Pacheco, with her final strength, leaped on Mrs. May, crooked one elbow around her neck, and held on.

The old woman fought back with the viciousness of a cornered animal. Louise whirled around to face them, moving the gun as if trying to get a clear shot. Fay ran to Louise and grabbed her arm, trying to wrest the gun from her, but Mr. May turned toward them and struck Fay with a lazy backhand that threw her aside as casually as swatting away a fly. Fay collided with one of the posts that held up the ceiling, and crumpled to the floor, stunned.

Mr. May, his face contorted with anger, then turned his attention toward his wife, still locked in a struggle. Marcia clearly was at the last extremity. She was holding on, but feebly. He reached out hands that were curled like claws, the silver light rippling from the fingers like an electrical discharge, and reached for Marcia's throat.

"Louise!" Reverend Bradley said. "You have to stop him. It's what you were meant to do."

Louise called out, "Mr. May!"

He turned, his mouth still in a nearly inhuman snarl.

"I hate myself for ever having listened to you." And she shot him squarely in the chest.

Mr. May staggered back, his anger turning to shock, and he looked down at the front of his shirt, which was stained with crimson. He fell to his knees, still staring at Louise with wonder and disbelief, and then pitched forward onto his face.

Kelly saw the lean, austere figure of Georgios Metaxas slip quietly aside, and like a shadow, he vanished through the still-open door of the pole barn. Power was one thing, but if Mr. May could be killed, there was a chance that everything was going to fall apart. Self-preservation came first. And clearly, risking prosecution for being an accomplice to cold-blooded murder was not part of his plan. A moment later, she heard the sound of a car engine starting.

That was when Marcia could maintain her stranglehold on Mrs. May no longer. Whether it was because her remaining energy had been taxed to its fullest, or because

Mrs. May had suddenly acquired a burst of power from seeing her husband betrayed and killed, Marcia's arm went slack, and she slithered to the ground, insensate.

Mrs. May took one step toward Louise. "You… traitor," she said in a hiss. "After what we have done for you."

"You've done nothing for me but to bring despair." Louise brought the gun up again, aimed at Mrs. May's face.

She hesitated a moment too long. Mrs. May swept one arm up and once again the gun went flying. Then Louise's body rose slowly into the air, her feet dangling like a hanged man's. Her face turned splotchy and congested, purple with suffused blood, her eyes bulging. "Despair?" Mrs. May said. "You will meet despair face to face. A pity you won't have longer to regret what you have done." One of Louise's arms twisted upwards and behind her, and she gave a choked cry of pain.

A voice spoke somewhere within Kelly Delahanty's brain: *The dream. Remember the dream. Now is the chance to use it.* Sudden comprehension dawned on her. And she said, her voice breathless, "Reverend Bradley! The Mechanism! You have to destroy the Mechanism! Grab the handles, it's the only way!"

Reverend Bradley darted forward, behind Mrs. May. She realized what was happening, but this time, she was the one who was too late. Louise fell to the dirt floor, forgotten, as Mrs. May reached for Reverend Bradley's arm, and missed by inches.

"No!" she shouted, but he had already grasped the bronze posts with an unbreakable grip.

As the power of the Mechanism surged through him, he said, through clenched teeth, "And your altars shall be desolate, and your images shall be broken… and I will cast down your slain men before your idols…" And then his mind was overwhelmed, and he knew nothing more.

But Kelly Delahanty saw what followed, and it was an image that haunted her for the rest of her life. The gears and pointers of the Mechanism were turning, faster, faster, making a grating, ruinous noise, as they drew power from the old man. Mrs. May herself shriveled, her face withering like a dry leaf, as the Mechanism pulled away what it had given her in a desperate attempt to save itself. She shrieked again, "No!" but her voice was weak, tremulous, and she backed away, unwilling to witness the final destruction of her creation.

Reverend Bradley's lean body was resonating like a bowed fiddle string. He was drawing energy from the Mechanism, but somehow reflecting it back inward, making it reabsorb was it was taking from him, from the surroundings, from everyone in the room. The Mechanism began to vibrate, its bronze workings shuddering, something inside making a sound like a gong striking midnight. A crack appeared in the steel frame. Then all at once, the whole Mechanism exploded apart, pins flying, springs uncoiling, gears sailing through the air. A long, thin pointer shot upwards, impaling itself an inch deep into a wooden ceiling beam.

The fragments rained down onto the floor, as the energy that the machine had accrued expanded outward like a bubble, shimmering as it moved, then winking out.

Reverend Bradley slumped to the floor.

Kelly ran to his side, knelt on the floor. She said, her voice desperate, pleading, "Oh, no, please, don't be dead, not you, too…"

She lifted his shoulder, trying to move him gently from the awkward position he'd fallen in. His face was quiet, tranquil, but whether in unconsciousness or death was uncertain.

Behind her, amongst the shattered ruins of the Mechanism, Stacy was helping Marcia to her feet. They came to Kelly and Reverend Bradley, and Stacy said, "We can't lose him."

Kelly looked around her. The room was littered with the fallen. Mr. May lay on his face where he'd collapsed after Louise shot him. Louise herself was still lying on the floor, motionless. Fay at least was stirring, but she moaned with pain, and one of her arms was bent in an unnatural way. Mrs. May was nowhere to be seen.

"Reverend Bradley," Kelly said. "Please. Please, you can't have died. There has been enough hurt and death. It's enough." Her voice became stronger, fierce, demanding. "Tell your God that. The sacrifices were sufficient. We have paid enough for our sins."

And he opened his eyes.

Kelly gave a cry of joy. Reverend Bradley would undoubtedly have an opinion about whether Kelly's plea was what did it, whether in response to her command the universe gave back some of what it had taken from them all. At the moment, she didn't care. Sometimes knowing the reason made no real difference.

"It's…" Reverend Bradley said, his voice hoarse. "The Mechanism."

"You destroyed it," Kelly said.

"And Helene May? And their friend, the one who helped them build it?"

"Both gone."

"Not destroyed, then."

"No."

"At least…" He stopped, coughed, and the cleared his throat. "At least we have prevented them from fulfilling their plans for the present."

"Yes. We have."

"And the others?"

"Mr. May is dead. Fay is hurt. I don't know about Louise. She hasn't moved since Mrs. May attacked her."

Stacy left Marcia, who remained standing, although wobbling a little on weak legs. She went to Fay first.

"Are you okay?"

"Arm's broken," Fay said, through clenched teeth. "Otherwise okay. But it hurts like hell. What happened?"

"The Reverend did it. Destroyed the machine. Mr. May is dead, Mrs. May gone. It's going to be okay."

"What about the other woman? The one with the gun?"

Stacy looked over at the crumpled form of Louise Middlebury. "I don't know." She stood, went and knelt beside Louise, and put a hand on her shoulder. "Unconscious."

She placed two fingers beneath her jaw, and said, "There's a pulse. She's still alive. But badly hurt, I think."

Reverend Bradley was struggling to sit up, with Kelly's help. "We need to get an ambulance out here. Fay and Louise need to get to the hospital."

"Louise was one of them," Stacy said, still kneeling next to where Louise lay in a heap. "I'm not inclined to help her."

"You can't really mean leaving her here to die," Kelly said. "And remember, she's the one who killed Mr. May. If it hadn't been for her, we might not have succeeded."

"I suppose not," Stacy said. "But I still don't like her."

"Agreed. But Fay needs medical assistance, and so, I suspect, do Marcia and I." Reverend Bradley shook his head. "So much pain and suffering and death. And all for what? But practical matters first. Kelly, do you have a cellphone? I'm afraid I've never gotten one."

"Yes."

"You need to call 911. Tell them to send the police and an ambulance, that we've got several injured and two dead."

"What will we tell the police?" said Stacy.

"I've no idea," said Reverend Bradley, giving her a weak smile. "But the truth. Most certainly the truth, or as much of it as we can. For myself, I think my career as a liar is quite ended."

34

Disengage All Gears

Late Winter into Spring, 2016

The January sun shone from a clear, pale blue sky, giving little warmth but bathing everything in a crystalline light, making the snow which had fallen the previous day glitter and flash. The little group gathered in the North Colville Cemetery stood in a semicircle, saying nothing, letting the day's beauty simply be. There was no need to question beauty. When it happened, it was enough.

They visited two graves that day. The first said, "Andrea Yarbrough, Loving Wife and Sister, 1967-2015." She had been laid to rest next to her husband. The second, in some odd twist, was only about twenty feet away from Andrea's, and they lingered longer there.

This stone read, "Keith Thomas Sparlin, October 26, 1982 - December 19, 2015. Onward Into the Next Great Mystery."

Kelly began crying when she read it, and Stacy put her arm around the girl, but said nothing and let her cry. Fay stood to the side, her face solemn, her arm still in a cast and sling inside her coat, leaving one sleeve hanging limply. Reverend Bradley stood and prayed silently.

Lord, Your mysteries are manifold, and I cannot fathom them except dimly. But I ask Your mercy on this young man, who gave his life freely for the sake of others. Although he did not know You while he was alive, I pray that You make Yourself known to him now. If he is the man I took him to be, in the short time I knew him, he will greet You as a long forgotten friend, whose face he has always known and remembered, but who he has not seen in years. I know Your Word says that salvation comes from belief, but my dear Lord, here lies a man who can only be said to have followed Your way, however, he didn't recognize the path his feet were on. I ask You to have mercy on his soul. In Your name.

Amen.

They stayed a while, finally separating and going back to their homes and lives, each carrying the bond they had created, knowing that they were not alone.

***

REVEREND BRADLEY SAW, on his way back home, that Robin's Nest Florist had a sign in front that said "Closed Due to Illness." On his periodic trips into Colville in the following weeks, he always made note of it. It didn't change as a month, then two went by. It wasn't until April and the advent of warmer weather that he saw it become "Opening Again Soon!" and finally, the third week of April, it was changed to "Open For Business!" He debated whether he should stop, but finally, his curiosity won the battle, and he pulled into the parking lot. The racks in front of the nursery were covered with annuals in full bloom, fat perennials bursting with life, and balled and burlapped shrubs covered with plump buds. He walked into the nursery building, remembering the last time he'd been there, after meeting an odd man in Colville Hardware who claimed to have a long-lost twin. It felt like ten years ago, not six months.

And Louise was there, behind the counter, and turned to look as he entered. Her face was paler than usual, and somehow older and more weatherworn. She had lost weight and moved with a caution that was wholly unlike her previous tough strength. Whatever the Mechanism had given her was gone, drained from her along with some core vitality she once possessed. She did not smile as their eyes met.

"I came to find out how you were doing," he said, his voice gentle.

She raised one eyebrow. "It's slow. I'm healing, but it's slow."

"The paramedics said you'd broken several ribs."

"Four. Plus a dislocated shoulder. I had deep tissue damage in my neck as well. Between the trouble breathing and the trouble swallowing, the first three weeks were as miserable as I've ever been."

"I should have visited you in the hospital."

"It's all right. I didn't expect it."

He looked at her, trying to catch her eye, but she looked away. "I still plan on buying my flowers here this spring, and my wreaths, next Christmas season. Unless you'd prefer I didn't."

"It's all one to me."

"Miss Middlebury. Understand that I do not harbor any ill feelings toward you. You and I both carried out God's will, in our own ways. You saved our lives on that day."

She grimaced a little and turned to pick up a plant catalog. "I don't know why I did what I did."

"Because it was the right thing to do, perhaps."

She looked at him, her mouth fixed in a little sneer. "You're wasting your platitudes on me, Reverend," she said. "I don't know why I did it. It wasn't for any sense of the greater good, that's for sure."

"I cannot help but think," he responded, "that even you don't completely believe that."

"I don't believe anything," she said, her voice flat.

He reached forward and touched her arm. She flinched away from him and looked down.

"I hope for you that your healing continues," he said. "Your body and your soul as well. I will check up on you every so often if that's all right."

"Suit yourself," she said, in a despairing tone.

The bell jingled as he left, and she turned, an expression almost of longing in her eyes, as she watched his car pull out and turn onto the highway.

AFTER THE NIGHT of December 20, Kelly had stayed with Stacy for two weeks, until her roommates returned from their holiday visits home, and then she went back to her house. At first, she was edgy and frightened and hardly slept. She kept an eye on the Mays' house, and its darkened upper floor window seemed to watch her as she lay in bed. She imagined its flat, dark, rectangular pupil, its gaze reaching right through her curtains, and she didn't get more than an hour's sleep for the first few nights home. But gradually the feeling receded into the back of her mind.

Mrs. May did not return to her house. Mr. May was, according to his obituary, buried somewhere in Colville, and Helene May was listed as "his wife, who survives," but the house remained unoccupied and dark. Later that spring, it was put on the market, and was sold to a young couple with twin two-year-old boys.

As FOR KELLY, she had no more dreams of Mr. May killing her with the hedge clippers, nor did she ever again have the familiar dream of the destruction of the clock shop.

Still, she was haunted by the thought that they hadn't finished. They had destroyed the Mechanism, but Helene May and Georgios Metaxas both survived. Between the two of them, there was enough knowledge to reconstruct the machine once more. The thought kept returning, like a persistent itch, keeping her awake at night.

It's not over. It could all start again.

In mid-January, she decided to call Marcia.

When Marcia found out what Kelly was proposing, at first she was aghast.

"No way in hell," she said. "Why would you want to go back there?"

"Closure," Kelly said. "I have to find out if there are still pieces of the thing left. If there is any way that someone could rebuild it."

"Helene May, you mean."

"Not necessarily her. When she ran, after Reverend Bradley destroyed the Mechanism, she looked… Well, do you know those mummies they find in caves in Peru, high up in the Andes?"

"I've seen photographs in *National Geographic*."

"Like that. Like whatever was alive in her had been drained."

"I wish I believed that," Marcia said. "That woman was evil. As long as she's alive, she's dangerous. She's got teeth still, I believe." She paused. "What if you find that someone has come back, and is starting to reassemble it? What will you do?"

"Try to stop it again. I don't know."

"I can't bear the thought of starting over with this."

"Me either."

"So why do you want to go back?"

"I have to know. I'll go alone if need be."

In the end, Marcia acquiesced, but added, "Stacy will strangle me if she finds out I'm doing this."

Kelly picked her up on a March afternoon, one of those rare early spring days when the sky is clear and the air cool but pleasant. There would be more snow to come, that was certain, but days like this were to be relished when they occurred. They made the drive down to Lamont mostly in silence. Both recognized that this was not a social excursion, it was a way of reaching the final chord of the piece—or to find out that the symphony had yet to conclude.

They turned onto the rural road that ended at the pole barn that had housed the rebuilt Antikythera Mechanism. Marcia said, "Are you scared?"

Kelly said, "Petrified."

"I don't remember much of my time there. Whatever that device did to me, it sapped enough of my energy that I didn't form any strong memories."

"You're fortunate. What happened that night will never be gone from me, I don't think."

The pavement turned to a dirt road, then to a pair of muddy ruts, finally petering out completely.

"Are we in the right place?" Kelly said, in a hushed voice.

The pole barn was not there. They got out of the car, and for a moment stood, the light breeze brushing their faces, birds chirping in the trees.

The only sign of the building was a rectangular bare patch of beaten-down earth. Rain and snowmelt had already turned the dry ground into a morass of mud. Goldenrod and aster and field grass would grow there this summer. After that, there would be no sign that anyone had ever built there, that it had been a place where people had struggled to prevent an ancient device from wreaking destruction upon the Earth.

Kelly walked forward, her boots making squelching noises in the wet soil. There were post holes where the corners had been, now rectangular pits of muddy water. Whoever had taken the pole barn down had been thorough. There was hardly a screw or a splinter of wood to be seen.

But fallen into a tussock of dead grass, near what had once been the north-facing wall of the barn, Kelly spied something that glimmered in the pale gold light of the March sun. She went up to it and picked up a small bronze gear, missing teeth, the bands that formed its central crossbars bent and scorched. Around its rim ran an inscription in Greek lettering, ending in a geometrical symbol, a seven-pointed star.

"What do you think that means?" she asked Marcia, holding it out in the palm of one hand.

"No idea," Marcia said, shuddering.

Kelly slipped the gear into her pocket.

"You're keeping it?" Marcia's voice registered shock.

"It can't hurt me anymore. I want to keep it as a reminder."

"Of what?"

"That friendship and courage sometimes triumph over ruthlessness and power."

They went back to Kelly's car, got in, and drove away.

Neither woman ever returned to the desolate dirt road near Lamont. There was no reason to. Whatever more would happen, would not happen there.

———

ALL OF THEM had been questioned by the police that night. Reverend Bradley told them, and the others substantiated, that Mr. May had broken Fay's arm, Louise had shot him, and Mrs. May had somehow struck Louise hard enough to break four ribs and dislocate her shoulder. Louise was never charged, the decision being that it was self-defense, a claim that was supported by the injuries sustained by the people who had fought against the Mays. The investigation was hampered by the bringing to light of a recent weird accusation against the Mays by a Miss Kelly Delahanty, who was also at the scene of the crime. The skepticism that this generated evaporated when it was found that the pistol that had been used to kill Mr. May was registered to Keith Sparlin, whose body was found in plain sight but covered by a piece of canvas, despite the fact that the two police officers who had been dispatched to the place the previous evening with a report of a dead body had seen nothing suspicious. Mr. May's fingerprints were found on the gun, and a search of the Mays' house turned up letters and emails between the Mays, Metaxas, and others that were sinister enough to be damning. Even if the correspondence gave little in the way of concrete information about what exactly they were trying to do, the final straw was a mention by Metaxas of two prominent archaeologists, Armand Soileau and Lise Verhoeven, who had died the previous year under mysterious circumstances.

No charges were filed against any of the survivors.

The fact that Mrs. May was nowhere to be found when the police went to her house also lent credence to the claim that the Mays had been attempting to harm or kill one or more of the survivors. Both Helene May and Georgios Metaxas were the subjects of an intensive search by the authorities, but no trace of them could be found. After the night of December 20, it was as if both Mrs. May and Dr. Metaxas had simply evaporated.

A NEWSPAPER STORY headlined "Mystery Surrounds Death of Two Colville College Professors" appeared two days after the events in the pole barn in Lamont. It had only mentioned Fay Kalivoda's name once, but it was enough. Her boss, Mrs. Vanlandingham, was completely old-school when it came to any improprieties by her reporters, and Fay was "regrettably terminated," as it was put to her.

It was remarkable how little this affected Fay's mood. She applied for, and got, a job as a clerk at the Flying Centaur Bookstore in Colville, and although it paid far less than her job at the station, she found herself relaxing into it. The lack of the necessity to keep the Right People Happy actually turned out to be something of a relief.

The third week of April, she was working the two to nine shift, and just as she was opening up her dinner—a container of leftover Chinese food from the previous day— the bell over the door tinkled, and in walked Kelly Delahanty.

There was a moment of frowns and puzzlement, then both women smiled in recognition.

"Fay!" Kelly said. "I didn't know you worked here. I thought you were a newscaster."

"Didn't work out."

"Oh. I'm sorry."

"I'm not," Fay said. "On the whole, I like working in a bookstore better. Even if the pay's less. I'd have paid the difference not to have to put up with misogynistic assholes."

Kelly laughed. "How's your arm?"

"Still hurts sometimes. I got the cast off about a month ago. I'm in physical therapy to build the strength back up, but it's slow." She gestured at Kelly. "How are you? You came through unscathed. The only one, I think."

"I don't know if I'd call it unscathed, exactly. I still fight with the memories of what we all went through. But physically, you're right, I escaped without a scratch."

"I don't know which one is worse." Fay shrugged. "But at least you and I survived. I wish I'd known Keith Sparlin. I'll bet he was an awesome teacher."

"He was. And a good person, too. I still feel guilty about getting him involved in this. If I hadn't gone to him that day…"

"Don't," Fay said. "You can't do that to yourself. We all got involved by chance. If you try to track anything down to its ultimate cause, you always end up with the answer that there was no reason things happened as they did. It was a chaotic jumble of little actions, any of which could have changed the outcome. No real pattern."

"Reverend Bradley would disagree."

"Yes. Yes, he would. But I can't buy into his 'God has a plan for everything' worldview, I'm afraid. It'd be comforting, but I don't see it."

"Me either. But I wish we could have avoided… avoided so much of what happened."

"Me too," Fay remembered the car, sunk in Carlisle Inlet. Who had died in that car? Surely someone unconnected to anything having to do with the Mays' grand plans. Collateral damage. An innocent who happened to be in the wrong place. "We can't change that, though," she said. "And I think that Keith would have believed that the cost was justified, to stop the Mays."

"I think so, too."

Fay straightened her blouse. "But you didn't come in here to discuss this. Sorry to divert the conversation into depressing topics. Are you looking for something I can help you with?"

"Yes," Kelly said. "A Greek dictionary."

One of Fay's eyebrows rose a little. "A Greek dictionary? Ancient or Modern Greek?"

"Ancient." Kelly gave her a wry smile. "So maybe the depressing topics were appropriate."

"This has to do with the Antikythera Mechanism, doesn't it?"

Kelly reached into her pocket and pulled out the little bronze gear she had found in the clump of grass near where the pole barn had stood, and handed it to Fay.

"Is this…?" Her voice trailed off.

"Marcia and I went back to where it all happened. Someone had taken down the barn, and hauled away everything—all of the pieces of the Mechanism, not to mention the entire barn itself. It was nothing but a square of mud. But they missed one piece."

Fay looked at it closely. "And you want to find out what the inscription says."

"Yes."

"Hang on." She handed Kelly the gear. "I'll be right back." She came out from behind the counter and had only been gone for a minute when she returned with a heavy hard-bound dictionary. The cover said *Yonge's English-Greek Lexicon*.

"I think it's only two words," Kelly said. "But they kind of run together." Fay peered at the inscription again, and saw the grooves in the metal spelled out:

ΣΤΕΡΙΓΜΟΣ ΚΟΣΜΟΥ

"I guess the first thing is to see what the English transcription would be, so at least we can pronounce it," Fay said. She opened the dictionary, and found a Greek alphabet, with the English letter equivalents, on the inside of the front cover. She took a piece of scrap paper and a pencil, and in a few moments, she had written out in English:

STERIGMOS KOSMOU

"Now, to find out what it means," Fay said.

They were unable to find the first word, but the second one they translated easily. It came from "kosmos," meaning the entirety of everything, the universe.

"Maybe we should look online," Kelly suggested.

"You've got me as curious as you are," Fay said. She turned the computer on the counter toward her, opened up a browser window, and typed in "Sterigmos."

The first hit was from a paper by Tony Freeth *et al.*, called, "Decoding the Ancient Greek Astronomical Calendar Known As the Antikythera Mechanism." And a little way in, they found the phrase, "… the word 'sterigmos,' translates as fixed point, or stationary point."

"So it means the 'fixed point of the universe'," Kelly said.

Fay looked at the little bronze wheel, sitting on the counter, in silence for a moment. "If the Mechanism had worked, it could have been the pivot around which everything else turned. Maybe that's what it means."

"Scary thought," Kelly said.

"The whole thing was terrifying."

"I wonder where Mrs. May ended up."

"I don't want to know," Fay said. "That woman gave me the screaming creeps."

"Me too." Kelly picked up the bronze gear and looked again at its inscription. *The pivot around which everything else turns.* "What if she does it again?" she said. "Tries to rebuild the Mechanism?"

"It'll be someone else's turn," Fay said firmly. "I can't do that again. I'm not made of hero."

"I don't think the real heroes are. They're just people, people who had circumstances thrown their way, and had to react."

"Maybe." She smiled at Kelly. "We did what we could, anyway."

"That's all you ever can do." Kelly slipped the gear back into her pocket. "And this time, it was enough."

NOTE TO READERS

If you would like to know more about the Antikythera Mechanism (with, I'm sure, no intentions of rebuilding it and using for evil purposes), allow me to direct you to the wonderful papers "Decoding the Ancient Greek Astronomical Calendar Known as the Antikythera Mechanism" by Tony Freeth *et al.* that appeared in *Nature* in 2006, and "The Cosmos in the Antikythera Mechanism" by Freeth and Alexander R. Jones that appeared in *Institute for Study of the Ancient World Papers* in 2012. Both are available online.

I also wish to point out, if Dr. Freeth or any of his colleagues should ever read *Gears*, that any dismissive comments that Dr. Armand Soileau made about the research others have done on the topic are opinions not shared by the author. Dr. Soileau was not, perhaps, best known for his modesty and circumspection, and any commentary he made should be taken in that light.

ABOUT THE AUTHOR

Gordon Bonnet has been writing fiction for decades. Encouraged when his story "Crazy Bird Bends His Beak" won critical acclaim in Mrs. Moore's 1st grade class at Central Elementary School in St. Albans, West Virginia, he embarked on a long love affair with the written word.

His interest in the paranormal goes back almost that far. Introduced to speculative, fantasy, and science fiction by such giants in the tradition as Madeleine L'Engle, Lloyd Alexander, Isaac Asimov, C. S. Lewis, and J. R. R. Tolkien, he was captivated by those writers' abilities to take the reader to a fictional world and make it seem tangible, to breathe life and passion and personality into characters who were (sometimes) not even human. He made journeys into darker realms upon meeting the works of Edgar Allen Poe and H. P. Lovecraft during his teenage years, and those authors still influence his imagination and his writing to this day.

This fascination with the paranormal, however, has always been tempered by Gordon's scientific training. This has led to a strange duality: his work as a teacher, skeptic and debunker on the popular blog _Skeptophilia_, while simultaneously writing paranormal and speculative novels, novellas, and short stories. Gordon explains this, with a smile: "Well, I do know it's fiction, after all."

He blogs daily, and is never without a piece of fiction in progress—driven to continue (as he puts it) "because I want to find out how the story ends." From historical fiction (*Kári the Lucky*), to murder mysteries (the Parsifal Snowe Mysteries, beginning with *Poison the Well*), to paranormal fiction with a humorous twist (*Periphery* and *Lock & Key*) to the truly terrifying (*Gears* and *Descent into Ulthoa*), Gordon's fiction has something for all tastes!

Find him conversing with his dogs (and perhaps his wife) in Trumansburg, NY, or the following platforms:

• YouTube *https://youtube.com/@skeptophilia1509*

• Skeptophilia blog *http://www.skeptophilia.com/*

• Books and stuff *http://www.gordonbonnet.com*

• Twitter *@TalesOfWhoa*

• TikTok *@GordonBonnetAuthor*

• Instagram *@skygazer227*

Or, ya know, the Google.

OTHER NOVELS BY GORDON BONNET

The Communion of Shadows

Sephirot

Descent into Ulthoa

The Shambles

Kári the Lucky

Kill Switch

The Fifth Day

Snowe Mysteries *(beginning re-releases 2023)*

Book 1: Poison the Well

Book 2: Dead Letter Office

Book 3: Face Value

Snowe Mysteries *(available now)*

Book 4: Past Imperfect

Book 5: Room for Wrath

Book 6: The Obituary Collector

Book 7: Slings and Arrows

The Boundary Solution Series (stay tuned for re-releases)

And More…

Stay tuned for releases *(and re-releases for ones you may have missed)*

Sign up for Gordon's Little Bustard Books Newsletter and Obscure Weird Tidbits at his website: http://www.gordonbonnet.com